Shocked

Elemental Magic Unleashed

Book Three

Serenity Ackles

Axellia Publishing

Shocked
Copyright © Serenity Ackles
All rights reserved.

First edition, June 2022
Published by Axellia Publishing

Print ISBN: 978-1-912644-40-7
eBook ASIN: B097TPRWDJ

Cover design by Moorbooks Design

Edited by Aethereal Press
Proofread by S. Harvell

CONTENTS

ALSO BY SERENITY ACKLES

Elemental Magic Unleashed

Grounded
Charged
Shocked

SERENITY ACKLES & J. S. LEE

The Goddess of Fate & Destiny

Cursed Luck
Stolen Luck
Twisted Luck

Coming Soon

Chosen Luck

One

Zera

"Javion is still in there!"

For weeks, I'd done little more than scream. My throat was raw. Considering the little conversation I'd had, it was a real effort to force the words from my mouth to be loud enough to be heard.

Now, as Carter flew upwards and the burning building that I'd just escaped from appeared smaller below us, I wasn't sure he was hearing me.

"Carter, we need to go back. Javion was right behind us. He said—"

Something shot through the air and dinged off Carter's skin.

"Hunter, get higher," Carter yelled at the other gargoyle. "They're firing at us."

"Javion." I tried again as, with a sudden movement, we seemed to go higher.

"Zeraora, he's gone."

"No, you don't understand. He's coming."

The arms around me squeezed tighter despite the electricity buzzing out of control over my body.

Metal shackles were still clamped around my wrists, but despite how exhausted I was and how much pain my body felt—especially beneath the shackles—I couldn't turn off the power.

Passing out was probably going to stop it. That was certainly what my body wanted, but if I did that, we'd never go back for Javion.

"Carter, he's still in there."

"Look at Knox. We need to get him out of here. He's hurt. *You're* hurt."

"Let Hunter take him. I'll go back. I can take them." It didn't matter how much pain I was in; I couldn't let Carter leave Javion behind. He was Knox's mate. He was my... I didn't know what he was, but he'd distracted the Lycans so I could get Knox out to safety. Javion was supposed to be right behind us.

"They have guns. Even if you have enough energy to destroy every Lycan that's still standing, you can't stop bullets, and your skin isn't made of stone like ours."

I wriggled in Carter's arms, trying to see the Lycan facility. We'd now flown so far that I could barely make out the glow in the distance. If he didn't turn around now...

"DB, are we clear enough to land?" Hunter called over. "Knox isn't doing well." There was a croak in Hunter's voice that I'd never heard before.

I didn't like it.

Knox had been... the Lycans had taken him, and I hadn't seen him for days. When they returned him to our room, he was missing a wing, and his body was covered in claw marks. There had been so much blood.

And there still was.

Gargoyles were supposed to have skin strong enough to stop things like Lycan claws. They'd done something to him.

"Over there." Carter called, pointing at something.

3

I wasn't sure what it was, but in the next moment, we were heading down at a rapid pace. It wasn't until we got lower that I could hear the wail of a siren. Below us, I could see red and blue flashing lights that we seemed to be following.

My throat hurt too much to ask why we were following it. Instead, with the wind making my eyes water, I stayed quiet. My thoughts were with Javion.

Carter wasn't going back for him.

Not long after, we landed. The thing we'd been following, an ambulance, had stopped across the street.

Carter set me down, but my legs didn't cooperate to let me stand. Instead, I leaned against a wall as Hunter gently set Knox down beside me.

"Are you suggesting we rob an ambulance?" Hunter asked.

"You think we can head to the nearest ER?"

Hunter glanced back at me and Knox. Moments later, he was running across the street.

When I'd woken in the glass cage, I didn't have my glasses. Hunter had quickly become a blur. So instead, I turned to the one I could focus on: Knox.

This was the first time I'd been close enough to see him clearly. A new kind of pain radiated from inside my chest as I looked at him. Knox was unconscious, and

4

his head was rolled to the side. The metal bar which had been in his eyebrow was no longer there. In its place, like dozens of other places over his near naked body, was a barely healed wound.

My vision went fuzzy as tears rolled down my face.

This was because of me.

Knox and Javion had tried to protect me because I wasn't able to stop the Lycans. And then, when they'd taken us away, the Lycans hurt him to make me produce electricity.

Ignoring the agony I felt when I moved, I shuffled away from Knox. His skin was supposed to protect him from everything, including me. If the Lycans could hurt him, so could I. The chains around my wrists meant that the electricity was still escaping my body uncontrollably.

"Zera, what are you doing?" Carter asked as he hurried over.

"This is my fault," I mumbled.

Carter gently grabbed my chin and turned my head to face him. "No. This is absolutely *not* your fault, Blue Eyes."

"DB, Go." Hunter appeared.

Strong arms slid underneath me, and Carter lifted me again. "Is he going to be okay?"

"Knox is going to be fine," Hunter replied, firmly.

"Can you carry these for me?"

As I nodded, Hunter placed a bunch of items onto my stomach. Without looking, I wrapped my arms around them and watched as Hunter picked Knox up.

It wasn't until we were back in the air and flying away from the ambulance that Hunter spoke. "Where to?"

"Follow me," Carter replied.

Clutching tightly to the things Hunter had given me, I closed my eyes. The pain was becoming unbearable, yet I still couldn't pass out for relief.

Finally, we landed for a second time. We were in front of a large house which only had one light on outside. Instead of going in, Carter carried me towards a building to one side. Using his shoulder, he rammed himself into the door, which flung open with a loud crack echoing across the ground.

Quickly, he and Hunter hurried inside, then shut the door behind us.

"Do you think we woke anyone?" Hunter whispered.

The two of them were moving around like they could see in the pitch-black room. They probably could.

Carter set me down on the floor. "Where are we?"

"Shhh." Hunter hushed me.

A sliver of light appeared on the other side of the room. "No lights have come on," Carter told us. "You get Knox's wounds dressed. I'll get those shackles off Zeraora."

The light disappeared, and I could hear the two moving around in the darkness until a warm glow suddenly appeared to my right. Carter turned around, holding up a light. He moved over to us and set it on the ground before he turned his attention to the benches.

Beside me, Hunter was busy cleaning Knox's injuries and wrapping them in stark white bandages. I couldn't watch. Instead, I focused on the room. It wasn't a house, but it reminded me of Knox's garage, but there was a lot of straw in here. A barn?

After a little while, Carter returned to me carrying what looked like an enormous pair of scissors. He crouched down beside me. "I've got to get these things off you," he said, lifting one of the chains. "This place doesn't have the same tool I used last time." He glanced at my wrists and frowned. "This is going to hurt, and I'm so sorry. But I need you to try not to make a sound. I don't want to wake up anyone in that house."

"It's okay," I told him. I doubted what he was going to do would hurt even half as much as being back in that glass prison had.

"These are bolt cutters." Carter explained. He brought them around the metal cuffs where the chains were attached. "Don't look."

I closed my eyes.

Carter was right. Whatever he was doing made a hideous noise as the metal pressed into my skin. Fresh pain erupted from underneath, shooting down my arms like fire.

The process wasn't as quick as I wanted it to be, but finally, they were off. My pain levels dropped, and my body felt like it was deflating. With a sigh, I opened my eyes and found Carter looking at the metal like he was going to rip it apart with his bare hands.

"How is Knox?" I asked.

"He's going to be fine, Zee," Hunter told me without looking up. "Gargoyles are quick healers."

"You're also supposed to have strong skin."

Hunter sucked in a deep shuddering breath but didn't answer as he continued to wrap a bandage around Knox's torso.

"Tough, but not impenetrable with the right tools," Carter told me as he reached over for one of the bottles beside Hunter. "Unfortunately, this isn't enchanted by witches, so it's going to sting."

I just shrugged. At that point, I was starting to just feel numb.

Carter gently poured the liquid over my wounds. He was wrong: it wasn't just a sting definitely more like a burn, but quickly, the biting pain eased up.

"Hey, Zeraora," Carter said softly, lowering his head in front of me. "Are you okay?"

Again, I just shrugged.

"What's up, DB?" Hunter asked without looking over. When he didn't get a reply and turned back, Carter shook his head. Hunter glanced at me, frowning, and then nodded before turning his attention back to his twin.

"Is he really going to be okay?" I stared at Knox. Despite the fact Hunter was pouring the same stinging liquid over his wounds, he hadn't moved once.

"Knox just needs to rest. There's a lot for his body to recover from." Carter explained. He picked up a bandage and started wrapping it around my wrists.

This was my fault. I should have been able to stop the Lycans. And now, not only was Knox hurt, but they had Javion. He was hurt when he'd left us—that had to be why he didn't get out of the building quick enough.

The Lycans would be mad, and they'll probably take it out on Javion.

Javion once told me that after he turned, he woke up a captive of the Lycans, who experimented and tortured him. What would they do to him now? He helped us escape... would they blame him for that?

"... Zera? Zeraora?" Carter waved a hand in front of my face which slowly came into focus. "I think it's time for you to rest. Go to sleep."

I stood, shaking my head. "I need to go back and—ah!"

When they'd taken us, they removed my shoes. My feet had rested on cold metal grates. Like the chains that were around my wrists, it was another place to get my electricity from. As I escaped, I ran, not caring what I was treading on as I tried to get Knox to safety.

When my legs gave out beneath me, Carter was at my side, catching me before I even hit the ground. "Zera, you aren't going anywhere."

"Javion—"

"Javion is gone." For the first time ever, Carter raised his voice at me.

My lips parted, and then I shook my head. "Javion said—"

Carter moved in front of me, trying to get me to sit down. "There are only three things that can permanently kill a vampire. Beheading, sunlight, and fire. That facility went up in a giant fireball. There's no way Javion could have survived that."

I knew how vampires died. And I'd felt the fire as we took off into the air. "You don't know that. He could have survived. We need to at least check."

"You're not strong enough to go up against the Lycans."

Ignoring the pain in my feet, I shoved Carter as hard as I could.

He took a step back, holding his hands up.

"I am going to get Javion, Carter. And I'm going to kill any Lycan that stops me."

"What about me?"

"What about you?" I demanded.

Carter let out a long sigh. "If you can use your powers on me, then I will take you back there myself."

"DB." Hunter started to protest but stopped as Carter shot him one of his silencing looks.

Turning back to me, Carter tilted his head. "I'm serious. If you can zap me, then I will go back with you."

"I don't want to hurt you."

"You won't."

Carter's dark blue eyes were almost buried beneath a frown. His face was filthy, and although he stood with a straight back, his shoulders were sagging slightly. He was exhausted. Even if he had tough skin, I wasn't sure if he was going to withstand my power.

But if I didn't do something now, I'd lose the Lycans again. And more importantly, we'd lose Javion.

I raised my arms in front of me. Despite Carter having removed the chains, they felt heavy. Drawing up the electricity inside, I aimed at Carter and…

Nothing.

Not even a spark.

A wave of dizziness hit me, and I quickly shook it off.

Sucking in a deep breath, I tried again.

Nothing.

Just as I shifted my weight, the dizziness came back. And then everything went black.

Two

Hunter

Our team—our family—had consisted of four people who all had their own roles to play. DB was our alpha, the leader who had the ability to step back, assess a situation, and lead us with a clear head. At home, his old man vibes meant that he looked after our home and gardens. And our stomachs.

Being a vampire and having limits set on him by the time of day might have stopped Javion from actively joining any of our missions, but he was always with us, supporting us in our ears and using his tech skills to hack places he needed to give us the eyes and vision we lacked. At Castle Viegls, aside from taking care of our security, he also cooked a mean barbeque—even if he no longer ate it himself.

Where Javion was technical, Knox was mechanical. His love of tinkering, taking things apart and rebuilding, meant he could hotwire a car or break into most buildings. There wasn't much he couldn't fix, and he was the reason we never went without heat at home.

Then there was me. I wasn't useless by any stretch of the imagination, but I didn't really have a specialty. Naturally, the last spot on any team went to a medic of some sort. I wasn't bad at stitching people up, but that wasn't my forte. The truth was, I didn't really have one. I was a jack of all trades, but a master of none.

And right now, as I tried to hotwire a car, my hands shook so much I could barely get the starter wires to touch, so that was as good as useless.

The power plant, which had been a façade for the Lycan facility, was about an hour south of where we were. The place had literally been exploding around us as DB and I grabbed Knox and Zera, and then took to the skies to get the hell out of there.

She had spent the entire journey here protesting, trying to get back to Javion. I wasn't mad about that, just surprised. She'd gone from hating him, to indifference, to clawing at Carter like he was pulling her away from her mate.

I rubbed a hand over my face. Whatever had happened there, I was not in a state to start processing.

"How's it coming, Hunter?" DB asked. The urgency in his tone was also laced with weariness. His previous injuries hadn't completely healed before we'd arrived at the Lycan facility, and an hour flight with Zera acting like a lightning storm was draining.

"Knox is better at this than me."

The car was probably older than DB, and disused. But the interior of the vehicle also didn't have the same level of dust as I'd expect for something that was barely used.

From the door of the barn where DB was keeping watch, I heard a scratch as his hand rubbed over his coarse beard. "You can do this too."

He didn't add *you've got to*, to the end of his sentence, but he might as well have.

I was running on fear, adrenaline, and a blinding rage.

Although I'd carried Knox for miles, I tried not to

look at him. He was a mess and barely hanging on. One of his wings was missing, and there were dozens of raw claw marks covering his body. He was unconscious despite me taking care of his wounds, as best I could anyway.

Zera was almost as bad. There were contact burns all over her body, and it took breaking into this barn to find tools that could get the shackles off her wrists again.

Finally, the old Toyota rumbled to life.

While I pushed open the doors to the garage, DB gently moved Zera and Knox into the backseat of the car. As I climbed into the driver's seat, he sat down beside me, wincing at the effort.

I felt only slightly guilty as we drove out of the garage and away from the house in the middle of nowhere. A car this old probably belonged to an older person and given the lack of security and the state the house was in, they were probably going to struggle to replace it.

Behind me, Knox moaned in his sleep.

If this car got us to somewhere safe, at some point, I'd return and do what I could to help them out.

Despite the millions of questions I had, I asked DB only one. "Where do we go now?"

Both Zera and Knox needed to see a doctor, but there was no way we could take a gargoyle and an elemental—no, a fae—to a hospital.

"I don't even know where we are," DB muttered, staring out the window at the blackness of the night.

That was not a DB answer.

"You okay?" I asked.

A hand was on his beard again, but DB didn't respond.

Now was not the time for him to zone out. I needed my alpha. I needed someone to tell me what to do because I had no clue.

I drove until we hit a twenty-four-hour gas station. Ignoring the signs, I left the car running as I filled it up and then went in to pay. The cashier didn't even raise an eyebrow at the fact I had pulled every item of medical supply the small convenience store had and set them on the counter. Along with several bags of snacks, bottles of water, and a map, I paid for my stash and then hurried back to the car.

DB hadn't moved since I left. Nor had the other two.

I hit the road, but this time, at least I knew where we were. Kentucky.

We weren't going to make it back to Castle Viegls

before the fumes I was running on dried up. But I also wasn't going to head back there anyway. Our home had been infiltrated by the Lycans once, and it wasn't safe there anymore.

DB had a second location in Tennessee. A few years back, he'd bought a couple of safehouses across the country. This was the closest to our current location.

The house was too far to get to tonight, though. Instead, with the help of the map I'd just bought, I started us in the right direction. After a couple of hours, I pulled off at the first roadside motel I saw, grabbed us a room, and with little help from DB, got the four of us inside.

The exhaustion was setting in, and it was all I could do to get Zera and Knox on one bed. DB moved like a zombie to the other bed before sitting down and staring at the black screen of the television.

After dumping the medical supplies on the floor by the bed, I busied myself with checking the wounds of my brother and our mate.

"There's no way he survived it," DB muttered, suddenly.

Although his voice was quiet, it was still loud in the room and made me jump. I sucked in a deep breath, more at the acknowledgment he was right over trying to calm myself. "I don't think so either."

I'd looked back at that power plant as we flew away. Flames had ignited the sky, trying to lick the clouds. Sirens blared across the valley, warning local residents that the nuclear power plant was suffering from some catastrophic failure. Headlights lit up the roads as dozens of cars all sped away from area.

Thankfully, it wasn't really a nuclear power plant, and no local residents were in any danger of nuclear fallout. But there was a blazing inferno.

Zera hadn't stopped screaming that Javion was still inside.

There was no way in hell he'd survived that.

I glanced over at DB now. Guilt was radiating from him like he was the thing in meltdown. He'd thrown Javion out of our home. As far as I knew, the last conversation they had was him telling the vampire he was no longer welcome at Castle Viegls.

No wonder he was shutting down.

"Get some rest, Carter," I told him.

Rubbing at his head, DB finally nodded and rolled over onto his side.

It took most of the time checking Knox over for DB's breathing to fall into a steady rhythm. After making sure Zera's wrists were still dressed, finally treating her feet, and then checking the other minor wounds all over her body, I slumped down against the wall.

There was space next to DB, but I didn't want to fall asleep—just in case.

Just in case of what, I wasn't sure. Something happening to one of them? Someone coming through the door? Javion miraculously calling me.

The last one was the least likely option. Ignoring the fact that my phone wasn't working, I doubted the Lycans had handed him his phone back…

I doubted there was anyone to hand a phone back to.

With nothing else left to do, I reached for the bag of snacks and pulled out a tube of Salt and Vinegar Pringles. After trying to get my fingers past the first five chips, I turned the can upside down and dumped the contents onto the tiled floor beside me, not even caring how clean this dump of a motel was.

With my hand and elbow propping my head up, I sat there, eating junk food. They tasted like cardboard. I just wasn't hungry. How could I eat?

Instead, I grabbed the map and stared at it, trying to find the small town DB's safehouse was in. That was what I could do: come up with a plan for what came next.

Assuming the worst-case scenario, the owner of the car we'd stolen would have discovered it missing and reported it to the police. We'd need another way to travel. Currently, we were close to the Kentucky-Tennessee border. It looked like a few hours' drive to the safehouse.

Or an hour's flight.

Stealing another car was risky, and I wasn't convinced that the Lycan's weren't looking for us. They'd found us once before from Javion's internet searches. Who's to say they didn't have access to the police—to our bank transactions?

We had all the things we needed to go into hiding back at Castle Viegls, including new identities and money. Only, we'd not brought any of it with us. I hoped DB had this in the safehouse too.

The motel was shitty enough that I was able to pay with cash and no ID. Hopefully that was enough to keep anyone off our trail, for a while, at least.

I didn't sleep. DB did. He slept through the day, not waking until after sunset. Neither Knox, nor Zera, even stirred as we picked them up and carried them outside.

"We can get another car if you think that's going to be easier?" I told DB.

"No. You're right. Flying is not only quicker, but will be much harder to trace," he responded, sounding much like his usual self.

Aside from Knox in my arms, the only other thing I carried was a bag of used bandages. Maybe it was lack of sleep, but paranoia was setting in. I didn't want to leave anything that could give clues as to where we'd been. The bag would be burned when we got to the safe house.

Under a cover of darkness, we set to the skies. DB had studied the map and assured me he knew where we were going. Trusting him, I let him lead.

At this point, I was too tired to do much more.

Thankfully, the late winter skies still provided a lot of cloud coverage, but with the detours we had to make around several towns and cities, it took us a while to get to the safe house.

DB's safe house was hidden away in the Great Smoky Mountains, not far from the border of North Carolina and Tennessee. We'd almost flown a full circle from leaving Castle Viegls and rescuing Knox and Zera from the Lycan facility.

Suddenly, DB dipped, dropping below the tree line. Hidden beneath the leafless hickories stood a large stone house. In daylight, I'd have seen it, but now, with no moon or stars to light up the sky, the house was hidden in darkness.

I landed heavily behind my alpha. Fatigue left me with aching muscles.

Gently, DB laid Zera on the ground beside me. "Let me check inside."

Shifting my weight, I prepared myself in case I needed to scoop Zera up and fly, but a short while later, DB came back outside.

"It's clear." He sounded relieved. "The local I paid to keep an eye on the place hasn't been out for a while. There's so much dust I can see my own footprints. No one else is here."

It wasn't until I had gone upstairs and laid Knox down on one of the double beds that I finally felt myself relax. DB had placed Zera next to him, and I quickly checked their wounds as best I could in the low light from an old oil lamp DB gave me.

DB disappeared, and eventually, a low grumbling started up. At least the local had kept the generator's fuel filled up. I waited until I rebandaged Zera's wrist before I leaned over to switch the bedside light on, turning off the oil lamp so I could clean up in better light.

"How are they looking?" DB appeared in the doorway. There was a smudge of oil on his cheek.

I rubbed at my jaw as I shrugged. "What's the chance we have some magical remedies here?"

Having moved over to the bed, DB perched on the edge beside Zera, carefully brushing her dark hair from her face. "There's a safe in the master bedroom. There should be some magical ointments and remedies in there, along with IDs and money. I'll go get it. You should rest."

"I'm not tired."

DB looked up; his blue eyes seemed blacker than usual thanks to the dark circles around them. "That's a load of crap, and we both know it. When was the last time you slept?"

"What if someone comes?" I protested.

"This place is protected by wards."

I folded my arms. "So was Castle Viegls."

With a sigh, DB lowered his head; his gaze dropped back to Zera's pale face. "The only people who know about this place are in this room. Get some rest, Hunter. We'll talk later when Knox and Zera are awake."

"What about you?"

"I slept last night. I'll stay with them." DB looked up and scanned his gaze over me. "At the very least, you should go clean up. I turned the water heater on, so we'll have hot water soon. Get a shower and rest for a while, even if you don't sleep."

That was DB's polite way of saying I looked like crap. I nodded before leaving this bedroom and heading to the next. The door closed with a soft click as I leaned against it and breathed in and out.

Alone in the darkness, not wanting to turn a light on, I stared around the unfamiliar room, not really seeing anything despite the nearly flawless night vision I had. Although I'd told DB that I wasn't tired, I was exhausted. The fumes I'd been running on had almost run out.

The prospect of sleep made me uneasy. Zera, Knox and Javion had been taken from Castle Viegls where there were also supposed to be wards protecting the place. Wards which were supposed to deter anyone— human and supe—from getting close. We'd paid the witches a fortune for those wards.

They were taken anyway.

Either the wards failed, or they were broken. I wasn't sure which was worse. But if they'd been breached at Castle Viegls, who's to say they wouldn't be here?

"And how are you going to do anything in this state?" I asked myself.

If Lycans were to burst through the door right now, I wouldn't be able to fight any of them off for long. Much as it made me feel uneasy, rest—sleep—was exactly what I needed. Rubbing my hand over my face, I pushed away from the door and half stumbled over to the bed.

Despite the local person coming to check up on the place, just as DB had said, there was a layer of dust indicating they'd probably not been here in the past couple of months. The bed had a protective sheet draped over it like the one in the other room did.

I was too tired to give a crap.

The water might have been warming up, but the pipes in this place hadn't been used in who knew how long. It wouldn't have surprised me if the water was lukewarm and clear as dirt.

Without even bothering to take my clothes off, I flopped onto the bed.

Tomorrow, I'd deal with all the shit piling up at a rapid pace.

Three

Hunter

It took Knox two more days before he woke up, and about two minutes in, he realized how much pain he was in.

"I've got some painkillers." I offered him a glass of water and six pills, helping him sit. They were human pills and not going to do too much for him, but DB and I decided that unless it absolutely came to it, we were not getting any other supe involved.

Wincing, Knox took the pills from me and washed

them down with water. He leaned back against the pillows and closed his eyes. "How is she?"

I took the glass and set it on the bedside table, taking a few steps back. Although there were enough rooms, we'd left Zera in the same bed as Knox.

She still hadn't woken up.

Knox slowly opened his eyes; his gaze drifted to the unconscious woman beside him. He started to raise his arm and then instantly bit back a cry of pain.

"For fuck's sake, just stay still." I snapped at him.

He had insisted on staying upright, despite the fact that it was putting unnecessary pressure on his back.

"You're still healing."

Knox's eyes narrowed as he glared at me. "Fuck that."

Throwing my hands in the air, I rolled my eyes. "You're a stubborn asshole."

Whether he was in pain or not, Knox flipped me the bird and then returned his attention to Zera. He reached out again, hands hovering over her wrists, but he didn't touch the bandages.

The door opened, and Carter walked in carrying a bowl of the stew he and I had eaten from earlier. "How are you feeling?"

"Like shit."

DB looked back at me. His eyebrows momentarily knitted together while he continued his path to the bed. "Your body has taken some serious damage. Have something to eat and help it continue to recover."

Knox finally brought his attention to our alpha. "Where's Javion?"

There was something in Knox's eyes telling me he already knew the answer, but he stared at him anyway, expecting DB to tell him otherwise.

"He didn't make it. I'm sorry."

"No," Knox said, far too firmly. "He said he'd be right behind us."

"Knox, I'm sorry—"

"Fuck you and your apologies." He yanked his covers back and attempted to get out of bed.

Reacting faster than DB who was still holding onto the bowl of food, I darted forward to catch Knox before he could fall out of bed. "You need to stay in bed. You're nowhere near recovered en—"

"Fuck you too." Knox snapped at me now. He tried to push me away but had no strength to do more than smack his hand against my arm. "Why are we here? Why aren't we going back to get him?"

"The power plant was destroyed," DB told him. "It went up in flames. We needed to get you and Zera out of there."

Knox stopped struggling against me to glare at DB. "Did you even try to save him? Or did you decide this was a convenient way to get rid of him permanently?"

"Knox!" I cried.

Behind me, DB inhaled sharply. "No matter what you think, I never wanted this to happen to Javion." Abruptly, DB turned. He set the stew down on a chest of drawers, sending it slopping over the side, and then walked back out of the room.

"That's not fair," I murmured.

The injuries to Knox's face had mostly healed; the bruises were a faint yellow. But the eyebrow where his piercing had been ripped out, combined with scars where Lycan claws had slashed his face had left him with a permanent scowl. There was no warmth left in his gaze as he stared me down.

"Then why didn't either of you try to save him?" Knox's voice cracked, but he didn't flinch.

"The place was exploding around us." I tried justifying our actions to myself as much as to Knox. "You were unconscious in my arms. Zera was—" I pointed at her. "If we hadn't left, neither of you would have survived. What you would have done?"

Knox turned his head. I wasn't sure if it was to look

at Zera or to hide the tear rolling down his cheek. "Javion went back to stop the Lycans so me *and* Zera could escape. You can try to justify your decision by saying that he didn't care for her, but he did."

My eyebrows curved upwards before I could stop them. Thankfully, Knox still had his head turned.

Javion cared about her?

"No one is saying he didn't care, and that wasn't even a consideration," I told him. "We had seconds to make our decision. *Seconds.* That's seconds to try to save you and Zera. None of us would have survived if we tried to get inside. We were barely in the air before they were shooting at us."

Knox whipped his head back to look at me, his eyes narrowed. "We're gargoyles—stone demons. Since when hasn't our skin protected us from bullets?"

Bullets maybe. But if we were still on the ground, we'd have been overwhelmed by Lycans. If we'd have gone inside, while our skin might have protected us from the fire, our lungs still needed oxygen. Knox was talking bullshit, and I suspected he knew that.

"And what about Zera?"

He didn't blink as he stared, and then after taking a shuddering breath, he closed his eyes.

"I'm sorry. I can't even begin to imagine how much

pain you're in right now."

"Fuck you," Knox muttered.

There wasn't much else I could say or do. The words were already starting to feel thick in my throat. For the past two days, my heart had felt heavy, sitting in my chest like there was something tied around it. Things hadn't been the same between me and Javion, but he had still been my friend.

Family.

He might not have been my lover, but he was still someone I loved.

I was hurting too.

Once, Knox and I had been close. Those days had long passed, but that didn't mean I wanted him in pain. We didn't have the same kind of connection twins supposedly had, but I could feel his pain as much as my own.

The urge to take him in my arms took over me, so I stepped towards him to do just that.

"Don't touch me," Knox said, not even opening his eyes.

Swallowing back the lump in my throat, I took a step back, turned and then picked up the bowl of stew before offering it to my brother. "You should eat."

Knox gave me a look of disdain. "Why? How much

food will it take to grow back a wing? Or what about a lover?"

"I'll leave it here," I said, setting it down on the bedside table, closer to him so he wouldn't have to get out of bed. "Would you like to be left alone?"

"No." Knox looked me in the eyes. As he did, something in me broke. All I could see in his gaze was despair and pain. "I want Javion." His voice cracked.

"I'll be back later to check on your injuries and Zera," I told him.

Knox turned away, staring down at the woman beside him. He didn't look up again as I left the room.

In the hallway, I bent over, resting my hands on my knees, and sucked in a few deep breathes. I might not have had the same relationship with Javion as Knox did, but he was still like family to me. And Knox *was* family. Having a knife stabbed in me would have hurt less than seeing him in pain like that—again.

My vision grew blurry, and I quickly wiped the tears away as I stood straight. The relief I'd felt from seeing Knox open his eyes earlier was gone.

I headed downstairs, looking everywhere for DB. It was only when I got to the last room, the kitchen, that I saw him outside. It was late afternoon, and the sun was already disappearing behind the tree line, sending a chill across the area.

At first, when I got close to DB, I thought his movements were from shivers, but then I heard him. "Carter?"

DB's hands flew to his face before he half turned to look at me. The dusk light was dim enough that no human would've been able to see the traces of his tears in the shadows cast on his face. I chose to ignore them.

"How is Knox?"

I shook my head.

"I think, when Zera is awake, we should have some sort of service for Javion."

Something told me that was the last thing Knox would want, but my heart hurt too much to tell DB otherwise. Instead, I looked out into the forest. "What do we do now?"

We'd been asking each other the same question since we got here and still hadn't come up with an answer.

Turning, I found DB staring back at the house. "I don't know. But I *need* Zeraora to wake up. Soon."

Four

Zera

Something didn't feel right.

Wherever I was, there wasn't much light. I was alone and in a place that felt very unfamiliar to me.

No, that wasn't quite right.

There was something familiar. Something close. I just didn't know what it was.

Holding up my hand, I tried to summon the energy inside me, hoping to create some light.

Nothing appeared.

Frowning, I tried again.

Nothing.

Was this the thing that didn't feel right?

"Carter?" I tried to call out, but barely any sound left my mouth.

Carefully, I walked forward with my hands stretched out in front of me. I wasn't wearing my glasses, and my eyesight was bad in daylight. It was almost gone in the dark.

At the last moment, I saw the wall, but only as my hand passed through it.

Astral projecting.

My body wasn't really here, wherever here was…

I stepped through the wall and was instantly blinded by bright light. Bringing my hands up over my eyes, I tried to shield them, but the light seemed to shine straight through my arms.

Turning my back to the light, facing the wall now, I waited until the light didn't hurt my eyes and I could see.

"Where are my clothes?" Again, no words seemed to leave my mouth as I tried to speak them.

No voice. No clothes.

No clue as to where I was or why I was here.

My gaze drifted to my wrists. There were no wrist guards or bandages to cover my skin. Although there was no blood, there were deep crevices carved into my flesh with red and black scabs making the wounds hard and dry. Black lightning bolts stretched down my arms from more injuries trying to heal.

Dropping my arms so I wouldn't have to look at them, I turned my attention to the place I was in. Now that my eyes were accustomed to the light, I realized it wasn't that bright. I was in the middle of a small platform. There were stairs leading up and stairs leading down.

Wherever this was, it had the hairs on my arms standing on end.

Lycans.

At the thought of the wolves, rage bubbled inside me.

They hurt me. They hurt Knox and they'd…

A gasp of pain—this time audible—escaped me.

Javion.

The Lycans will need to pray to all the gods, because if I came across any of them while I was here, I would show them no mercy. They would all die.

I went up the stairs until I came to a door. Whether it was locked or not, I didn't know nor care. Instead, I

Shocked

walked through it and found people on the other side.

None of them looked in my direction.

Did that mean they were human? Or were they Lycan and unable to see me?

Hunter once told me that supes could naturally sense when another supernatural creature was near, even if they couldn't necessarily tell what they were. There was something about these people that had my hairs standing on end again.

The building we were in reminded me of Castle Viegls. The walls had paintings on them, and below my feet, I was now walking on carpet. Lots of doors with numbers all starting with four were spaced out between the paintings.

I walked through the closest one. On the other side was a bedroom with its own bathroom. This one had no people in it, but there were clothes piled on a chair under the window. I moved over to the window and stared out. From here, all I could see were trees below us.

Frowning, I turned around, trying to find anything that would give me a clue to where I was, but nothing looked familiar. And I still didn't know enough to even know what to look for.

Heading back towards the door, I stopped when I

saw a picture on the back. It looked like a map with writing on it. "M-a-i-s-o-n d-e-s l-o-u-p-s." I read the letters out, but even as I tried to sound it out like Carter had taught me, I didn't know what it said.

If there were no answers in this room, I would look in the next. I turned to the right and walked through the wall. This room was almost identical to the other, except everything seemed to be the opposite way around. This room was empty too.

The next one had a person in it. They were stretched out on the bed, watching television which flickered as I walked by. The woman frowned, but it was at the television, not me.

For hours, I walked up and down each floor of the building. There were six of them in total. I went up. I went back down.

It took me a long time to remember the word for it, but I was sure this was a hotel. I was also sure that everyone inside was a supe.

And I had no clue why I was here.

On the bottom floor was a big dining room with people coming and going at all hours. Behind it was a kitchen that was much, much bigger than Carter's. There were people in white clothes cooking meals. Everything they put on a plate looked delicious. Leaving the kitchen behind, I walked through to where a woman sat behind a desk, and opposite, two large doors led outside.

The other thing confusing me was how long I'd been here for. Normally, whenever I'd astral projected anywhere, it hadn't lasted for long. Here, day had become night, and people had started to sleep.

It was only at these doors that I felt different. The closer I got, the weaker I seemed. And when I looked down at my body, it would go even more see-through.

As I watched the sky start to get lighter, I made a decision. I walked through the door.

Five

Zera

Before I opened my eyes, I could feel everything—like warmth from the body curled around me.

And pain.

A lot of agonizing pain radiated from my wrists.

"Zera?" I could hear Knox's voice behind my ear, and the grip around me loosened.

With my eyes still closed, I ignored the movement around me, as well as Knox's shouts. Instead, I focused on the pain. It was like my body had forgotten what that felt like and was suddenly remembering.

It took a few moments for my body to adjust, allowing the sensation to become familiar. When I opened my eyes, Knox wasn't the only one in the room with me; Hunter and Carter were too.

"I'm fine," I said. Or I tried to. Words didn't come out of my mouth, just a hoarse hiss.

"Don't force yourself, Zee. Just take a few minutes and sip this." Hunter helped me raise my head enough to drink the water he offered.

"I'm glad you're awake," Carter said.

The cool water eased the pain in my throat slightly. After drinking my fill, I lowered my head and closed my eyes, yet not wanting to sleep. "My head feels fuzzy," I mumbled.

"You've been asleep for a long time," Hunter told me. "Just rest up for a little longer."

In the darkness of my mind, a light appeared, illuminating a familiar figure. Although I could only see an outline, I knew instantly who it was. Abruptly, I sat upright. "Javion."

As I said his name, everything started spinning. Before I could fall, however; arms wrapped around my waist to steady me.

"Careful," Knox muttered in my ear. He didn't let go.

"Where is he?" I opened my eyes and asked both of the Carters that I saw.

Instead of responding, Carter dropped his gaze to the floor.

"Zera, baby, Javion didn't…" Knox's voice cracked.

I turned to face him, frowning. "Didn't what?"

A hand took mine, drawing my attention to the owner.

"Javion didn't make it out," Hunter told me.

"Then we have to go and get him." Tugging my hand free, I wriggled out of Knox's grasp and swung my body around. As my feet hit the floor and I tried to stand, more dizziness hit me, along with a wave of pain, this time, coming from my feet.

I lurched forward, but Hunter caught my waist. My hands fell to his shoulders as I steadied myself. Almost upright, everything seemed to start hurting all at once.

The pain from my wrists was the worst. They throbbed, and with each pulse under the bandage, it felt like they were being thrust into a fire. The soles of my feet felt like I was standing on broken glass, even though they were bandaged up too. And every time I swallowed, I was almost sure I was swallowing knives. Over it all was a dull ache that seemed to have settled into all of my muscles.

But none of that was important if Javion was still captured by the Lycans. Had I destroyed everything enough that the prison he'd been held in wouldn't hurt him? Or was he in as much pain as me because I wasn't there to power the things stopping the fake sunlight?

Pushing off Hunter, I stumbled past him, trying to ignore the pain in my feet as I walked across the room.

"Zeraora, there's nothing you can do now."

I ignored Carter and pulled the door open. Javion said he would meet us. What if he was waiting for us?

Although I was aware of the three gargoyles following me, I wasn't listening to whatever they were saying. It was taking all of my energy just to keep from falling down the stairs. Vaguely, I was aware that this wasn't Castle Viegls anymore.

My determination masked my pain...

Until I reached a door and pulled it open.

Outside, it was raining heavily. With almost no wind in the air, the water seemed to be falling in straight, visible lines.

Dizziness hit me again, only this time, I couldn't move.

I couldn't breathe.

Although I was upright, it felt like someone was standing on my chest. My heart was pounding as hard as the rain fell.

All I wanted—needed—was to go out and get back to Javion, but terror had me rooted to this spot, and my vision was slowly going dark.

"Zee? Zera?" Hunter stepped in front of me, raised his wings and blocked out the view of the rain. He leaned over and took both of my hands in his. Until his warm ones were holding mine, I hadn't realized how cold they were.

"Ja… Ja…" The words weren't coming out.

"Zera, you need to breathe. You need to take a deep breath."

I was breathing. Fast. But I couldn't feel the air was not doing anything.

Hands appeared out of nowhere, settling on my hips. And then I was lifted out of the doorway, despite Hunter holding on like I was being pulled away.

"Knox, let your brother handle it."

"By standing in the fucking doorway? She needs to come inside, away from the rain. Look at her."

Hunter followed me in, kicking the door closed behind me. "Look at me, Zee," he said, firmly. "Don't focus on anything else. Can you do that?"

I locked my gaze onto his green eyes. Although he had a slight blur to him as I wasn't wearing my glasses, I could still see the concern in his expression.

"Zera?" he said again. "You need to inhale. You've stopped breathing."

It took me a moment to process what he was saying before I opened my mouth and gasped. Air seemed to leave me, but I couldn't get it back in.

"Get something to eat," Knox said. "That's what you did last time."

As I started to look in his direction, Hunter shifted his weight, drawing my gaze back to him. "Focus on me. Just me."

I nodded.

"Tell me something you can see."

"You." I gulped in a mouthful of air.

"What else?"

"How the fuck is I Spy going to help her?"

"Knox." Came Carter's firm tone. "Either shut up or leave."

"On me, Zera." Hunter squeezed my hands. "What else?"

I glanced at him before dropping my gaze to the floor. "Wood."

"Good. Anything else?"

With a sideways glance, I spotted a picture. "Horses."

Hunter arched an eyebrow but nodded. "One more thing."

"Bandages."

Squeezing my hands again, Hunter nodded. "What about something you can feel?"

"Pain."

This time, Hunter winced, but he nodded again. "Anything else?"

"Cold." The cold from the wooden floor was seeping through my bandages, but my feet were starting to feel blissfully numb at that. "And warm." That came from his hands.

"And can you smell anything?"

I sucked in a deep breath through my nose. Although I wasn't sure what I was smelling, I nodded. "Food."

Hunter smiled. "Anything else?"

"You." Hunter always had a fruity smell to him. Even now, it was there. Like the warmth from his hands, there was a familiarity that came with it. He was the sweetest smelling person I knew... not that I knew many people.

"What else?"

"Clean." The smell mixed strangely with the delicious aroma of whatever was cooking, but it was the same as when we would clean up. There were several different liquids that we'd use depending on if we were cleaning a floor or a cabinet. And something called polish: that one smelled the best. "It doesn't smell like Castle Viegls though."

Although Hunter had asked me to keep my attention on him, I couldn't help but look around. This room wasn't like any in our home. The door to the outside was in a large hallway. This one was to one side of a living room. The floor was cold, but the room was warm, despite there being no fire.

"We're somewhere else," Hunter told me. "Somewhere safe." Using his chin, Hunter nodded towards the sofas. "Why don't we go and sit down? DB can get you something to eat. That food you smell is his pie. It's good."

I started to let him lead me to the sofa, but I stopped and shook my head. "What about Javion?"

"Javion didn't make it." Hunter's voice was so soft, I could barely hear him.

"Then we need to go help him."

"No, I mean…" Hunter sighed.

"He's dead."

My lips parted as I turned to face Knox. "He's a vampire. He's supposed to be."

Knox's gaze met my eyes, and then he closed them. "He's dead, Zera. Dead and not undead. He's gone." He turned on his heel and limped away.

I looked back at Hunter, and then Carter, confused. "No, he was right behind us. He was going to follow us out."

"I'm so sorry," Carter said.

"Why are you saying sorry? We need to go get him." I pulled my hand free of Hunter's grip and started to move back towards the door.

Hunter was back in front of me, blocking the way. "Javion is gone, and we can't get him back. There's nothing to get. Like when you killed the vampires that attacked us?"

I'd turned all the vampires I could into ash.

Did that happen to Javion? Did I do it?

A wave of dizziness hit me again, and I swayed on my feet. It was Carter who swooped in, catching me before I fell. "How about you sit down now?"

"Why didn't you go back?" I looked up into Carter's dark, blue eyes. "Did you hate him that much?"

Zera fainted in my arms, but her question had me frozen to the spot.

"Don't misunderstand her." Hunter stepped forward, taking Zera from me. "It's Zera. She doesn't understand the weight of her words sometimes."

I watched as Hunter carried her over to the sofa and gently set her down. With tenderness, he brushed her hair from her face as she started to stir beneath him.

Although I did banish Javion from Castle Viegls, I didn't—hadn't hated him. Angry and disappointed in him, yes. Even betrayed, considering he'd allowed the vampires to gain access to our home. But it was never hate.

Death was the last thing I'd ever wish on him.

There was a lump in my throat that had been there for weeks since we'd arrived at this house. One that had me constantly on the brink of tears at the loss of my friend, and right now, the lump was growing.

Leaving Hunter to look after Zera, I walked into the kitchen and stopped when I reached the worktop. Using the side to brace myself, I leaned into it and closed my eyes.

For nearly three weeks, I'd waited for my Zeraora to wake. Although that inner demon was constantly assuring me that she was going to be fine, that she'd used a lot of energy and just needed to rest. The me that had been married once and lost the first love of his life had felt like his second chance had been taken away from him.

If Zeraora hadn't woke up, I wasn't sure what I would have done.

Now the relief was rushing through me, mixing with the sorrow from losing Javion.

"DB?"

I turned. Before I could process how close Hunter was, he pulled me into a hug. We stood like that for a while, not saying anything. And then Hunter stepped back and ran his hand through his hair.

"Zera's sleeping."

Remaining silent, I went to the cupboard and pulled out two glasses. After getting ice from the freezer, I poured some whiskey into the glasses before handing one to Hunter. After taking a large gulp, I eased myself into one of the chairs at the kitchen table.

Hunter slid into the chair beside me, setting his untouched glass on the side. He pointed at it. "What's wrong?"

"Zeraora." I rubbed at my beard before taking another sip.

"She's going to be fine once she sleeps it off. I mean, as much as she can be, afraid of rain thanks to the traumatic life she's lived."

I let out a long sigh. "She didn't spark."

"Come again?" Hunter cocked his head as he stared.

"Anger, distress, fear... she experienced every one of those emotions and not one spark."

Realization hit Hunter as his lips parted. "Shit!" He

glanced back at the door before returning his attention to me. "Maybe it's normal, right? She's powerful. Knox said they were constantly forcing her power from her, and then she destroyed a power plant. Maybe it's like using your energy in a fight. Once my adrenaline has worn off, all I want to do is sleep."

I took another mouthful of whiskey, holding the liquid in my mouth for a moment before swallowing it.

"I have no idea. And I have no idea who to ask. Whether Zeraora is an elemental or a fae, who knows anything about them? And if they do, can we trust them?"

"What do we do?" he asked.

Hunter and I had avoided having this conversation. Or rather, I'd avoided having this conversation, blaming the need to have Zera and Knox present, but the truth was I had no idea what to do. All three of them would be looking at me for the next steps, yet I had none.

"Do we go after the Lycans?"

After reaching for the bottle, I topped my glass up. "I've not given up on ending them," I told him. "But we stand no chance as we are. There's nothing we can do or say now to keep Zera or Knox from that fight."

Hunter glanced towards the window, fixing his attention on something outside. "I'm not sure Knox will survive another encounter with the Lycans."

I didn't disagree.

"We can't do anything in the state we are in right now, but if we do nothing, we're going to spend more time making sure Zera doesn't go on a suicide mission by herself. And if we stop her, are we any better than the—"

"Do not say it. We are nothing like them."

Nodding, Hunter looked at me before taking a sip of his drink. "I know. I just don't know if she will see it that way."

"The Lycans infiltrated Castle Viegls. I think it was that mongoose shifter who figured out our connection to Zeraora, but even if she had, the wards should have stopped anyone from infiltrating them like that." I leaned forward. "That's the first thing we need to do: find out why. We can't stay here forever."

"Do you think the witches sold us out?"

I shrugged. "They're the ones that performed the wards. If not the Daughters of the Twilight Goddess, then another coven."

"We should talk to Liberty."

"She's one of them, Hunter."

"She is, but there's some rift between her and her coven. She's not the greatest witch." He bobbed his head from side to side. "Okay, she's a shit witch and a little loopy, talking to herself, and they don't like it. She works as a hairdresser, doing piss-poor jinxes on the side. But I trust her."

If I remembered correctly, he and the witch had hooked up in the past. "You trust her enough to stake Zeraora's life on it?"

Hunter's gaze dropped to the whiskey he'd barely touched as he swirled it around. "Yes," he responded, eventually.

"What are you talking about?"

I looked up at Knox, who was standing in the doorway. Once, when he was younger, I was willing to bet that anyone they ever met struggled to tell the difference between the twins. Even when I first met him and he had scars on his face, the similarity between them remained.

Now, it was almost like looking at a stranger.

As he stared the two of us down, I stood and walked over to the cupboard before pulling out another glass. After filling it with ice and whiskey, I walked over to the injured gargoyle and offered him the drink.

Knox took it, but not without giving me a death glare. Animosity radiated off him. Fully expecting him to make some biting comment, I was surprised when he walked over to the table, trying to hide the pain and limp from us. He sat down and continued to glower.

"What do we do next?" Hunter asked.

"We find the Lycans and turn each one of those fuckers into a pelt."

Hunter rolled his eyes. "Somewhat unsurprisingly, that's not what we're going to do."

"So, not only do you not care what they did to us, but you're going to let them get away with it?"

Javion and Knox always made little sense to me. Both carried this burning rage inside of them which I expected would consume them both and burn them out. It didn't. Somehow, it worked. Somehow, they kept each other in check.

"You can barely walk," I told Knox. "Your wounds are healing, but slowly. The Lycans did a number on you, and you need time to heal. You're not the only one who wants revenge. Their ledger is getting bigger and bigger, and it is long overdue collection."

"Then let's go after them."

On his lap, hidden from Knox by the table, Hunter's hands curled into fists. "What do you think we've been trying to do for the last ten years? They have evaded us time and time again."

"Then we go back to the place they held us and find

clues." Knox glared at the pair of us. "We don't just sit around doing fuck all this time."

"You're not the only one who wants revenge, Knox," I said, quietly.

Knox's eyes narrowed further.

Before he could say anything more, I gestured in the direction of the other room. "You think she's ready to go?"

For the first time, Knox's expression softened. "She's not ready."

"Zeraora was ready to go marching straight into the Lycan's camp when she can barely walk, and I don't know if you noticed, but she's not giving off any electrical charge. She has no way of protecting herself." I moved over to the table and took my seat. "We need time to look, and more importantly, we need time for Zera to heal."

"You're going to let her fight the Lycans?" Knox shot me a look of disbelief.

Drumming my fingers on the table, I didn't answer. Of course, I didn't want to let her. The alpha in me knew she shouldn't be allowed to leave my sight, whilst also keeping her far away from the Lycans. My duty was to protect my mate.

I was sure the same thing was true for the twins.

She was ours, and we were supposed to protect her, to keep her safe. We couldn't fail her again.

"We're going to investigate why the wards failed," I told him instead.

"You're going to waste time instead of going back?"

"The facility the Lycans were using is nothing more than rubble now, and humans will be crawling all over the site."

Knox arched an eyebrow. Or tried to. The injury to his face made it look more like a sneer. Hell, maybe he *was* sneering. "The Lycans had that place listed as nuclear to keep humans away."

"Use your head, Knox." Hunter sighed. "If a nuclear power plant went up in smoke, they'd be checking the radiation levels in the air, and as soon as the humans discovered it wasn't really nuclear, they'd be investigating what really happened."

"Our wards failed." They were designed to keep humans and supes away, so unless the supes knew we were there, they shouldn't have been able to get close without the ward essentially sending them in a different direction. It was a diversionary ward that had never failed us before.

Even I couldn't fault Javion for that one. His

invitation did give the vampires entry, but the wards should have repelled them before that.

"The attacks themselves might be separate incidents, but the only way for them to fail is magic," I continued. "And if the witches sold us out, maybe they can lead us back to the person who paid that price."

That had both of the twins sitting up, looking at me.

"You think the Lycans went to the witches?" Hunter asked.

The more I thought about it, the more I did. Maybe not directly. More like, they paid an intermediary like the mongoose shifter. However, that could lead us back to the Lycans. I highly doubted going back to where I'd seen the mongoose shifter last would work. Even if I could find the location again, they'd have moved on by now.

"When do we leave?" Knox asked.

"Don't get too excited," I told him, shaking my head. "We're going nowhere until you and Zeraora are healed."

"Fuck that!" Knox snarled. He swiped his hand, sending the barely touched glass of whiskey soaring across the room.

"Knox." There was a warning to my tone.

Hunter turned in his chair to angle himself at me. "Let him go. There's no car here, and we're further from civilization here than we were at Castle Viegls."

Knox glowered. Then suddenly, he stood. Although he sent the chair flying, I could also see him hiding a wince. "Fuck you."

Hunter waited for Knox to storm out of the room before he sighed and took a sip of his drink. "I'm starting to think one of our parents was a berserker, and Knox inherited those genes."

Seven

Zera

Every time I tried to do anything, I got tired. Going up and down the stairs exhausted me. Watching television made me want to sleep. Even just sitting had my eyelids feeling heavy.

More importantly, my powers were gone.

I held my hand out in front of me, trying to get even a small spark, but nothing came.

"You just need to rest," Carter said.

He reached over and took my hand, holding it in

his as he rested them both on his lap. We were in the small living room, sitting on the sofa.

Hunter sat on the other side of me, doing something on a computer.

That was proof I was broken. Back in the castle, no one would let me near one of Javion's computers.

Blowing out an impatient breath, I sat upright. "You need to teach me to fight."

I could see Hunter turn his head to look at me from the corner of my eye, but I kept my attention on Carter. "If I can't use my powers, I need to learn to use my hands."

Carter licked his lips. "You can barely stay awake to watch the television."

In the two weeks since I'd woken up in this house, Hunter had ordered me new glasses. My eyes hurt less when I was wearing them, but they did nothing to stop the heaviness in my eyelids.

"I don't want to watch television. Watching people fight is not the same."

Carter shifted his weight to face me fully. "You are not ready."

Irritated, I pulled my hand free and stood.

"He's not saying it to be mean, Zee."

Ignoring them both, I stalked upstairs. By the time

I reached the top, I had to lean against the wall and rest. Maybe I did get tired easily, but all Hunter and Carter would let me do was… nothing.

After wiping a bead of sweat from my forehead, I continued back to my bedroom. Knox was inside, sitting on the bed, half curled up against the wall. He spent all his time in my room.

The gargoyle looked up as I walked in, frowning. "You look angry."

I walked over, climbed into the bed and crawled into his arms. "I want to fight, but they won't let me."

Knox's laugh was dry and hollow. "Tell me about it."

If something was wrong with me, there was something wrong with Knox too. The curtains in the bedroom were never opened, and the only light came from a dim lamp which made everything have an orange tint and long shadows. Carter would cook several times a day, but Knox rarely left the room.

"You should teach me." I turned in Knox's arms so I could look up at him. "We can go destroy the Lycans on our own. That will stop Carter and Hunter being scared."

Knox's fingers tapped on my arm, but his attention was on a spot on the wall across the room. "They're more scared of losing you," he said with a sigh. Finally, he looked down at me. "Not doing anything, not getting revenge for Ja…" He swallowed. "Being here and doing nothing is killing me, too. But as much as I hate it, right now, I can't fight one Lycan, never mind a whole pack. And you don't even have enough energy to stand upright, much less power a torch. We've been after them for years. We're not giving up. We're just… getting stronger first."

Javion was dead. Knox was injured. Carter would barely look at any of us, and even Hunter rarely wore his cheerful smile. I hated how much the Lycans had hurt all of them, even more than how much I hated them for what they did to me.

My need for revenge was as strong as my need to make sure my men were safe. We all needed the Lycans gone forever. All of them. As soon as possible.

"If you teach me to fight—"

"Zera." Knox stopped staring at the wall and took hold of my waist, twisting so he could look at me. "Do you honestly think you can fight the Lycans right now?"

I was angry enough, and I wanted to say yes, but when I opened my mouth, nothing came out. Instead, I raised my hand and tried to get the spark to appear.

Outside, the wind was howling, lashing rain against

the window. The noise made me jump before my body froze. And still, not one jolt of electricity appeared.

Even if I could find my powers again, I couldn't go anywhere because of *rain*.

"I'm sorry."

Knox tilted his head. "What are you apologizing for?"

"I couldn't stop them."

Realization hit Knox as he quickly shook his head. "No. None of this is your fault."

"But it is. When we were trying to leave, and they got into the castle, I should have been able to destroy them all. But because of the rain—"

"Zera, stop it." Knox placed his hands on my cheeks. "They are the ones that did that. Not you."

"Javion—"

"—didn't die because of you." Knox sucked in a deep breath and closed his eyes. I could feel his hands trembling against my cheeks. "The Lycans killed Javion."

A tear fell from Knox's good eye, but before I could do anything, he pulled me to him, wrapping his arms back around me. "You're insanely powerful, and I know your charge will come back, but right now… I can't lose you too. Just wait with me, and we'll go after them together."

Knox fell asleep not long after. He'd been sleeping more than I had. For once, I didn't fall asleep. Instead, I rested against Knox's chest, listening to his heartbeat. Hunter told me his brother was heartbroken, but it still sounded the same in his chest. I wasn't sure how you could fix something that wasn't really broken, but I needed to work out how.

I lay there for a while, trying to listen to his heartbeat and not the rain. Hunter had brought me a music player to listen to when the rain got loud, but I didn't want to disturb Knox, even though the rain made me cling to him.

Even if I got my electrical charge back, how could I save any of them? I was scared of water.

"No."

Knox stirred, but he didn't wake up.

Pushing myself away, I wriggled free of his grip and got off the bed. After leaving the room, I found the hallway dark and quiet. Carter and Hunter had both come in and said goodnight a while ago before going to bed.

There was a chill in the air. Although struggling to see properly in the dark, I didn't turn a light on as I went down the stairs and pulled the first coat I touched from the closet. It smelled of Carter. Wrapping it tightly around me, imaging he was there with me, I walked towards the door.

My stomach felt strange, like it was being squeezed, and that made me feel like I wanted to be sick. Instead, I raised my hand; it was shaking.

I *had* to go outside.

If I couldn't, how was I going to protect Carter, Hunter, and Knox? How was I going to find and kill all the Lycans?

I wasn't sure how long I'd stood there, but finally I made my shaking hand wrap around the door handle and open the door.

The house we were in had a porch wrapping around the outside of it. On the days it didn't rain, Carter would sit outside with me. He said fresh air would help me get better quicker, but I never felt any different when I went inside.

Now, the floor was wet, but the rain wasn't really blowing under the small roof. There was another squeeze in my stomach and then I felt dizzy. Stumbling, I leaned against the door frame, clutching it to keep from falling.

The rain was louder now. The way it fell against the roof sent tremors down my spine. The squeezing in my stomach moved to my chest as I clutched the door frame.

Eventually though, I got my feet to move. Walking was suddenly a strange sensation. They didn't feel like they were even mine.

When I got to the edge of the porch, a gust of wind blew the rain in my face.

Like the bones had been taken out of my legs, I fell face first, off the porch and landed heavily in a shallow pool of water. It was icy cold, and yet my face felt like it was on fire as the rain fell over me.

My body locked up. Every muscle went tight, and I couldn't move. The tightness in my chest got worse, and I could barely breathe. Carter's coat offered little protection, soaking up all the water that fell on me, making me feel heavier and heavier.

My body shuddered yet I wasn't able to inhale fully. Even though they were wrapped in bandages, my wrists felt like they were still attached to the shackles.

For the first time in weeks, little white bolts of electricity started crackling over my hands.

The rain picked up before suddenly, I wasn't on a mountainside. Glass walls grew around me. The ground turned to metal, and that agonizing pain was back.

The tightening in my chest increased as my muscles

got so tight, I was sure they were all going to snap.

Somehow, I managed to roll onto my side. More than anything, I wanted to close my eyes and have it all stop, but I couldn't even get my eyelids to shut. Rain poured over my face and into my eyes, sending my bad vision blurry beneath my dirty glasses.

"No chains," I muttered. "No chains. No chains."

This was all in my head.

I was outside in the rain.

The Lycans didn't have me.

There were no shackles around my wrists.

It was just rain.

The words repeated again and again.

All that mattered was I could endure this. It was just *rain*.

I had to survive this.

I had to be ready when the Lycans came again.

I had to be able to protect the men I loved.

Next time, I had to kill all the Lycans before they got close.

Then, as a shadow loomed above me, everything went black.

Eight

Zera

The bright light was unfamiliar and painful. The house we'd been staying in was up a mountain, just like Castle Viegls was. When it rained and the clouds covered the sky, unless there was a light on, the house was very dark. But each room had some sort of clock or television in it, and somehow, the glow from those things made the rooms feel safe and familiar.

During the day, although it was dull, the light was comfortable. No matter which room we were in, Carter and Hunter would have only a soft light on as anything brighter and I couldn't see again. Only Knox liked the darkness, but even his room had a little bit of light in it.

This light was like staring into the sun. A white haze had settled over my vision, and the brightness was making tears stream down my cheeks.

At least the rest of my body wasn't in agony.

Covering my eyes with one hand, I reached out with the other, stumbling towards a wall. Only, when I reached it, I walked straight through it.

On the other side, the light was much more tolerable. I lowered my hand, waiting for the dancing white dots in my vision to fade away. When I could finally see again, I looked up and down the corridor.

The bright light might have been unfamiliar, but this corridor… I'd been here before.

Or, I think I had?

As I walked towards the door, curious to see if I was right, I realized that once again, I had no clothes on. Even the bandages on my wrists were gone. The ugly, angry wounds beneath them stood out against my pale skin. Just looking at them made me feel angry and sick. So, I ignored them and focused on the door I was

71

walking towards.

I walked straight through it.

On the other side, there were stairs.

Just as I suspected.

Feeling like I'd walked this route before, I went up.

On the next floor, I went straight through the door and into a corridor. This one was much brighter than the first. There was a soft carpet beneath my feet and the walls had pictures on them.

There were a lot of doors along this corridor too, each with numbers on them. Something about this place was familiar to me. Did it remind me of the castle?

While trying to figure that out, I headed for the door and walked through it. On the other side was a bedroom, and just by the door I'd passed through, a small bathroom. It was light and clean looking, and also empty.

Where was I?

I turned to the left and walked through the wall into an almost identical room. Again, it was empty.

There was a strange feeling in the pit of my stomach. It wasn't uncomfortable, but it had the hairs on my arms standing on end.

After looking around this room, I went back into the corridor, following it around the corner. It opened up into large room with a desk. Behind it, a woman was talking to a man who was standing on the opposite side.

There was something about the two of them that made my instinct to fight kick in. They seemed harmless enough, though, so why did I want to send all the electricity I could conjure through their bodies until they were twitching on the floor?

Could I even do that?

I raised my hand and tried to summon my electricity, but again, not even a spark appeared.

Biting my lip as I frowned at my hand, I stared at it, trying to imagine the white arcs of the electricity. Finally, as my hand flickered like it was going to disappear altogether, a small lightning bolt fired off from my finger. The lightning was small and it wasn't going to get far, but maybe it was enough to work like one of those taser things I'd seen in those cops shows Bacco used to watch when he wasn't watching pornos?

The sound of a sniff had me looking up. The man at the desk had raised his head to smell the air. Slowly, he turned and then it felt like he locked eyes with me. His eyes changed color, from brown to something more yellow.

Lycan.

No wonder I had the desire to fry them both.

Bringing up my hands in front of me, I aimed my palms at him, ready to send whatever power I had in me.

And then he looked away.

They couldn't see me.

Was the woman a Lycan too? I had the same urge to kill her as I did the man.

Did that mean there were other Lycans here?

Without turning my back to the two at the desk, I quickly looked around the large room. There were chairs around small tables. These, along with all the bedrooms I'd walked past, had to mean I was in… my brain searched for the word… a hotel.

One that I'd been to before?

But how could I have been here before? It felt familiar, but I was pretty sure I'd never seen this place.

Frowning, I rubbed at my head. It felt like there was a memory trapped in there, but I had no idea what it was, or how to get at it.

The man at the desk picked his bag up off the floor and turned to leave, heading straight towards me. Suddenly, he stopped, right in front of me. For a moment, it felt like he was looking right at me again, but then he turned back to the woman.

"Thanks, Viv. I'm going to head down before I go

to my room. Can you arrange for some dinner to be sent up later?" he called over.

"Of course, Mr. McVey."

McVey turned back. At the last moment, I sidestepped out of the way, not wanting him to walk straight through me. And then, for a reason I wasn't entirely certain of, I followed him.

He went towards to the stairs I had walked up and headed back down. Although he couldn't see me, I didn't get too close.

The dark hallway he walked into lit up as we walked through it. Each time the light flickered on with a loud click, I couldn't help but jump and glance behind me. All the while, I tried desperately to get my hands to light up with electricity.

Why wasn't it working?

McVey stopped so suddenly, I nearly walked straight through him. He held his hand up to the wall and something beeped before the door opened.

I followed him into a room that reminded me of Javion's basement—the one I wasn't allowed in because all the computers were there. I didn't know enough about what I was looking at to know what everything was, but a soft sound hummed in the air, calling to me.

Moving over to the side of the room, I placed my

hand on the metal objects, wondering if there was enough power in me to make these stop working. While it wouldn't be as helpful as stopping the Lycan from working, it would be funny watching him get mad.

A small smile grew on my face, but it quickly faded as I realized everything in this room would remain intact when I left it, Lycan included.

Unfair.

"Wakey wakey."

I turned, eyes wide. But McVey wasn't talking to me.

He wasn't even looking at me.

His attention was on the wall of black glass in front of him. Before I could figure out what he was doing, the glass suddenly changed to a blinding white as light streamed through.

Spots covered my vision. Raising my hands to shield my eyes had little effect, and I had to turn and wait to be able to see again. When I turned back around, McVey was seated at a desk in front of the window.

All of a sudden, my stomach lurched. I covered my mouth, thinking I was going to throw up.

Even though he looked nothing like him, I felt like I was taken back in time. This was just like the room I was kept in—or, rather, this was just like the room

Bacco used to stand in as he'd watch water pour over my head. As I screamed in agony, he jerked off.

"Bacco is dead. Bacco is dead. Bacco is dead." I chanted the phrase over and over. Eventually, the feeling of needing to vomit subsided, although a bitter taste remained in the back of my throat.

"How are you doing in there, leach? Apparently, we can't make a jerky out of you, but we're getting some interesting results."

Curious as to who the Lycan was talking to, I walked closer to the desk. The bright light from the other side of the glass was hard to look at. It took some time before I could see a person in the room, huddled up in a sliver of darkness.

Javion.

Without giving it a second thought, I charged through the desk and window, and into the white light.

Nine

Zera

I bolted upright; my eyes widened, and my heart was pounding.

"Zera, you're safe, calm down." Hunter wrapped his arms around my waist while the comforting scent of fruit wafted around me. "It's just a dream."

As I leaned into him, my gaze drifted around the room at Carter and Knox who were both at the foot of the bed, watching me with worried expressions. I tried to figure out what this strange new feeling was.

Carter moved around and perched on the edge of the bed by my feet. "What were you doing, Zera?" he asked me, softly.

The inside of my head felt like it was full of those mushy apples Carter put into his pies. It was stopping me from getting my thoughts together. "Where am I?"

Hunter handed me my glasses. I put them on, squinting while looking around the dark room. My bedroom. My bedroom in the strange house that wasn't Castle Viegls.

"You don't remember?" Carter asked.

"I was with Knox?" I looked over at the other gargoyle.

Slowly, he nodded. The worried expression didn't leave his face.

"And you don't remember going outside?" Carter moved closer, resting a hand on my leg.

Outside?

Was that where I had been? When I leaned forward, my hair fell in front of my face. It was wet, like I'd been in the bath. After reaching for it, I took a small lock and examined it.

"The Lycans," I said, slowly.

"They're not here." Hunter reached for my other hand.

Before I could stop myself, I flinched.

Hunter sighed. "Sorry, Zee."

"There are no Lycans here," Carter told me.

"Are you fucking serious?" Knox's reaction had the three of us looking at him.

"Knox…"

The youngest gargoyle rolled his eyes. "She was out there because of you two."

Hunter looked back at me, his lips parting. "Is that true?"

Was it? I couldn't really remember why I was outside. Had these two sent me out? As I looked between him and Carter, I figured that probably wasn't the case as they both seem horrified.

"You two have been promising us that we're going to go after the Lycans for days, but instead, we've sat around doing nothing—"

"Healing." Hunter cut Knox off. "You're both still healing. Look at your state: you'd fall over if the wind was strong enough, yet you think you can take on a Lycan?"

"I was not the one out there in the rain," Knox snapped back. "Zera thinks we're doing nothing, and while we do nothing, the Lycans are going to get away."

Rain.

Being out there triggered a memory that had a shudder running down my spine. But I *had* been outside... "I'm not going to let the rain stop me anymore."

"See?" Knox gave his brother a pointed look.

"Zeraora, did you go outside to try to find the Lycans?

I shook my head. "Not then."

"Not then?" Hunter repeated. "You've been outside before?"

"Or plan on doing so again?" Carter asked.

"I couldn't stop them. I should have been able to kill them all, but I couldn't. Next time, I won't be stopped by the rain. I won't let any of you get hurt. Not again." I wasn't going to lose any more of the only people I cared about.

Hunter rubbed at the back of his neck. "That's really not the best way to get over something like that."

"How do I?" I asked.

"Let's discuss this later."

I focused on Carter, frowning. *Later.* This was one of those imaginary terms, because whenever someone said that to me, it never happened.

From the foot of the bed, Knox snorted. "And you're amazed that she decided to go out in the rain by herself."

"If you've got nothing sensible to contribute," Carter said. "I suggest you stay quiet."

We were back to the three of them arguing again. Over the last few weeks, this was how things ended up if they were all in a room together for more than a few minutes. And like most times, I found myself agreeing with Knox.

If I had my powers, I would have zapped Carter and Hunter. Since I didn't, I pulled my hand free from Hunter's and started to wiggle off the bed.

"Where are you going?" Hunter hovered over me.

I wasn't sure if he was trying to stop me or help me up.

"All you two do anymore is argue with Knox, and you're doing it because of me."

As I stood up, so did Carter. "We're not arguing because of you."

"You wouldn't be arguing like this if I wasn't here. And Javion would still be here, and you'd be happy in your castle…"

Javion.

As I said his name, something twinged.

"Javion's death is not your fault," Knox told me, firmly, before the others could.

"Then why are you all shouting at each other all the time?" I thought I had learned a lot about these three men since I'd been with them, but the longer I was with them, the more I could see how little I really knew. Frustration forced tears from the corner of my eyes. Angrily, I pushed my glasses up and wiped them away with the back of my hand.

Carter let out a long breath as he held out his hand. When I took it, he pulled us both to sit on the edge of the bed. "We are shouting a lot, you're right. We're sad and we're angry, and we all miss Javion—"

"You made Javion leave," I told him. "You've said that before, but if you care about someone, how do you make them leave?"

"That's not fair," Hunter said as Carter's breath caught. "You don't understand."

"No, she's right," Carter said, drawing in a deep breath. He exhaled heavily as he rubbed at his beard. "I did send Javion away. The fact is, you got hurt because of him, so even if we did it over, I would still do the same thing."

"I'm not Manon," I told him.

"Zee!" Hunter's tone was high pitched, He looked at me like I'd said something wrong.

"But Carter said he did it because of what

happened to Manon, and I'm not Manon." This was getting frustrating again. There were things I could and couldn't say or do, but no one telling me what they were or why I couldn't.

Carter waved Hunter off. "No, you're not. You're not even close."

"Then why—?"

"I've had to live through losing one mate. I won't survive another. And I don't even need to look at Knox to know that he feels the same. None of us want to lose you."

"We're going to if you keep treating her like this," Knox told him.

"Knox!"

"Stop it," I said before Carter could shout at Knox again. "Stop arguing. I don't like it, and I don't understand why you do. None of this makes sense to me."

Hunter crouched back down in front of me. "What doesn't make sense? I can try to explain it."

"Will you?" My head was pounding again. "Because whenever I ask something, you say you'll answer later, but then you don't answer at all. You don't listen to me, and you don't talk to me. I don't know why or what I've done wrong. Then when I try and do something to help, you all end up shouting at each other and saying it's each other's fault…"

"And you wonder why she walked out that door," Knox muttered.

"You should have stopped her," Hunter shot back.

Knox puffed out his chest. "If she'd have woken me, I'd have walked out with her."

"Enough." Carter didn't shout, but it was enough for any words to die in Hunter's throat. "It's late, and it is cold. Zeraora, I want you to change into some dry clothes and then join us downstairs."

"Why?"

"Because you're right. We're going to talk. Properly. About everything. But we can't have this conversation with you soaking wet." Carter got up and stared at Hunter until he did the same.

"Are we actually going to talk?" I asked as he ushered the twins towards the door.

Carter looked back at me and nodded. "Yes."

The door was barely closed before I was ripping my wet clothes off. Even though my body was exhausted, and sleep was an appealing option, I wasn't going to let this time go. There was something about the way Carter answered that made me sure that, finally, they were really going to talk.

In a new outfit, I hurried downstairs. Someone, most likely Hunter, had started the fire going, and it was already starting to warm up the room. The fire was for my benefit. These three gargoyles could fly through the icy night air with virtually no clothes on and feel nothing. Until I got close to the flames, I never realized how cold I was.

Knox was already seated on the couch, but instead of joining him, I chose a chair close to the fire. Carter came in carrying a mug of cinnamon milk—my favorite—and I took it from him gratefully.

Carter sat down on the opposite side of the couch while Hunter continued to stand on the other side of the fireplace. And yet, none of them spoke.

"Well?" I looked around at all of them.

Rubbing at his face, Carter let out a long sigh before leaning forward. "Firstly, let's all agree to have this conversation without raising our voices."

Considering my voice was naturally low, even more so since the second time I'd been held prisoner by the Lycans, I was sure this wasn't aimed at me, but I nodded along with the twins.

After seeing Hunter and Knox were in agreement, Carter looked at me. "Even before you joined us at Castle Viegls, things weren't as peaceful as you seem to think. Yes, we got on, and we certainly didn't disagree as much as we do now, but we still argued."

Knox snorted. "Is it an argument when you always win?"

Ten

Knox

Zera was right. This unit, this family—whatever it was—was falling apart, and not just because we'd lost Javion.

Just the thought of him had my heart twisting in pain, like someone was actually squeezing it, in the center of my chest. It hurt more than any of the physical injuries the Lycans had inflicted on me, and yet, in a somewhat sadistic sort of way, I liked it. The pain reminded me that I was alive, because some days, I felt so numb that I wasn't sure.

I turned my attention to the light in my life. When I woke to Hunter yelling and discovered Zera wasn't beside me, I thought what was left of my ravaged heart was going to give up.

DB was right about that—if something were to happen to Zera, I wouldn't recover. Her and Jay? I wouldn't want to. If my heart didn't give up on me completely, I'd run a blade through it myself.

As I ran down the stairs, I barely felt any other pain from my damaged body. All I could concentrate on was Zera.

Right now, she was staring at DB, ignoring the drink in her hands. Even in shades of gray, she was the most beautiful thing I'd ever laid eyes on.

Her hair was still damp, but she'd changed into some clothes DB had found for her. They weren't anything like the ones she'd chosen. At some point early on, he got some clothes for all of us—another thing that was pissing me off. He had us all dressed like fucking lumberjacks.

Clenching my fist, I tried to push my anger down.

Yes, I had anger issues. I'd had them since I was a kid. Back before me and Hunter reached our *aibidh*, that was how people could tell us apart. Hunter always had a smile on his face, whereas I looked like I wanted to punch someone.

The differences were a lot more obvious now.

But since I woke up, the anger that had been simmering below the surface was bubbling away like magma, ready to spew forth from the volcano. The only things holding me back from beating the shit out of DB were Zera... And Javion.

Fuck.

"DB's not doing it to be a dick, you fuckwit. He's in charge for a reason. I listen to him for a reason... He sees the bigger picture, and he's trying to look out for all of us. He's just really shit at telling us that."

Even now, Javion's lecture was still clear in my mind.

"Well?" Zera's voice pulled me out of my memories.

That was my mate. Direct and often blunt to the point of being tactless. And it was just one of the many things I loved her for. Before, when we were in the bedroom, she was asking questions. I knew she had no malice in them, but it was amusing to watch DB and Hunter squirm.

"Even before you joined us at Castle Viegls, things

weren't as peaceful as you seem to think. Yes, we got on, and we certainly didn't disagree as much as we do now, but we still argued," DB was telling her.

That was a fucking joke. "Is it an argument when you always win?"

"What did we just agree?" Hunter shot me an irritated glare.

I raised a brow. "Did you hear me raise my voice?"

"Boys." DB held up his hands and shook his head. When I didn't say anything, and Hunter also remained silent, DB fixed his attention on me. "Aside from asking Javion to leave, have you had any real issue with my decisions?"

"Aside from?" I asked in disbelief. "That decision is the reason he's dead."

DB winced.

He actually winced.

"If the roles were reversed and you were in my shoes..." he kept his voice level. "What would you have done? Honestly."

The most annoying part about this whole fucking situation was that I probably would have done the same thing to keep my mate safe. "Irrelevant. Because the fact is, it was the wrong decision."

"That's kinda the whole point," Hunter told me.

I glared at my twin. "Why the fuck do you always have to take his side?"

"Why was it the wrong decision?"

My mouth fell open as I looked at DB. "Are you fucking kidding me?"

"He was my friend too, Knox."

Another of life's mysteries. I'd asked Javion on countless occasions to tell me how he had ended up choosing to stay with DB—much less end up being friends with him—and he'd always give me his annoying, *I've got a secret and I'm not telling you*, grin.

The memory of that smile pierced my soul.

Fuck. I needed him back. How was I supposed to do this without him?

"This entire time, we—*I*—have been underestimating everything," DB said, softly.

For the first time since we met, I saw vulnerability in DB's eyes. "What?"

"The Lycans—how powerful and dangerous they are. And us."

"Us?" Hunter sounded as confused as I felt.

"How powerful we are."

"I haven't," Zera said with that beautiful matter-of-factness she often spoke with. "I am dangerous and powerful, and I can destroy them all."

I chuckled. Even DB managed to quirk the corner of his mouth.

"Yes, you are. And I've been underestimating you, too."

In an instant, Zera was on her feet, not noticing that she was sending the warm milk she'd been holding onto over the edges of the mug. "Good. Let's go destroy the Lycans."

With her powers MIA, it was like looking at a wasp without its stinger. She was all fierce and angry, determined to have revenge while protecting us, yet with no powers to back it up.

"Okay." DB agreed.

It was a rare moment when Hunter and I managed to have anything vaguely resembling a twin connection, but right then, with our mouths hanging open, we both looked at DB. "What the fuck?"

DB stood and walked over to Zera, gently taking the mug from her. He set it down on the sideboard before he led her over to couch and sitting her down beside me. "Not so fast, Blue Eyes."

Zera's beautiful face screwed up in anger, and she jerked her hand free from DB's. "You always say that."

"You're right." He sat back down but angled his body to face the angry elemental. "But this time, we really are going to do it. Only, we need to do this correctly. And we need to do it together."

"I can destroy them all."

"When you're at full power, yes, you have the power to do so. I believe that, but you can't do it without us—all of us—working together. Being separate is what led us here and to this position in the first place."

I couldn't keep the surprise from my face, even if raising my eyebrow still hurt. Was DB admitting he was... wrong? That he'd fucked up?

"Yes." DB looked at me, meeting my disbelieving stare. "You were right. It was the wrong decision."

"Then why did you ask?"

"Because I wanted to know if you understood why." DB sucked in a deep breath. "In the same situation, I would make the same decision, and so would you. We all would. Because all we want is to protect Zera."

"Are you saying we shouldn't protect her?" Hunter asked before I could.

"I can protect you," Zera said, scowling at Hunter.

I expected DB to tell her a fly zapper had more power than she did right now—or something with a little more tact—but instead, he spoke again.

"It's instinct to protect our females," DB said, although I wasn't entirely sure if he was telling Zera or us. "But usually, our females are gargoyles. They're built differently than you." He reached over and tucked some hair behind Zera's ears.

"Because I'm not made of stone?"

"We're not quite made of stone either, but yes. Female gargoyles are strong and have skin that can protect them from most things. By comparison, you're smaller and fragile. You might have the ability to simultaneously power one city while wiping out another, but you get hurt much more easily." DB pointed to her wrists. "And we're reminded of this every time we see you."

Instantly, Zera's hands disappeared behind her back.

This woman had no problem saying what was on her mind. She had no shame in her body—not that she needed any—but I'd never seen her shy away. Until it came to those scars on her wrists. Scars that were now re-opened and once again hidden behind bandages or wrist guards.

"You don't need to hide them, Zee. I want you to know we love you, including your scars."

"They're hot. Makes you look a little more

dangerous. But that doesn't me we don't want to kill the fuckers that did that to you," I growled, but nodded in agreement.

"And we're going to," DB told her. "All of us. Together."

"Then let me."

"We can't right now. It's going to take all four of us at full strength. Knox can barely walk up the stairs, and you can't stop a Lycan. But..." he said quickly before Zera could object. "We *are* going to teach you to fight. We're going to build up your strength, and we're going to make sure that, if you need to use a blade to fight the Lycans, you know how to use it. More than that, we're going to work together to overcome your fear of rain. And while we're doing all of that, we're going to get our home back."

"Of course," I muttered.

DB arched an eyebrow. "Tomorrow, we're heading to Atlanta to talk to that witch."

Considering we'd already had this conversation, and nothing had come of it, I wasn't going to bother holding my breath, but before I could remind him of this, Zera was moving in front of him, tilting her head.

"The witch who cut my hair?"

"Liberty," Hunter told her, nodding.

"Is she working with the Lycans?"

"No," Hunter said.

At the same time, DB shrugged. "I don't know."

Zera looked between them both before turning to me.

"That's what we're going to find out."

Eleven

Zera

At first, I believed Carter when he said we were going to Atlanta, and then, as the day turned back to night, I started to doubt him. He told me I could do things a lot and then I wouldn't.

Carter had left us after the sun had set and hadn't returned until after I had gone to bed. When I woke up the next morning, I discovered he'd gotten a truck to take us to Atlanta.

Now, we were in the truck driving back to the city.

We'd been in it for hours.

It was big and black. Carter was driving, and Hunter was in the front beside him. Knox sat beside me in the back with his hand wrapped around mine as we both stared out of our windows.

I was glad Knox was there. Carter tried to tell him he needed to stay behind and rest, but Knox insisted he come with me. We weren't going to fight any Lycans, so if it was safe enough for me, it was safe enough for Knox.

"Why does Liberty know where the Lycans are?" I asked as we got closer to the city.

"Liberty is part of the Daughters of the Twilight Goddess—that's the name of her coven," Hunter told me.

"A coven is a group of witches who all follow the same High Witch," Knox added.

"And the coven knows where the Lycans are?" I asked. "Are we going to kill them too?" Carter had said this visit was just going to be to talk to Liberty, but I wouldn't mind if I had to kill witches to find out where the Lycans were. I would do what I needed to.

Hunter turned in his seat to face me. "We're not killing anyone, especially not Libby," he said, firmly. "We're just going to chat with her."

"She knew I was an elemental, and then we were found by that mongoose shifter," I said.

"I know." Hunter glanced at Knox before looking back at me. "But I don't think she would hurt you, I really don't. So can you promise you won't try to kill her?"

As I stared at him, thinking about whether or not I was prepared to make that promise, Carter let out a loud sigh. "There will be no killing today. We are just going to ask some questions."

I didn't say anything. I thought it over and decided that if anything threatened any of these men, I'd kill it. Even if it was Liberty. I was hoping I wouldn't have to, though. She seemed nice...

The streets finally started looking familiar, but before we could get to the hair salon Liberty worked at, Carter pulled over. "We can't go into the salon."

"Then why did we come here?" I asked.

Carter pointed at the store we'd parked in front of. The windows were full of brightly colored cakes that had my mouth watering at the sight of them. "We're going to ask her to meet us here. It's neutral ground." He looked at me through the mirror. "We have to assume that the whole supernatural community is looking for us."

"Why?" I asked, frowning.

"Someone is working with the Lycans. There's a good price on your head. Either it's the witches, and that's why the wards failed, or it's someone who paid the witches. Until we know which, we don't know who our enemy is, and we have to assume it's everyone for our own safety."

"If the Lycans are looking for me, it should make destroying them easier."

"Maybe Zee should wait in the car with Knox."

I scowled at the back of Hunter's head. "No."

"If we were going to do that, we should have left Zera and me back in the safehouse," Knox said.

"No one is being left anywhere. I said we were going to do this together, and we will. This is just a conversation with an old ally—nothing more. We're just going to make sure we don't bring any unnecessary attention to ourselves." Carter was looking at me as he said that.

"I won't EMP the city again." Not that I could if I wanted to. I was still barely able to get a spark to appear.

Knox, who was still holding onto my hand, ran his thumb over the back of it. "That's my girl."

Only after Carter had walked up and down the street did he allow the rest of us to follow him into the store. Inside were even more cakes and lots of tables, although there was hardly anyone seated at them.

Knox led me over to a table in the back while Hunter and Carter stood at a counter. A few minutes later, they joined us at the table. "What were you doing?" I asked.

"Ordering you some cake." Hunter grinned.

Carter set a tray down on the table. There were several small cakes on a large plate.

I reached for a red one with white icing. Although there were enough cakes for all of us, none of the gargoyles ate any despite each selecting one and placing it in front of them. The one I was eating was delicious, so if they didn't eat theirs, I would happily help them with theirs.

When a bell at the door jingled moments later, all three of the men surrounding me sat up straighter. I glanced over at the door and saw Liberty walking over. She was pretty and curvy. Her long hair started off pink at the top and was blue at the bottom with purple blended between the two. It was also unbelievably bright. I really liked it.

Liberty was alone. She did have a familiar—a strange creature Knox had called a honey badger—which was very angry and liked to drink. But it hadn't come with her.

She glanced at the space beside her before she moved over to the table. "Hi guys. I wasn't, uh, expecting to see all of you." She narrowed her eyes as she looked at Hunter. "What do you want?"

"Why don't you sit?" Hunter suggested, pointing to the only free chair at the table, across from me.

Although still eyeing Hunter suspiciously, Liberty sat down. She looked over at me and smiled. "Your hair looks much healthier. You do too, actually."

"You seem surprised to see us," Knox said.

Liberty nodded. "I mean, the last time you guys were in Atlanta, the city had a black out." She glanced around the room before continuing. "Kinda figured you might be avoiding major cities for a while."

"Did you tell anyone?" Carter asked.

The witch, as well as being pretty, was tall—taller than me. But she wasn't taller than any of the gargoyles, and she had to tilt her head to look at Carter. "We've not met before."

"You didn't answer the question."

"Libs, this is Carter Harlow. Carter, this is Liberty Talbot of the Daughters of the Twilight Goddess." Hunter's introduction was brief.

"Did you tell anyone these three visited your

salon?" Carter asked.

The cake I'd been eating was temporarily forgotten about. The only other people I'd seen Carter talk to, aside from the twins and Javion, were the vampires, and he was talking to Liberty like she was one of them.

"I haven't told anyone," Liberty said, frowning. "Is that what you think?"

"The wards at Castle Viegls failed. Lycan were able to infiltrate the grounds," Hunter told her.

Liberty's eyes widened. They were bright blue, like mine. "You think *I* had something to do with that? Hunter, the Lycans are my enemies too."

"Then explain how our wards failed."

Chewing at her lip as she looked around the table, Liberty slowly shook her head. "You really think I would do that?"

"Actua—"

"I think a lot of people would do a lot of things if the price was right," Carter said, cutting Hunter off.

Liberty slammed her hands on the table, making the plates rattle. "I don't know who the fuck you think you are... but fuck you." With a screeching sound that had me cringing, Liberty pushed her chair back and stood.

Before she could get far from the table, Carter

blocked her path. "We're not done."

"What are you going to do?" Liberty grabbed her hips as she glared up at Carter. Once again, next to the tall gargoyle, she looked tiny. But it didn't make her back down.

All of a sudden, a mug shot through the air, narrowly missing Carter's head before it sailed passed him and hit the wall.

"What the fuck was that?" Knox asked.

"Can't witches do things like that?" I asked, even though Liberty looked just as bewildered.

"Not without an incantation, or at the very least, a wand. And Liberty is not good enough to pull that off without either," Hunter muttered, getting to his feet.

"I can fight my own battles," Liberty hissed before Hunter got to Carter's side.

"I didn't say anything," Hunter told her.

With a sigh, Liberty swung her head to give him an irritated glare. "I wasn't talking to you. And I'm *done* talking to you."

This time, it was Hunter who stepped in front of her. "Libs, I'm sorry. Look, you'll know what it's like when you find your mate—"

"Consort."

Hunter shook his head. "The point is, someone

came after Zera—no, not just someone. The Lycans came after Zera. They got into our home, through our wards, and they took her. They took Knox, and they took Javion. Javion's… gone."

Liberty stared at Hunter before she slowly turned to look at Knox. Although his hand settled on my thigh, squeezing slightly, he seemed to be staring straight back at her.

"Excuse me, but do you need help?"

The question came from the store owner who looked very old, and yet was carrying a broom like she was prepared to hit Carter over the head with it.

"If she attacks Carter, am I supposed to kill her?" I asked Knox, confused.

"Sorry, ma'am. Just disagreeing with my father," Liberty said, casting Carter a side eye. "He'll pay for the mug."

Whether the woman was scared of Carter or not, I couldn't tell, but she shuffled back to behind the counter, keeping an eye on the five of us.

"So much for not drawing attention," Knox muttered as the three of them sat back down.

After shooting Carter a wary look, Liberty turned her attention to Knox. "I'm sorry about your mate."

The hand on my thigh squeezed me again, but

Knox just nodded.

Liberty sucked in a deep breath and, ignoring Carter, focused her attention on Hunter. "Yes, I need the money. Who doesn't?" Rolling her eyes, she sighed. "Maybe not the people who live in a castle. Whatever. It's irrelevant. But I need the money because my hair salon barely makes enough money to pay the rent, and my hexes are bought by humans, not supes." Liberty's cheeks went a similar color to the roots of her hair. "Because my magic skills are crap. There's a reason why the coven doesn't include me when they perform any spell, never mind wards."

"That doesn't mean you wouldn't tell someone about Zeraora if they offered the right amount of money for the information." Carter's eyes fixed on the side of Liberty's head.

Liberty kept her attention on Hunter as her eyes narrowed. "Fuck you."

"Is that aimed at me?" Hunter arched an eyebrow. "Or DB?"

"You."

"You didn't even give me the chance to say anything," Hunter protested.

"That's because you had the chance to say this *before* you turned up here, questioning me. So, fuck you."

Folding her arms, now ignoring Hunter whose mouth had dropped open, Liberty turned to Carter. "I would never sell out another woman. I'm not stupid. I see the bandages. Whatever she's been through, I'm not going to send her back there." All of a sudden, she whipped her head around and glared at Knox. "That's not the same."

Knox's eyes widened. "I didn't say anything."

"I'm talking to Mingi, not you."

"Who's Mingi?" Carter asked.

"A ghost," Hunter replied.

I turned in my seat to stare at Hunter. "You said ghosts don't exist."

Hunter sighed. "They don't."

"Send her back where?" Knox cut off the conversation. We all looked at him, but his eyes were locked on Liberty's.

"You know where," Hunter told him, frowning slightly.

"I do." Knox raised his hand and pointed at the witch. "But how does she?"

Liberty's hands disappeared under the table. From the movements of her arms, it looked like she was rubbing her hands on the top of her legs.

"We had a coven tea morning, and one of my

Sisters was talking about how a mongoose shifter had been seen in Atlanta, asking about an elemental. An elemental who had hurt her mate, stolen something from him, and he was looking for her."

It took a moment for me to realize the elemental she was talking about was me.

"My mate? Who did I hurt?" My eyes skimmed over the three men at the table, pausing at Knox. He was hurt because they came for me, and I couldn't stop them like I should have been able to.

"I know what you're thinking. Stop it," Knox told me. "She's talking about a Lycan."

"I've never had a Lycan mate."

Hearing those words had my blood running cold. Bacco once told me they planned to make me have babies to replace me. That same night, I escaped, and he was killed by the ghost that helped me.

"They never said it was a Lycan, but there was something about that shifter that gave me the heebie-jeebies." Liberty shuddered. "Either way, I stayed quiet. I didn't tell anyone anything."

"Thank you." Hunter gave her a small smile.

Liberty nodded, her head then her attention drifted back to me. "They found you anyway."

My answer got stuck in my throat.

"Look, I didn't break the ward, and I don't know exactly who did, but realistically, it's one of two options." She raked a hand through her hair. "Yeah, the witches who cast a ward are also the witches who can break it. Or they found a more powerful witch. You just need to know what the base incense is, and that just needs a bit of trial and error."

"You think someone in your Coven could do it?" Carter asked.

Liberty chewed at her lip before shrugging. "I think they're hiding something, but I don't think it's this. The Daughters of Twilight have built a high reputation of being able to create secure and reliable wards. That is a more secure and regular source of income than a one-off payment to break a ward and destroy a reputation."

"You got a list of witches who could pull it off?"

"I should be flattered that you think this highly of me and my abilities, because my Coven doesn't. I'm that family member you don't like to speak of and keep hidden at social occasions." Liberty sat back into her chair and looked away. "I'm the witch with no real power. They keep me hidden. Why do you think I have a hair salon?"

"Thanks anyway, Libs."

Carter held a hand up. "So, what you're saying is

that no matter what wards we have up, someone could still infiltrate them if they're powerful enough?"

Liberty raised a shoulder. "It's not easy—it takes time—but yeah. It takes the course of a moon cycle. I guess if you had the wards reinforced more regularly, then it would be a *lot* harder, but still not impossible. And hella expensive." She leaned forward and put her elbow on the table as she propped up her head. "If you want to keep Lycans out, you could plant wolfsbane, but it has to be silver wolfsbane—common wolfsbane is purple."

"Where do we get that?"

"Actually, forget that idea. I've never seen it, and one of my Sisters mentioned that the Lycans destroyed it all decades ago. There might be some *somewhere*, but who knows." She laughed. "You need to find an earth fae. Apparently, they can make anything grow."

"Where would we find one of those?" Carter asked.

Slowly, Liberty stopped laughing, growing serious. "Fae aren't real. They're stories—fairy tales."

"No, they're—" Knox's hand clamped over my mouth, making me jump.

"Never mind," Hunter said, loudly.

Looking between the twins and me, Liberty's eyes narrowed until Knox lowered his hand. "I can't help you with mythical creatures, but if you're up for a road trip, you might want to visit Florida."

"Tinkerbell is not going to help with this one." Carter's tone was dry.

"No, but Dean might."

"Who the fuck is Dean?"

Liberty glanced at Knox. "He's a warlock. British. Grumpier than this guy." She jammed a thumb in Carter's direction. "Take him baked beans."

"Who is Dean?" Carter asked, looking less than impressed.

"The last time I met Zera, she shut down an entire city for weeks. Since we've been here, I've not seen one spark and…" she looked over at me. "I thought maybe you'd gotten your powers under control, but then Knox startled you, and somehow, the lights are still on."

"Liberty—" Hunter was using the same tone Carter used on him and his brother.

Liberty quickly waved her hands. "I mean nothing by it, and I don't want to bring up whatever the Lycans did to you. But whatever they did, Dean is probably the only one who might know how to fix it."

Twelve

Zera

"You really think after everything, the Daughters of the Twilight Goddess can be trusted?" Knox asked Carter.

We were back in the truck, heading out of Atlanta. I was in the backseat again, curled up next to Hunter this time, while Knox sat in the front next to Carter.

"Mmmm." Carter didn't really seem to be listening as he turned off the street into the parking lot of a fast-food burger place. He parked up and we all followed him into the restaurant.

While Knox and I went and claimed a table in the far corner, Carter and Hunter went to order the food.

It didn't take long for the two of them to join us, both carrying trays piled high with burgers and fries, which smelled delicious. Hunter passed me some food, and I dug in, enjoying it so much that I had to keep stopping to lick the salt from my fingers.

"You've started something, DB," Knox muttered, watching me eat. He was already on his second burger.

"I'm close to trusting nobody right now," Carter said.

I blinked a few times, trying to work out how the two things were related.

Seeing my confusion, Carter used a fry to point at Knox. "Before, he asked if we could trust the Daughters of the Twilight Goddess. And my answer is, that I don't know who to trust, but trusting no one would be safer."

"If we trust no one, we live a life in fear," Hunter said.

"You told Liberty to arrange with her coven to put the wards back up. Doesn't that mean you trust them?" I reached for the chocolate shake they'd brought and took a sip.

Instead of eating more of his food, Carter

drummed his fingers on the table. "What do you three want to do?"

While Knox's eyes widened, Hunter's lips actually parted. Even I was surprised.

"You're asking us?" Knox dropped what was left of his burger into the box.

Carter nodded.

"Castle Viegls is our home," Hunter told him.

"What about you, Knox?"

After a long pause, Knox shrugged. "Whatever you guys want to do."

"I want to kill the Lycans," I said, firmly. I was not going to let that mission be forgotten.

The side of Carter's mouth quirked up as he nodded. "And we will. But first, I propose we go see this warlock the witch spoke of. We know little about Elementals, and Zeraora is still without her powers. Maybe he knows how to help with that."

Knox glanced at me. "Can we trust him?"

"I think we can trust Liberty," Hunter said when I said nothing. "I know you're all questioning if the witches can be trusted, which is understandable, but I do trust her."

"She said he was in the Everglades. That's at least a ten-hour drive." Knox stared at Carter, still frowning.

"If we can find out how to help Zeraora, I'd drive until I wore the tires out, and then I'd start walking."

I only vaguely listened to Carter explain how, if nothing else, the Lycans would be highly unlikely to consider looking for us in Florida. Instead, my attention was on the palms of my hands as I tried, once more, to get a spark.

My gaze dropped to my bandaged wrists. They were throbbing again.

The pain, I was used to, but the lack of power felt wrong. Like the Lycans had done something to me that was permanent. And I couldn't let that happen. This needed to be temporary because I needed my power to destroy the Lycans.

But it wasn't just about my powers anymore, or even the need for vengeance.

"I want to go see the warlock," I said. Looking up, I found the three gargoyles staring at me.

"Hand," Hunter muttered before reaching over to take mine in his. Once his warm hand enveloped mine, he cocked his head to look at me. "Are you okay, Zee?"

"Liberty said he should be able to help me, so he'll know what I am, right?"

The three men shared a look, but it was Carter who spoke, leaning forward and keeping his voice low, despite there not being anyone seated close to us. "We'll go see him, but you *cannot* tell him that you're fae. According to Liberty, he knows about elementals. But do not tell him anything else, understand?"

"Yes."

After finishing the meal, we headed back out to the car. I wasn't really sure where Florida was in relation to where we were now, but ten hours was a long drive.

We drove for a while before Carter stopped to fill up the truck and Hunter disappeared inside to get snacks. Knox, who had returned to the back seat to sit beside me, glanced down. "You've been quiet."

"I don't have anything to say."

Knox let out a long sigh before nodding "I get that."

"Do you mind that we're going to Florida?" I asked him.

Knox leaned over and pulled me to him, allowing me to rest my head against his chest. "Not at all. I want you to get better."

"I want you to get better too."

Without responding, Knox held me tighter, turning his attention to what was going on outside the car.

It was dark, but it no longer felt like we were moving. At some point, I'd fallen asleep, but now that I'd woken up, I wasn't sure where we were.

We... I was alone. There wasn't anyone with me.

Sitting up, I waited for my eyes to get used to the darkness, but even after a few minutes, I couldn't make anything out. An eerie sensation set into me, like I'd been in this situation before.

The only time I'd been somewhere this dark was when Bacco had finally turned the lights out to my cell.

All at once, the hairs on my arms stood up as fear seemed to seep through the air like an invisible fog that I couldn't help but breathe in.

Forcing myself to take deep breaths, I stood. With my arms stretched out in front of me, I took slow steps forward until I was suddenly in bright light. This time, I had to stop to allow my sore eyes to get used to the brightness.

When the dazzle turned dimmer, I discovered I was in a cold, gray hallway. Like the other room, there was something familiar about this place. My instinct was to head to the right, so I started to do that, but then I stopped and glanced back over my shoulder. Going right felt... wrong.

I wasn't sure how walking in one direction over another could feel right or wrong, but I still found myself turning around and heading in the other direction.

"I've been here before," I said to myself.

Stopping, I looked around. Which was when I discovered I wasn't wearing any clothes. I reached for the wall. I wasn't completely surprised when my hand went through it.

Astral projection?

To where?

The corridor was long and dark. The lighting, which had seemed so bright before, dimmed to a dull orange glow from hanging lightbulbs every dozen steps. There weren't many doors along the corridor, despite how long it was. The air also smelled musty, like people didn't go down here very often. The ceiling was covered in long pipes and more than one spider web.

There was nothing about this place that looked familiar.

But it *felt* familiar.

I continued walking the hallway until I reached the first door. Something was stuck on it. The only word I could read was *danger*, but the rest was just a bunch of letters in an order I didn't understand.

Danger meant I should keep away. And yet, I felt something pulling me towards it.

Like I *needed* to go through the door.

Even if this was an astral projection, it didn't mean that I couldn't be seen. That didn't stop me from walking through the door.

Walking into the corridor before felt like I had been blinded, but it was nothing like the light that hit me the moment I walked in this room. I'd barely been in a second before I snapped them shut, and yet I had white dots dancing across my eyes.

"Sparkler?" The question was followed by a hollow laugh that quickly turned into a wracking cough.

Through squinting eyes, I tried to find the source of the voice. "Javion?"

"Zera?" The voice was stronger and more serious this time. "Is that really you?"

Slowly, the room started to take form. Lights as bright as the sun shone down, bathing the whole room. Except for a sliver of darkness under a thin bed against the far wall. In the shadow, his body as flat to the wall as possible, was Javion.

I ran over, dropping to my knees in front of him. "Javion?"

"Is it really you, or am I just hallucinating?" His

silver eyes narrowed into a squint. "You have no clothes on."

"Neither do you."

Javion closed his eyes. "My body and sunlight is somewhat combustible. Clothes don't stand a chance."

Tears appeared in the corner of my eyes as I looked him over. There was barely a part of his body that wasn't covered in burns. Some parts were still red and wet.

"Everyone thinks you're dead. Really dead, not vampire dead."

Javion turned his head away to face the wall. "I wish I was."

"I don't." I stuck my arm out, ready to lower my wrist to his mouth when I saw my own wounds, still as angry and fresh as Javion's. "Can you reach my neck?" I asked as I lowered my head towards his.

"Wha—?" Javion fell silent as he turned his head back. Our noses were almost touching. "What are you doing?"

"You need blood."

Unblinking, Javion stared at me.

I stared back.

"I can see through you," he whispered.

Confused, I sat up. My head passed straight through the top of the bed he was hiding under. "Oh."

"I appreciate the thought though, Little Sparkler."

Once again, my gaze skimmed over his burned body. He used to have drawings—tattoos—on his skin, but now, I couldn't make them out.

"Are you checking me out?"

I stared blankly . "I don't understand."

"I can feel your eyes burning into my ass."

My eyes went wide before I quickly covered them with my hands. I had that power too?

I could sense Javion shifting his weight slightly in front of me before he sighed. "I don't mean literally. How the fuck are you still alive?"

"You helped me escape with Knox."

"How is Knox?"

Javion's voice had gone deep and husky on that question, making me lower my hands a fraction. He'd turned his head as much as he could without exposing more of his body to the light, and now his silver eyes were fixed on me.

"The Lycans tore off his bad wing and destroyed the other. He's got more claw wounds on his body too." I lowered my hands completely. "But mostly, he's sad. He thinks you're dead, and I think that hurts him more."

Javion closed his eyes. Without him breathing, he looked like he was dead.

"Javion?"

"Still here, Little Sparkler." His mouth opened enough for me to see him rubbing his tongue over a fang before he opened his eyes.

"I'll tell him you're okay—"

"Don't."

Tilting my head, I frowned. "Don't what?"

"Don't tell him I'm alive."

"Why not? How else are we going to get you out of here?"

Javion shook his head, wincing as he did. "You're not, Zera. Look at me. I'm not surviving this place. I don't know where I am or how far away I am from you, but I'm not going to survive much longer."

"But I'm here and I can—"

"Don't. Don't try, don't tell him, don't fucking do anything."

My hands slammed on the floor, but they made no sound. "I'm not going to let you die here, again."

"I'm already dead."

"You're undead. Not dead-dead." I wasn't sure if I was using the right words, but Knox had used them before and honestly, I didn't care.

Javion stared at me before finally giving me a smile. Unlike the usual sly smirks he would give me, this one was soft. "Careful, Little Sparkler. Someone might think you care about me."

That had me sitting back. "You helped me get Knox out."

"And you saved Knox, so we're even. There's no debt to settle. Zera, forget about me." With a lot of effort, he rolled onto his other side, wincing as his shoulder caught the light before he was able to flatten back against the wall. "I mean it, I'm not leaving this place alive—or unalive. The only reason I'm still here is because letting my body atrophy is less painful than rolling out into that light, but so help me, I'll fucking do just that if you think of telling Knox I'm here."

Javion was glaring at me, but with burnt skin and hiding under a thin plank of wood, there wasn't anything vaguely threatening about him anymore. However, with the way his silver eyes locked onto mine, I knew if he did pull himself out from under the small shelter, there would be nothing I could do to stop him.

"Why not?"

"I've not got long left. If you tell Knox, he'll spend the rest of his life looking for me, only to never find me. Hope like that isn't a gift, it's a curse. He deserves happiness, but he won't get it unless he lets me go. If you want to help me, you do that. Make sure he's happy."

"We could find you."

"You won't."

For some reason, as I stared at him, my chest started to hurt. That had never happened before, not while astral projecting.

"I know you can't lie—or don't know how to—so if any of them ask…" He closed his eyes. "Fuck, I wish you could lie."

Thirteen

Zera

"Zera?"

At the sound of Knox's alarmed voice, I opened my eyes, fighting off sleepiness as I tried to sit upright. "What is it? What's wrong?"

Knox grabbed my upper arms as he let out a long sigh of relief. "Nothing, you were just crying in your sleep."

I wiped at my cheeks, surprised to find they were wet.

"You had us worried there."

Carter had pulled the truck over on the side of the highway, and all three of them were watching me with worried expressions.

After being accustomed to all the pain I was used to feeling, I was surprised when I felt a new pain—a dull ache in the center of my chest. Rubbing at it with the heel of my hand, I frowned. *What was that from?*

"Are you okay?" Knox asked me, watching my hand move back and forth.

Was I?

"Where are we?"

"Still in Georgia," Carter replied like I had any idea what that meant. "Zera, why were you crying? Do you need some painkillers? Knox can redress your wrists if you need some more balm."

Before we left Liberty, she gave us a jar of healing balm from the bottom of her bag. It wasn't full, but Carter didn't want to stick around in case someone saw us, so he accepted the half full jar. Just a small bit of it had soothed my wrists, and they weren't hurting now.

"They are okay."

From his twisted position in the front seat, Carter continued to stare at me until a huge truck drove past us, making ours shake slightly. "I'm going to get moving again."

As Carter got the truck going again, Knox pulled me back to him. "Bad dream?"

"I don't remember," I muttered as I settled back against him.

As we continued the drive towards the Everglades, stopping occasionally for us to get out and stretch our legs, no matter how hard I tried to remember what made me cry, I couldn't. All I knew was I had this dull ache in the center of my chest, and I felt... sad.

Even when Hunter returned to the truck with snacks which included cake, I couldn't manage to get a smile on my face.

Finally, we reached Florida, and outside of the truck, the weather was getting brighter and sunnier. There had been gray clouds since we left the safe house, and everyone in the car was worried it was going to rain, so when the sky turned blue and stayed like that, everyone seemed happier.

Everyone except me.

The bright sun in the sky just continued to make me feel sad.

It wasn't until the sun set and the sky darkened that I felt more at ease, even though the ache was still present, just dulled. We stopped to eat, and then got back on the road. A short while later, Carter declared we were almost there.

The warlock's house was in the middle of nowhere. Unlike Castle Viegls, which was on the side of a mountain, everything here was flat. It just looked like tall grass everywhere.

I started to walk towards the grass to give it a closer look, but Carter's hand wrapped around mine, gently pulling me back. "It's the Everglades, Blue Eyes. You can't see it in this light, but most of that out there is water."

My nose wrinkled. "Why would anyone want to live here?"

"To each their own," Carter muttered.

Hunter appeared at my other side. Using his phone, he lit the ground in front of us, illuminating a trail of dirt about the width of the sidewalk. It wasn't wide enough for the car to get down, which was why we were walking, but either side of the loose stone walkway, the grass grew tall, and I could make out the water.

"There's definitely gators in there. It's smart really, because he has a place with a natural moat and very dangerous creatures to keep the humans away."

"More dangerous than me?"

"You know, if you had your powers, I bet you

could stick a finger in that water, zap it, and kill them all at once." Hunter declared as Knox joined us. "But right now, I think a gator would win."

"It's a good thing you've got three hunky gargoyles to protect you," Carter said.

"Hunky?" Hunter repeated, looking at Carter like he was speaking another language. "The nineties called and asked for their slang back."

Carter gave him a sideways glance. "I'm not above shoving you in that water, you know."

"I'm surprised you're not telling him to shut up and stop making so much noise," Knox said.

"The guy is a warlock. He will have wards up to let him know someone is here that we've already activated. If we sneak around, he's more likely to see it as a threat." Carter glanced down at me. "Remember what we said?"

I nodded: don't tell him I'm a fae.

The path snaked through the tall grass before turning into a wooden bridge over the water. Out here, with only the light from Hunter's phone and wind rustling through the trees, it was strangely peaceful.

Except for the fact we were walking over water.

Eventually, the winding bridge led us to a small island. A single-story house stood in the middle. Despite it being on an island, the house sat on stilts, raising it higher above the ground.

Carter moved me behind Hunter and Knox, and then made his way up the steps. Before he could knock on the front door, it opened. Lit from behind, the silhouette of a tall man stared down at us. I could barely make out the top of his head from behind Knox's shoulder.

"Evening, chaps. I don't know what you've been promised, but you're not going to find it here." The man had a strange accent. "And if you try, you will end up alligator bait."

"You Dean?" Carter asked.

"If the price is right, I'll be who you want me to be, but…" He cocked his head and grinned. "You can't afford me."

"Liberty Talbot sent us," Hunter told him.

"And Liberty just got removed from my Christmas card list. Whatever she said, I don't care. You all can do one."

"Do one what?" Carter asked confused.

"Do one. As in fuck off."

"You don't even know why we're here."

"Either you want something of mine, or you want something from me. I can't be arsed with either. So do us all a favor and—"

"What do you know about elementals?" Carter asked.

There was a pause. "You've been spending too much time around kids, mate. Elementals don't exist."

It was then that I realized it had gone silent. Since the moment I got out of the truck, there had been all kinds of bugs and frogs chirping away, and the wind was rustling through the grass. But now, the only thing I could hear was water lapping against the legs of the bridge and up against the shore of the small island.

"Hunter," I muttered, tugging at the back of his jacket.

"I noticed, don't worry," he said in a voice low enough for me to hear, but not loud enough to carry over to Carter and the warlock.

"We're not here for trouble, just information. Liberty said—"

"I don't care what the witch said." Dean snapped, cutting Carter off. "She shouldn't have said anything, and if you know what's good for you, you'll all fuck off now before she has to compete with the gators to get to your dead bodies."

From nowhere, a jet of water about as wide as Carter's truck shot at Carter, sending him soaring through the air. He landed with a loud splash, far enough away from the house that I couldn't see him in the darkness.

"Unless you want to join him, you might want to do one too."

I barely heard him as rage shot through me. How *dare* he attack Carter?

Ducking under Hunter's arm, avoiding Knox who tried to stop me, I ran to the bottom of the steps, ready to kill the warlock. Summoning every bit of power in me, I created a ball of electricity and launched it at the man.

Even as a child, I'd produced more electricity—but the orb was bigger than anything I'd produced in weeks.

"Zera, no," Hunter yelled from behind me.

It was too late.

The energy ball soared through the air, catching him on the shoulder. It might not have been very big, but it was big enough to send him flying backwards into the door frame, making him slump to the ground.

Just as Dean hit the ground, Knox was behind me, wrapping his arms around me to stop me moving. "Happy as I am to see that power of yours back, you shouldn't have done that. We need to get out of here."

"Why not? He hurt Carter."

"DB is fine. Look." Knox turned my body to face

the direction Carter had been flung.

He was completely drenched, with mud and grass was hanging off him as he charged towards us. The water he ran through only came up to his knees and was churning and splashing everywhere. "What happened?"

"She shocked him," Hunter said, then let out a sigh.

Carter came to a stop in front of me and ran his wet fingers over my face. "Are you okay?"

"She's fine. She thought you were hurt," Knox told him before I could respond, though he did let go of me.

"What about the warlock?" Carter looked over at the body against the door.

Hunter moved past us, up the steps, and then crouched down in front of Dean. He turned back. "Unconscious." He glanced at me, and then at Carter. "Now what? I can't see him wanting to help us now."

Carter rubbed his hand over his wet hair, sending water dripping off him. He let out a loud sigh. "Take him inside. Maybe he'll be more amenable once he wakes up."

Hunter did as he was told, picking the smaller man up and carrying him inside.

Without moving from in front of me, Carter leaned down and kissed me. When he stepped back, he sighed. "While I appreciate your need to protect me, you can't do that, Blue Eyes."

"He hurt you, and threatened Hunter and Knox. And he sounds funny."

"Wet," Carter said, waving at his torso as drops of water continued to drip from him. "He got me wet. And that funny accent is because he's British." He glanced at the house and then back to me. "I can see how that looked, but you can't attack people like that."

"What's British? And he attacked you."

"We have a long drive home. We'll discuss it later." Carter moved away, walking into the house.

I turned to Knox, confused. "Why is he angry? If someone attacked me, he would do the same thing."

"Fuck that, Zera, your powers."

Even though I had just attacked someone, I'd been too distracted to realize that I *attacked* someone. I raised my hands and stared at them, willing the sparks to appear.

Nothing.

Fourteen

DB

The stone demon inside of me was screaming to get Zeraora, throw her over my shoulder, and take her back to the safehouse.

Protect her.

Hard as it was to fight that instinct, I refrained.

Although I'd told her not to reveal she was fae, to do whatever she was instructed to do by us—including run, if needed, I'd never expressly told her not to use her powers. It had been so long since I'd even seen a spark from her, that it hadn't crossed my mind to tell her otherwise.

If anything, I was actually somewhat flattered that she would do that for me.

But it did now mean that this warlock knew she was the elemental we needed the information for, rather than a being we were hunting, which had been the original plan.

And that made Dean a threat.

I walked into the house and looked around. Outside, it had the appearance of a dwelling lived in by a hunter. The entire building was made from wood and didn't look like it would survive a strong breeze, much less the hurricane seasons this state was famous for.

Inside, I felt like I'd been transported to Atlantis. The walls were painted to look like the sea crashing against the shore with big, white-tipped waves. The floor was sand—actual sand. Hopefully, this guy didn't have a cat familiar, otherwise this place was one giant cat box. The furniture looked like it was made from driftwood and old sails.

Considering the guy was wearing a brick red suit, complete with waistcoat, and looked more like he was going to a wedding, the setting and his appearance did not coincide.

On the other side of the room, Dean, the warlock, was laid out on the couch. Hunter crouched beside him.

"Tie him up."

Hunter looked over and arched eyebrow. "Really? You think he'll talk if we do that?"

"If he didn't want visitors before, he's not going to want them after Zeraora's attack. And now he knows what she is, so I'd rather have him tied up so we know where he is. If he doesn't want to talk, we can make him." I frowned. "And make sure you take his wand away."

Hunter stood, shaking his head as he did. "I can't find it. Maybe he dropped it outside when he fell?"

"I'll go look." I really wanted to go grab a towel and try to dry some of the swamp water off me but making sure a warlock didn't have the means to cast a spell was more important.

I walked over to the door, reaching it as Zera and Knox walked in.

"Where are you going?" Knox asked.

"To find his wand." I paused and directed my attention to Zera.

Before I could say anything, she raised her hands at me. "It stopped working."

Although it had crossed my mind to ask her not to

use her powers, that wasn't what I was going to say. I'd already told her we would discuss it on the ride home since I didn't want the warlock to know too much, and that was still my intention.

"We'll figure it out," I said, instead.

Turning my attention to the doorway, I flicked one of the light switches by the door frame. I was wondering why the warlock hadn't bothered turning that on before, but it wasn't working.

At least my night vision wasn't bad.

Outside, I rubbed at my chin and let out a breath. I still had the urge to run off with Zeraora. I felt I needed to figure out how to protect her from herself before dealing with protecting her from everything else—not the other way around.

There was no wand on the porch. I headed down to the ground, searching around the stairs and just under the house. There were plenty of twigs and debris, but no wand.

"DB." Hunter called from inside the house.

After giving the ground one last scan, I turned and headed back up the stairs into the house. Sure enough, Dean was awake, struggling against his restraints.

Hunter had tied him with some rope, probably from one of the many sea-themed ornaments lying around, making sure his hands were in front of him where we could see them.

Now that he was in the light and his eyes were open, I could see how bright they were. Turquoise, almost. No doubt he had a glamor like the witch had. It was standard practice amongst them, that it was now rarer to see a witch or warlock in their natural form. Like chameleons, they hid themselves behind good looks.

Or in Liberty's case, whacky hair.

His gaze was locked onto Zeraora, and I didn't like it.

Before I could move over to her, he spoke. "I thought your family was dead."

"You know who I am?" Zera asked.

"A member of the Ceraun Court."

"I don't know what that means." Zera looked at me.

I didn't know what that meant either.

The warlock raised his hands. "How about you get these ropes off me, and I can make us all a cup of tea so we can discuss."

Knox snorted. "Don't fucking think so."

Dean fixed his attention back on Zera. "Interesting company you keep. I suggest changing it."

"No." Zera's response was as blunt and simple as

ever, but it made my heart soar.

"What is a Ser-whatsit court?" Hunter asked.

Tilting his head, Dean carefully looked at each one of us. "You really don't know, do you?"

I still couldn't gauge this man. He clearly knew a lot more than we did, and most likely, held the answers we needed. But even if we had been led to him by someone Hunter trusted, none of us knew him, and I wasn't about to put my trust in him just yet.

"We came for information on elementals," I told him.

"And I think we all know that elementals are just another word for fae."

I folded my arms. "Fae don't exist."

Dean glanced down at the ropes around his wrists and ankles before shifting his weight to get more comfortable. "About three hundred years ago, two races of fae walked this earth: seelie and unseelie. The rule that all supes remain hidden from the humans was instituted by the fae."

"They were real?" I asked, still not believing him. "Then why is there no trace of them? The Council has records of all supernatural races, and yet there's nothing for fae. What you're talking about is the human's fae lore. Stories."

The warlock let out something between a snort and a sigh. "Which was exactly what they wanted you to think."

"Why?" Zera asked.

"A fae seer foretold the end of the earth." Dean cleared his throat and looked at me. "Can I at least have a glass of water?"

"The end of the earth?" I ignored his request. "Seems a little melodramatic. What did they do? Leave the earth and head to the moon?"

Dean smirked. "Not quite the moon."

"But they left earth?" Hunter arched an eyebrow, looking as skeptical as I felt.

Three hundred years ago this world had barely hit its industrial revolution. There was no way a whole ass race was jumping ship to another world.

"Another realm. Their realm. Parallel to this one. At that time it was accessible by passing through fairy circles, but now it's locked, even to the fae who remained in this realm."

"Why?" Zera asked, again.

I glanced over at her with a frown. She didn't know much about where she came from, but that had never seemed to bother her. I'd made a mistake assuming it wasn't important to her since she hadn't mentioned it much, and I mentally kicked myself for that. This was a woman still learning to express and trust herself, and unless you asked her outright, she wouldn't volunteer information like that.

Right now, her gaze was fixed on the warlock, and I could see the curiosity there. She didn't know enough yet to be able to tell if someone was pulling her leg.

"The seer said that the end of the world would be caused by a fae, so the seelie court, the governing fae, summoned *all* fae to return to their realm where they closed the gates behind them. Unless you are of royal blood, the gate cannot be opened from this side."

"If all the fae were summoned back, how come you think Zera is one?" Knox asked.

Dean looked over at him and arched an eyebrow. "Because, obviously, not all fae returned when summoned." His tone said he thought Knox had asked an idiotic question.

Knox bristled. "And yet there's no such thing as fae."

"When I was told that gargoyles had the reputations of having skulls so thick there wasn't much room left inside, I didn't believe it. But seeing you, I understand where that idea comes from." He looked Knox up and down. "Judging from the state of you, you don't know who to pick your battles with either."

With no warning, Knox stormed over, grabbed the warlock by his shirt and lifted him off the couch with little effort. "Say that again."

"Knox," I uttered in a low tone.

Knox glanced over at me, let out a short breath through his nose, and then shot the warlock a dark look before dropping him. He moved to the back of the room to stand behind Zera.

"Are you okay?" Zera turned to the seething twin.

Even though he responded like he was, I knew he wasn't. Knox had a short temper, but his fuse was never that short. Any other day, he'd blow off comments like that.

"Am I going to get that glass of water?" Dean looked over at me.

"If some of the fae stayed, how does no one know about them other than in human fairy tales? There is no mention in our histories."

Knox hadn't asked a stupid question.

"Because those fae made themselves the enemies of the seelie court. And because there were members of the unseelie who stayed."

Behind Zera, Knox snorted impatiently. I was beginning to agree with him. This man was testing my own patience.

Zera moved towards him, moving Hunter's arm to the side as he tried to stop her. "You think I'm fae?"

"There is no being in either realm who can generate electricity other than the fae of the Ceruan Court."

"Zeraora," I said in a low tone. I don't know why I bothered as that tone never worked with her.

Ignoring me, she crouched down in front of him and tilted her head. "Am I your enemy?"

"You attacked me in my own home."

"You were outside."

"My home includes the land it stands on."

Zera shrugged. "You attacked my mate. I'd do it again."

"Wouldn't that make you my enemy?" Dean asked. For some reason, he seemed slightly amused.

After a moment's pause while she considered the question, Zera shrugged. "I think it makes you stupid. I'm not someone you want as an enemy."

"Do you want to be my friend?" The warlock's gaze roamed over her. "Or my lover?"

"Like fuck." Knox growled, marching across the room.

Before he could get there, Zera wrinkled her nose. "Why would I want you as a mate? I would destroy you.

My mates are perfect. You're…" This time, she looked him up and down before reaching over and pinching the collar of the man's jacket. "I don't even know what this is."

Knox faltered and came to a stop. As Dean's mouth dropped open, so did Knox's, but only for laughter to come bellowing out.

I arched an eyebrow as Zera looked around, confused. It had been a long time since we'd heard Knox laugh. I think she was more unsure about why he was laughing.

"I love you," Knox said as he sucked in a deep breath. He leaned over and kissed her forehead. "You keep being you."

"What did I do?" Zera asked.

Zera took Dean's question seriously, only she didn't realize that while answering, her response was insulting. Although, to be fair, I wasn't sure how to describe that monstrous red suit, either.

"You lot are all insane," Dean muttered. "And this is a limited-edition Dior suit."

"What door?" Zera narrowed her expression at the warlock.

"*Dior*, not door." The warlock let out an irritated sigh. "I know the fae went into hiding, but it's like you've been living under a damn rock."

"The Lycans held me prisoner most of my life."

Seeing the shiver go down her spine, Knox leaned forward and gently put his hands on the top of each arm to pull her to her feet.

The warlock's eyes widened, then his gaze roamed over Zera once more, only this time, it looked more like he was examining her than admiring her.

Either way, I didn't like it.

"Eyes up top." I warned him.

The warlock's gaze settled on the white bandages poking out from under the cuffs of the plaid shirt Zera was wearing. We still hadn't stopped to buy her the style of clothes she preferred, nor had we replaced the wrist guards she loved to wear.

"What are those?" Dean asked.

Seeing where he was staring, Zera pulled her sleeves down; her cheeks turned pink.

"Off limits," I said, taking a step towards him, ready to rip his tongue out if he asked another question that made Zera feel uncomfortable.

Slowly, Dean's gaze inspected each of us before settling back on Zera. "The seer foretold that the fae would cause the end of the world. But not alone. The fae would encounter a Lycan, and that would start off the chain reaction."

"And that's me?

Fifteen

Zera

I didn't want to destroy the earth, but if that was what it took to hunt the Lycans down, I'd do it. I had enough power.

Dean gave me a smile and shook his head. "You're of the Ceruan Court."

"You keep saying that, but I don't know what it means."

Pursing his lips, Dean leaned back into the sofa and continued staring at me. "How old were you when you were taken?"

"That's none of your business," Hunter told him.

Dean's gaze didn't leave mine.

"Five," I replied. "I think. I don't really remember."

The warlock had bright blue eyes, but looking at them, they made me think of ice. They were cold and unfriendly.

But my response made them change. Somehow, like they had melted, they looked liquid. "You know nothing."

I shook my head.

Inhaling deeply, he turned to Carter. "Why exactly are you here?"

"You're not in a position to be asking all these questions," Hunter told him.

"You seem to think you're the one with all of the power, and yet I can just stop answering."

"And then we kill you," Knox said with a snort.

Dean rolled his eyes. "Living up to that reputation again, aren't we, stone-for-brains? If you kill me, you still don't get any answers."

"My powers don't work anymore," I said. "Not like they should. Not since the Lycans took me the second time. It's like they took my powers away." I wasn't sure why I told him that, but I shrugged. "When I get them back, I will be powerful enough to destroy the world."

A smile grew on Dean's face. Despite his suggestion, I had no intention of making him my mate, although he did look very handsome when he smiled.

"You are not the fae that will destroy the world."

"That's good. I don't want to destroy the world. I just want to destroy the Lycans."

"How do you know it's not Zera?" Knox asked.

"The fae are split into two races. The seelie and the unseelie. The seelie are ruled by the royal family of the Aurora Court, and the royal family of the unseelie by the Lunar Court. The Ceruan Court is part of the seelie. No seelie would ever destroy the world. Unseelie, yes— they're crazy enough—but that's why they were all summoned back and the gates closed." Dean frowned at me. "Your parents didn't teach you this?"

I shook my head.

"You still haven't explained why no one else knows about the fae," Knox said, his grip around me tightening slightly.

Dean let out a long sigh before casting Knox a dark look. "Your voice it at a pitch that is very annoying. Too low." He shook his head like there was something in his ear. "Like a hornet buzzing around."

"Yeah, and like a hornet, I can cause pain."

"Where is the Ceruan Court?" I asked. "The other realm place?"

Over the years, I hadn't thought much about my parents. I didn't remember my father at all, and the small memory I had of my mother might have been another woman altogether. It was easy when you didn't remember something to not miss it. It also made that life slightly more bearable because I didn't have anything to miss.

"You cannot get to the other realm. Only one with royal blood can open that gate, and it hasn't opened once in several hundred years. As for any members of the Ceruan Court who stayed in this realm, I couldn't say. There weren't many who stayed—or weren't hunted down by the seelie guard. Those that did went off the grid."

"This still doesn't add up." Hunter drew my attention to him. His lips were pursed.

"Like everything else, it's all a bunch of fairy tales." Carter scoffed. Unlike Hunter, he looked like he didn't believe a word Dean had said.

When it came to things I knew about this world— the supernatural and human one—I didn't know much. Carter knew a *lot*. More than the twins, who were both really smart too. But Carter knew everything. Hunter said it was because he spent a lot of time reading.

But there was something about what Dean had said that felt... familiar to me. I had exactly one memory of before the Lycans took me—a party. I couldn't remember my family, I didn't know if I had any friends... I didn't even know my name.

And yet, there was something about this that felt true.

"No." Hunter disagreed with Carter. "I mean, maybe? But it was Knox who asked earlier: how come no one knows about the fae. Maybe they disappeared or maybe they're all really good at hiding, but even if this all happened hundreds of years ago, you can't erase a species from the earth and leave no trace." He moved closer to Dean and folded his arms. "We've tried to hide every trace of supes from humans and now we're stories. Hell, at some point we changed from creatures to be feared to creatures that are lusted after. But we're here."

"And fae are your supernatural equivalent," Dean told him.

"You can't compare the two." Hunter let out an exasperated sigh. "Supes have always been hidden from humans. That's why they're not in the history books. You're saying fae walked this earth with us, albeit hundreds of years ago, and then vanished without a trace? Without an actual trace. We should have records of them. There are some supes who are immortal and would remember them."

"Hunter, let it go," Carter said. He sounded annoyed and tired. "He's wasting our time."

"Why does no one know about the fae?" I asked the warlock. Although I understood what Hunter was saying, I still couldn't stop feeling like there was some truth to what Dean had told us.

Dean's gaze locked onto mine. "A spell. A very powerful member of the Lunar Court cast a spell. A spell which went wrong. And now, even most fae who remained don't know what they are."

"And you do?" Knox's voice was laced with skepticism.

When the warlock didn't answer, Carter shook his head and moved closer to us. "Enough. We've wasted enough time."

"I believe him," I told Carter.

Carter's dark eyes widened, and then he sighed, bowing his head as he rubbed at the back of his neck. "Zeraora, baby, the warlock is just spinning a very elaborate tale."

"It's fucking bullshit, is what it is," Knox muttered.

Pulling myself free from Knox's arms, I stepped to the side so I could look at my three mates. "I believe him."

"Zee, I'm sorry, but I've got to go with DB and Knox on this," Hunter said, gently. He gave me a sympathetic smile. "There's no evidence to any of what he's said." He turned and looked at Dean, pursing his lips. "Is there evidence?"

Using his chin, Dean gestured towards me. "She's right there."

Hunter rolled his eyes and turned back to me. "There's no evidence."

"I believe him."

Carter stepped in front of me, reaching out to cup my cheek with his palms. They were cold. "I know you want to believe, you want to find your family, but—"

"I already have."

A small smile appeared on Carter's face. "You did. But don't you want to find your other family? Your own kind?"

"I want to destroy the Lycans. And I want to be with you." I frowned. "And sex. I want more of that."

Carter's smile grew. Knox was grinning his crooked smile, while Hunter chuckled. Even Dean snorted. I wasn't sure how that was funny. It was the truth.

"Javion believed it. And you all did too until now. What changed?" I asked.

Carter rubbed at his temple as the smile slipped from his face. "Okay then. Why do you believe him?"

For as long as I could remember, the only thing I had ever wanted was to die.

Living the life I had, in excruciating pain with no relief, I hadn't thought there was anything worse and that death would bring a sweet relief to that. Then, when I'd gotten free, all I wanted was to kill every last Lycan and make sure they suffered like I had.

If I hadn't found my mates, then I would still be trying to do that.

Now, I wanted two things: to kill the Lycans and to spend the rest of my life with my mates, knowing they were safe.

Nothing else had been important before, and I couldn't see how anything else would be important after.

The only problem was that... something was wrong with me.

"I don't know," I told Carter, glancing past him at Dean. "But I do. And I think he can help me."

Hunter's mouth dropped open. Even Carter looked surprised. "Help you with what?"

Holding my hand, I stared at my palm. Despite the small surge I'd had earlier to attack Dean, now I couldn't even draw out a spark. "I'm broken."

Carter reached out, this time, curling my fingers up so he could wrap his hands around my fist. "You're not broken. I know your powers aren't like they used to be, but I think I was wrong to bring us here. I think this idiot is only going to get your hopes up."

"What's wrong with your powers?"

"Zeraora, don't answer that," Carter said, looking at me.

I scowled. "I want to know what's wrong."

"Let her ask, DB," Hunter sighed, moving over to the couch sitting down at the far end. "Zera's not going to let it go. We both know that."

The two of them stared at each other a bit, and although they didn't say anything, it felt like they were having a secret conversation.

Finally, Carter shrugged. "Fine."

I stepped around Carter so I could see Dean. He was looking at me in curiosity. "It's gone," I told him.

Once more, Dean's gaze dropped to my wrists. "What happened?"

"The Lycans used her as a fucking power source. They did it before, she escaped, then they caught her, and they did it again. Only worse. Then she blew the whole fucking thing up." The explanation came from Knox. He moved beside me like he needed to protect me, although I wasn't sure what from.

Dean's eyebrows knitted together, but his anger was quickly replaced with concern. "Do the Lycans know what you are?"

"No."

"Yes," Carter said, making me look at him in surprise. "When I…" he glanced at Dean and then frowned. "Yes."

Slowly, Dean licked his lower lip. "Fuck."

Sixteen

Zera

Knox took a step towards him. "You need to follow up on that."

During our time here, despite being tied up and surrounded by four people prepared to kill him, I'd not seen fear in the warlock's eyes until now.

"The spell wasn't just used to hide fae from the Seelie. It was used to hide from the Lycans. Those that stayed in this realm knew that if the Lycans got ahold of them, they were in danger. The spell wiped us from the

Lycans. If they know about you, about the fae, we're all in danger. Are you sure all they did was use you as a power source?"

I nodded.

Dean sucked in a deep breath but didn't look any less concerned. "Your powers haven't gone. They can't just disappear."

"But I can't do anything." I raised my hands, willing the power to appear in my palm like it used to. Once again, there was nothing.

"The fae succeeded in hiding by claiming to be elementals. You know why that is?" When I shook my head, Dean sighed. "Because fae don't just use the power from the world around us. They can create it. You are a power source."

"Don't call me that." I snapped at him.

"Why not? It's what you are."

"It's what the Lycans called her," Knox told him, gruffly. "Don't call her that."

Dean's lips thinned as he nodded his head. "The power of the Ceruan Court is Lightning—Electricity. Most things have current to them, no matter how small. Didn't you do that experiment in science class where you power a light bulb with a lemon?"

Whether it was my confusion or him remembering

that I had spent my life with the Lycans, Dean sighed.

"You draw that current in, channel it, and can unleash it in several different ways. But when that power isn't there, you can create it. The Lycans used you for as long as they did because even when you'd used all the natural energy in the atmosphere, you could just keep creating it. If it worked any other way, they really would have sucked you dry."

"Fae get their power from the air?" Carter didn't sound as disbelieving as I expected, but he was eyeing the warlock warily.

"Seven Courts, seven sources: the air, water, heat, earth, sun, moon, and electricity. There are certain spaces in this world where those levels may fluctuate depending on the fae, but those sources are everywhere." Dean's eyes seemed to twinkle as he stared at me. "But that's not the important part. The important part is that you can create that electricity. That said, emotions play a factor too. That's different for whether you're Seelie or Unseelie."

"If I'm Seelie, what does that mean?" I asked.

"Seelie's draw their power from light: the positive emotions. Unseelie, from darkness. The opposite dampens that." Dean glanced around at us before settling his gaze back on me. "You four are carrying some form of sadness about you. I'd guess that's not helping anything."

"So, she should just…" Knox shrugged. "Be happy?"

"I didn't feel happy when the Lycans had me and nothing like this has ever happened to me before."

Once more, his gaze dipped to my wrists. "Every supe has a weakness, including fae. The Lycans worked out what yours was." He glanced away, closed his eyes, and sucked in a deep breath. When he turned back, the irritation was back on his face. "Am I ever going to get that glass of water?"

I took a few steps towards the kitchen to get him a drink, but Carter stepped in front of me. "How do you know so much about the fae?" Carter's attention stayed on Dean.

"You know, I've asked you several times for a glass of water, despite helping you out, and you've now stopped her from getting me one…" Dean glowered at Carter. "I'm not a patient person, and I live out here. I avoid people because I don't like them."

Something strange was happening to the air in the room. There was a smell like you would get just before a storm. But the air was also… wet. As we'd gotten close to this house, Hunter had muttered something about the humidity, which was the cause of my skin feeling sticky and damp, and it started to feel like that again.

But as I moved my hand through the air, it felt like I was collecting water.

As I glanced over at the twins and saw they could sense it too, panic started to build in the back of my throat, choking out the air, making my chest tight.

Knox leapt to my side, hands on me as he muttered into my ear. "Zera, you're fine."

"What are you doing?" Carter took a step towards Dean. Before he could get closer, Hunter grabbed the warlock by his shirt, jerked him off the sofa, and flung him on his back onto the floor.

Dean stared up at him. "If you won't get me water, I'll get it myself."

Water droplets appeared from nowhere, hanging in the air. Then, they rushed around, joining together in one long snake of swirling water. The tail flicked Carter, sending him soaring into the kitchen before the head of it got between Dean and Hunter.

Knox grabbed me in his arms and charged towards the door before I could see what was happening. He ran along the wooden bridge, only stopping when we were a safe distance away.

"Carter and Hunter." I gasped, trying to get air

back into my lungs as I fought against Knox to go back into the house.

The bridge started to vibrate, and I stopped, clutching at the handrail as Knox wrapped his arm back around my waist to help steady me. Below us, I could just make out the water vibrating too. "What is it?"

"I don't know." Knox started to pull me back again. "But we should move."

"Not without Carter and Hunter."

The vibrating turned into a rumbling, and I looked up in time to see a wall of water moving towards the house.

"Oh, shit," Knox muttered.

The water hit the house before I could tell Knox to let me go, but the crashing noise drowned out my yells anyway.

Somehow, the water didn't touch us, staying in front of us like we were watching one of Hunter's movies. As the water flowed away, the house disappeared with it.

I slid out of Knox's grip, hitting the bridge with my knees.

Knox's hand settled on my shoulder as we stared, in silence, at what little we could see in the dark night.

"I am going to kill that fucking warlock."

My heart soared at the sound of Hunter's voice. The grip on my shoulder tightened. Straining to see in the dark, I stood, looking around. I heard him splashing through the water before I saw the dark figure.

"Hunter!" I ran towards the edge of the bridge, back to where the house had been.

"Zera? You okay?" Finally, Hunter emerged from the water, jogging across the small, empty island, to the steps leading up to the bridge. Water poured off him, but I threw myself off the steps and into his arms.

My hug was short as I pulled back, glancing over his shoulder. "Where's Carter?"

Hunter lowered me to the ground and looked up at Knox, who was shaking his head. Hunter turned his attention to me. "Wait here."

Before I could protest, he stepped back, shook himself off, and then spread his wings. With a graceful leap, he jumped into the air, beating his wings a couple of times until he was high above us.

"Anything?" Knox called to Hunter.

"I don't see anything. I'm going to circle around."

"The water went that way." Knox pointed to the right, and Hunter flew off.

"Is he going to be okay?"

Knox didn't answer me.

My stomach was churning painfully, like it had when I waited for Javion to come out of the Lycan prison.

"There." Knox let out a sigh of relief.

I wasn't sure where *there* was, until Hunter was almost back to the island, carrying Carter in his arms.

Knox and I ran over as Hunter landed. Before I could ask if he was alright, Hunter was setting Carter on the ground. The eldest gargoyle took one look at me and then wrapped his arms around my waist. "Thank the gods. Hunter said you were fine, but…"

"Are you okay?"

Carter released me and stepped back. "We've got tough skin, remember? I'm all good. Just wet—*ter.*"

"What the ever-loving fuck happened in there?" Knox asked, looking around at the destruction.

"I'd bet the deeds to Castle Viegls that we just met a second fae." Carter rubbed at the back of his neck as he looked around. "And I don't think the fae should ever be underestimated."

I just stared at Carter.

He held his hands up and shook his head.

"What do we do now?" Knox asked. "Go after him?"

"He's long gone, and I don't care for another dip

in the Everglades tonight. I'm sure there's only so many times before I have to fight a gator, and I don't have it in me tonight." Carter let out a long sigh. He looked exhausted. "Let's find a hotel for the night."

We walked back to the truck in silence where Carter and Hunter then stripped out of their wet clothes and changed into some of the spares they'd put in the back of the truck.

Was Dean really a fae? I'd not met a warlock before, but they were supposed to be magical. How did they know that Dean wasn't just performing a spell?

Maybe the same way I did.

I wasn't sure how or why, but while we'd been in that house, I didn't feel in any danger. And it's not because Dean was tied up the whole time.

Although Carter's plan was to spend a night in a motel, Hunter drove for several hours at Carter's instruction until we put a large distance between us and what was left of Dean's place. He pulled off the highway to a hotel, which sat right next to it.

"Stop or keep driving?" Hunter asked.

Carter looked up at the hotel and shook his head. "This place is fine."

Inside, the place was bright and cheerful. Hunter and Carter went to speak to a woman while Knox hung back with me. She was lucky my powers weren't working because she kept staring at the scars on Knox's face, looking like she was about to run.

"Let her be," Knox muttered, somehow knowing what I was getting angry over. "People stare. They always have."

"When I get my electricity back, I'm going to shock everyone who looks at you like that. I don't like it."

Knox gave me his lopsided grin. "You can't go killing people over a look."

"I never said I was going to kill them all." I folded my arms and glowered back at the woman.

Carter and Hunter returned to us, each carrying a plastic card. "Come on, Zee," Hunter said, taking one look at me. "Leave the woman alone." He slowly reached out to put his hands on my shoulders so he could direct me to the elevator.

When it stopped on our floor, we followed Carter out of the elevator and along the hallway to our room. Inside was one large bed and a couch.

"This is starting to feel familiar," Knox muttered, heading straight for the couch. He sank into it, turning his attention to the pile of papers on the table next to it. "And there's a pizza menu. Any requests?"

Seventeen

Zera

Darkness was all I saw when I opened my eyes next. Strangely, I was standing instead of lying on a bed, curled up in Carter's warm arms.

Something wasn't right.

"Carter?" I called out, even though I was certain I was alone. "Hunter? Knox?"

No one answered.

I fell asleep in the same room as them, and there was no way they'd all leave me alone.

The room also wasn't this dark. Carter made sure the lamp stayed on, and Knox volunteered to stay up and keep watch, while watching television.

Wherever I was, it wasn't where I was supposed to be. And the last time I was somewhere I shouldn't have been, the Lycans had captured us.

Closing my eyes, I took in several deep breathes, refusing to let the panic that was building up, take me over. If the Lycans had me, I would feel pain, and I felt nothing.

Nothing.

I didn't feel *anything*.

My eyes snapped open. Wherever this was, I wasn't in the hotel room.

Finally, I'd found my powers. Maybe being able to attack Dean earlier had sparked something in me?

The question was, where had I gone? We'd spent a long time trying to get me to astral project to Hunter, but Hunter, Knox, and Carter—they were all in the same room. And I wasn't in that room.

I'd once visited Liberty. Was this her place?

Stretching my arms out in front of me, I took a couple of steps forward. Then, with no warning, everything got bright. I had to clamp my eyes shut and then peak open very slowly until the light didn't burn my eyes.

When they were finally adjusted, I looked around. The light actually wasn't that bright, coming from a few flickering lights down a long hallway. A hallway that seemed familiar… and yet I'd never walked it before.

Where on earth was I?

It wasn't Liberty's salon; I was certain of that.

As if my feet took on a life of their own, I started walking along the hallway. Once more, a sense of familiarity took over as I made my way to a door at the end of the hallway, ignoring all the others as I went. When I walked through this one, I was in a stairwell. The only option was to go up.

Still allowing my feet to lead me, I went up one flight of stairs, and then through the only door on that floor. This hallway was brighter, with strangely patterned carpet. This place looked similar to the hotel I was supposed to be in.

Had I projected to a different part of the hotel?

Confused, I walked to the window and looked out. It was still dark outside, but lights were illuminating the grounds. There were a lot of trees where we were, but there were none outside here.

Turning around, I then made my way in the opposite direction. The hallway exited into a large reception area. There was a desk with someone behind it, staring at a computer screen.

My attention was on the sign on the front of the desk. Words I couldn't read, and even when sounded out like Carter had taught me, they still made no sense: M-a-i-s-o-n d-e-s l-o-u-p-s.

I had been here before. I just wasn't sure when or—Javion.

Javion.

Out of nowhere, a memory of him appeared in my head. Hiding underneath a strange bed in a room of bright sunlight.

My gasp wasn't loud, but the woman behind the desk peered out to an empty reception room. Even though she couldn't see me, I ran back to the stairwell.

I'd been here before, and somewhere, Javion was here too.

Charging back down the stairs, allowing my feet to lead me again, I ran back through the door and into the dim corridor. I ran until I reached a particular door. There was a sign on it, but the only word I could read was *Danger.*

Ignoring the warning on the door, I walked straight through it. The new room was illuminated by a bright light coming through a window. There was no one in there, and the only computer was turned off. I walked straight past the desk to the door beside it and went through.

Although the light had been bright in the other room, in here, it was blinding. The last time I saw light this bright was when the Lycans had recaptured me and were using it as a means to get power—create power to lower the blinds and save—

"Who's there?"

The voice was quiet, hoarse, and pained. But I recognized it instantly. "Javion?"

"Sparkler, is that you? You're back?"

Tears streamed down my face as I fought with the light to see properly. Finally, I could just start to make out a bed—a thin board hanging from the wall—on the other side of the room. The bed was empty, but I hurried over.

As I dropped to my knees, my sight finally started to come into focus… But I wish it hadn't. He looked… awful. If I didn't know it was Javion, I would never have recognized him.

Javion was tall and muscular. I'd never seen him in the gym with Knox, but Javion had bigger arm and thigh muscles. Knox might have been part stone, but Javion's body was just as hard and cold.

Only now, it looked like all his muscle had dried out. His arms and legs looked twisted, like gnarled bark. There was barely any hair on his head, and his face looked like... well, he looked dead. *Actually* dead, not undead-dead.

And that was all underneath charred skin.

"What have they done to you?"

Javion closed his eyes. "Nothing."

I scoffed. "It doesn't look like nothing."

"Nothing. They've done nothing. They just shut me in here, turned the lights on and walked away."

Turning, I looked at the window. This place reminded me of where they'd held me. But on the other side of that window there was no one watching him.

They left Javion alone, and I didn't know if that was better than them keeping an eye on him.

"Why?"

"I have nothing to offer them." Glancing back, I found Javion's eyes squinting. "Why do we have this same conversation every time? You didn't tell Knox, did you?"

"Every time?" I frowned. "What do you mean? I've not been here before."

"You have..." Javion moved his head back to be able to get a better look at me. "You don't remember.

Maybe you really are a ghost?"

I wasn't quite sure what that meant, but I hadn't been here before. I'd remember Javion looking like... that. I'd have gone straight back to Knox, Carter, and Hunter, and we'd have gone to look for wherever this place was to rescue Javion. "Where are we?"

"Hell."

That was something I could relate to, but this looked worse than anything I'd been through. I glanced down at his body again. He had to be in so much pain.

"Blood," I said, suddenly remembering what would make him feel better. Sweeping my hair to the side, I lowered my neck close to his mouth.

"What are you doing?"

"You need blood. That will help, right?"

"You're not really here."

Slowly, I turned my head, my face inches from his. "I... I want to help."

Javion smiled. A sad smile. "You always do." With an effort, he raised his hand, reaching for my face, but he never touched it. "Thank you."

"I didn't do anything."

"You did."

Something didn't sound right. I pushed myself back and cocked my head. "Why do you sound like that?"

"Like what?"

It took me a moment to work out what I meant. And then my breath caught in my throat. "Like you're giving up."

Silver eyes fixed on mine. They weren't as bright as they used to be. "Keep talking like that, and I'm going to start thinking you're going to miss me, Little Sparkler."

"Of course I'd miss you," I said before I could even think about what I was saying. My eyes widened at that thought.

Javion stared back at me before eventually nodding. "I think I'll miss you too. I've gotten used to your visits. They might even be why I'm still here. But it's time you stopped coming."

"No." I shook my head. "I'm going to get you out of here."

"How? You can't even touch me." Javion closed his eyes. "We need to stop having this conversation. My body isn't going to last for much longer anyway, and even if you could figure out where I am, I won't be here when you arrive."

"Knox—"

"Zera, you promised me."

"Promised you what?" I demanded.

"Don't tell Knox. You can't. You can't let him get his hopes up. He needs you now." Reaching up, his hand stayed just in the shadow before he curled his fingers and lowered it. "You have to look after Knox. He's grumpy and stubborn. His fuse is short, and he reacts with white-hot anger to the smallest of things. But you bring out a softness to him. I never told him I liked it. That he needs it. But he needs you now."

"Javion." I went to shove his shoulder, but my hand passed through him. Javion didn't react other than to close his eyes. "Javion. Javion!"

The strangest sensation washed over me.

Everything went black, and I felt like I'd fallen backwards. My stomach felt like it had jumped out of my body before I hit something soft.

My eyes shot open. "Javion!"

"Zera?"

A hand touched my shoulder, and I shrieked, dodging out of the way. The next thing I knew, I was falling again, only this time, my landing wasn't as soft.

In an instant, Carter's head was above me. "Zeraora, I'm sorry. Are you okay?"

Something in the corner of the room banged. "What's going on?" Knox shouted.

A second later, Hunter was crouched down beside me, ignoring his brother. "Can I touch you?" he asked, holding his out in front of me. "Help you up?"

My heart was still pounding, but I took his offered hand and sat up.

"What the fuck is happening?" Knox demanded. He was completely naked and soaking wet.

"Zeraora had a nightmare. Go back to your shower."

Knox looked over at me. "You okay?"

"My back hurts."

Hunter sighed. "You fell out of bed. Why don't you lie down and take it easy? Knox, finish your shower. I've got this."

Giving me one last look, Knox disappeared into the bathroom, shutting the door behind him.

With Hunter's help, I eased back onto the bed. "What happened?"

"You had a nightmare," Carter said. "You woke up shouting, and I scared you. I apologize for that."

"I was asleep?" My heart was racing, and I wasn't sure why, but it didn't seem like it was because Carter had scared me.

"You don't remember?" Hunter shared a look with Carter.

My gaze drifted to the television. Hunter had been watching one of the Marvel shows we'd watched a while back, but I wasn't really paying attention to it. Instead, I was trying to get my mind to remember what had woken me up.

"Javion." The name left me in a whisper as it suddenly came back to me. As I remembered, I gasped, covering my mouth with my hand. "Javion."

"It's okay." Hunter perched on the bed beside me. "I sometimes remember like that too. Out of nowhere, the pain—"

"He's alive," I told him. "I saw him."

Hunter's lips pressed together, but instead of telling me I was wrong, he looked at Carter.

"There's no way he survived," Carter muttered. Slowly, he turned to me. "What do you mean?"

The memory of his charred body had me swallowing back nausea as I realized how much pain he had to be in.

"I went to him. I don't know where he is, but the Lycans have him. He's… they kept him in light. He's been hiding under a bed, but he's hurt. Really hurt. We need to go rescue him."

"Are you sure it was him and not a dream?" Hunter asked.

"You don't believe me."

Hunter set his hand on my knee and shook his head. "It's not that we don't believe you, Zee. It's Knox—"

"And you." Carter added, gently.

"We don't want either of you to get your hopes up and start chasing after ghosts." Hunter gave me a sad smile. "I promise you, we all want Javion back, but we just want to be sure."

"You haven't been able to use your powers correctly since we left that Lycan facility. That warlock may have given us some tips, but you're still not getting a spark." Carter glanced over at the bathroom door. "And Hunter's right: Knox won't be able to handle this if you're wrong."

Eighteen

Hunter

Zera had been quiet since we checked out of the hotel. DB took the first shift for driving home—home to Castle Viegls—while I'd tried to get some sleep.

Sleep hadn't been easy. I kept looking back at Zera in the sideview mirror, unsure if she was going to say something to Knox. He would believe her in a heartbeat.

And it wasn't that I didn't... I really wanted to...

But it had been months, and Zera couldn't use her powers. How was she able to get to Javion? How could Javion have survived?

"You thinking about that fae?" Knox asked Zera.

Instead of being curled up against him, she was upright in her seat, staring out the window. I was sure she wasn't really that interested in all the trees lining the side of the highway.

"No," Zera said, softly.

Glancing over at DB, I found him staring back at Zera in the rearview mirror.

"I'm thinking we should stop for snacks," DB announced. "Donuts."

That earned him a surprised look from Knox and... nothing from Zera.

"We're on a highway. Where are we going to find donuts here?" Knox asked.

DB pointed at the upcoming exit. "You missed the signs. There's a place here."

We'd not given Zera a donut yet, and I was sure, with her sweet tooth, she would love them. But this distraction tactic wasn't going to work for long. We still had a good six hours left till Castle Viegls.

And then what?

DB took the exit, turning to a donut shop. He

found a space and parked. "Hunter, why don't you and Knox go inside and get something for us."

Before I could even arch an eyebrow, Knox leaned forward. "You're fucking joking, right? If anyone should be going in, it's Zera. Let her pick which one she wants."

"It's fine," I said before DB could respond. "I'll go with Zee." I turned in my seat. "Come on. You and me are going to pick all the donuts."

Without even questioning what a donut was, Zera nodded and got out of the truck. She followed me in silence into the store and stood in front of the display beside me. This number of sweet treats should have given her some kind of reaction, but she just stared.

"Zee?"

She turned and looked up at me.

"Donut?"

When she didn't respond, I gave her a small smile. "Hand?" Once she let me take it, I led her over to a table, away from the window in case Knox could see in. "You're thinking about that dream?"

She nodded.

"I know you two had a strained relationship, but it's okay to miss him. And it's also not unusual to dream about someone when they're gone." I didn't know that for sure, but grief hit people differently.

"I don't remember it."

"That's normal too. I remember hardly any of my dreams."

Zera lowered her gaze to the counter, frowning at it. "I think I should."

"You woke up pretty upset, so maybe it's okay that you don't."

"Why are you so sure it's a dream?"

I sucked in a breath and exhaled slowly before answering. "Honestly, I think the chances of Javion being alive are virtually none. That place went up in flames, and there are very few supes who cope well with fire, but it's a weakness for vampires."

Zera looked up at me, her bright blue eyes, unblinking. "What if he did?" she asked in a whisper.

"Why now?" I asked, gently. "You've not been to him before now. And how? I would assume astral projection takes some energy. You're still struggling to get a spark out of your hands."

"But what if I did go to him?"

I held up my hand up and waited for her to acknowledge it before setting it on top of hers. Her hands were cold. "What do you remember?"

She stared at the back of my hand as it rubbed hers.

"I don't… I just…" Zera pulled her hand free to press it against her heart. "Here. I feel it here. It hurts."

My own heart was beginning to hurt as I watched her. She looked broken, confused, and scared. I hadn't even realized she'd grown that close to Javion.

"It's okay to be sad," I said, hoping I was reassuring her. "We're all sad. We just show it and experience it differently."

Zera nodded and then looked out of the window on the other side of the room. I sat, watching her, wondering if I should just grab a box of mixed donuts and let us leave, or if tempting her with sugar would work as a distraction. Seeing her like this was killing me. She'd been upset before, but now she just seemed so lost.

Maybe it wasn't just Javion. Yesterday, we confirmed what we'd suspected—she was fae—and all of her kind were trapped in another realm she'd never get to.

Suddenly, Zera gasped as her gaze locked onto something outside.

"Zee?" I turned my head, trying to see what she was staring at. There wasn't much out there aside from a bunch of cars in the drive-thru. "What's wrong?"

Slowly, she turned her head towards me. Tears

were in her eyes. "It was real. It is real. He was real."

"Zera?"

She stood, her hands hitting the table. "We need to go get him. He's hurt. Really, really hurt."

I stood, ignoring the people who were staring at us. "Javion?"

"They took him and put him in a room with light. The same fake sunlight from when I was with him. Only there's no shutter and no me to power it. He's burned badly." A tear rolled down her flushed cheeks. "He said they don't come anymore."

Before I could process what she was saying, she darted out from behind the table and ran for the door. I tore after her, catching up before she stepped outside. In an instant, both DB and Knox were getting out of the truck and charging across the parking lot.

"What the fuck did you do?" Knox asked, reaching us just after I'd pulled Zera back from running in front of a car.

"He's alive," Zera told him. "We need to get him."

"It was just a bad dream," DB said, trying to calm our elemental.

"Alive? Javion?" Knox looked at DB. "You knew?"

"She woke up from a nightmare this morning. That's all."

"No, it was real," Zera shook her head.

"Zeraora." DB sighed, stepping closer to her.

Zera shook her head again. "It was real. He was real. And I've been there before."

"You…" Knox's lips parted but some form of choking sound came out. "You've seen him *before*? Why the fuck aren't we going to get him?"

I was used to seeing anger on Knox's face. Usually, it was directed at me. But I'd never seen him look at Zera the way he was now. My own anger simmered, and I stepped forward, putting myself between the two of them.

"Do you really think Zera would be able to keep something like that from you? She's just remembering it. You need to calm down."

Sucking in a deep breath, Knox glanced over my shoulder. His expression softened. "I'm sorry, Zera."

"Let's go sit down and discuss this somewhere that isn't in the middle of a parking lot." DB pointed to the truck.

We followed him back to the truck; this time, DB ushered Zera into the front passenger seat while I slid in the back beside my brother. I could feel the tension radiating off him.

"Let's start at the beginning—"

"Where is he?" Knox cut DB off. "Where are those fuckers holding him?"

"I don't know."

"You just said you'd been to him before! Please, Zera. Where is he?"

I turned in my seat and glowered at Knox. It was only because he sounded desperate and not angry that I refrained from punching him, although my hands were clenched into fists. "Calm the fuck down. Stop yelling at Zera."

"But Jav—"

"Knox!" DB snapped, making all of us jump. But it was enough for Knox to fall silent.

DB turned his attention to Zera. "Start at the beginning. Tell us everything you remember."

"He's by himself. He's in a room, and they have bright lights on him—lights like when the Lycans had us last time. Javion said it was artificial sunlight. It burns him." She winced. "He was hiding underneath a bed? It wasn't big. But he was already burned. So many burns." Her gaze dropped to her bandaged wrists. "Every part of him was burned. But he looked different last night. He didn't look like he normally did. He was thinner."

I leaned forward and gently placed my hand on her shoulder. "We're right here with you."

Zera stared at Knox before looking at me. "They haven't given him any blood."

Beside me, Knox inhaled sharply. "I'm going to fucking drain them of all their fucking blood."

Aside from Zera, the only supe I'd ever heard of being able to survive without some form of nourishment for long periods were ghouls. They might have been undead like vampires, but eventually, even they needed something.

From what I'd heard, vampire's bodies did weird things without nourishment. Of course, I'd never witnessed it firsthand, but if the stories were true, their bodies turned on themselves, seeking all the nourishment from what was left of their flesh and bones. Only, being dead, their bodies were slowly poisoning themselves.

Their immortality turned them into mummified corpses.

Except they were still undead. And once they got to that stage, they couldn't be healed. It was either eternal pain and suffering, or someone killed them and put them out of their misery.

If Javion was still alive and heading to that stage, I was praying to any god that would listen that we wouldn't find him like that. That he wasn't in that much torment.

"When did you go there?" I asked Zera.

"Last night." She frowned. "And I know I've been before. I think... I didn't remember until just now." She turned in her seat to look at Knox. "I would have told you had I remembered."

Knox nodded. He'd gone pale. "How do we know that it was the same time?"

Zera absently rubbed at her temple. "I don't understand?"

"You went back in time to Javion before, right?" Knox asked. "Jay turned up at the castle, and you'd been to visit him, only it was weeks before. How do you know that last night was really last night and not a month ago?"

"How...?" Zera looked at me. "How would I know?"

"How would she, Knox?" I asked. "Unless there was a calendar in there with him, or they gave him a newspaper daily, which even if they did, Zee has no clue how to read it."

"We need to rescue him," Zera said.

I turned and found her eyes locked onto DB's.

DB rubbed at his beard and nodded. "What do you remember about where he was? Anything that could help us."

Nineteen

Zera

The only thing that kept flashing in my mind was Javion. His twisted, burned body, and his silver eyes that had gone gray and dull. "I don't know."

"Okay, we'll take this slowly."

"You believe her?" Knox asked Carter, in astonishment.

Carter didn't answer, instead, he continued watching me. "Don't force it. Just tell me anything you can remember, even if it's small."

My heart was pounding inside my chest. Javion was alive.

Somewhere.

And I was the only one who knew where. I just couldn't remember where...

He said he didn't have much time left.

"Zera, baby, don't panic. Take a couple of deep breathes. You remembered this, you'll remember more." Hunter squeezed my shoulder.

I did as he said, inhaling a couple of times. Breathing didn't stop the pounding in my chest though.

"What do you remember about the room?" Carter asked. "You said he's in a room with bright light. What color was the room?"

"White," I replied. "The floor was white too. And shiny. It hurt to look at it."

"And what else can you remember about the room? Were there any windows? Could you see outside?"

I shook my head. "There weren't any... there was a window, but it didn't look outside. There was a room, and it had a computer in." I frowned, trying to grasp at a memory dancing in my head. "There was a man in it once."

Like the man had walked into the car, I could

suddenly smell awful scent he'd had, and it made me shudder.

"Do you remember what he looked like?" Hunter asked.

"He was a Lycan. He had hair like Carter's." I pointed at the gray hairs near Carter's ears. "...I followed him there."

"That's good." Carter gave me an encouraging smile. "What did you see when you followed him there?"

A journey along a musty corridor with no windows and lots of dark spots came to my mind. The stairs, the ugly-colored carpets, and all the identical looking bedrooms I'd walked through.

"A hotel?" Hunter suggested after I'd told them the little I could remember. "What are you looking at?" I turned around and found him staring at Knox who had a phone in his hand. Hunter leaned over. "Knox, you're never going to find the hotel based on that description of a carpet. And you can't see colors."

"It's a start," Knox said, before gritting his teeth.

"Can you look for hotels by their carpets?" Did people really care enough about what they walked on when choosing where to spend a night?

"Can you remember anything else about the

hotel?" Carter asked

There *was* something else. Something I'd seen... writing. "I... I don't know what it said."

"Am I okay to go in the glove compartment?" he asked, pointing to the thing in front of my knees. When I nodded, he leaned over, opened it, and pulled out a book. It had a picture of the truck on the front of it, but before I could work out what it was for, Carter had flicked through it, found a blank page, and tore it out. "Either of you got a pen?"

Hunter arched an eyebrow. "Dude, who writes anymore?" He went into his pocket and pulled out his phone. Then he sighed. "Damn warlock." After tossing it behind him, he plucked Knox's phone from his hand.

"Hey!" Knox objected.

Hunter handed the phone over and leaned closer. "Can you type the letters you saw?"

"I don't know what it means."

"It doesn't matter. You type it ,and we'll try to guess it."

Using my finger, I typed the letters that I could remember. *Masondelopes*. Hunter took the phone from me, cocking his head as he read it.

Beside him, Knox leaned forward. "Is that a word?"

Carter took the phone and looked at the screen. He frowned as his lips moved, but no sound came out. And then he let out a long sigh. "It can't be that obvious."

"It's not," Knox said, dryly. "What the fuck does it say?"

"Maison des Loups," Carter said in a strange accent. "It's French for House of Wolves." His lips pressed into a thin line.

"House of... Wolves?" Knox squinted at the phone. "The Lycans—wolves—are hiding in a hotel called... House of Wolves?"

"Are you sure that's right?" Hunter asked.

"You think Zera learned French to fuck with us?" Knox leaned over and snatched the phone back, quickly tapping at the screen. "Fuckers have three fucking hotels in the US. They used to have four, but one in Maine shut down last year. The others are Texas, Nebraska, and Oregon."

"None of those are a close drive," Carter said.

I nodded as though I had a clue what Knox was saying.

"Was there anything else, Zee?" Hunter pointed at Knox's phone. "Anything that could help narrow it down?"

"Maybe the fucking carpet?" Knox muttered under

his breath. He pressed something on the phone and then pushed it in front of my face. "Like this?"

"I don't…"

"Knox, you gotta dial it back a bit. This is Zera, and she's on our side." Hunter warned him. He reached for Knox's hand and pulled the phone away from my face. "This is a photo gallery of the first hotel. Use your finger to swipe the screen and see the next one. Don't worry if it doesn't look familiar. We can look at them all."

My attention was on the men in the truck and not the phone in front of me. There was a strange atmosphere in the truck, like the air was something I could touch and press my hand against.

Carter had been the quietest, but his eyes hadn't left me once. Not even to look at the image on Knox's phone. Hunter was trying hard to be calm, but I could feel something radiating from him. And Knox was cycling between anger and desperation.

But all three of them were… I wasn't sure what it was. It had never been there before…

Before I could work it out, Knox was leaning over to change the photograph. "Like this. Anything, Zera?"

I looked at the phone and started swiping. Nothing looked like anything I'd seen before, except the name of the hotel. I shook my head.

"Not Oregon, thank fuck. That's got to be a forty-hour drive, at least." Knox was muttering to himself as he tapped away on his phone. Seconds later, it was back in front of my face. "What about this one?"

"Knox, you can't rely on carpeting. What if two of them have it? What if none of them do?" Carter sighed.

"What the fuck do you propose we do? Wait until Zera projects back there so she can ask for directions?"

My eyes widened. "I could try."

"Why don't we try the photos of the hotel first," Hunter suggested. "It doesn't have to be the carpet. This place looks different than the last one. These hotels don't look like those big chains where everything is the same. What do you think, Zee?"

Still thinking about trying to astral project back to Javion, I looked at the phone, barely paying attention as I swiped through the photographs. And then something caught my eye. The picture was of the outside and a small garden area with no grass.

I'd seen that.

Hadn't I?

Swiping through a few more pictures, I stopped on another. It was a large dining room with lots of tables. That felt familiar too. Another with a pool.

"Here."

"This one?" Knox asked. "Texas?"

"I think so."

"Fuck, Zera, it's at least a twelve-hour drive between Nebraska and Texas. You need to be a little more positive than, *I think so*," Knox told me.

"You need to calm down," Carter said, using his warning tone.

I glanced back at Knox as he narrowed his eyes at Carter, but I could see the concern in his expression. "I don't know how to explain it, but it feels like I've been there before, and I don't remember it."

"Hunter, program the address into the GPS," Carter said.

"You believe me?" I asked him as Hunter leaned through and started typing on the truck's little computer screen.

There was a pause but then Carter nodded. "I do."

Warmth filled me. Not the burning heat he could switch on when he looked at me like he wanted to devour my body, but a warm, satisfying feeling. Like I'd slipped into a warm bath, or he'd wrapped his arms around me. It took me a while to work out what it was.

Since joining this group, I'd found it difficult to get them to listen—really listen to me—when I told them how I felt. I'd found myself repeating my words a lot, and even then, for some reason, they still wouldn't believe what I was saying.

For Carter to believe me, just like that… I felt happy—despite the thing that he was believing.

But the happiness was quickly drowned out by the growing desperation I felt. No matter what I did, I couldn't get myself to calm down as I worried about Javion. Had I remembered him in time? Were we going to be too late for him?

We stopped to put more gas in the tank, and then we drove. Every so often, Knox would tell Carter to drive faster, and Carter would tell him to be quiet. But I still felt the car speed up.

"Why do you think I didn't remember?" We'd been driving in silence for a while, and I had been asking myself that question more times than Knox asked Carter to go faster.

"I don't know," Carter answered.

Hunter leaned forward. "I think it's because you're still healing. You always seem tired when you astral projected in the past, and if your body is trying to use what energy you have to get better, maybe you're funneling it away in other directions, and you're probably too exhausted to remember."

"I should remember something like this. We

should have gone to Javion sooner."

I felt a hand on my shoulder, but when I glanced down, I realized it was Knox's and not Hunter's.

"You remembered. That's the important part."

For some reason, Knox's words didn't fill me with any comfort.

"How much longer?" I asked.

Carter glanced over. "A long while yet. Don't worry, Blue Eyes. We'll get there, and we'll get him out."

Leaning back into the seat, I tried to get comfortable. Sitting here, unable to do anything was making my skin feel like something was crawling over it. I quickly glanced down, hoping it was my electricity back... but there was nothing there.

Knox set his hand on my shoulder and started to rub the back of my neck, moving in large circular motions. As I reached up and put my hand over his, somehow, I knew he was feeling the same way.

We stopped a couple of times for Carter to put more gas in the tank and grab food. At some point, he switched with Hunter for driving. Otherwise, we didn't stop. Although it was a long time in the car, none of us slept, even as the sun disappeared, and we drove through the night.

Finally, Carter, who had switched back with

Hunter, pulled over.

"Why are we stopping?" Knox demanded.

I had no idea where we were, but the truck's little computer said we were close. Surely, now wasn't a good time to stop.

"You and Zeraora are going to stay here—"

"I'm not!" Both Knox and I said that at about the same time and with almost the same irritation.

"You are both injured. We can't go into a hotel that's probably swarming with Lycan and be expected to rescue Javion *and* protect you."

"I am prepared to risk my life to get Jay back," Knox told him. "You have no right to stop me."

Before I could add in my agreement with his statement, Carter turned the engine off and jumped out of the truck. Hunter was out seconds after him. I scrambled to follow, like Knox, but before I was out, the two gargoyles had taken to the air.

"Get back here, you fucking bastards!" Knox bellowed into the air. He turned around and punched the car; his fist went straight through the window.

With my blood boiling and my mouth hanging open, I turned to Knox. "They left us?"

Twenty

"They are going to murder us when we get back." Hunter called to me.

"If we make it back," I muttered, my words, lost in the night air.

For most of the drive, I'd been trying to come up with a rescue plan. One that would ensure all five of us would return to Castle Viegls safely. Although I wasn't sure if I believed her at first, by the time we'd left the donut store's parking lot, I was certain Zera had found

Javion.

Her astral projection ability was new territory for me. I'd witnessed it, and the twins had told me what she was capable of, but it still seemed too incredible of a gift.

Though if anyone was going to have a gift that powerful, it would be my Zeraora.

With it being so unpredictable, and her still being unable to control her powers, the safest place she could be was anywhere apart from that hotel. If she—and Knox—wanted to murder us if we came back, they could. So long as they were safe.

There was also the fact that maybe we weren't going to get there in time. The last thing *I* wanted was to find Javion if he hadn't survived. Neither Zeraora nor Knox would cope with that sight, and I was not running the risk of that happening.

I'd come to the conclusion about halfway through Louisiana that the only way we had any chance at succeeding was if Hunter and I went alone. So when we switched back on the driving, I told him when we stopped, we would get straight in the air and leave the other two.

Hunter hadn't questioned it. He hadn't even asked for more information. He'd just gotten back in the car like the exchange hadn't happened.

"Do you have a plan?" Hunter asked, flying a little closer.

"Javion will be held prisoner in a part of the hotel that isn't available to the public. Throw in some artificial sunlight and the most likely option is he's in the basement."

"We need to take out the power. It will knock any security cameras down. I figure if we take out the power for the local area, it's going to look less suspicious and buy us a little more time." Hunter pointed west. "There's a substation the hotel is on over there."

I arched an eyebrow. "You worked that out in the back of the car?"

"Why are you so reluctant to use technology?" Hunter rolled his eyes. "You can Google anything on your phone these days."

"And did Google tell you how to turn the substation off?" I ignored the jab, and instead, changed direction. It's not that I was reluctant, so much as I'd grown used to Javion, or even Hunter, doing all that.

"Make it go boom?"

I paused, hovering in the air. "What?"

Hunter glanced back and then turned around. "What?"

"I'm all for taking out the power for a few hours, but we can't just leave a whole town without power for days—if not weeks."

"We just need to take out a few transformers. If the power company is paying attention, they will reroute the power from somewhere else. In fact, we don't want them paying attention because they could fix it too quickly." Hunter shrugged. "But I figure it might give us an hour, and that should be all we need. If we're in there for longer than that, we've got bigger problems, including the sun that will be rising in a few hours, and we'll need to get Javion somewhere safe."

We continued flying towards the substation and landed on the peak of a hill to get a good view of it, and the town behind. Hunter pulled out a phone, sighing. "Knox is really going to kill me later. Good thing we have the same face."

Milliseconds later, the phone unlocked.

Quickly, he pulled up the map of the area. I leaned over, stared at the screen, and then looked back out at the town. "That's the hotel over there."

"Let's do this and bring Javion home."

As Hunter took to the air again, aiming at one of the transformers, I stared at the hotel and sucked in a deep breath. I'd tried to play out various scenarios in my head as I drove, but it was Javion who was my go-to for fine-tuning a plan. He had the ability to step back and look at the whole plan to find the weaknesses, and he was good at thinking on his feet. That was why he usually stayed behind, manning the comms.

Too often, our plans were reactionary now. I hated not having the upper hand or the ability to plan things out. Under different circumstances, we'd have studied this place, found out how many people were staying there, and we'd have floorplans.

Small bangs started to fill the air as Hunter took out transformer after transformer. And then the town in front disappeared into the darkness. We were working with a lot of cloud coverage and the likelihood of rain. Good cover for a rescue mission.

Before Hunter could return to me, I jumped in the air, leading the way to the hotel. We landed just to the rear of the property after diverting around. The place stunk of Lycans. I hadn't doubted Zera's ability to astral project here, but the scent, despite turning my stomach, reassured me, giving me hope that Javion was inside. I just hoped we weren't too late.

There were only a few vehicles in the parking lot, which I was taking as a good sign that there weren't too many guests—Lycan or otherwise—currently in the hotel. And as an added bonus, looking at the hotel that was as dark as the town, the place didn't have a backup generator.

"In and out," I told Hunter. "We work on the assumption that the power will be back on in half an hour. We stick together. It might be quicker to split up and divide the search, but Javion will need help getting out of there, and we need to watch each other's backs."

Hunter nodded.

Without another word, we moved forward, keeping to the shadows. As we got closer, it seemed some rooms were lit, but the little light suggested candles. It was late, so most people were asleep and probably unaware the power had gone out.

I led the way to an emergency exit, testing it.

Locked.

Reluctant to break it down just yet since the noise was likely to travel in the still night, I carried on around the building. At the side was an outdoor seating area— and an unlocked door leading to a large dining room. One look at Hunter was enough to let him know to be on guard.

With him keeping behind me, we crept inside. There was noise in the distance, but not much. Likely the few employees on the night shift still awake, trying to deal with the blackout.

On the drive here, Zeraora had been able to recall a few more memories. It wasn't much, but as we followed the corridor away from the reception area and the area that would be the busiest, we quickly found the elevator and the stairwell she had likely spoken about. There was a slight squeal as the door to the stairs opened. My hearing strained to check if anyone had heard it.

Without sticking around to find out, Hunter and I hurried down the stairs. The emergency lighting wasn't on, but our eyes had adapted to the darkness quickly.

The door to the basement had a security panel, which was still working thanks to the battery backup. I glanced at Hunter, wondering if he'd ever learned to pick one of these, but he just shook his head.

Holding a deep breath, I shoved my shoulder at the door. It popped open with a crash that echoed up the stairway. We paused, just for a moment to see if anyone reacted to the sound, but when no one came, I finally let out my breath.

The deeper we went into this hotel, the more dangerous it got. Less ways to escape, greater chances of being discovered.

Several doors lined each side of the corridor.

Working in silent unison, Hunter took the opposite side to me. Slowly, carefully, we pushed each door open. The first few were storage rooms. And then they changed.

Rooms with operating tables. Rooms with chairs that looked like they belonged in a dentist office— except for the straps hanging from the side. As I closed one door, I looked over at Hunter. His grim expression told me he was as alarmed as me.

Under different circumstances, I would burn this place to the ground. Not tonight. The thought made me more grateful that I'd not brought Zeraora here. Her impulse control would have faltered, and we'd be trying to stop her from destroying the place while still searching for Javion.

My beautiful elemental with a short fuse and a slightly wonky moral compass. My heart once again swelled for her.

The next door had a sign on it: DANGER. KEEP OUT. AUTHORIZED PERSONNEL ONLY. Expecting some form of furnace room, I pushed the door open and glanced inside. Instantly, I knew this was the room Zeraora had told us about.

"Hunter." I hissed.

He was behind me, following me inside. We crossed a control room lit by one dim emergency light.

The far wall had a large window in it, but the other side was pitch black. The light and our shadows reflected off the glass.

The door to the other room was unlocked. I pushed it open. "Javion?" My eyes picked up the slightest movement on the far side of the room.

"DB?"

I barely recognized Javion's voice, but it didn't stop me from darting across the room and slamming a hanging bed back out of the way.

"Fuck," Hunter muttered behind me.

The smell was stomach turning. I couldn't see the charred flesh, but I could tell it was bad.

"What are you doing here?" Javion croaked.

"Rescuing you." Using a claw, I sliced my wrist and shoved it at Javion's mouth. He didn't resist, sinking his teeth into my arm. I'd never had a vampire feed on me before, but I knew enough to tell he was in a bad way if the bite hurt: there were no endorphins being released into me.

"Make it quick. I don't have a good feeling," Hunter muttered, edging back to the door.

I didn't let Javion drink much, quickly switching places with Hunter. Even though he clearly needed it, so did we if we wanted to get the three of us out of here.

There should have been enough to keep him going, and then we'd work on getting him all the blood he needed.

Carefully, I scooped him into my arms, trying to ignore the feeling of his skin. I wasn't even sure his healing abilities would return his body to what it was. "We're getting you home," I told him. "Just hang on."

Javion slumped against my chest, but as I turned, his silver eyes glinted in the darkness.

With no further communication, I followed Hunter, allowing him to take the lead back up the stairs. Everything was going well until Hunter stepped outside. He took to the sky, and I crouched, ready to follow.

As I straightened my legs and jumped, something barreled into my side like a cannonball. Javion slipped from my arms; his body rolled across the ground as mine slammed into the side of the hotel.

Twenty-One

Zera

The number I could count to was much lower than the number of times I'd paced back and forth alongside the truck. Restless energy filled me, and I could do nothing with it other than walk the same short path, over and over.

Knox had spent half the time swearing with his head under the hood as he tried to get it started, and then he'd beat the back door until it could no longer be opened. Finally, he slumped down, leaning against the tire.

I was angry.

I was angrier than angry, but I wasn't sure what the word was for that.

Carter and Hunter had no right to leave us behind like this. I should have been there: I was sure that if I saw a Lycan, I would find my power and destroy them.

The Lycans deserved nothing less for what they'd done to Javion.

"Hunter."

Turning, I found Knox scrambling to his feet, staring at the sky. He looked worried. I glanced up, unable to see what he could. "Javion?"

"He's alone."

Although it never left my body, my stomach felt like it had fallen out of me. Air got caught in my throat. "No."

Finally, Hunter landed in front of us. Just as Knox had said, he was alone.

"Where's Carter and Javion?" I asked.

Hunter just stared at me.

"Where are they?"

Knox's hand settled on my shoulder. "We need to get out of here."

"No." I pulled myself free from his grip and

glowered at him. "No, not without Carter and Javion."

"They're not coming, Zera." Knox no longer sounded like himself. His voice was hollow, and his eyes were empty. "We need to go."

"No." I shook my head. "No, we did this last time when we should have gone back to save Javion. We need to go to the hotel—"

"They're dead, Zee." Hunter's voice was strained. "I saw it. I couldn't stop it. The Lycans... they're both dead."

"We need to go." Without any warning, Knox scooped me up into his arms and started jogging away from the truck. As I glanced over his shoulder, I saw Hunter following.

"Knox, put me down. Put me down or turn around."

"There's nothing to go back for." Hunter joined Knox's side. "We need to get somewhere safe." He glanced up at his brother. "The next town is about eighteen miles away."

"Take Zera." He handed me over like I was a bag. "Go. Get out of here."

Hunter shook his head as he continued running. "We stick together. I flew in the wrong direction before circling back. The Lycans don't know where we are."

"Hunter—"

"I'll take Zera if I have to."

"No." I objected, wriggling in Hunter's arms. "We need to go back."

"They're gone, Zee."

"That's what we thought about Javion."

Hunter's pace slowed, and he looked down at me. His eyes, usually a slightly brighter green than Knox's, were dull. "Zee, I saw it with my own eyes. The… They killed them. Dead, not undead. They're gone."

Staring up at him, I tried to understand what he was telling me, but it didn't make sense. How could Carter be gone? With me no longer struggling, Hunter picked up the pace.

It seemed like a long time had passed before the twins slowed to a walk. I wasn't really paying attention as numbness set in. It was only because something bright blinded me that I realized the sun was coming up.

"There," Hunter muttered.

I wasn't sure if he was talking to me or to Knox, but I glanced in front of us. We'd left the road a long time ago, running over dirt and stone, but finally, there were some buildings ahead of us, and the area was lit with dull streetlights.

"Where is this?"

"Fort Gawin, I think," Hunter replied. He glanced over at his brother. Knox was dripping with sweat and his breathing was heavier than Hunter's, but despite his obvious discomfort, his face was blank. "He's… he'll be fine," Hunter told me.

As we got closer to the outskirts of the town, they slowed further. Hunter set me down on the ground, and we walked to join the side of a road. Several cars were passing us by now. Their headlights were on despite the rising sun.

Knox was walking behind us, staring ahead, but I wasn't sure he was really looking at anything. I kept turning around, but Hunter took hold of my hand, keeping me next to him. "Just let him be. He's still with us."

After that, we walked in silence to the only motel in town. We got a room and Knox walked in, heading straight for a dirty looking armchair by the window. He sat down in it, staring at the curtains.

Now I knew why Javion hadn't wanted me to tell Knox about him.

Hunter moved behind me, sitting down on the corner of the bed. Just as distracted as his brother, he stared down at his hands, unblinking. Tears started rolling down his face, but I wasn't even sure he'd noticed them.

Carter and Javion…

They were really… gone…?

My legs felt weak beneath me, so I sat down and leaned against the wall, not far from the door we came through. The numb feeling that had encased me was cracking, and pain was leaking through.

This pain wasn't like anything I'd felt before. The pain the Lycans had caused me had hurt my skin, my flesh, and my bones. This was different. This was deep inside me. Not my stomach or my lungs… I couldn't pinpoint where it was, other than everywhere.

And it hurt worse.

I never thought I'd *want* to go back to being chained up by the Lycans, but that hurt less.

Loud sobs escaped me as water seemed to stream from my eyes.

Carter and Javion were really gone…

Twenty-Two

Zera

The bed sheets were itchy, but I had no energy to move. We'd been at the motel for... I wasn't even sure how long. The sun had risen and set a few times, but I hadn't counted.

"Zee, come on, it's pizza. You like pizza." Hunter was waving a slice of pizza in front of my face.

The smell, which had once made my stomach grumble, made it moan. Already lying on my stomach, I turned my head away. "I'm not hungry."

"You've not eaten since we got here. You need to eat something."

No, I didn't. I wasn't hungry. I wasn't tired. I was… sad, and I couldn't control my eyes anymore. They would just leak tears until there were none left. And then, after time passed, they would leak some more.

"Even Knox had a slice. Just one, please?"

I knew Knox had eaten a slice. I'd watch him eating like he was feasting on the motel's curtains. His actions seemed automatic. Aside from the occasional trip to the bathroom, he stayed in the chair, staring at the wall, until Hunter pushed a drink or some food in front of him.

He hadn't said a word since we got here, either. I could understand that. I didn't want to speak either. I didn't want to do anything other than lie there.

Everything still hurt.

Hunter let out the longest sigh as the bed dipped beside me. His hands were in my hair, gently stroking it.

"What happened?"

Knox's question made Hunter's hand still. In all the time we'd been here, Knox hadn't asked. Neither had I. I didn't want to know.

"I don't think you need to—"

"I will decide what the fuck I need."

Turning my head back to face Hunter and Knox, I

found the younger brother still in his chair, not looking at us. His fists were curled so tightly around the arms of the chair, that they were crushing them.

"We found him. We gave him some blood—it was going to take a lot more than we both had to get Javion back to... he was in a bad way. Real bad."

The chair arm creaked as Knox's grip tightened.

"DB was carrying him out. We'd gotten out. I was in the air, and I thought DB was right behind me—"

"You left him."

"No, he was with me."

"If he was with you, he'd still *be* with you. They both would."

Hunter bit his lip. "The Lycan came out of nowhere. They were both knocked to the ground... I went to help, but before I could reach them, two jumped at me. Javion..." Hunter swallowed. "He couldn't get up. A Lycan in human form came out with a blade..."

A strange noise left Knox. One I'd never heard before. It wasn't quite a sob, and it wasn't quite a screech. Something in between... whatever it was, the sound of his pain hurt me just as much.

I closed my eyes, clutching at the rough bedsheets.

"The Lycans got at Carter..." Hunter stopped and

didn't continue.

"And you managed to get away, completely unscathed."

Knox sounded angry about that, but I wasn't sure why. He and Hunter had a difficult relationship sometimes, but did he wish Hunter hadn't returned?

"It wasn't unscathed."

My attention went to Hunter. "Are you hurt?"

Hunter looked down and then shook his head. "Don't worry about it."

With an effort that had my head feeling like it was full of water, I pushed myself up and turned to face Hunter. "Are you hurt?"

With a small nod, Hunter sighed before lifting his shirt. Underneath was a bright white bandage.

"You never said anything." I leaned forward. "You carried me, and you were hurt."

Dizziness hit me, and Hunter was quickly steadying me with his hands on my shoulder. "I'd do it again. It's healing now, don't worry about it."

The pain levels in me flared. Hunter had been hurt too—and I'd not even noticed?

"Are you really okay?" For the first time, Knox was looking at his brother. Any anger left from before was gone now.

"This wound is healing." Hunter let out a long sigh and rubbed at his face. His skin was pale, and there were dark circles under his eyes. "We can't stay here forever. We need to go back to Castle Viegls. Even if we just get some stuff and go."

Without a word, Knox turned his head back to face the curtains.

There was no warning as tears started leaking out again. I leaned back and closed my eyes, not bothering to wipe them. I'd learned it was pointless.

"This was my fault," I muttered.

"No." Hunter's voice was sharp. "Don't start that."

"The Lycans attacked because of me. Javion and Knox were taken with me, because of me. I couldn't get Javion out—"

"Zera, we've had this conversation before," Knox's tone was as firm as Hunter's was.

"But I visited Javion. I visited him a lot, and I didn't remember it. If I had, we'd have known where he was sooner. He would have been—"

"If anyone's at fault, it's DB."

Both my eyes and mouth opened as I looked at Knox.

"Knock it off. There's no one to blame besides the Lycans." Hunter snapped.

Knox whirled around, making me jump. "Are you fucking kidding me? He left us behind and decided to take on the Lycans by himself. If we'd all been there—"

"You'd what?" Hunter asked, calmly. "You're still injured. Zera is injured. None of us would have gotten out of there alive. And you can be as pissed off as you like, but you *know* that's true."

With no warning, Knox swiped at the chair, sending it soaring across the room. It broke into several pieces as it hit the wall and fell to the floor.

"We tried, Knox. We tried as soon as we could." Hunter looked at me, reaching for my hand. "And if you'd have remembered sooner, it would have been just as difficult, if not more so. You and Knox would be more hurt, and the Lycans would have been prepared. We attempted a rescue mission, but that would have been a suicide mission."

"Then I should have gotten Javion out of—"

"Javion went back to save us," Knox said. He sounded broken as he looked at me. So broken that I wasn't sure if I'd ever see him smile again. "You didn't send him down there. Hunter's right. This wasn't..." Instead of finishing the sentence, Knox shook his head and walked out of the room.

"Where is he going?" I struggled to get back up.

Hunter helped me upright. "He'll be back. I think fresh air will be good for him." He let out a long sigh and lowered his head into his hands. "I think maybe we should just head west. It doesn't rain much in California."

"We need to go back to the hotel."

Another sigh came from Hunter as he turned to look at me. "They're gone, Zera."

"The Lycans. I am going to kill them all."

"Zee... we're not... there's three of us—"

"I can destroy them. I have the power."

Hunter turned, bringing his legs up and folding them beneath him so he could face me. "You don't. You can't even light a lightbulb. Look, I'm not saying that we give up, but we can't fight this battle now. We need to rest and recover, and then plan to get some help—"

"We don't need help."

"Yes." Hunter leaned forward, fixing his darkened expression on me, unblinking. "We do. You do. I know you are crazy powerful, and I know you can probably destroy a small country, but you can't do this alone. None of us can. I know you deserve to get revenge more than anyone, but you can't do it alone."

"But—"

"This is not me saying you're not capable. It never has been. Zera, you're incredible. You really are, but you are not invincible. You need someone to watch your back—we all do." He leaned in again. "Please, please, understand that. You need us as much as we need you, and we need to do this together. We can't go back in time and change what happened, but we can make our next moves more carefully. Together. So, we all come back alive."

I stared at him. "I can protect us."

"We protect each other." He reached for me and cupped my cheek. "We protect each other."

As I continued to stare, the strangest sensation started. The pain and the sadness was still there, but now it was mixed up with other things. Warmth. And tingling.

"I've never had anyone protect me."

"I know." Hunter leaned forward, resting his forehead against mine. "I know this is hard for you, but it's not you against the world. It's us, *together*. And if you're really struggling with that, just remember where going it alone has gotten us. Let's at least try it together, try protecting each other. Just try."

"Together." I closed my eyes.

The tingling sensation increased.

Hunter pressed his lips against mine. It had been so long since I'd kissed anyone that I almost forgot how much I loved it. I leaned into Hunter, enjoying how incredible he tasted, how warm his mouth was... how his lips had the ability to send sparks dancing across my skin.

Two thoughts hit me at the same time, causing me to sit back with a gasp. The first was that there were actual sparks. Staring down at my hands, there was electricity zapping between my fingers. And for the first time in a long time, it felt like my power was really there—for now, at least.

More than that, I could sense the charge around me.

And then the second thought had me bursting into tears.

"Your powers?" Hunter's face seemed to light up as he smiled.

I couldn't return the smile. My second thought was that I couldn't remember my last kiss with Carter.

With a sob, I threw myself at Hunter, kissing him through my tears.

"Hey, hey, Zee." Hunter gently pushed me back. "It's okay."

It wasn't. It wasn't at all.

"Why don't you lie down and get some sleep. I'll work on getting us out of here. Okay?"

While I couldn't stop the crying, I nodded and then lay back down, pulling the pillow to me so I could wrap my arms around it. Although Hunter said he was going to do something, he instead stayed beside me, stroking my hair until I fell into an uneasy sleep.

Only, I wasn't really sleeping, so much as lying there with my eyes closed. I wasn't trying to deceive Hunter, but as I felt on the brink of sleep, an idea began to form.

An idea Hunter would never approve of.

He wanted us to do things together, but we weren't together. Not without Carter and Javion.

More importantly, this was something only I could do. Something I had to do before my powers disappeared again: Stop this from happening.

If I could use my astral projection, I could get a message to me. Go back to before Carter and Javion had died.

I'd done it before.

Somehow, I'd gone to Javion—long before he was taken by the Lycans—but I'd not only traveled the distance between Castle Viegls and the apartment he'd been staying in, but I also managed to go back in time.

Opening my eyes, exhaustion disappearing from my body, I sat up.

Hunter glanced over at me, now busy gathering things together on the other side of the room. "Are you okay?"

I slid out of the bed and walked to the bathroom. My legs were stiff from not being used much. "I'm taking a bath."

Apparently, most motels didn't have baths in them anymore. Hunter tried to tempt me into the one in our bathroom, telling me this place was old and special because it still had one.

Hunter frowned but didn't stop me.

Thankfully, he didn't ask any more questions.

And I didn't really want a bath, I just needed somewhere I could be for a bit while I tried to figure out how to get back to a past version of us to make sure we knew about Javion sooner.

Hunter meant it when he said he wanted out of here, and I had a feeling as soon as Knox returned, we'd leave. I needed some time alone first. And I needed it now, before the power I had disappeared again.

But, more than that, I couldn't take this pain anymore. And I didn't want Knox and Hunter in pain either.

As the water filled the bathtub, I stared at my reflection in the mirror. I looked more like I had when I first escaped the Lycans. The color that had been in my cheeks and lips had gone—almost ghostly.

The bathroom door had a lock, but I didn't use it. If Hunter or Knox wanted to get into the bathroom, it wouldn't stop them anyway. Hopefully, when I left the bathroom, Carter and Javion would be waiting in the other room.

I climbed into the warm water, still wearing my clothes. Lying down, I took a deep breath, closed my eyes, and hoped for the best.

Twenty-Three

Javion

My first memories after being turned into a vampire were of pain. I was held captive by the Lycans— tortured and experimented on—for years before they let me go. In that time, I discovered there was no end to their cruelty. Me and the other supes—I knew there were others—were just subjects to be experimented on.

Last time, I was put in a hole with actual sunlight shining down. I endured it then, and I would endure it now. But Knox... yeah, he'd suffered thanks to the Lycans, but he had *never* experienced anything like what they were doing to him now.

I'd step willingly into that light if it meant Knox wouldn't suffer anymore.

I was close to making the same offer for his female too.

Fuck, I'd been wrong about her. I was so sure she'd been sent to us and that she would betray us.

After I'd been turned and held captive by the Lycans, they had let me go to see what I would do, to lead me to others, and to eventually try to kill me.

With Zera, they brought her back to use her as... a fucking power source. We'd been here for days now, and not once had they let up on her. I had my reprieve when she powered the blinds shut. Knox was taken away but returned.

She'd been chained to a spot, and not once had they let her take a break from powering whatever the fuck she was powering. I wasn't even sure why they were using her like that. We'd found her in a power station— this was probably another—why weren't they getting electricity like normal folk?

Was this another experiment to see how much she could take?

The glaring white light in this room was at its strongest. I had only a sliver of shade to stand in, and if I moved, it caught my skin. But she was lying unconscious on the floor of a metal cell, still having electricity pulled from her.

Until she woke up, that blind was staying up.

If *that* was her reprieve, I would stand in this too-small shadow for as long as I needed to, trying to ignore the searing pain in my toes, where they were exposed to the artificial sunlight.

"How you doing, Knox?" I called over, trying to distract myself from the fact that my toes were probably going to burn off before the Lycans ever let me out of this cage.

"Fucking fantastic." He grunted trying to move but cried out from the pain. "Motherfucking cocksucker."

"Now, now. This isn't the time for using pet names."

With shuddering breathes, Knox finally forced himself into a slumped, but more upright, position. "Zera?"

"Still unconscious."

"How the fuck are we getting out of here, Jay?"

There were only three ways out of this place. Death, the Lycans letting us "go," or two lone gargoyles managing to find us and successfully pulling off a rescue mission in a building swarming with Lycans.

Before I could answer, the female started to stir. And then, before she'd even opened her eyes, the energy levels coming off her shot up. Through gritted teeth, she was letting out an almost inhuman sound that had me shuddering more than nails on a chalkboard.

The hell with the blinds. I was in pain, but she was in agony.

"Zera, stop it."

On the other side of the room, Knox was trying to get to his knees. "What the fuck is she doing?"

I pointed at the lights. "She powers the blinds. Zera, I told you to stop it."

She ignored me; her face was screwed up in pain until the blind slid shut, sending the room into a dimmer light which didn't restrict my movements. "That female is a damn idiot," I cursed as she finally stopped what she was doing and slumped to the floor.

"One who cares about you," Knox said.

I glanced over at Knox who just managed to give me something close to a shrug, as though daring me to tell him otherwise.

She cared?

The idea seemed absurd considering our

relationship was frosty at best.

But she'd gotten that blind lowered in less than a minute, and it was obvious to anyone and everyone that she was torturing herself to do that. My gaze lowered to meet hers.

She wouldn't deny it any more than I could.

Now that she'd stopped putting herself through that, feeling seemed to come back to me in one massive explosion of pain. Doing my best not to let her see it— I really didn't want to let her do *that* all over again—I eased myself down and leaned against the corner of my cage.

Getting comfortable was hard. If I had blood, these wounds would heal, but the Lycans hadn't rolled out the welcome drinks.

I didn't need to look at my skin to know it was a mess. If I was alive, I'd be dead. Or whatever the fuck that was supposed to be. Humans with wounds like this would be in some special ward in a specialist burns unit with some poor fucker of a doctor fighting a lost cause.

"I'm sorry."

The female sounded like she'd been smoking two hundred cigarettes a day for a century. Now I knew why her voice always sounded so low and gravely.

"Shut up," I told her, not sure if I was talking about

the apology or wanting her to rest her raw throat.

"Zera, are you okay?" Knox called over.

"I saw Hunter and Carter."

Hunter and DB? She'd projected to them?

My eyes went wide as alarm set in, shaking my head in warning at Knox.

"In a dream?" Knox asked.

Good Betrothed.

"No, I—"

"They might be listening, Little Sparkler." I pointed up at the security cameras positioned on the ceiling just outside of our cells. "If you can't lie, just don't say anything."

"Okay." The female clamped her lips together.

There had been a point where I was sure her not being able to lie would make my life easier, but now I saw it as a curse. Mustering my strength back, I pulled myself up to my feet, once again, trying to hide the pain.

"I guessed that might have happened. Your energy levels dropped completely."

The female stared at me. She'd lost her glasses, and I could see her squinting like she was trying to assess how hurt I was. With her hands clenched into fists, she gathered the energy to push herself into a sitting position.

"Whatever you're thinking right now, don't," I warned her. Maybe it was a threat…

I glanced up at Knox. He met my gaze before nodding. "Stop worrying about us, Zera."

Knox, the fucking martyr over there…

Sighing, I glanced around the room for the umpteenth time. I was holding out on some stupid hope that there was a way out of here.

DB walking through the door was more likely.

If I had a beating heart, it would have stopped when, moments later, the door opened. It wasn't DB, but some Lycan female strutting like she was walking a red carpet.

I figured out she was the one pulling the strings in this room, and she seemed to be some kind of scientist… which felt like an insult to science.

Lead sadistic bitch.

In her bright red high heels, she marched up to Zera's cell. Stopping, she jutted her hip and stared down at the elemental.

"What happened there? In all the years you've been with us, your levels have never dropped like they did then. Even now, they're lower than they should be, despite you managing to shut those blinds at record speeds. What happened?"

I'd been keeping an eye on her energy reading too. That was how I guessed she'd been projecting somewhere. But this female couldn't lie. "Maybe you've pushed her too far, and she's finally running out of energy." I suggested before Zera spilled something she shouldn't.

If they found out she had the ability to astral project, being chained in that cage was going to feel like a picnic compared to what they'd do to her.

The sadist turned to face me, arching an eyebrow. "No. This battery has a much longer shelf life than she's letting on. I think she just needs more motivation."

Zera seemed to work out what she meant at the same time I did.

I leaped back against the edge of the cell just as the bitch pulled a remote from her pocket and set the blinds rolling up.

"Shut them," Zera shouted. "Please, shut them."

"Zera, you need to stop that," I yelled at her as she curled up, forcing electricity from her body. Above her, the energy readings shot up.

The sadist bitch looked at me and then at Knox. "And there's the other motivation."

Two men who'd been lurking in the doorway made their way towards Knox. As soon as they unlocked the shackle around his wrist, Knox swung at them. Instantly, the two Lycans started attacking him.

"Leave Knox alone, you fucking bitch."

I'd never felt so helpless in my life.

Watching them torture Knox hurt me as much as any burn from that artificial sun.

Knox put up a weak fight before he was knocked unconscious. Then the two mutts dragged him out of the room; his legs smeared blood behind them.

"Wait," Zera shouted, straining from the chains. She fell to her knees, clawing at air as she tried to free herself again. "Wait. Bring him back."

The bitch doctor looked down at her like she was a smear on the floor. "We'll bring him back when you learn that your consistent output is what's going to keep your friends alive."

"I can do that," Zera told her. "I can. Just bring Knox back."

"Let's see how well you do first."

"Just give me two minutes alone in a room with you," I muttered under my breath. I wouldn't need two minutes, but that extra time would get the fear pumping around her body.

She heard me, walking over and flashing me a smile, which I desperately wanted to rip off her face.

"Your kind are nothing more than a plague in this world. I'm surprised you found a non-vampire betrothed. But then, she probably doesn't know any better."

The tips of my toes crossed into the sunlight, but my reaction wasn't from the pain. "Fuck you."

"Delightful." The female Lycan pulled the device out of her pocket and tapped at the screen again. "And now you've just doubled the required output to get those blinds lowered. Let's see how much you really mean to her."

She walked out of the room then, leaving us alone.

My attention returned to Zera. If I had a heartbeat, it would be speeding up right now. The female was still on her knees, but she'd curled over, and I could see the little neon blue and white lightning bolts increasing around her hands like she was a plasma ball.

"Don't hurt yourself, Zera. That bitch is only going to keep moving the goalposts."

She ignored me. She always ignored me.

It might not be comfortable, but if I flattened back against this cage, I could survive.

I could practically taste the pain she was feeling, just from the chains being clamped around her wrists, and she wanted to make it worse?

For me.

That made no sense to me.

How could someone who didn't like me want to put herself through that much pain just so I could have a few extra feet to move in?

How could I not like someone and yet want them to not help me so they wouldn't be in pain?

The sound of water gurgling though the pipes above us appeared, and I had to brace myself, knowing what was about to happen next.

And I was powerless to stop it.

Gushing out of the hole above our heads, water rained down over Zera. The moment it hit her, I could tell something was different. I wasn't sure what it was, but the scream that ripped from her throat was one of the worst I'd heard: it started loud, and then almost instantly, went silent... yet her mouth didn't close.

The numbers on the display above her cage shot up.

"For fuck's sake, just stop it," I yelled at her. "What you're doing isn't worth it. They'll just bring the—Zera, fucking stop—"

Zera raised her head, and my voice dried up. She'd always had unnaturally blue eyes, but now they were glowing. If the room was in darkness, they'd be there, lit up like an LED display.

She wasn't looking at me, even though she was staring straight in my direction. Then, she closed her eyes, wrapped the chains around her hands, and somehow got herself standing, in spite the joules of energy pouring from her body.

"Zera, I said, stop it."

Her eyes opened, and with them, so did her mouth. From out of it, came the eeriest sound I'd ever heard. A scream, combined with the low rawness that came from her throat. But it wasn't just a scream. It was like she was forcing everything from her body at once: pain, electricity, air…

The numbers on the display went crazy as the electricity started pouring from her. It rolled down her arms and went shooting at every angle across the room. I had to duck several times just to avoid being knocked on my ass.

With a bang, the shutters slammed down. Behind them, the bulbs exploded, overloading from what Zera was sending them.

She still didn't stop.

Zera's powers lit up the room, and every dial in the place was going into red zones.

Avoiding another stray bolt of electricity, I moved

towards the bars. "Zera! Zera, you're going to hurt yourself. You need to stop this. Now!"

One by one, every bulb and display in the room— both in the ceiling and on the equipment lining the walls—lit up, glowing brighter and brighter until they exploded, shattering glass everywhere.

"Zera!"

I was locked behind bars. Zera, behind glass.

And then she wasn't. A single crack ran down the glass in front of her, expanding almost as quickly as the electricity that just hit it until the glass exploded.

Shards of glass flew through the air, and even though I ducked my head, I could feel it shredding through my skin and what was left of my clothes.

When I looked back, one of her chains had come loose.

She still didn't move. If anything, she seemed to be summoning more of her power—fuck knows from where.

"Stop," I yelled at her as an alarm rang out. I wasn't sure if it was from the electrical surge fucking something up somewhere else, the smoke now filling the room from all the damage, or just because her restraints were broken.

Then the main door flew open, and Lycans poured

into the room, a mixture of those in their wolf form and more in their human form. I was too shocked to laugh as they were all hit by bolts of electricity, one after another, before they could get close, all dropping to the floor.

Dead.

Not even dead.

Obliterated.

I could only gape at Zera. I hadn't been wrong when I said she was powerful, but I never realized she was *this* powerful. No wonder the Lycans wanted her back.

The other chain holding her down snapped, and she walked out of her cell like she was taking a leisurely stroll through the park, oblivious to the destruction and danger around her.

Or the danger to herself.

There's no way that level of power was sustainable. Or that she wasn't going to do some serious injury to herself.

"Zera? Zera, it's time to stop now."

She turned to me, and for half a moment, I thought she was listening. Then she raised her arms, pointed at my cell door, and let it rip. I only just managed to fling myself out of the way.

When I picked myself up from the ground, dust and debris raining from me, she had already left the room. I ran my hand through my hair. Knox was going to murder me if something happened to her…

Knox.

Charging after Zera as quickly as I could limp on my injured feet, I caught up with the crazed elemental. She was destroying everything in her path—which, again, I wasn't completely unhappy with—but she still needed to turn that power off.

"Zera?"

Either she couldn't hear me calling her or she was ignoring me.

I stepped in front of her, cutting her off. "Zera, stop now."

She ignored me, stepping around me.

"Dammit."

I followed her, keeping close behind, making an effort to avoid the energy blasts she was regularly shooting off at Lycans who were too stupid to stay clear, or at doors, to open them.

Finally, after a dozen or so damaged doors and easily, three times as many Lycan kebabs, she blew open a door and stopped.

There was Knox, lying on a table.

Sticking with her, I stepped into the room, just behind her.

Knox was strapped to a table and unconscious.

Inside my chest, my heart felt like it was twisting, seeing my betrothed lying there.

The sight seemed to have the same effect on Zera as the power she was generating finally started to die down. We both made to move over to him until I caught the scent of wet dog.

Turning around, I saw a Lycan in human form barreling into the room. I didn't see his weapon until it was ramming through my stomach. Unless a blade was used for decapitation, it couldn't kill me but that didn't mean it couldn't hurt. And my body, struggling from the lack of blood and wounds I'd already received, could do little more than slide off the blade to the floor.

A Lycan in wolf form leapt into the room, heading straight past me for the bigger threat.

Thankfully, she was still amped up, and Zera blasted him. Seconds later, the Lycan that stabbed me fell to the floor.

I closed my eyes, clutching my side.

In theory, it took a shit ton of sunlight, decapitation, or fire, to kill a vampire. But if a vampire's body was damaged past a certain point, no amount of blood would allow complete recovery. And I was certain I was about to hit that point.

Sensing the female in front of me, I opened my eyes and glared. What was she still doing here? "Get Knox out of here."

She ignored me, trying to look at my latest wound. "Why aren't you healing?"

Talking was an effort. I closed my eyes, irritated that I had to repeat myself. Why did this female never fucking listen?

"I've gone too long without feeding. Don't worry about me. Just get yourself and Knox out of here."

The scent of sour candy was suddenly stronger.

"Heal."

I opened my eyes to find Zera's arm in front of my mouth. "You said you didn't want me to do that."

Like fuck was I going to take a bite and risk her hating me. Besides, I wasn't important. She needed to save whatever energy she had to get her and Knox out of there. I wasn't in a good state anyway, and I doubted I'd last much longer. With a surprising amount of effort, I shoved her arm away. "Just go."

The stubborn female shook her head and thrust her arm back under my nose. "I don't want to leave you behind. Take what you need."

Shocked

Before I could stop myself, I laughed. What I needed was more than she could ever give me. My body was fucked. "You don't have enough blood for what I need."

"How much would it take to get you out of here?"

Twenty-Four

Javion

Fucking woman was going to make whatever was left of my time here even more insufferable. I reached out, grabbed her arm, and slammed it against her, pinning it down.

Why the hell did she want to help me?

My side protested as I pulled up into a sitting position. I fixed my attention on the one thing I wanted badly, but I also knew this could be a deal breaker for her. "I need an artery, not a vein. I need your neck."

Shocked

Before I could get a horrified response, something outside the room exploded. Without thinking, I threw myself at Zera, covering her body with mine. Something rained down on us—dust... rubble... the whole fucking building? I wasn't sure, but I kept her under me anyway.

The falling sky didn't feel like the floor above us, just the ceiling and the stupid tiles.

Beneath me, I felt Zera's blood pounding through her body. Vampires did get bloodlust, and I was close to hitting that point... the point where I would have no self-control until I drank all the blood my body needed.

"Knox?" Zera spoke, bringing me to my senses.

I pushed myself up, closing my eyes as I dragged my thoughts back to why I hadn't succumbed to the bloodlust yet.

Knox and Zera.

"You need to get Knox out of here."

"Not without you."

"Zera—"

"Not without you."

Insufferable, stubborn, annoying female glared as if the three of us walking out of here was an actual possibility.

And then I smelled it. My gaze dropped to her throat. Despite my efforts to shield her, she'd gotten scratched—the smallest of scratches—and yet the scent of her blood was suddenly overwhelming.

Fuck.

"Just drink."

If I didn't... If I let the bloodlust win, she wouldn't survive it...

I leaned down and sank my teeth into her neck, creating access to that beautiful, *needed*, source of everything. Almost immediately, my tastebuds sprung to life.

Blood wasn't fizzy but hers seemed to fill my mouth like I was drinking soda. And the taste... she tasted like she smelled—sweet and sour combination of... Nerds.

Her blood was as exquisite as Knox's.

With a moan, I let the endorphins into her bloodstream. Enough to take the edge away and make the experience more enjoyable than the last time, but not enough to have her coming on the floor.

Not draining her took an effort I hadn't experienced for a long time. I hadn't been close to a bloodlust for decades, but I also hadn't tasted blood like this. There was something about it that excited me in a way that was different to how Knox's did.

Her taste... it made me want more.

Suddenly, I knew to stop. I'd taken enough to help heal me, but not enough to have her fainting. Hopefully… we still needed to get out of here.

Only when I pulled back did my brain seem to reengage properly. Her blood… it didn't taste like *any* blood I'd had before. "Is it normal for fae blood to taste like Nerds, or is that just you?"

Before I could get an answer, the sweetest taste was followed by the sweetest sound: Knox's voice.

"Jay? Is that you?"

His question was followed by coughing, which had me scrambling to my feet. Knox was awake, and he looked as shitty as he sounded. Unfortunately, the blood he needed could only come intravenously, otherwise I'd have made him drink Zera's blood instead of me.

With Zera's help, we started unfastening the straps that'd pinned him down to the bed he was laid on. "You look like shit."

"You look like you just fucked." Knox's narrowed his eyes, staring at Zera' neck.

I rolled my eyes but couldn't help but find his comment amusing. Despite everything, he almost seemed a little jealous. Of her or me, I wasn't sure. Maybe of both of us. If we got out of here, maybe I could do a little experiment where I got to fuck the female in front of him.

But not now.

"In case you haven't noticed, the two of us broke free, and this place is literally falling down around us. So as much as I like taking some risks to make fucking more fun, now isn't the time."

With his free hand, Knox flipped me the bird.

As we freed him, he looked around the room, confused. "What the fuck did you do?"

I pointed at Zera. "Your mate turned into a walking lightning storm and—"

Another explosion shook the building.

Storytime could wait. I hurried around to the other side of the bed then pulled Knox's arm around my shoulder. "You think you can walk?"

Knox nodded as he slid off the bed.

Thankfully, I'd had my doubts and was holding him tightly, so when he did get off the bed and collapse, I was able to keep him upright. Zera took Knox's other arm, helping support him. "Let's go," I muttered.

We had no idea how far it was to the exit, nor what was standing between here and there. The sooner we moved, the better.

Whether Zera had succeeded in destroying all the Lycans on her murderous rampage to Knox, or they came to their senses and ran, the corridor was empty. Nothing tried to stop us other than rubble from crumbling walls and ceilings, making our progress slow.

We burst through the door to the stairwell only to be greeted by thick, black smoke. Whereas Knox and Zera were already coughing, I didn't have the same issue. Instead, I steered us towards the stairs. The smoke was coming from below us, but I was certain we were underground.

Maybe it was because we were close to an escape, but Knox seemed to have found a second wind and was working with us to climb the stairs.

Were we going to escape the Lycans?

No sooner had I thought that, when a sudden burst of noise came from below. It sounded like footsteps and shouts. They could have been trying to escape whatever fiery hell was down there, or maybe they were after us. Either way, if they caught up, we were dead.

Unless…

I had no idea what time of day it was anymore. Being under here had fucked with my internal clock. My chance of survival up there was fifty-fifty, at best and down here, it was zero.

But so was Knox and Zera's.

I stopped and turned, facing the love of my life, and

then kissed him like I was never going to see him again. When I pulled away, his only good eye was staring questioningly at me.

"I love you."

"Jay?"

If I responded, I would... nope. Not happening.

Instead, I turned to Zera and felt... regret. After all this, she wasn't *that* bad. She loved Knox—I could see that now. And that was what he was going to need.

"When we get out of here, we should try again, because I think I could end up loving you too, Little Sparkler."

"Javion!" Knox bumped me with his hip to get my attention.

I gave it to him. "Get her to safety."

"What about you?" Zera asked.

The noises in the stairwell were getting louder. I glanced back down before looking to her. "You're nearly at the top. The stairwell is an emergency exit, so the door up there will get you outside. I'll be right behind you. I'm the only one who doesn't need oxygen. Let me go stop these fuckers, so we can all get out of here without needing to watch our backs. Go."

Before I could change my mind, I pushed Knox onto Zera and then ran back down into the smoke. I only had to go a single flight of stairs before I met the Lycans. Six of them were in human form, all kitted out like they were some black ops team. Here was campus security.

"Blood sucker."

I rolled my eyes. "Highly original."

The first two Lycans charged at me. I knew I stood no chance at winning against these six. I had the advantage of not choking on the thick smoke, but they had strength and numbers. But all I needed was to give Knox and Zera enough time to get out.

The stairway gave me a second advantage that they couldn't attack all at once, but after only gouging the face of one Lycan, I was hit in the gut and then the side of the head by a hand that was half human, half wolf. Claws raked through my skin.

I fell to the ground and closed my eyes, waiting for death.

It didn't come.

Instead, I was flipped over, and my arms jerked behind my back. I felt them get something—a zip-tie, maybe—around one wrist.

And then the two Lycans pinning me down disappeared. Craning my neck, I looked up, finding Zera a few steps above me. Her hair was floating around her like she was in a sea of static, her eyes glowed like lighthouse beacons. And from her hands were orbs of white-blue electricity.

I ducked just in time for a ball of electricity to go soaring over my head. Then another and another.

Just like that, the Lycans weren't a threat.

Shoving my hands onto the step, I pushed myself up. "Not that I'm not grateful, but what the fuck, Sparkler? I told you to get Knox out."

Her glowing eyes dimmed, and she seemed to focus on me. She burst into tears and flung herself at me.

I braced myself to catch her, but she went straight through me.

Whirling around, I found her a few steps below me, steadying herself above the dead Lycans. With the thick smoke behind her, I could see her better. She wasn't corporeal. Although her flying through me proved that.

"Zera, where is Knox? Why are you like that? And what are you wearing?" Her clothes weren't the important thing, so much as the fact that she was now in jeans and a sweater which looked like it had come from Wrangler, or wherever the hell it was DB shopped—not the skintight leather bodice I'd last seen her wearing.

"Move. Move now!" She yelled at me like nothing

I'd experienced before.

Surprise made me move slow, but I turned to head up the stairs.

"Not this way. This way will explode. We need to find another way out."

I followed after her, glancing back over my shoulder. "This way is on fire. Look at the smoke."

Zera flung her arm towards a door, shooting a bolt of lightning at it to make it bang open. "The place they'd held me had another way out. This place must too. That can't be the—"

We'd only gone a few steps down the new corridor when the ground shook as, simultaneously, a loud explosion sounded above us. Barely a second later, I was flung forward. Soaring through the air from a blast behind me.

The emergency lighting went out.

"Javion? Javion?"

I blinked, realizing I had blacked out too. And I was now pinned beneath something. Groaning, I pushed my hands to the ground, braced myself, and then pushed half a wall off me. The corridor was still full of smoke, but I sat there, dizzy.

"What the hell just happened?"

"You're not safe. I don't know if they got you

before or if they're coming back. I just know they got you."

"What do you mean?"

"I don't know. But you're dead. You were dead. And so was Carter—"

"What?"

Zera closed her eyes and swallowed. Not that I thought she'd make something like that up, but the distress expression on her face was enough for me to know, whenever she'd come from, I was dead.

Really, dead.

"Start from the beginning," I told her.

"No, you need to get out of here." She took a few steps towards me and attempted to pull me up before remembering she couldn't. "Javion, leave. Before more of them come. Carter makes us leave. You can't be left behind again." She flickered.

"You need to tell me what happened."

"I don't know. You were taken by the Lycans to a hotel in Texas."

Arching an eyebrow, I cocked my head. "You're telling me I won a holiday or some bullshit?"

"You need to get out of here." She tried to push me again. "I can't lose you again."

The last part was said with a sob. I stared at her,

trying to work out why she was getting so upset... "You're from a future where me and DB are both dead?"

She nodded. "Please, move. Help me save you both. I want to go back to you being there."

Using the wall for support, I pulled myself up. I was in desperate need of blood. But if she needed me to keep going, I would. I took a step forward, frowning as I moved. She'd already proved that she could project herself into the past, but she hadn't ever changed it before. This, if it worked, would change everything. And she knew more about the Lycans than I did. "Tell me about this hotel."

"How is that important?"

"Walk and talk. I'll decide what's important."

"Knox is important. You need to get to him. He needs you. I need you."

My heart wasn't beating, but that didn't mean I didn't feel anything. "Walk and talk," I said again, taking steady steps down the corridor, climbing over rubble she just walked through. "Hotel."

"It means House of Wolves." She looked like she was struggling, but she was giving me something.

"And I was there?"

She nodded. "In a room with sunlight. You were...

it was bad. You were burned all over. Really burned. They hurt you."

The burn marks currently on my body felt like they were heating up. "Where were you?"

"A mountain. A house in a mountain. Carter's safe house. Javion, this isn't important."

If I got out of here, we were changing the future. She wasn't going back to what she'd left.

This version of her and all of her memories—gone.

DB had two safehouses: one in Tennesse and one in Wyoming. The one in Tennessee wasn't exactly up a mountain, but the one in Wyoming was on an island in the middle of a small lake.

"How did you find this hotel?"

"You." Zera let out an exasperated noise. "Why aren't you moving quicker? They will go. They will go without you, please, Javion."

I picked up my pace. "Me?"

"I visited you. A lot of times. I astral projected, but I didn't remember. I was looking around in the hotel."

However much time had passed, they hadn't bothered working on her vocabulary or knowledge much.

We were getting closer to the end of the corridor, and I was certain when I stepped outside, she would disappear.

"What else, Zera? What else did you do? How did you know to come back here? This seems intentional, not accidental."

"I was supposed to go back to me, but I went to the last time I saw you. I don't know how, but Dean said my power came from everything, so I found it and used it, and came back."

"Who is Dean?"

"He's a warlock. But he's not. He's fae too. I think. Liberty knows him. But I don't think she knows he's fae."

We reached the door and I turned. "Zera—"

"Go, please, just go," she yelled at me. She flung her arm at the door, then a bolt of lightning left her hand, blasting it open. "Now." She flickered again, but this time, she stayed almost see-through.

"Thank you."

I stumbled through the ruined door into another stairwell. It was filled with as much smoke as the last, but the stairs here seemed intact. They also only led down.

"Go." Desperation was still in here voice, even if she was barely more than a faint outline.

Hoping she knew where this led, I hurried down

the stairs. With each step, my body protested more and more, but I didn't stop. Eventually, I got to the bottom. Down there, I found a tunnel full of pipes and wires.

The smoke wasn't as thick, and I paused to look at the signs on the walls. I was almost certain this was another power station. Which, if they were pulling all the energy from Zera, made sense. It was hard to store electricity.

"Javion?"

Zera was getting fainter and fainter. I hurried on, her ghost of a shadow keeping close. "Tell me more about Dean."

"He attacked us, then I zapped him, but not much. I haven't been able to use my powers. But it was enough. Then Hunter tied him up. He was strong, though. He controlled water."

"And he knew what you are?"

Zera nodded. "He said I was part of some Ser-something Court."

Up ahead, I saw an emergency exit, just as the tunnel descended into darkness. There were more explosions, and although they sounded far away, there was rumbling and shaking that sent dirt cascading from the ceiling.

Never mind DB leaving me, if I didn't get a move

on, I'd get buried alive.

My side was protesting as much as my legs and bare feet were, but I picked up the pace, slamming into a door. It wasn't unlocked and opened easily. And then we were outside.

The light was dim, either dusk or dawn. If it was the latter, I didn't have time to find shelter. Before I could even consider keeping shelter in the tunnel until there was darkness, a much louder explosion rang through the air—the shear force sent me flying.

Although the world was thankfully getting darker, I could still feel the heat prickling at my skin from the lingering daylight. Somehow, I managed to drag myself to a tree. It barely had leaves on it, but its trunk was thick enough for some temporary shelter.

"Javion? Are you okay?"

Somehow, Zera was still with me, although I could barely see her. "Out of the frying pan and into the fire."

"What pan—? What was that?"

Gunshots echoed through the air, but they sounded far away. "Someone's shooting at someone."

Zera stared up at the sky. "No," she whispered, although her eyes were wide with horror.

I glanced up, spotting two dots on the horizon. No doubt that was my getaway option.

"They can't leave without you." Before I could tell her that it was okay, she started to glow brighter and brighter until she was almost too painful to look at. Then, with a look of determination, she flung her arms into the air, sending a stream of light into the clouds.

And then, just as suddenly as she appeared, she was gone.

Twenty-Five

Zera

"Hunter, get higher," Carter yelled at the other gargoyle. "They're firing at us."

"Javion." I tried again as, with a sudden movement, we seemed to jump higher.

"Zeraora, he's gone."

"No, you don't understand. He's coming."

The arms around me squeezed me tighter despite the electricity buzzing out of control all over my body.

"Zera—"

"Stop using that voice on... Carter, over there." I tugged at his arm, pointing at the strange lightning bolt I could see behind him. I'd never seen anything like it in my life, but I could also feel it calling to me.

Carter sighed, but slowly glanced in the direction I was pointing. "Zera, he's... Hunter!"

Just ahead of us, Hunter looked back. His attention went from me and Carter to the strange light. "The hell is that?"

Just as suddenly as it appeared, it disappeared. "We need to go there."

"We don't—"

"Carter, please!" I was desperate. I couldn't explain it, but I needed to go towards the light. The electricity still dancing over my skin could feel it too. "Please."

The older gargoyle looked at me, then over at Hunter and Knox. "How is he?"

We were still flying away from the burning Lycan building, but our speed had slowed. Hunter glanced down at Knox, biting his lip. "Not good."

"Please," I begged. "We need to go there. I don't know how I know, but I do."

Carter's face was getting harder to see in the growing darkness, but I could see his face as he sighed. He nodded to the ground, and then the four of us descended. "Stay with Hunter. I'll go check it out. *Alone.*"

"But—"

"There's no other option, Zera. Either you stay here, or we go. If it's a trap, I'm not risking you, and I need Hunter to get you all out of here." He turned to Hunter as, in the distance, wolves howled. "If I'm not back in fifteen minutes, go. Get them to the Tennessee safehouse."

Carter took to the air and flew away.

Hunter lowered Knox to the ground, checking him over. All I could do was stand there, watching. The chains, still shackled to my wrists, hung down by my sides. The skin beneath them felt like it was on fire, but it didn't hurt anywhere nearly as much as looking at Knox did.

He and Javion were... Javion... "Is he going to be okay?" I asked Hunter, not sure if I was talking about Javion or Knox.

Sucking in a large breath, Hunter stood up and walked over to me, pulling me into his arms. "You both stand a better chance away from the Lycans. His wounds need dressing, like yours. And you both need some food in you."

I wasn't sure why, but Hunter didn't sound

convinced. Closing my eyes, I leaned into him. This was why I wanted to leave and destroy the Lycans myself. Carter, Hunter, and Knox meant everything to me.

This should never have happened.

This was all my fault.

"He's got Javion."

As I looked up, my mouth dropped open. Flying low but back towards us, was Carter.

And Javion.

The relief flooding through me was so overwhelming that my legs suddenly felt weak. Clutching at Hunter's shirt, my gaze was locked onto Carter until he landed in front of us.

"Shit," Hunter muttered.

"Is he...?" I couldn't bring myself to finish the question.

"If he was really gone, he wouldn't be here," Hunter said, gently. He took a step backwards and looked at me. "Zee, are *you* okay?"

My attention was stuck on Javion. "He needs blood."

"All three of you need medical attention," Carter said with a firm tone. "We are too close to the power plant, and with the Lycans evacuating, I don't feel comfortable staying here. We need to get further away."

Hunter looked at Javion, then at Knox. "We're not going to make it to Tennessee like this."

Carter nodded. "We head north and fly as far as we can until we can't. Find a motel and a pharmacy. Or a Walmart—whatever's still open at this time." He turned to me. "Zeraora, I'm going to need you to climb onto my back and hold on tightly. I can carry both of you, but I can't hold both of you. Do you understand?"

I nodded and started to move over to him, but as I did, the chains slammed against my legs. Wincing, I looked down, seeing the electricity still there. The relief I'd felt seeing Carter and Javion safe somehow temporarily muted the pain, but now I was aware that the power hadn't stopped. "I don't want to hurt you or Javion."

"I carried you here, Zera. You're not going to hurt us."

"But Javion—"

"Is undead. You won't hurt him, either." Carter looked at me and sighed. "I promise, if it seems like either of us are in pain, we will stop. And as soon as we get somewhere safe, I'll get those chains off you, but I don't have the tools to do so now. We really need to go before the Lycans find us."

They were still howling, and they did sound closer.

"Please, Blue Eyes. Let's get out of here and get us all somewhere safe."

A howl, loud enough that I expected a wolf to burst through the trees, had me turning my head. I raised my arms, ready to finish what I'd started, but Hunter stepped in front of me, taking both of my hands in his. "Please, Zera. Knox needs help."

Even though I felt compelled to stay and destroy them all, the look in Hunter's eyes had me nodding. With a sigh, he let go of my hands and watched me as I walked over to Carter.

Still holding onto Javion, Carter dropped to his knees. I climbed onto his back, trying not to hit him with the chains. His wings came from a spot about a hand's length from the base of his neck, making it difficult to hold on.

"Wrap your legs around my waist and your arms around my neck. It will be easier when we're flying." Carter promised.

I did as he asked, as best as I could. Then we were back in the air. This time, Carter was flying with his body angled, which did make holding on a little easier.

With Hunter just behind us, carrying a still unconscious Knox, Carter led the way. I wasn't sure how far we flew for, but the longer we went, the colder it was getting, and the harder it was to hang on.

Finally, Carter called over to Hunter. "Whatever's in that town, we're taking it." He directed us to the lights on the horizon, but as we got closer, he landed on the ground. "You think you can walk, Blue Eyes?"

I slid off Carter's back. My body was freezing, especially my feet. "How is Knox?" I asked as Hunter landed.

Hunter looked at Carter before answering. "We'll be fine once we've got a roof over our heads."

With five of us to a room and only one bed, there wasn't much space. There were more rooms available, but Carter wanted us all in one.

So did I.

Knox and Javion were on the bed, both still unconscious. Hunter was busy trying to treat Knox's wounds. Of the three of us, he was in the worst shape. I sat on the edge of the bed, trying not to move since I already destroyed the television, and Hunter needed the lights to see what he was doing.

Carter went out for supplies, promising to be as quick as possible. He wouldn't let me go with him—not that I wanted to leave the others alone anyway.

Once again, I found myself feeling helpless, only this time, it wasn't chains holding me back. So to get rid of my nervous energy, I started walking a path on the floor.

"Zee, do you think you could run a face cloth under the water?" Hunter asked, making me stop pacing.

Eagerly, I nodded and hurried into the bathroom. Hunter had already been in, claimed the towels and ripped them up. One small square of white cloth was left on the towel rack, so I ran the water and dunked the cloth under it. Once it was soaked, I hurried back to Hunter and held it out to him.

Hunter gave me a small smile as he took it from me. "We don't need it quite so wet this time. I'm sorry, I should have told you." He squeezed it out, letting the excess water soak the floor by the bed.

As I started pacing again, Hunter held it back out to me. "Why don't you help Javion?"

I stared down at him. "I don't know how."

"Hand?" he commanded, softly. When I held out a hand, he took it then turned it over. A scowl flickered across his face as he looked at the chain but then focused on the underside of my arm. "Dab his forehead, gently. Like this."

I paid close attention to what he was doing. Hunter gave me a reassuring smile as I took the cloth from him and then hurried around to the other side of the bed.

Javion was lying on his back, eyes closed. I'd never thought about it before, but as he was dead, his chest wasn't rising like Knox's. That was a strangely unpleasant sight.

"You don't have to do it if you feel uncomfortable."

Looking over at Hunter, he nodded towards my hand. It was hovering over Javion's head as I stared at his unmoving chest. "It's fine," I muttered before gently pressing the cloth to the vampire's forehead.

Moments later, Javion moaned.

"Is he going to be okay?"

Hunter glanced over. "I'm confident Javion just needs blood and rest."

"If he's dead, why does he need to rest?" I asked, curious.

"Vampires don't need sleep, so much as down time to let the blood do the healing it needs. Most don't sleep anyway. They just stay still."

"How can you make the complicated healing process of a vampire seem so lame?" Javion's voice croaked, making me jump. He was promptly rewarded by the hanging chain smacking into his side. "Fuck's sake, Sparkler." Javion groaned, reaching to grab his ribs. "I haven't had any blood, and you're already hurting me."

Instantly, I backed away, dropping the face cloth on the side of the bed.

Hunter hurried around to take the spot I'd just been in. "How are you feeling?"

"Like shit."

"Here." Hunter sat down next to him and pulled up his sleeve.

"It needs to be an artery," I told him.

Hunter looked at me, then turned back to Javion, arching an eyebrow.

"The elemental offered me her blood. I wasn't in any position to turn it down."

My eyes narrowed. "You said it had to be my neck."

"Because I wanted you to get Knox out of there. I figured after the last time a vampire bit you that you'd refuse." Javion reached for Hunter's arm, but Hunter moved it out of Javion's reach. "Come on."

"I can't believe you went for her neck."

With some effort, Javion turned his head; his attention was on Knox. "I thought if I said that, she'd get herself and Knox the fuck out of there. Didn't expect her to give me her neck like that." He closed his eyes, turning his head back to Hunter before reopening them.

"Fuck's sake," Hunter muttered before thrusting his arm at him. "Drink up so I can punch you."

He had to lower his wrist to Javion's mouth because the vampire couldn't raise his head. Javion's mouth clamped down.

My nose wrinkled up, but I couldn't look away. When I'd seen Javion drink Knox's blood, sex had been involved, so Knox's reaction had been like he was having an orgasm. It wasn't like that when Javion drank mine, but it hadn't hurt like when the other vampire bit me. Now, even though he was scowling at Javion, Hunter didn't look in pain.

Eventually, Javion moved his hand, grabbing hold of Hunter's arm. Not long after, Hunter pulled his arm back, earning a snarl from Javion.

"Chill." Hunter warned him. "I only have so much blood, and I need to take care of your boyfriend. DB will be back soon. You can have his blood then."

"Do you need my blood?" I asked.

"No," Hunter said, sharply. He got up and moved over to me, gently pointing to my shackled wrists. "You need your blood to heal these."

"Why the fuck are those things still on her?" Javion managed to pull himself into a sitting position with some effort.

"We're in a motel, not a fucking Home Depot. DB's out getting something to get those things off her. Unless you can get them off with your bare hands?"

Javion shot him a scathing look, but then fixed his attention on me. His gaze softened slightly. "You okay, Little Sparkler?"

I wasn't. The constant buzzing from my powers that wouldn't go away was making my whole body feel like it was being pressed by something heavy.

The sensation was like being back in the glass prison, making me want to pass out and find relief, but unable to. Escaping, finding Javion, getting here… for a while, everything made me forget about the feeling, but now, there was nothing left to distract me.

The main light in the room flickered, and Hunter looked over at me. "I'm going to see if the motel owner has some tools I can borrow." He moved to the door, but as he went to pull it open, Carter was on the other side with a key in one hand and several bags in the other.

"What's wrong?" Carter asked.

"You got something to get those chains off Zera?" Hunter took the bags from him. Without waiting for an answer, he seemed to find what he was looking for, pulling a box out of one of the bags.

Carter stepped into the room before pulling the door closed behind him. He glanced over at the bed and saw Javion. "You're awake."

"Get those things off Zera, and then we'll talk."

Hunter was already pulling a strange red tool out of the box, staring at the black rope hanging from it. "Wired?"

"We're in the boonies. There was one small Walmart open, and it had the smallest selection of power tools I've ever seen. I've got bolt cutters and some other things in the other bag if that doesn't work, but we managed to get the last lot off Zeraora without her shorting it out." He turned to me. "You can do it again, right?"

He seemed so confident in my abilities, but right now, I wasn't sure if I had a hold on my powers at all. Carter walked over to Hunter and took the thing off him.

The room had a small table with a single chair in it, but the table was up against the wall. Carter went over to it, poking the rope—the *wire*—into the wall. "Come sit down, Zeraora. Put your arms on the table."

Doing as he requested, I sat down and placed my

arm on the table, eyeing the thing in his hand suspiciously.

"Do you remember what happened last time?"

I nodded.

"Same thing. But I need you to keep very still. It's going to be very noisy, and it might even spark, but you need to stay still because I don't want to hurt you. Okay?"

Hunter moved beside me. "I'm going to cover your ears so it's not as loud. Why don't you close your eyes or look away?"

I closed my eyes as Hunter's hands pressed against my ears. The thing Carter had was loud, even with my ears covered, but I kept my arm as still as I could. It seemed to take longer than last time, but I could tell the moment the chain was removed.

Even with the other one still on my wrist, the relief was instant. And although it still felt like someone was pressing something against my chest, at least I could take in a breath. And the agonizing pain on my wrist lightened up, too.

Twenty-Six

Zera

One side of me felt hot, and the other, ice cold. The inside of my head felt like someone had taken it and squeezed. And the burning sensation in my wrists was close to bringing tears to my eyes.

I'd gotten used to not feeling pain, but now it was back.

Before I opened my eyes, I sucked in a deep breath. It really wasn't any worse than anything I'd experienced before. I just wasn't used to it.

Finally, I opened my eyes. I was laying between Knox and Javion, which explained why my body was confused with whether I was hot or cold. Both were asleep still. Or I assumed Javion was asleep and not dead. His lack of moving chest was still strangely creepy.

Biting my lip, I pushed myself up, feeling dizzy almost immediately. From nowhere, hands pressed against my back, helping me up.

"Take it easy, Zee."

As my vision cleared, on the opposite side of the room, Carter suddenly sat upright. I think he'd been leaning against the wall, but it hadn't really registered as I sat up myself.

"You're awake."

"Go back to sleep, DB. It's your turn to rest. I'll take care of Zee."

Carter rubbed his hand over his face and then shook his head. "It's nearly time to switch."

"Switch what?" I asked.

"We're taking turns looking after all of you." Hunter let go of me and reached for a bottle of Coke, unscrewing it with a satisfying hiss before handing it to me.

The sweet liquid almost made me tense up, but it

came with a burst that took away the lingering dizziness.

"Take small sips," Hunter told me, reaching to pull the bottle back. "I could do with you not choking."

"Are you hungry?" Carter asked.

I nodded before drinking more.

A dark look crossed his expression, but it was quickly gone as he turned and started looking in one of the many bags. He pulled out a loaf of bread, taking a few slices from it. Quickly crossing the small room, he held it out to me.

"I know it's not exciting, but with Coke and not eating for some time, I think you should take it easy."

My stomach was hurting, so I didn't care. I didn't need to eat any food, but since having it, I missed it. Eating felt like something I had to do now. I took the bread and ate it as quickly as I could.

"Give it a little while, and you can have some more." Carter promised me. "I don't want you to be sick on top of everything else."

Nodding, I turned to look at Knox. The ripped-up towels Hunter used before had been replaced with bandages. And there was a lot of them covering his nearly naked body. Most of the remaining skin was covered in blacks and blues.

"Zee?"

Blinking, I looked up at Hunter.

"I said, how are you feeling? Are you in pain?"

"Yes."

Carter sucked in a deep breath. "Zeraora, you need to tell us when you're in pain. We can give you medicine to help. If you don't, you're just going to suffer."

As he spoke, Hunter held out his hands. One held the half-drunk bottle of Coke, and the other had two white tablets. "It's human medicine, so it won't help as much as anything a witch could give us, but it should help some."

"What about Knox?"

"There's plenty for him when he wakes up too."

I took the tablets and swallowed them, wincing as they scratched against my throat on the way down. Somehow, they were harder to swallow than the bread had been, even though I took a drink right after.

"What do we do now?" I asked.

Hunter looked at Carter, who was sitting on the edge of the bed, and turned to face me. "It's nearly dawn. We're going to stay here for today because of Javion, but tonight, once the sun sets, we're going to head somewhere safe. As far away from here as possible."

"Your safehouse in Tennessee."

The comment had come from Javion, and I turned to watch him sit up. Before I could ask him what that meant, Carter was responding.

"Wyoming. I don't like being so close to the Lycans. We'll get a van—"

"Tennessee. We need to go to Tennessee."

Carter's lips thinned as he stared at Javion. "Why?"

"I…" he frowned before groaning and rubbing his face. "I don't know. I just know it needs to be there." He glanced down at Knox, his expression turning grim. "I think we need to get Knox settled somewhere closer."

Carter stared at Javion until the vampire looked back at him. "You're hiding something."

"I'm not hiding it intentionally. There's a reason, I just can't remember it yet."

"What's a safehouse?" I asked.

Instantly, Carter's expression softened. "Pretty much what it sounds like. It's a place I have that no one else knows exists. It has supplies, and it's in the middle of nowhere."

"How are we going to get there?"

"I'll go out and get us a vehicle later. Don't worry about anything, Zee." Hunter moved in front of me, pointing at my wrists. "Can I change the bandages?"

I nodded. As Hunter set to unwinding the bandages, Carter moved over to the table in the corner and leaned against it. "What happened?"

"Turns out she was right, and they used her as a fucking power source," Javion replied.

"Before that. How did they manage to take you?"

There was something about Carter's tone that felt like he was accusing Javion of doing something wrong, and it made me wince.

"It wasn't his fault. It was mine."

At the same time, Javion arched an eyebrow. "You think it's my fault?"

"No one is blaming anyone," Hunter said, quickly. "DB found a group of shifters who were working with the Lycans. They were distracting him while the Lycans made a move on Castle Viegls."

"But it was my fault." I hung my head. "They came, and I couldn't stop them."

"It was raining." Javion added. "And we were outnumbered."

"No." I whipped my head around and glared at him. "I should have been able to stop them."

"Why? Because you can power a city? Because you can EMP a county? Fuck all that when you've got no clue what you're doing with it. Throw in a bit of trauma and you're unstable. You're either firing at two hundred percent or not at all. You've got no idea how to control any of it."

"Javion." Carter snapped. "Do not talk to Zera like that."

"You think I'm doing it to be a dick? You three have spent the last few months pussyfooting around her or giving her mixed signals instead of being straight to the point."

I didn't think Javion was being mean, but for some reason, Carter stood up and marched over to the vampire before grabbing him by the throat. "The whole reason you all ended up captured by the Lycans is because they traced the searches back to you."

"Carter, let him go," I cried.

Javion didn't fight Carter, instead, stared up at him. "If you want to kill me, why did you save me?"

"Because Zeraora fought to save you."

"She did?" Even though Carter's hand was still around his throat, Javion looked at me, then his eyes went wide.

"She did." With a grunt, Carter let go and stepped back. "I'm going to find a vehicle." Without another word, he marched out of the door, slamming it behind him.

"Zee?" Hunter tapped my knee.

I'd pulled my hands free when Carter went after Javion, so I held them out so that Hunter could continue bandaging them up. I kept my attention on Javion, partly because I didn't want to look at the ugly, painful wounds, but also, because Javion hadn't taken his eyes off me, either.

Twenty-Seven

Zera

We arrived at Carter's safe house in the middle of the night. Carter had found what Hunter called a van. He took the soft half of the bed from the motel and laid it in the back, and then made Hunter get on it with Knox and Javion while I sat in the front with him. Only, I'd spent most of the ride sleeping.

My wrists were throbbing, but sleep gave me a much-needed break. They were still hurting when we arrived at the house in the middle of nowhere.

Inside, it smelled a little musty, but it was a lot more comfortable than the motel. Knox was still unconscious and had been taken upstairs by Carter, with Javion right behind them both. Hunter sat down in the kitchen, leaning his head against the table.

"Are you okay?" I asked him.

Without lifting his head, he nodded. "I gave Javion some more of my blood, so I'm feeling a little light-headed from it."

"How is Knox?"

Hunter paused before raising his head. "DB should have some better medical supplies here—enchanted things with a higher potency." He frowned. "We should get some for your wrists. It will help."

"What about Knox?"

"There will be plenty for the both of you."

"I have it. Stay where you are." Carter walked into the room carrying a box. He set it on the table and then looked at Hunter. "Can you do this? I'll get some food cooking. You look like you need it."

"I think we all need it," Hunter muttered.

While Carter turned his attention to the kitchen, moving around and opening all the cupboards to look inside, Hunter focused on my wrists. I couldn't help but look at them, turning my nose up. Most of the area was black, going down below the top of my skin, but there were also patches of wet blood.

"Monsters." Hunter growled. Despite the anger in his voice, he applied the cream carefully. The initial contact had me wincing, but almost instantly, the magic started to work.

"What do we do next?" I asked.

Carter, who had been cutting something on the other side of the kitchen, turned. "Tonight, nothing. We're going to eat and then we're all going to get some sleep. We all need it. We'll discuss everything tomorrow. Knox should be awake by then."

"Are you going to make Javion leave again?"

Hunter looked at me and then at Carter.

The older gargoyle let out a long sigh. "We will discuss everything tomorrow."

"You can't make him leave again," I told him.

"Zeraora—"

"No, he must stay." I wasn't sure why I felt so strongly about that. It wasn't just that he helped me when the Lycans had us, but something else. Like, if he wasn't with us, something really bad was going to happen.

Carter rubbed at his forehead and sighed.

"Zeraora."

"Carter, he needs to stay."

"Fine." He shook his head. "Fine."

I still couldn't explain why I felt relief at that, but being satisfied that Javion would be safe, I sat back into the chair and actually relaxed. I glanced at Hunter and found him staring at my wrist, frowning.

"They're uglier than before." I sighed.

"Huh?" He looked up and then firmly shook his head. "No, I was just... Zee, I don't care what they look like. I just... you haven't shocked me."

"Why would I want to do that?" I asked in alarm.

"You wouldn't, but there hasn't been a single spark. There hasn't been since we took them off you and I've just realized it."

"There was nothing on the drive either," Carter added.

Holding up my free hand, I tried to summon the electricity to my fingers; something that had been easy in the past. Now, there was nothing.

"Don't worry about it," Carter said, suddenly. "We're all tired, hungry, and your body is injured. You just need some rest, and I'm sure it will be back in the morning."

It wasn't.

Three days later, my powers were still missing. As I sat beside Hunter on the couch, watching television, waiting for Knox to wake up, I tried again to find a spark.

"Just wait," Hunter muttered, reached over and took my hand in his. "You've been through a lot, and your body has a lot to heal from."

"I slept and ate."

"And you still look exhausted. Think about how you felt when you first came to us."

I frowned at him. "But when I first came to you, I was still able to use my powers."

On the other side of the room, the door opened, and Carter walked in. He left while I was sleeping to get 'fresh' supplies—whatever that meant.

"How far did you have to go?" Hunter asked him.

"Next state." Carter looked thoroughly exhausted. He set the bag down on the side and then rubbed at his face. "Have you been to check on Knox recently?"

Hunter shook his head. "Before lunch. His breathing had strengthened, and some of the worst wounds were starting to look better."

Carter reached into one of the bags and pulled out a bag of blood. "I'll go." He disappeared upstairs with a few other items in his hands.

"When will Knox wake up?"

Sliding his arm out from under me, Hunter stood and moved over to the window, staring. "Soon, I hope."

"Why is it taking so long?"

"It's not," Hunter said then let out a sigh. He bowed his head. "He has a lot of injuries—injuries that no human would survive. Gargoyles, like most supes, heal fast. It's just he was... really hurt."

Hands in my lap, I curled my fingers into fists. No matter what any of them told me, the fact he—and Javion—were hurt was because of me. The Lycans came for me, and they tried to protect me. The Lycans wanted me to give them more power, so they hurt Javion and Knox to make sure I'd provide it for them.

I was going to destroy all the Lycans, and if my powers didn't come back, I'd do it with my bare hands. The wolves needed to pay for what they'd done, and I needed to make sure they *never* came for us again.

"Stop thinking that, Zee." Hunter's voice was weary. "I can practically read your thoughts over here. It's not your fault, and we will get our revenge *together*." He turned to look at me. "And if you try to go on some solo suicide mission, so help me, we're relocating to New Zealand."

I had no idea where New Zealand was, but I wasn't going to let Hunter take me anywhere until I made the Lycans pay.

"Hunter? Zera?" Carter called from upstairs. "If you're not too busy, someone wants to see you."

Hunter and I stared at each other before we both worked out at the same time that Carter meant Knox. I scrambled off the couch, helped by Hunter, and together, we hurried up the stairs. Hunter stayed right behind me.

Carter had given Knox and Javion a room at the end of the hall. Hunter had mentioned it was north facing, and the trees growing outside blocked out most of the sunlight, so even if the thick curtains failed, it wouldn't be too bad for Javion—at least for him to stay out of direct sunlight.

Since the first night here, Carter and Hunter had been swapping with each other, letting Javion feed. Fresh blood was apparently the best for him. Even though I'd offered to let Javion have some of mine, he refused.

Carter got angry at me for even offering. He said I was too injured to be giving Javion my blood.

When we walked in their room, the vampire was sitting up in bed, looking better than we'd seen him all week. And he was smiling. Which I thought was creepy. But then I was distracted by Knox, who was awake and propped up on pillows beside him.

"Zera." Knox let out a breath.

"I told you Sparkler was okay."

I flung myself at Knox, wrapping my arms around him tightly.

He froze momentarily before hugging me back.

"You're awake."

"I'm awake," Knox murmured in my ear.

"Zee, baby, take it easy. Knox is awake, but he's still injured. You don't want to hurt him"

Horrified, I pulled back. "Did I hurt you?"

"I'm fine." Knox assured me. "Thanks to you."

Staring at him, I slowly shook my head.

"You're hurt because of me."

"I thought we covered that bullshit back in that gross motel," Javion said before letting out an impatient snort. "Those at fault are the Lycans. They chose to take you. They chose to hurt us. You didn't."

"Jay!" Knox turned and looked at Javion in disbelief.

From the foot of the bed, Carter straightened his

back. "I swear to the gods, I'm going to throw your ass out into the sunlight."

"No, you are not." I turned and gave Carter a murderous look. "I'm not letting any of my mates get hurt again."

The anger slipped from Carter's face, morphing into confusion. "Mate?"

"Clearly she didn't mean that," Hunter said. "She doesn't even like Javion."

"I don't not like Javion."

Hunter let out a long sigh and moved in front of me before lowering himself to his knees so that he was eyelevel with me. "I understand that you want Javion to stay, but he can't be your mate."

"Why can't he?" I asked. "I claimed you and Hunter and Knox."

"We wanted to be your mate too," Hunter replied.

Frowning, I looked over at Javion. His silver eyes were locked onto me. "Do you want to be my mate?"

"Do you want me to be your mate?" He arched an eyebrow, curious.

"Okay, enough. I get your point. Javion doesn't have to leave," Carter said. He shook his head.

Javion's attention switched to Carter. "Do you want me to leave?"

Carter stared back at him.

"DB, do you want me to leave?"

Twenty-Eight

Zera

"I don't know. Honestly, I'm so damn angry at you." He sighed. Arms folded, Carter looked away, jutting out his chin. "But you're... family. And even if I do want to murder you, we need to stick together because I actually can't stand the thought... I thought you were gone... Gods be damned, Javion, I'm so pissed at you."

Javion closed his eyes. He sat there, unmoving for a while before opening his eyes to look at Carter.

"Look, I admit that I didn't like Zera at first, and I should've been more careful when talking to that vampire, but I swear, I never wanted to bring the Lycans to Castle Viegls. I had no idea they knew what she was. I didn't think that trying to find information would trigger anything from the Lycans. Fuck, I'm pissed at myself for underestimating their abilities to break through my defenses. I was masking my servers, and they still managed to find us. I'm sorry."

Carter continued to stare, and then he nodded once.

"But they came because of me," I said, frowning at Javion.

Hunter, who hadn't moved from in front of me, groaned, but it was Javion who spoke.

"See, this is why we need to be fucking blunt. Look, Sparkler, the Lycans came because they are Lycans. They don't let supes go, and they hunt them down if they do. They were going to find you, regardless, because that's what they do."

"But if I led them to you…"

Javion rolled his eyes. "We'll ignore the fact that DB found you and brought you home with him because you're doing that anyway, but okay, sure. It's your fault."

"Javion, I swear to the gods—"

"No, let's play this out," Javion said, though his gaze was still locked onto me. "You got taken when you were a kid. So clearly, that's your fault. And then you get tortured by them—fucking *tortured*—by them for what? Two decades? Also, your fault because you clearly wanted that pleasure. Then you had the audacity to try to escape that nightmare. I mean, that's clearly on you."

"Jay, you're going too far," Knox said in a low tone. Javion ignored him.

"And then, hundreds of miles away from the mutts, you made them come chasing after you, capture you and throw you back into your nightmare. I mean, that's a whole ass level of skill there, but still, your fault for wanting it."

"I didn't want it." I wasn't sure how the words came out of my mouth. My heart felt like it was pounding in my throat. "Any of it."

"You must have." Javion gave a casual shrug. "You must have asked for it. Otherwise, why would they come after you? Which also means you clearly wanted me and Knox to get captured and tortured too. I bet you wanted DB and Hunter with us as well."

If my powers had been working properly, they'd be exploding. But they weren't, and the only thing exploding was my anger that Javion.

"I didn't ask for any of it," I yelled at him. "And I certainly wouldn't want any of you to be hurt."

With lightning quick speed that surprised me, Javion's face was instantly in front of mine. He was on his hands and knees over Knox's legs, but he was close enough that even without my glasses, I could see his eyes clearly.

"So, if you didn't want it, and you didn't ask for it, how can any of it be your fault? Because either it's all your fault or none of it is."

I stared into his silver eyes, breathing heavily.

Could what he was saying be right? I would never, ever have wished to go through what I had, and having lived it for most of my life, I would rather die than ever let any of my mates have to experience it, either.

"Jay, that's enough." With a groan of pain, Knox leaned forward and tapped Javion's shoulder, making the vampire sit back.

"Think about it, Little Sparkler. Because when you do, when you *really* think it through, you'll see the only ones to blame are those mother-fucking Lycans."

"Okay, on that note, I think it's time for a hot chocolate." Hunter leaned up and held his hand out to me. "Or maybe DB found some cinnamon, and we can have cinnamon milk."

In a daze, I took Hunter's hand and followed him downstairs into the kitchen. "It's really not my fault?"

"No, it's really not."

Javion's words stuck in my mind for several weeks before I started to believe him. Sometimes, it still didn't make any sense—the Lycans would never have come to Castle Viegls if they weren't following me.

But as everyone was quick to remind me, the Lycans made their own choice to find me. And now they were going to know what it was like for me to look for them.

Knox was taking too long to heal. Hunter kept telling me he'd been really hurt, and it was normal that it would take him a few weeks to recover, but I didn't like seeing him this way. The furthest he'd gone from his bed was to the bathroom, and that had only been last night.

After drinking more bags of blood, Javion was moving freely around the house once the sun set.

"Are you going to glare at me all night?" he asked me.

"You look normal."

Silver eyes narrowed. "Somehow you make that sound like an insult."

Carter tapped his fingers on the page of an open book in front of me. "Concentrate."

I returned my attention to the words in front of me. Carter decided that while we waited for Knox to feel better, I needed to continue learning how to read.

Glancing at the page, I sighed and then focused my gaze on Carter.

Carter shook his head. "You can make all the faces you want, but I'm not teaching you to fight until we're back home, and we're not going home until Knox will be comfortable in the truck."

My powers still hadn't returned, and I had been trying to convince Carter and Hunter to teach me to fight the Lycans with a different weapon. They were both being annoying and refusing. *Nothing* I did convinced them otherwise. Carter even bought books back with him when he drove for supplies.

Another sigh escaped me as I rubbed at my eyes.

Before I could focus on the words, Carter reached over and touched the back of my hand. "We'll finish there tonight. It's late. Go to bed."

Although my eyes itched, I wasn't tired. But I also didn't want to stay there and continue to read a story about some child who was at school. Unless that was a Lycan school—which it wasn't—I didn't care.

Without giving Carter a chance to change his mind, I stood, leaned over to kiss him, and then hurried upstairs.

Although I had my own room, I wasn't using it. After being separated from everyone, I was sleeping in a different bed every night. Even with Knox and Javion, although Javion didn't really sleep and spent most of his time sitting in a chair in the corner of the room.

Tonight, I pushed open the door to Hunter's room. He was lying on his bed with his head hanging off the end.

"What are you doing?"

Without moving, Hunter looked up at me. "Nothing." With a groan, he rolled onto his stomach and propped his head up with his hands. "Want to join me?"

I narrowed my eyes. "What do I need to do?

Hunter patted the bed next to him, so I walked over, climbed up, and lay down on my back beside him.

"Nothing," Hunter finally said. "We're just lying here." He rolled back onto his back, this time, keeping his head on the bed, before scooting closer to me.

Lying there, I stared at the ceiling and then turned

my head to look at Hunter. "This is boring."

Hunter chuckled.

"Bringing you closer," he announced before sliding his arm under me and pulling me to him. As I curled into his side, I felt him kiss my head. "That's only because we've never really done nothing together. I was lying here, imagining you, and now you're here. Just try doing nothing with me for a while."

I moved my head to rest on Hunter's chest. "I don't think I like doing nothing."

A hand gently started to play with my hair. "Why?"

"Because I think about how everyone got hurt and how the Lycans are still there, and how I need to be able to stop the—"

"Not tonight." Hunter continued stroking my hair. "You're still healing."

My gaze drifted to my wrists. Somehow, in the time we'd been here, Hunter had been able to get me new wrist guards, as well as clothes that I liked. When we first arrived, Carter had given me some of their clothes, but once Knox woke up, both he and Hunter decided I needed my own clothes again.

I would have worn whatever Carter had given me since it made him happy, but I felt more comfortable in these clothes. The wounds on my wrists weren't healing as quickly this time. I really liked the wrist guards there to cover the bandages.

"You just need time," Hunter added. He reached for my hand, linking fingers with mine. "I know it's frustrating. Everyone feels the same when they recover from something."

"Javion healed quickly."

"Javion's a vampire. He's completely different than you."

I frowned. "Maybe I should become a vampire."

Hunter chuckled again before kissing the top of my head. "You don't want to be a vampire. And I don't want you to be one either. I like a warm body to cuddle."

"Knox likes both."

"Knox can like whoever and whatever he wants. The same goes for you. But I like warmth." He tightened his grip around me.

I liked the warmth. But I'd not tried cold. How cold was Javion? Cold couldn't be too bad because Knox liked it. And Javion wasn't really that cold to touch. He was warmer than the cans of Coke Hunter put in the refrigerator for me.

"What are you thinking about now?" Hunter asked.

"How cold is Javion's cock?"

Hunter spluttered, rolled out from under me and then onto his side. He stared at me, arching an eyebrow. "Seriously? You're thinking about Javion's... cock?"

I nodded. "It doesn't look cold. I know he is but—"

"Nope." Hunter gently placed his hand over my mouth. "I can't talk to you about Javion's cock. I just can't."

"What about Knox's?" I mumbled through Hunter's hand.

Hunter's eyes narrowed as he slowly licked his lower lip. "I think I'd rather your mouth talk about mine."

"What about it?"

Something flashed on Hunter's face, and suddenly, it was like his eyes were somehow heating me up.

"About how good it feels buried deep inside you."

When I was caught by the Lycans, there were times I thought I'd never escape their prison again.

I'd never get to eat food again... and I'd never be able to see my mates again. Or, see them, but not touch them.

Knox might not be fully healed yet, but he was here. He was alive.

And while there might have been something wrong with me, the way Hunter was looking at me now had heat rushing through my body, straight to that sensitive area between my legs.

My eyes narrowed. "Are you going to let that happen, or are you going to tell me that's not what I want?"

Twenty-Nine

Hunter

lthough we hadn't discussed it, DB would probably have something to say about just how hands-on we could be with Zera.

Maybe not because she didn't know what she wanted like she was implying—although that may have been the case previously. More likely, it's because she had been through something bad enough that Carter removed yet another shower from one of the bathrooms and had us play music loud enough to block out the sound when it rained.

But fuck DB.

Not literally—Zera could do that.

I closed my eyes and sucked in a deep breath. In less than five minutes, I'd reluctantly had various images of Zera riding a cock, and not one of them had been mine.

I didn't want just images of Zera riding my cock, I wanted to be buried deep inside of her for real. If she thought she was ready for that, I was more than happy to oblige.

"You want to stop at any point, you tell me, and we stop. Okay?" I told her, ignoring the twitch in my dick.

So help me, when Zera looked at me with those wide, blue eyes...

"Why would I want to stop?"

In one fluid movement, I pulled her body beneath mine, using my forearms to prop me up so I wasn't completely crushing her. "I'm going to kiss your lips until they're too sore to talk. And then I'm going to work on the rest of your body."

Despite my threat—or was it a promise?—my kiss was firm, but gentle.

Zera responded with a low moan. Her hands slipped around my neck; her fingers played with my hair. Gods, I'd missed her touch. Eyes closed, I enjoyed the kiss and the softness of her lips. As I teased it with my tongue, her hands moved higher, then she massaged my head with her fingers.

Before I could even process what she was doing, she started stroking my horns. I swear, my eyes rolled into the back of my head. As I felt my horns grow, I pushed myself up, bracing my weight on my legs as I hovered over her.

"Zee, you can't do that," I told her, practically breathless.

"You're hard," she said.

Of course, I was hard. I was like a pubescent teen around her most of the time but playing with my horns was like flicking a switch.

She ran her fingers over my arms, and it took me a moment to register that she was talking about my skin and not the raging erection that was desperately trying to break free of my pants, like my cock had a mind of its own.

I breathed in deeply. "No touching the horns."

Zera's blue eyes seemed to take on a mysterious glint as her gaze drifted from my arm to my own eyes. "What if I want to touch somewhere else?"

This woman was going to kill me, and my death

was going to be glorious. "You sound like you know what you want."

She pushed herself up, so I leaned back to allow her to sit up.

"I want you." Zera reached for the hem of my T-shirt, pushing it up.

I helped her, taking it off and quickly tossing it aside.

With a wicked smile on her face, she leaned into me, her hands trailing over my chest as she pressed her lips just over my heart. I didn't move, curious what she was going to do next.

"Not the horns," I whispered.

Zera didn't respond. Instead, she slid out from beneath me so she could get on her knees. As her mouth sought mine, kissing me more fiercely than I'd been kissing her, she explored my chest with her fingertips. She crept her hands lower until reaching my waistband. My pants were quickly unbuttoned.

She pulled away, her lips red and plump from kissing me, then she tilted her head. "I need these off."

Who was I to deny a request like that?

Obliging, the pants joined the shirt somewhere on the floor. Only, the moment I looked back at Zera, the strongest urge to shed her of her clothes hit me. Much as I wanted to let her set the speed, her body was a shrine I was ready to worship.

As I stared at her, Zera's cheeks turned pink. "Why are you looking at me like that?"

"You are the most beautiful thing I've ever seen."

Her gaze dropped to her wrists.

My heart seemed to plummet at the same speed. While I wasn't surprised, knowing she thought any other way about herself tore a hole in my soul. I took her hands in mine.

"Zee, you are the most beautiful thing I've ever seen."

Slowly, I raised her hands and turned her arms over to bring her wrists upright, then I placed a gentle kiss on each, keeping a tight hold as she tried to pull her hands free.

"I'm not taking the wrist guards off."

The idea that she thought I would ever think anything less of her because of a few scars tore another hole in my soul. I sucked in a deep breath and then wiggled an eyebrow.

"What about the rest of your clothes?"

She nodded, pulling her hands out of mine so she could unbutton her pants. "They can come off."

I helped her make short work of them, then gently

lowered her back onto the bed, pressing my weight into her again. My cock throbbed between us, and I desperately wanted to bury it deep into her, but it had been a while since we'd been together, and I needed to make sure she was going to be okay first.

My mouth claimed hers, and I pushed my tongue in, kissing her until she was gasping for breath beneath me. Kissing her was intended to make up for all the kisses I'd not been able to give her while she was chained up again.

I pulled away, moving to her neck. There was a spot just below her ear that had her moaning in mine. My cock throbbed again. Sitting back, just long enough to figure out how to unfasten her top, I returned my lips to her neck before trailing kisses down to her breasts.

Latching my mouth over one of her nipples, I caught the tip between my lips and gently sucked.

Zera arched her back, then her hands were wrapping around my horns.

The sensation was like she'd wrapped her hand around my cock and brought me to the edge of an orgasm. Only it also awakened the stone demon in me.

Mine.

I bit down on her nipple, harder than I ever wanted to.

Zera let out a cry. "Hunter."

The control I'd been keeping weakened. The voice in my head quieted. My body moved how it wanted to. As I sucked hard on her nipples, massaging her breasts, my tail was between her legs, stroking her clit.

As she moaned and writhed beneath me, my tail continued to rub, harder and faster.

Zera came with a loud cry.

I stopped only long enough to pick her up and move her down the bed so I could replace my tail with my tongue.

Her taste was intoxicating, and I wanted more.

I pinned her thighs down, my tongue alternating between licking and sucking. Looking up, I found her panting, red lips parted, her cheeks, flushed. "Beautiful," I muttered into her.

Wanting to give her more, I brought my tail to her entrance, not letting up with my mouth. As she whimpered my name, I pushed it inside. My tongue was hard and firm, my tail, moving slow and gentle.

"Hunter... I... I can't..."

Zera reached down, her hands in my hair.

Letting go of her thighs, I went to stop her, knowing my actions were teetering on the edge of control, but as her hands curled around my horns again, that resolve disappeared.

I had just one goal: I was going to make my mate feel good as she came around my tail and then my cock.

As she rubbed harder, my tail action picked up, moving faster and deeper. With my face still buried deep inside her, working her clit, I gripped my cock, pumping my hand up and down.

Her grip around my horns tightened.

In response, I sucked hard at her clit. My instinct was taking over, and I only just stopped myself from ramming my tail into her.

There was a pleasurable white haze settling over me, and I was probably seconds from losing all control. If that happened and she said stop, I couldn't.

Before that happened, I pulled back, removing my face from her pussy and making her to let go of my horns.

Her mouth parted into an 'oh' of disappointment, but it quickly changed as I swapped my tail for my cock.

I wanted her to come around both, but I was about to come myself, and I was only going to do that buried deep inside of her.

She let out a loud moan as I pushed my cock into her welcoming body.

Leaning forward, I took her hands in mine, pinning

them down beside her head. Locking my gaze with hers, I started thrusting into her: if I wasn't going to last long, I wasn't going to let her either.

She came, crying loudly. As she squeezed my cock with her orgasms, at the last minute, I remembered I'd not put on a condom.

"Fuck." I roared, pulling out as my cum spilled onto her stomach.

Rolling to the side, I lay on my back, catching my breath. Annoyed was an understatement. That had been incredible, but it could have been better, for both of us.

I turned and pressed a kiss to Zera's temple. "Stay there," I told her. She didn't look like she was in any hurry to move, but I disappeared to the bathroom, grabbing a damp cloth to clean her up.

It was the least that I could do.

Zera curled into my side, her eyelashes tickling my chest. "Why do you tell me I can't play with your horns? It didn't seem that bad. You looked like you were enjoying it."

"I was." I admitted.

"But if you like it, why not let me touch them?"

Bringing my hand up, I ran my fingers through her hair, frowning at the ceiling before answering. "Gargoyles are stone demons. That demon part of us is what gives us our strength and our tough skin. But it's fueled by basic instinct, and there's nothing more basic than desire. I wasn't sure I could stop myself. I had to fight with myself, making sure not to hurt you."

"You're big. Not as big as Carter, but still big, and it hurts a little. And then it doesn't. Then it feels really good." Zera's voice was low and husky, like she was ready to fall asleep. "Really, really good. I don't mind if you hurt me."

I was going to ignore that comment about DB while my ego focused on everything else. And then I sighed. "Not in that way, Zee. I mean, a little, but more that when instinct takes over, I might not be able to stop."

Zera twisted, propping herself up to frown at me. "Why would I want you to stop?"

After brushing her hair over her shoulder, I cupped her cheek. "Maybe today you didn't want me to stop, but one day, you might. And you have every right to ask that as well as expect me to stop. I would. But when that instinct takes over, it's unbelievably hard to stop. I don't want there to be a time where I can't, where you get hurt. Sometimes, emotional pain can hurt a lot more than physical."

The frown didn't disappear from Zera's face. "I don't understand."

"Honestly, I hope you never do."

"That doesn't make any sense either," she muttered as she settled back down beside me. "What's the point in having those horns if you can't have fun with them?"

Gargoyles usually paired with gargoyles. I hadn't known anyone else who'd ever mated with a different supe. Sure, there were hook-ups. I had a few myself, but I'd never allowed another to touch my horns unless they were gargoyle too. Female gargoyles had horns. If they were being touched, we were both touching, and it didn't matter about holding back.

Zera didn't have that luxury, nor did she have a body built to withstand our strength.

More importantly, she'd been through enough in her life already. I was not going to be the one to add to that. She didn't deserve it, and I wasn't sure I'd survive if she looked at me in any other way than she did now.

I lay there, stroking Zera's hair until she fell asleep.

One thing that I noticed tonight was that there had been no electrical discharge at any point. Even now, there was still nothing over her skin. I wasn't going to let Zera know how much that worried me, but I was damn sure hoping that Knox was feeling well enough to travel back to Castle Viegls soon.

We needed to work out what those Lycans had done to Zera, and what we needed to do to reverse it.

Thirty

Zera

"Are you going to watch me eat all of this?" Knox pointed at the bacon and eggs on his plate.

Carter cooked it, and I brought it up to him, but because Javion was sitting beside Knox, I decided to stay too.

"She's going to finish off what you don't eat." Javion pointed at me. "Look at her eyeing that bacon."

"I've already had my breakfast," I told Javion.

The vampire arched an eyebrow. "Since when has that stopped you? You're like a black Labrador, waiting for scraps."

"I don't know what one of those is."

"A dog."

My lips settled into a thin line as I stared at Javion. "I am nothing like a dog."

"How about you two stay here, and I'll go eat downstairs?" Knox asked.

"No," I said. "Carter says you need to stay in bed and rest."

As Knox let out an irritated sigh, pushing his plate to the side so he could get out of bed, Javion's silver eyes flashed at me. "Smart move, Sparkler. Knoxlyn, get your sexy injured ass back into this bed."

Shaking his head, Knox ignored him and continued to the door.

I got off the bed and ran after him, ducking around to block him from leaving. "You need to stay in bed and rest."

"I need a piss."

"Oh." I stepped to the side and let Knox walk out of the room.

"You fell for that?" Javion arched an eyebrow.

"I didn't fall. I moved to the side."

Rolling his eyes, Javion pointed out of the door. "He's going downstairs."

Wondering why Javion didn't care enough to stop him, I ran after Knox, catching up to him as he reached the bottom of the stairs. "You need to be in bed."

"Zera, I am not staying in that bed any longer. I need to stretch my legs and see sunlight and have fresh air." He pointed out the window.

Outside, the sun was shining brightly, filtering down between the trees. *That* would be why Javion hadn't followed. "But Carter *and* Hunter said—"

Knox turned around and then placed his hands on my shoulders. "I know what they said, but I feel well enough to walk downstairs, I promise."

"About time," Hunter said, appearing in the doorway to the kitchen. He looked his brother up and down.

"Is he really ready to be walking around?" I asked, peering around Knox. "He's still covered in bruises and bandages."

Knox stepped to the side and blocked my view. "If I still felt like shit, I'd be in bed. I don't. I need to walk around."

"You can relax, Zee." Hunter joined Knox's side. "It took a little longer than I expected, but I think he's good to be up and about. Bruises are usually the last thing to heal because the body heals the most important things first: the injuries under the bruises."

"I suppose we should all talk then." Carter was in the doorway to the living room. "Zera, please could you draw the curtains so we can have Javion join us? It seems a little unfair to go back upstairs when Knox has just left."

Before agreeing, I peered back at Knox. "Are you sure you feel okay?"

"I know I look even worse than I did before, but I do feel better, I promise."

"You're still gorgeous." I hated seeing the claw marks on his body because they were a reminder that the Lycans hurt him, and I hadn't been able to stop that soon enough. But they didn't make him look worse. He was my Knox.

Knox leaned forward and kissed my temple. "Go close the curtains. Let's get that grumpy vampire downstairs."

I wrinkled my nose. "Do we have to?"

"I can hear you," Javion called from upstairs.

As Knox let out an amused sigh, I moved past him, heading into the living room to pull the curtains closed, as requested. Hunter explained that when Carter had bought this place, he made sure there were things called black-out curtains hanging over the windows because the house didn't have a basement.

Before I could close the last one, Hunter had switched on all the lights. As I turned around, Knox was easing himself into one of the chairs. I hurried over to sit beside him before Javion got there.

The vampire appeared just as I curled up into Knox and poked my tongue out at him. Javion rolled his eyes and moved to the side of the room before leaning against the wall.

"Now that everyone is healed enough, I think we need to discuss what happens next," Carter said.

With a look of surprise, Javion looked at Carter. "Do you want me in this conversation?"

Despite their early talk, things between Javion and Carter had been strained. When they were in a room together, which was on very rare occasions, there was a strange atmosphere. I knew I couldn't touch air, but it felt like I could push against it.

The same was happening now.

"I am still mad at you, but you're a part of the family," Carter told him, gruffly. "And we should *all* agree on what we do next."

Javion stared at him, and then nodded. Suddenly,

the strange feeling in the room lifted.

"What do you want to do?" Hunter asked.

"Find the Lycans and destroy them." All four men looked at me. I stared back at them. "Knox is better. Javion is better. Why wouldn't we go after them?"

"We haven't forgotten about the Lycans, but we need to be ready before we do that," Carter told me. "Yes, Knox is better, but he's not going to be able to protect himself, never mind you. And you still don't have your power back, and we have no idea where the Lycans are. There are a few steps we need to take before we can begin to hunt them down again."

Knox patted my thigh. "I want to kill them too, but I need a bit more time."

Looking up at him and seeing the healing claw marks on his face made me want to find the Lycans right now. "I can protect you."

There was a snort from the other side of the room. "You couldn't protect him in a pillow fight."

Grabbing the cushion from beside me, I threw it at Javion's head. Annoyingly, he batted it away.

"If you two are going to have a pillow fight, could you at least do it with no clothes on?" Knox grinned.

That seemed like a strange request, but I reached for the zipper to my corset. Before I could get it halfway open, Hunter was beside me, placing his hand gently over mine. "He didn't mean that literally."

"That's what you think," Knox muttered under his breath.

"Look, we need to discuss what we do next, preferably without arguing. Either we stay here, and we turn this into our home, or we return to Castle Viegls." Carter picked up the cushion from the floor and tossed it onto a spare chair. "What do you all want to do?"

"I want to go home," Hunter said.

"Same." Knox agreed. He looked over at Javion. "All of us."

"If I have any say in this," Javion said. "I would prefer a basement over this place."

Carter's lips thinned as he looked at Javion. "You have a say." He turned to me. "As do you—but this is about where we go next, which is either stay here and recover, or go back to Castle Viegls and recover. Only once everyone is healed, we'll start looking for the Lycans again."

"Where we are doesn't bother me. I just want to be with you all," I told him.

"Then I guess we're going back home," Knox said with a nod.

Carter ran his hand over his chin before letting out

a long breath. "Not straight back home. The wards around Castle Viegls were breached. That should never have happened. We'll need to find out how."

"How do we do that?" I asked.

"The Daughters of the Twilight Goddess were the ones who created the wards." Knox frowned. "Either they fucked up their magic, or they sold us out to someone—probably that mongoose shifter, seeing as though they don't like the Lycans either."

"You think they'd just tell us?" Javion asked.

"Castle Viegls was infiltrated somehow. If we go back, we need to go back somewhere safe. I don't want us to go after the Lycans, nor do I want to start a war with the witches," Carter said. "There's a coven in Charlotte. I'll call them and get them to put up new wards. Once we get home, we can investigate why the original wards failed."

"Put in the call, but we need to go to Atlanta." Hunter pulled his phone out of his pocket, and I expected him to hand it to Carter so he could do that, but he held onto it.

"Liberty?" Knox asked, surprised. "You think she can be trusted? She's a Daughter of the Twilight Goddess."

"Liberty?" Javion said her name like he'd not heard

of her before.

"She helped us out once. Hunter got friendly with her. Shitty witch with pink and blue hair." Knox explained, looking at Javion with concern. "Jay, you know her: she runs the hair salon we brought Zera to before she took the power out in Atlanta."

Slowly, Javion turned to look at me, frowning slightly, before looking back to Knox. "Yeah, I just…" he shrugged. "Continue."

"Yes and no," Hunter said before frowning. "I mean, I trust her. But as for her being a part of that coven, it's only that the coven doesn't like her. She's like the runt of the litter. She's not a great witch." He shook his head as Knox gave him a look of disbelief. "Alright, she's a terrible witch. But if they really thought highly of her, she wouldn't be in the city by herself trying to survive as a hairdresser doing cheap tricks on the side."

"We should go speak to her," Javion said, slowly.

"Why?" Carter asked.

Javion shrugged. "Like Hunter said, she's part of the coven. If anyone was going to tell us whether someone in that coven did something—sell us out, fuck up the wards—it's going to be her. And at least it's not a full-on war with the witches, right? Besides, it's only a couple of hours drive. We can go there tonight, see her, and then head back home after."

I wasn't sure why, but Javion was staring at me while he said that.

Carter nodded, turning to Hunter. "Call Liberty. Have her meet somewhere neutral. I'll call the Sisters of the Silver Moon."

As Carter and Hunter walked out of the room to make their calls, Knox stood and moved over to Javion and stood in front of him. "What are you doing, Jay?"

"What makes you think I'm doing anything?"

Knox snorted. "I've known you too long."

Reaching up, Javion threaded his fingers through Knox's hair. "You're overthinking. I just want us to be able to go home. I miss my bed."

"I thought vampires didn't need to sleep," I asked.

Javion glanced over Knox's shoulder. "Who said anything about sleeping?"

"You mean sex?"

With a smirk, Javion ran his tongue over his fang. "I do indeed. Maybe you can join us."

Before I could respond, Knox let out a long sigh. "Will you quit fucking around with her?"

"What if I want to fuck around with her?"

"I give up," Knox muttered before walking off.

Javion's silver eyes lingered on me, and for some

reason, the longer he stared, I was pretty sure that was one of those statements that had a different meaning.

Thirty-One

Javion

I t had taken about a day after arriving at the safe house before my memories came back—the strange conversation I'd had with Zera. Or rather, the Zera from the future.

The way that opaque elemental just looked at me, compared to the looks the Zera in front of me now was giving me told me she was completely clueless. If she had no recollection, it meant the future—her future— had changed.

I hadn't told any of the others how I escaped. Knox hadn't spoken of our time there much at all, and Zera hadn't brought it up either. Hunter asked one evening, but I kept Zera's part out of it.

I wasn't hiding that for the sake of being a dick, but because I had the strongest feeling that I shouldn't tell anyone. From what I figured out, Zera came to me from a good distance in the future, and something about this felt wrong.

Wrong to the point that if she could travel through time and change the future, there was likely some kind of repercussion from it. We had enough to deal with.

But she did mention the witch, Liberty, and a warlock who was really a fae, called Dean. That guy, I was sure would have some answers. I just wasn't sure how to find him without drawing attention to everything.

The witch agreed to meet us, but not until the following day, and only at a quirky Dutch pancake house she'd picked. We waited for the sun to set before driving down. Heading up to the safe house, I'd barely been aware of what was happening with my body so weak from lack of blood.

"You okay?" Knox asked me. It was just the two of us in the back of the van. "You're quiet."

"I'm always quiet."

"Not always." Knox smirked.

I arched an eyebrow but didn't comment. Instead, I swapped sides of the van, so I was sitting beside him and pulled him against my shoulder. "What's this witch like? Can she be trusted?"

"We worked with her in Savannah once, remember?"

"You were in Savannah, I was at home. But that doesn't answer my question."

Tracing patterns on my thigh, Knox shrugged. "She's good at illusion magic to create disguises. But otherwise, compared to all the other witches I've ever met, she's really bad. Means well but keeps blowing shit up that she's not supposed to. And that's with a wand. She'd be a hazard if she didn't have one." Knox's hand stilled. "And she talks to herself, in the *I see dead people* kind of way."

"Dead people? Ghosts?" I snorted. Ghosts didn't exist.

"Aside from the crazy and fucked-up magic, she's alright. I know Hunter fucked her once. Why? You worried?"

I was, but not in a way I could tell him. Not about the witches, anyway. Even the Lycans weren't ranking high on my list of concerns.

But a time travelling fae was.

Since being turned over thirty years ago, I'd been searching for the Lycans. Technology had improved, and my skills had increased with them. Yet, the only time they sought us out was after I started searching for fae and not Lycans.

After being in that facility, I was absolutely certain they knew nothing about Zera's astral projection, and definitely not about time travelling. But she was fae. And this warlock that the witch was supposed to know was also fae. Did the witch know what he was? Zera from the future had implied he was hostile—was their visit a set up? If it was, all this circled back to the witches being untrustworthy and us being back on the wrong side of the Lycan's crosshairs.

We arrived in Atlanta a few hours after nightfall. The pancake house was one Hunter knew of in the center of the city. The smell from the restaurant greeted us as we walked around the corner, and I glanced at Zera in time to see her eyes light up.

Predictable.

Inside, the place was busy. We were led to a round table at the side of the room.

"What about all of the people?" Zera asked,

looking around.

"Last minute reservations mean this place is more likely to be full of humans than supes," Hunter told her. Instead of whispering, he was talking in his normal volume, but it was still hard to hear him. "And this is a family place which means everyone is busy talking to each other. So as long as we can get through the meeting without attacking each other—"

"Which is the plan." DB cut him off, giving us all a stern look.

"Of course. I still think if anything happened with the witches, Liberty wasn't a part of it." Hunter stood back up. "I'm going to wait by the door for her."

As he walked away, DB passed Zera the menu. "Are you hungry?"

Was she hungry? When wasn't she?

The witch arrived after our food, muttering some bullshit about traffic. When we worked together last time, I ran an obligatory search online. She was one of those people who had every social media account under the sun and posted pictures of her job and food. If this gathering was a social thing, I'd expect her to pull out her phone and take a picture of the pancakes.

Instead, she glanced around the restaurant before looking at the empty space beside her. I didn't miss the slight shake of her head, but I wasn't sure what it was for. My eyes narrowed as I scanned the room, looking for anyone paying attention to us.

"When you said you wanted to meet, I wasn't expecting there to be so many of you," she said, sliding into the vacant seat between the twins.

"Liberty, this is Carter Harlow." Hunter pointed to the oldest gargoyle. "And that's Javion Moore."

"The guy on the other end of the radio mics."

I stared at her, unblinking.

"Anyway…" she glanced at Knox and then did a double take, sucking in a breath—a reaction making me want to hit her. "Knox, what happened?"

"The wards at Castle Viegls failed. The Lycans took us."

The witch's lips parted, then her eyes went wide as she whipped her head around to look at Hunter. "You think that was something to do with me? Why? You're my friend, and you know how much I hate the Lycans."

"I think, if the price is right, hate can be set aside," DB told her.

My instinct was to get her out of there and into a room alone. Without an audience, I'd be able to get the truth from her.

Annoyingly, as she started to bristle, I knew

violence wasn't the right approach. I assumed this to be the conversation where they found out about the warlock, and I highly doubted yelling at each other was how they'd obtain that information.

"Actually, no. We don't, otherwise we wouldn't have met with you. But it was your coven that set the wards on Castle Viegls, and as we know your coven is one of the most skilled when it comes to wards, so you're likely to know who would be able to break them."

I could feel the looks of disbelief from DB, Knox, and Hunter boring into the side of my head, but I ignored them.

"It's not that we think you did anything, but you might know who did. They took me, they took Knox, and they took Zera. We just want to make sure it's not going to happen again."

The witch's gaze scanned my face before looking at Knox, and then Zera, taking on all the bandages and healing wounds between the three of us. "I would never sell anyone out to the Lycans. And the coven has lost members to them before. We hate them just as much as you do."

"But you know something?" Hunter asked.

Liberty nodded. "I overheard two of my coven

sisters talking. A mongoose shifter had been asking about elementals." She glanced at Zera. "Apparently, you hurt your mate, stole something from him, and ran. He was looking for you."

A frown appeared on Zera's face as she looked around the table. "I hurt one of you?"

The way Zera's gaze lingered on me, stopped me from responding. She wasn't looking at me out of suspicion, but concern.

"She's talking about a Lycan," Knox told her. "Not one of us."

"It's a good ruse to track you down, making it seem like you're the one in the wrong," I added.

"But I never dated a Lycan." Zera wrinkled her nose like a Lycan had died and rotted under the table, and she'd just caught the scent of it.

"I didn't say anything, but I did ask my sisters if they knew what the shifter was talking about. They didn't."

"Which leaves us exactly nowhere." DB's eyes were still narrowed at the witch.

"I don't know who broke your ward. The easiest way to do so is to get the witches who cast it to break it, but I know my coven didn't do that. Our reputation is our livelihood. If they broke their trust when it came to casting spells, no one would come to them. What's more likely is the Lycans went to another coven to break them."

DB's frown deepened. "You're telling me that regardless of how much and how regularly we've been paying to have the wards strengthened, they could still be broken, and anyone could infiltrate them?"

"You make it seem like that's easy," the witch said before shaking her head. "Breaking a ward takes time. There's a lot of trial and error to know what goes into the spell to break it down. And time. You're looking at the very least, a moon cycle."

"What about a warlock?" I asked. "Could they do it?"

Liberty shrugged. "They tend to use more offensive spells, but it would still be the same process: they'd have to work out how to break the spell apart." She glanced over at DB. "Unless you're prepared to pay for the wards to be cast monthly, the only way you're going to keep the Lycans out is with wolfsbane. Considering the Lycans destroyed it all, you need to pay for the wards."

"Wolfsbane? That's not been destroyed," DB said. "We have some growing at Castle Viegls."

"Silver wolfsbane," the witch said. "You'll have the

common version, that's purple. Which, as you know, can be brewed to coat weapons that hurt Lycans, but it won't repel them. You need silver. It's just a shame it doesn't exist anymore."

One of DB's hobbies was gardening. He had all kinds of things growing around the castle, including purple wolfsbane. I'd never heard of silver. Judging from the way DB tilted his head, he hadn't either.

"There's no such thing as silver wolfsbane."

"Exactly. The Lycans destroyed it all. If you could find an earth fae, you could probably convince them to grow it—"

"Fae don't exist," Knox said, instantly.

"Where would we need to look to find one? Florida?" I asked at the same time. Again, I earned stares from the gargoyles.

"Florida?" The witch ran a hand through her pink and blue hair. "Like Knox said, fae don't exist. It's a stupid legend, a fairytale. I don't know what you'd find in Florida other than the Florida Man, and unless stupidity can make wolfsbane grow, I'd avoid that guy."

Frowning, I diverted my attention to Knox. "Florida?" he mouthed at me.

I looked back at the witch. "I heard there was a warlock there that might be able to help us."

"A warl... Dean?" Liberty tilted her head, her eyes narrowing. "Why do you want to see him?"

Once again, I could feel everyone's eyes trying to bore into my skull. "I heard he might be able to help us."

"Dean isn't part of a coven," Liberty said, her eyes, still watching me carefully. "I'm not sure he has the power to break the wards by himself."

"Liberty?" Hunter said, after a glance in my direction. "Are you hiding something?"

"You do realize I came here to help you, right? I could have stayed away, especially considering all the trouble you've been causing, but I came. Why would I be hiding anything? I've told you everything I know." She slammed her hand on the table, making Zera jump. "You're an ass."

As she made to get up, Hunter grabbed her arm. "Libby, wait. The Lycans breached the castle walls and wards, to take Zera, Knox, and Javion—"

"And that wasn't my fault."

"I know. I do." Hunter let go of her arm but leaned forward. "I thought we'd lost them. It's made us all a little on edge."

Liberty looked around the table before her gaze settled on me. "How do you know about Dean?"

"His name came up." Once again, I could feel DB's gaze boring into the side of my head. I was no doubt, going to get an earful after. The witch wasn't going to be the only one I lied to.

"I really don't think he's the one who broke through your wards." She pulled her phone out of her pocket and started tapping on the screen. Moments later, the phone in Hunter's pocket chimed. "I've sent you the address. If you really want to waste time heading to Florida, go for it."

She didn't stick around long after that. The moment she was out of earshot, DB turned to me with his eyes narrowed. "Dean?"

"His name came up."

"Where? When? How is this the first we've heard about him?" DB asked.

"Without my computer, I couldn't say specifically where his name came from. Until the witch mentioned warlocks, I hadn't remembered." The lie was smooth enough that each of the gargoyles seemed appeased by my excuse.

"That's not true," Zera said.

Folding my arm, I rubbed my tongue over my fang. "You're accusing me of lying? How would I be able to remember every site I've looked at?"

"I don't know because I've never used a computer."

"Then how is what I said not true?" I kept my face as expressionless as possible to hide my irritation. Yes, it was a lie, but how the fuck did she know that?

"You're the one who mentioned warlocks," Zera told me. "I don't know what one is."

"Zeraora is correct," DB said. "You are the one who mentioned warlocks."

I gave him a dismissive wave of my hand. "Her? Me? Whatever. Witches and warlocks: it makes sense. Witches are known for their defensive magic, and warlocks for their offensive magic. If a ward was broken, maybe a warlock could do it. Either way, that's what reminded me about the name."

DB waited for a small family to filter past us, but his gaze never left my face. "We should go. It's a few hours' drive back home, and I'm sure you'd appreciate not driving in the daylight."

There was nothing about his tone convincing me that he believed me.

"Have you seen the dessert selection?" Hunter said, suddenly.

I looked over and found him talking to Zera—big fucking surprise.

"It's a long drive back. Let's go pick something to take with us."

If only it was as easy to distract DB with food as it was that female.

I settled back into my seat and waited for Hunter to lead the elemental away from the table.

"Spill." The request came from Knox, not DB.

"Your mate is a lot more powerful than any of you realize. Unfortunately, she's far too naïve to understand the consequences."

"Is that supposed to be an explanation or an insult?" DB asked.

"She came to me. She's how I got out of the facility alive."

"You said you fought the Lycans and found a way to escape." DB's tone was accusatory. Knox looked confused: I'd told him the same thing.

Glancing over at the far side of the restaurant where Zera was distracted by the cake display, I pursed my lips. "I lied."

"What? Why?" Knox demanded.

"The way she was talking, it was like she had come from the future. A long way in the future. She's done it at least once with me before now. As far as I could tell from that conversation, she didn't do anything to change the future." I looked back at DB. "In the future she came from this time, you and I were both dead."

The two men stared at me like I was speaking in another language.

"Dead?"

"Why didn't you say anything?"

I glanced back at the female before looking at DB. "According to her, yes. Dead. And I didn't say anything, because... I think this is something we shouldn't tell her."

"Are you fucking kidding?" Knox asked. "Of course, we should tell her."

"Knoxlyn, do you have any idea how dangerous it is?"

"And yet we can have this conversation in a fucking pancake house?"

I rolled my eyes. "I will quite happily continue this conversation elsewhere, but the reason we came here was because we knew there'd be no supe. Can you sense any? The humans sure as hell aren't paying us any attention."

That last part wasn't completely true. Knox was getting a lot of side eyes and open stares thanks to the scars on his face. Years of experience had taught me not to react, but that didn't mean I didn't want to rip the throats out of every single human who looked at him with a revolted expression.

But that was a different kind of attention, and we weren't close enough to another table for them to hear our conversation.

"Just because there are no supes in here—"

"Time travel. The Lycans had her because she could power whatever fucked up experiments they were doing, and fuck knows what else. Can you imagine what they would do if they knew she could go back in time? More importantly, I do not think it's good for her."

"And you're suddenly concerned about her health?" DB asked.

Annoyingly, yes, I was. The female was... growing on me like mold in a bathroom with no ventilation.

"You should be," I said, pointedly ignoring his suggestion.

Thirty-Two

Zera

"You keep staring at me."

Instead of going back to the castle, Carter said we were going to Florida to see the warlock that Javion heard about. We arrived somewhere—I assumed Florida—and went straight to a motel since it was too close to sunrise for us to go straight to the warlock's home.

Almost instantly, Carter and Hunter left, saying they were going for supplies. Knox laid down on the bed and went to sleep. I was next to him, with Javion sitting up on Knox's other side.

He'd been staring at me for a while.

"Mmmm."

"Why?" I asked.

"You should be asleep."

The bed was comfortable, and Knox's body beside me was warm and comforting. I was tired, but I couldn't fall asleep if I tried. "You keep staring at me."

"Have your powers come back yet?"

"No. Why do you care?"

Javion shrugged.

"I can make sure you're the first to know when they do. I can destroy you, you know."

Running his tongue over his fang, Javion shifted his weight onto his side, and the covers slipped, exposing more of his torso. "You could, but you won't. If you wanted me dead, you would have left me with the Lycans."

My gaze dropped to his chest, following the lines down to his waist, which was just peeking out from under the covers. He'd taken off his top but still had his jeans on. His arms and chest were covered in tattoos, much like Knox, only because of his dark skin, they weren't as easy to see as Knox's were. I could see them better when my glasses were on.

"Like what you see, Little Sparkler?"

"You don't have any burns anymore." The Lycans had kept us in a room with fake sunlight, and although I tried to make sure the light didn't hit him, he was burnt anyway.

Javion raised an arm and looked at it. "Advantage of being a vampire." He lowered his arm and looked back to me. "Thank you."

I frowned. "I didn't make you a vampire."

"No, but you did make sure I stayed one. I'm alive because of you."

That didn't make much sense to me. "I thought you weren't alive?"

Javion chuckled, but then he stopped, frowning, before shaking his head. "Go to sleep, Little Sparkler."

I rolled onto my back and stared at the ceiling.

Javion was acting strangely. It wasn't a bad strange, but it didn't seem normal for him.

As soon as the sun set, we drove somewhere called the Everglades. As far as I could tell, that was a fancy name for a giant pond, even though Carter claimed there was a difference.

After that, Carter insisted he take the lead. With Knox and Javion on either side of me, and Hunter behind, we followed a path through tall grass. I glanced over the edge at the water beneath us, which was as black as the sky. The moon was large and round, and lighting up the sky, but I was still struggling to see much.

The winding path seemed to go on forever, but eventually, it led us to a small island with a house in the middle. The house looked funny, standing on tall, wooden legs. And there were a lot of steps leading up to the front door.

The five of us paused, but when I went to go towards the steps, Carter crossed in front of me and shook his head. "Stay back here. He's a warlock and will have wards up that have already warned him of our presence. You need to be ready to escape. I'll go."

Before Carter could move off the bridge and onto the island, the front door opened, and light shined onto us. A figure stepped into the light, but I could only see his outline before Knox pulled me behind him.

"Evening chaps. I think you've made a wrong turn somewhere along the way." The man had a strange accent.

"You Dean?" Carter asked.

There was a long pause before the man answered. "Never heard of him. I suggest you turn back and get new directions. Whatever you're looking for isn't here."

"Liberty Talbot is a mutual friend," Javion said. "She said we should talk to you. That you might be able to help us."

There was another pause. "Whatever help you think you need, I doubt I'm qualified to help you. You might want to—"

"We know you're fae—" Javion said.

"Do we?" Knox hissed in a whisper, and I stared at the vampire, surprised.

"—And we need your help."

Something changed in the air. I wasn't sure what it was, but the area that was just full of bugs making noises, and the wind playing with leaves, went silent. The air also seemed... thicker. And wetter.

"There's no such thing as fae," Dean said.

"And yet we all know that's not true. Because as I said, I know you are one." Javion took a step forward, moving past Carter. "Judging from the increased humidity, and the water, I'm going to say you're a water fae."

"Javion, what are you doing?" Carter's tone was low. The expression on his face told me he was close to jumping Javion and pinning him down.

"Dean has answers," Javion said, not turning back to look at us. "And I know he's about to attack, but I'm hoping he's going to change his mind and help anyway. Because our female is the same as him."

Before Hunter could stop me, I stepped out around Knox, but my attention wasn't on the warlock. It was on Javion.

Our female?

Since when?

Dean said something, but I didn't hear it. When I looked in his direction, he was walking down the steps, making his way towards us. As he stopped, he locked eyes with me. "You're supposed to be dead."

"The Lycans tried."

"The Lycans had you?"

When I nodded, the warlock growled.

"Fuck." Without explanation, he turned and headed back to his house, pausing at the bottom of his steps to turn and look back at us. "Are you coming or not?"

"Is that an invitation?" Javion asked.

Dean looked at him. "Vampire?"

"Yes."

"Yeah, you can come in." Dean walked into the

house, leaving the door open.

Javion shrugged. "Let's fol—"

Before he could finish his sentence, Carter grabbed Javion by the collar and pinned him against the closest fencepost. "We agreed not to mention Zeraora being fae. I ought to use this damn fence to stake you."

That seemed a strange thing to say. I knew the television vampires could be killed that way, but Javion said daylight, fire, and cutting a vampire's head off was the only way to kill one.

"You remember what I told you in Atlanta?" Javion wasn't attempting to break Carter's hold.

Carter looked over at me before turning back to Javion. "When we're done here, you're going to tell me everything, and this time, you're not leaving anything out."

I glanced at Hunter. "Do you know what they're talking about?"

With a sigh, Hunter took my hand. "They're still working through things. Why don't you and I go wait back at the car."

He tried to lead me back the way we came, but I stood my ground. "No, I go too. You promised."

"She'll be fine," Javion told Hunter.

Thirty-Three

Javion

Whatever I was expecting from talking to the fae, it wasn't this.

After my searches started pulling up hints of fae-related results, I looked at anything fae on the various internets. Most was on the human internet.

Stories—fairy tales.

And here was a second fae in front of me, talking about seelie and unseelie courts, and how the fae disappeared from our realm to save the world thanks to a prophecy, all hidden by an incredibly powerful spell.

"What was this prophecy?" I asked.

"What *is* a prophecy?" Zera asked.

"It's a prediction of something that will happen in the future." Hunter started to explain. Since we'd walked into the house, which was decorated like he lived on a beach—the dude lived in Florida and could have just headed a few miles to the coast–Hunter was lingering beside Zera like he was her bodyguard.

"*Could* happen," DB said, stressing the word.

"What's the prophecy?" I asked the warlock.

Dean moved over to a bookshelf, looking at the titles as though the answer was in one of his true crime novels.

"A fae, one of the most powerful, will meet a Lycan. Doing so will set off a chain reaction resulting in the world ending."

"Zera met Lycans. She was held captive by them. And when she's at full power, she's strong enough to take out cities with little effort at all." As I said this, I could feel DB's death glare in the side of my head again. He was still pissed that I chose to divulge this—or any—information but curious enough that he wasn't stopping me.

"The prophecy said it was an Unseelie. Zera is

Seelie. She might be powerful, and maybe she can destroy the world, but this one isn't her. Not in this prophecy, anyway." Dean glanced at Zera. "What do you mean, when she's at full power?"

"I can't do anything." Zera held up her hand. Like every other time she tried, there wasn't even a spark. "My power is gone."

"What happened?" Dean narrowed his eyes.

"The Lycans took her, *again,* and used her as a fucking power source. *Again.* We got out, and now, she has no powers." Knox moved behind Zera, placing his hand on the small of her back.

The warlock's gaze dropped to Zera's wrists. "Do the Lycans know what you are?"

"Fucking doubt it," Knox muttered.

I shook my head. "They've never referred to her as fae. They think she's an elemental—"

"—They know," DB said, cutting me off.

The warlock ran his hand through his hair. "Fuck."

There was panic—genuine fear—in the warlock's eyes. I was almost convinced he was about to bolt. "The Lycans have targeted all supes."

"The spell I told you about; the one that was cast to by the unseelie to hide from the seelie guard? It wasn't just to hide from them. It was to hide from the

Lycans. The unseelie may have stayed, but that prophecy... if the Lycans got hold of them, they knew they would be used, that the prophecy would be fulfilled."

"What is this end of the world? What does it look like?" Hunter asked.

Dean shook his head. "The prophecy didn't go into specifics. It could literally be the world disintegrating, or it could be something so powerful that it wipes out all life on earth. Either way, it doesn't matter. If the Lycans know about you, then we're all in danger."

I glanced at the female. She might not be unseelie, but surely, time travel was enough to fuck the world up?

My heart hadn't beat in decades, but right then, it felt like something was squeezing my chest. Not because I was worried about the world ending...

Nope, not addressing that one...

"I know her powers have disappeared, but are you sure she's not going to be the cause of the end of the earth?" I asked.

"Really?" DB shot me a scathing look.

My question wasn't because I didn't like or trust the female, but I didn't have time to address that because the warlock was talking to Zera.

"Have you tried?"

"No, she's just fucking stood there." Knox snapped at him.

The warlock shot him a dark glare, then returned his attention back to Zera. "You assume your power is finite."

Zera stared blankly.

"That there's a limit to it, and it has run out," Hunter explained. He looked at Dean. "Are you saying it doesn't?"

"Of course not. The powers a fae has can't just disappear, because you never possessed it to begin with."

"That's not true. The Lycans took my power from me for years," Zera told him.

Dean got up from the chair he was sitting in and walked to the middle of the room.

"All magic takes it root in some form of elemental energy. Humans don't have a clue. Some worked out how to harness it and called it science and technology, but none of them, like most supes, can wield that energy without a tool of some description. Those that come close to really using it are witches, but even they don't truly understand. As fae, we don't use it. We create it."

"You create electricity?" Knox arched an eyebrow.

"I am from the Uisce Court." Dean shot him a

contemptuous look.

"And for those of use that don't speak fae?" DB's lips were pressed into a thin line, unimpressed.

"Just give us a minute," I said, suddenly. DB arched his eyebrows as I walked over to him. I nodded in the direction of the door. Without any further instruction, I walked outside.

DB didn't disappoint and followed me out. "What's wrong?"

I didn't stop until we were a safe distance away, and then I turned back. "You're still pissed at me."

"You say that like there's supposed to be an off-switch." DB folded his arms. "I was starting to… and then you pulled this. What are you still hiding?"

"I'm not. I told you back in Atlanta, that Zera came to me from the future. That's huge. That's… that's the kind of power that anyone—not just the Lycans—would kill to wield." I pointed back to the house. "Zera has no clue as to how powerful she is. I know she keeps saying it, but what she thinks is just the tip of the iceberg. And yet, right now, she has no power. DB, I can't search this on any of the webs for answers. There was fuck all the first time, and oh yeah, it brought the Lycans to our front door."

"But you think some random warlock—"

"Fae."

"—will suddenly be able to help us? How can we even trust him?"

I shrugged. "Ask him."

Cocking his head, DB gave me an unimpressed look. "Ask him. You think he's not going to lie?"

"Actually, no. The little I could find on the fae is that they don't lie. They go out of their way to twist their words to avoid speaking the truth, but they don't lie. And I think that's true. When has Zera lied? Think about the questions he's been asked. If he's not wanted to answer them, he's diverted; answered the question with another question."

"What if he *can* lie? What if we *can't* trust him?"

"Maybe we can't, but right now, there's no other way of helping Zera."

DB unfolded his arms and took a couple of steps closer, his eyes narrowing. "Why are you so suddenly set on helping Zeraora?"

"She saved my life. I died, and then you died. And yet she came back to save me, and to save us both, when she could have just gone for you. I owe her." I was glad that I wasn't dead. That was the truth, it just wasn't all of it. "Fuck."

Realization hit me.

"What?" DB asked, instantly.

The fae that you three gargoyles are so infatuated with has managed to weasel her way into my heart. Not just my heart, but the bond. The bond I only share with my betrothed.

Like hell would I admit that out loud to myself, let alone DB.

It probably wasn't a bond anyway, just some stupid need to repay a debt.

"We need to know as much as we can about her. If the Lycans know she's fae, like you say, we need to know what they know. We're going to have to go after them."

I'd known DB for a few decades now, but he wasn't just my friend. Even though I was almost twice his age, I joined his family and accepted the gargoyle way of life. It wasn't that different from vampires. Mainly, I'd accepted that DB was in charge.

There were few vampires who knew this—most of them were now gone thanks to Zera—not that I really gave a shit. They'd turned up their noses, and half were less than impressed with Knox being my betrothed. But I'd stuck around because of him and my shared goal of finding the Lycans.

DB rubbed at his jaw, glancing out over the water before he lowered his head and sighed. "Let's go ask this fae some questions."

I nodded, following DB back into the house. The room was strangely quiet until Zera looked over at us. "Good. Hunter said we couldn't speak."

"I said we shouldn't talk about this stuff..." He gestured vaguely, "Because we'd need to repeat ourselves when these two came back."

DB gave Hunter a brief nod of acknowledgement but walked straight over to Dean. "Are you fae?"

"I'm not exactly gargoyle—"

"Yes or no."

The corner of Dean's lip quirked up into a smirk. "Yes."

"And are you our enemy or friend?"

"The enemy of my enemy is my friend, right?" he asked.

"That depends on who your enemy is," I said.

Tilting his head, Dean considered my words and then nodded. "That's true."

"So, who is your enemy?" I asked.

Knox stepped closer to me. "What are you doing?"

"I'm trying to work out if we can trust Dean."

"It's a bit late now, isn't it?" Knox muttered. He glanced over at the warlock before stepping back.

Dean had been watching the two of us, clearly

hearing the conversation, and yet smiling, clearly amused. "Your friend has a point."

"Can we trust you?" DB asked.

Slowly, Dean turned to face him, looking him in the eye. "You shouldn't trust anyone. Power corrupts."

DB didn't blink. "Can we trust you? Yes or no."

Dean pulled at the bottom of his bottle green waistcoat as though his eccentric suit had become ruffled, then he moved towards Zera.

Her wide, blue eyes watched him, but she didn't react, unlike Hunter, who was ready to pull her out of the way.

"Seelie or unseelie, right now, in this realm, our enemy is anyone who isn't fae. Our biggest threats are those who wish to control us and use our power for their gain. Do you trust these men?" he asked her.

"Yes." There was no hesitation in her answer.

"All of them?"

"Yes," she said, again.

Although I kept my expression blank, I was surprised. While I was aware that something had shifted between us, what I hadn't realized was that her acceptance had gone as far as trust. Then again, she probably didn't understa—

"With your life?"

"Yes." Zera frowned. "Why wouldn't I?"

Instead of answering, Dean turned to face DB and me. "I'm not sure I trust you."

"And that wasn't the question," DB told him.

"Personally, I do not care whether you trust me or not," Dean said.

I already concluded that dealing with fae would be tricky. In all of my research, one of the few consistent things I found was that fae couldn't lie. Which of course, meant that if they didn't want to admit the truth, they would do everything they could to avoid doing so.

Only, my patience was wearing thin.

"You think we care that you're fae? I don't give a fuck that you're a fae. The only thing we care about is Zera. We need to know if we can trust you to keep her safe," I laid it all out. Bluntness was best here.

A smile grew on Dean's face. "I will help you. While I have no intention of telling anybody who Zera is, I make no promises if the fae find me."

DB looked at me. Something told me this was going to be the best we would get.

So I nodded.

DB glanced over at Hunter.

"If he can help Zera..." Hunter shrugged.

"Help us protect our mate," DB asked.

Dean walked over to Zera, looking her up and down, before he turned back to us. "Your mistake is going to be not realizing she's the one protecting you."

Zera's eyes grew even wider, seemingly delighted, before she set her hands on her hips. "See?"

That warlock had no idea what he'd just done.

I couldn't help but grin too.

With a long sigh, DB rubbed at his chin. "That may be true, but it doesn't mean we won't do everything we need to, making sure she doesn't *have* to protect us."

Dean winked at Zera, then the smile slipped from his face.

"Your power hasn't gone. Fae are the only supernatural beings with true power. Others claiming to have power, don't. They borrow it. Witches and warlocks must ask to use these powers by casting spells and using conduits—wands. They use words, power, and magic interchangeably. They shouldn't."

"Then where has mine gone?" Zera held up her hand, palm up.

"Not only do you create power, but you can control it. These are two skills as easy as breathing. The problem is, that because you do it naturally, learning to do it with intent is much more difficult. The fact that you cannot create the electricity is only because of some block you've placed on yourself."

"How do I take it off?"

Dean pursed his lips. "Only you can figure out what that block is. However, while you work that out, I can teach you how to control the power."

"How can I control something I don't have?"

The smile on Dean's face told me he thought the question was stupid, and Zera being Zera, hadn't realized that yet. It wasn't a stupid question, but it did give me the urge to punch the warlock in the face.

"Each of the seven courts rule an element. These elements are all around us. I told you I was from the Court of Uisce. That means I have the power of water. While I can create water from nothing, I can also find the water around me and control it." Dean step back and pointed to the window, nodding towards it with his chin.

Zera walked to the window with Hunter following close behind her. When her mouth dropped open, Hunter looked just as amazed.

DB, Knox, and I moved so we could see outside. It took me a moment to figure out what was happening there.

A wall of water was surrounding the house. However, he did it, Dean had created what looked like a ten-foot waterfall from the water in the swamp.

Zera spun around, her eyes wide. "How are you doing that?"

"There is water all around us: in the air, outside, in plants, and in us." Dean raised his hands in front of him.

In the air, materializing from nowhere, he created a sphere of water the size of a basketball.

I gave Knox a sideways glance and found him staring back at me.

We all underestimated Zera, but we had also underestimated Dean. If he could create water from nothing and combine it with all the water outside, I was willing to bet he had the power to turn Florida into Atlantis if he wanted to.

"But there isn't electricity everywhere," Zera said, disappointed.

Glancing at Dean, Hunter moved into Zera's eyeline. "Most things have a current, an electrical charge." He pointed at Dean's television. "TVs, phones, power outlets, telephone wires—that's the obvious stuff. But then there are the things you don't think about: living things. I have a current, animals do, even trees. And you can't see it, but there's a small electrical charge in the air—atmospheric electricity."

"How come I've never seen your electricity?" Zera

stared at Hunter's hands, practically stunned.

"What they have isn't power, not like what you have," Dean told her. He arched an eyebrow then turned to Hunter.

I rolled my eyes. "She was held captive by the Lycans," I said dryly. "Do you think they taught her *anything*?"

The ball of water disappeared in the blink of an eye as Dean's expression darkened.

"Anything alive has an electrical charge. That's all you need to remember. If you can learn how to draw in that power, being able to create it from nothing should naturally follow." The warlock pointed to a power outlet under the window. "Put your hand on that."

"Are you fucking serious?" Knox asked.

"She's a fae from the Court of Ceraun."

Knox smacked his palm against his chest. "And I'm a gargoyle—a stone demon. That doesn't mean it's not going to hurt if you throw a rock at my head."

"You don't control the rock." Dean looked at Zera. "It won't hurt you."

Zera looked at the power outlet, but hesitated. Instead of sticking her hand in it like I expected her to, she looked at Knox.

I could see the conflict raging in his eyes. "I know

it seems crazy, but I don't think he's lying."

I could feel DB's eyes boring into the side of my head, but I didn't say anything else. I still believed that as a fae, Dean wasn't going to lie, but I wasn't going to admit aloud that I'd trust him not to hurt Zera.

In an instant, the hesitation disappeared.

Zera crouched down and placed her hand over the power socket.

"Can you feel it?" Dean asked.

Her head tilted to the side, and a small, rare smile appeared on her face as she held her hand up. As she opened up her fingers, dozens of miniature bolts of lightning jumped up, hitting an invisible forcefield, like she was holding a plasma ball.

"I'm not sure how I feel about seeing this," Knox muttered.

I wasn't quite sure what he meant by that.

"It's back!" Zera jumped to her feet, but the moment her hand left the socket, the electricity disappeared. As soon as she noticed, the smile fell from her face. "What? Why?"

"If you can pull the electricity from the power socket, you should be able to control it from where you are too," Dean told her. "Give it a go."

Thirty Four

Zera

I felt it. It was back, and this time, there was no pain.

Then, just like that, it was gone again.

"How?" I demanded.

Dean moved over to his couch and sat down, crossing his legs as he leaned back into the seat. He was a strange looking person. Not unattractive, though nowhere near as good looking as my mates.

But he did wear strange clothes. The only time I'd

seen anything close to what he was wearing was when Carter, Hunter, Knox, and Javion had dressed up for the winter equinox on the night the vampires attacked. Only their clothes weren't as bright and patterned as Dean's.

"Can you remember how that electricity, that power felt?"

Of course I did. Not only had I felt it dancing across my skin, but it was also inside me. There was blood pumping around my body that I could feel if I pressed my hand against certain parts of me, otherwise I couldn't actually feel it. The electricity, I could feel that thrumming.

I nodded.

"Then call that electricity to you."

I raised an arm and pointed it towards the power socket, then, frowning, I tried to seek out that same thrum of electricity, beckoning it to me. For a moment, there was nothing.

And then I felt it.

Opening my other hand, I smiled as the ball of electricity reappeared there. The thrum was back. I turned and looked at Carter, my heart, swelling as he smiled and nodded.

Hunter stepped in front of me with a big grin on

his face. "That's brilliant, Zee."

"Nicely done, Zera." Knox, who was beside me, reached up and cupped my cheek.

"Well done," Dean said, although he didn't really seem impressed. "Now find the electricity without using the power socket."

It wasn't until I lowered my hands and the electricity stopped that I realized my powers hadn't actually returned. My lips parted.

"It's okay, you've got this, Zee."

I held up my hand again, summoning the electricity back. A little surprised, it reappeared almost instantly.

"Nope," Dean said. "You're just pulling it from the power socket again. I need you to find it from anywhere other than there."

"But I've got it. What does it matter where it comes from?"

"It matters when you're in the middle of the Everglades without a power socket close to you."

"Why would I be in the middle of the Everglades?"

"What are you going to do if you end up in the middle of the woods with the Lycans chasing you?" Javion asked me.

I looked over at the vampire and frowned. That made more sense.

"Just remember, almost everything holds a current," Hunter told me, then gave me a reassuring smile.

"You're going to be tempted to find that electricity from anything electrical," Dean told me. He pointed to the television, and then the light above us. "Sure, that's an easy source, and yes, you can use it if you wish, there should be nothing stopping you from that. However, you need to be ready, just in case you're in a place where there's no electricity, no appliances, no power cables, or anything like that around. You need to find the current that's there. For now, ignore the obvious and find another source."

Everything had a current?

No, things that were alive had a current.

The only things alive in here were my mates. I gave Javion a sideways glance.

"Don't waste your time worrying about it," he told me before rolling his eyes.

I narrowed my eyes. How did he know what I was worrying about? I wasn't even worried. But I was curious if he had a current. He was a vampire, so he was dead.

"Let me help you," Dean said. He pointed at the other four men in the room. "Which of these do you have the closest bond with?"

"All of them," I replied.

Dean shook his head. "No, which one do you have the strongest connection with?"

"All of them," I said again.

"There must be one of them."

"Why?"

"Don't worry, Zera," Knox told me. "He's not asking you to pick a favorite."

"How could I pick a favorite?"

Carter tilted his head as though I'd said something strange, but before I could ask, he smiled. "No, you couldn't. And nobody's asking you to pick a favorite."

"Dean is."

Dean let out a long sigh. "Those Lycans really did a number on you." He got to his feet and walked out of the room.

"What did I do?" I asked.

"You didn't do anything," Carter assured me.

Javion ran his tongue over a fang before smacking his lips. "All things considered, he's being patient."

"Jay, don't be a dick."

Arching an eyebrow, Javion glanced at Knox, but before he could say anything back, Dean walked back into the room.

"How old were you when the Lycans took you?" he asked.

I shrugged. "I don't remember, but I think it might have been my fifth birthday."

The warlock stared at me, anger in his expression. "Five? And who else did they take?"

"I don't know," I told him. "I remember a woman giving me a balloon. She was smiling."

I had no memory of my life before being with the Lycans. I didn't really remember waking up in the glass cage. And I wasn't really sure how much of my younger years being trapped in the cage that I could remember, because I wasn't sure if it was because I was too young, or if it had all just turned into one big memory.

Although I could barely remember that woman, I was sure she was my mother. I couldn't remember her face, just her smile and her dark hair. But whenever I thought of her, I had this feeling she was someone important to me.

"Once Bacco said there was another one like me, but she had died," I told Dean. "I don't know if she was taken with me, or who she was, because I never saw her."

"Do you know of any other fae still here, that didn't go back to your home realm?" Carter asked Dean.

"A few, but none from the Court of Ceraun." He seemed to share a look with Carter.

"Is that important?" I asked.

Knox took my hand in his suddenly, making me jump. "Sorry," he said. He quickly squeezed it, but then turned his attention to Dean. "Javion."

"What about me?" Javion asked.

"The bond," Knox said. He squeezed my hand again. "If I was going to pick anybody, I'd say she has the strongest bond with you."

"How the hell do you figure that?" Hunter asked.

"I don't think so," I said. I looked at Javion and found his silver eyes gazing at me. "I don't have a favorite."

"It's not that you have a favorite, but a connection," Knox said. He shrugged. "Think about it. All those times you have projected, it was to Javion—"

"What do you mean, projected?" Dean cut Knox off. He was staring at us like something was about to go wrong.

"Fuck," Hunter muttered.

"I can astral project," I told him. "I can leave my body and go somewhere else."

"No." Dean shook his head. "You shouldn't be able to do that."

"But—"

A hand clamped down on my shoulder, making me jump. Before I could acknowledge what it was, instinctively, I turned and fired a bolt of electricity. The bolt came from the power socket, but it hit Javion's shoulder, making him stagger backwards.

"Don't do that," I told him.

Knox stepped between us. "The fuck are you doing, Jay?"

"I was going to... The hell with it, it doesn't matter at this point." Javion turned to Dean. "What do you mean she shouldn't be able to do that?"

"That's... your parents..." Dean shook his head and started pacing, staring at me as he did. Finally, he stopped and spun on his heel. "You can never, *never*, allow anyone—never mind the Lycans—to find out about this."

"You'd best start explaining," Carter said, a growl in his tone.

"That's not a power a fae from the Court of Ceraun should have." Dean's gaze was locked onto me, and I stared back. "It's not a power any fae should have. Fuck, if the fae were still here, you wouldn't be alive."

"What the fuck?" Knox demanded.

"Why not?" I asked.

Dean walked over to the table and sat down heavily in one of the chairs. He let out a harsh breath as he raked his hand through his hair, leaving it ruffled. "It's too much power."

I walked over to the table, bypassing Carter as he made an effort to stop me, and then sat down beside Dean. "I am already powerful. Why is this a problem?"

Dean raised his head and looked at me. "Fae like you..."

Carter stepped up behind me, drawing Dean's attention to him. "Be very careful how you answer that."

"Careful?" Dean arched an eyebrow. "There's no careful way to answer this. She's a nuke. A bloody nuclear bomb. All fae, we have power. We can create damage, but this? You say that you want to protect her, but you have no idea what you're up against, if anyone finds out what she is."

"We're not going to let anything happen to Zeraora."

"How can I be too powerful?" I asked.

Surely, having power was a good thing?

"It makes you a weapon. A very powerful, a very dangerous weapon. It may not feel like it, but you're lucky the Lycans were just using you as a power source."

Dean turned to Carter, and then looked at each of my other mates. "I realize you're not sure if you should trust me, and what I said before still stands: you shouldn't trust anyone. However, if there's one thing that you listen to, it has to be this: no matter what, do *not* try to develop those powers. Astral projection must end. If you don't, and anyone gets a whiff of what Zera can do, you'll spend what's left of your short lives running. And that, is the *best*-case scenario."

"You're saying I should stop?" I asked.

Astral projection was tiring, and I still didn't know how to do it right, but when the Lycans caught me, I was able to project to Carter and Hunter, and they came to find us.

"We can make sure that happens," Javion said, sharing a look with Carter.

"But I don't understand why," I told them. I knew I was still learning how to do it right, but surely, it had to be useful? "Why would that mean we would have to run?"

When I wanted to learn to fight, Hunter took me to the gym and said I needed to work on my stamina by running on his torture machine. I hated running.

"I don't want to answer this," Dean said, but his attention was back on Carter. "I sense she doesn't understand the implications, but you guys do." He looked around the room. "Or maybe some of you do. I don't want to say something that will give her ideas."

Carter nodded. "We understand."

"Ideas? You can't hide this from me!"

Dean stood and looked at me, unblinking.

"There's very little more that I can do to help you. I think it would be safer for everybody if you left now. Hopefully, your visit was short enough, should anybody have been following you, they will not visit."

Then he turned to my mates.

"Anyone who knows what she is and what she can do are either in danger or are the danger you should be running from. You've already made enemies with the Lycans. If I were you, I'd get out of here now."

Thirty Five

Zera

Despite my protests, Carter agreed with Dean's suggestion.

We were somewhere on the way back to the van, crossing the wooden bridge, when I stopped and unfolded my arms. "Why won't you explain anything? I'm not stupid, I just don't know things, but I won't know things unless you explain them."

"We will discuss this when we get home," Carter told me.

I shook my head and refused to move. "No, you won't. You'll do what you always do and pretend this didn't happen, and when I ask questions, you won't answer them."

Carter stepped towards me. "We have a long drive back home, and the sun will be up soon. Sun that we can't be out in because of Javion. Let's go home, where it's safe, and we'll discuss this together."

Biting my lip, I glanced over at Javion. It was still pitch dark, but I didn't know what time it was nor how soon the sun would be rising. After seeing him burned by a fake sun, I didn't want to see him getting burned by the real thing.

"We'll explain it all when we get home, I promise, Zee." Hunter gave me a smile. "But we need to get somewhere safe."

"It doesn't sound like anywhere is safe."

"The wards were reinforced while we've been here," Hunter told me. "The Lycans will not be able to enter the castle grounds again."

"If we need to leave and go somewhere else, we will." Carter added. He held out his hand to me. "We need to go now."

I didn't move, continuing to stare at Carter. "I want you to promise me that you'll explain things fully when we get home." Promises were funny things that I also didn't get, but I knew Carter took them seriously. And I knew we had to go, but I didn't want to go, only for us to get home and then everyone pretend this didn't happened.

"I promise."

Knowing Carter would keep his promise, I took the hand he offered. Carter wrapped his around mine, and we continued walking back towards the van.

For the journey home, I returned to the back of the van again with Javion and Knox. At first, I tried to get them to explain, but it was Javion who shook his head.

"DB said we would discuss it when we're home, so we'll wait until we get home." He had gone back to being his normal, grumpy self.

In the end, I spent most of the journey home sleeping, curled up against Knox. It was late, and with no windows to look out of and the van rocking, I closed my eyes.

When I woke up, I was still next to Knox, but this time, we were on the silk sheets of the bed he shared with Javion. And Javion wasn't with us.

"Where is Carter? Why didn't you wake me?" I asked.

Knox stretched. "You slept the whole way home,

but DB and Hunter drove. They got home and went to bed. I figured if they were sleeping, I would let you sleep, too. Why don't you go get a bath, dress, and by the time you come back downstairs, I'm sure they'll be awake."

"Where is Javion?" I asked.

"Next door." Knox sat up and rubbed his face. "He went to check on his computers."

"Carter isn't going to make him leave?"

"I don't think so," Knox told me.

"I don't think he should leave again."

Knox leaned back against the headboard. He frowned at me. "Can I ask you something?"

"Yes."

"How do you feel about Javion?"

"I don't know what you mean."

Knox's gaze seemed to scan my face. "I know things changed between you when the Lycans had us, but since then, you've called him your mate. Is that what you think?"

"He is one of us."

"He is, but what I mean is, do you think of him like you do me?"

"No."

That was a strange question. Why would I think

that? I didn't think of Knox in the same way as I did Hunter or Carter either. They were all different people. So was Javion.

"Huh…" Knox looked away and shrugged. "I figured you thought he was your mate too."

"I do."

Carter once told me that a mate was someone you wanted to be with. Javion was strange, And I didn't understand him a lot of the time, but he didn't keep the truth from me, even if it wasn't a nice truth. He belonged with us. His body was cold, and I didn't want to hug him like I did Knox, but I didn't want him to go anywhere either. I also found him attractive.

Knox's gaze was back on me in an instant. "You just said you don't think of him the same way you do me."

"I don't."

Knox let out a long sigh. "Why don't you go have that bath now?"

I leaned over and kissed him before leaving him in the bed and heading upstairs. Doing as he said, I took a bath and changed the dressing on my wrists while trying not to look directly at the ugly mess, before I got dressed.

Knox was right. By the time I got into the kitchen,

Carter was already in there cooking something that smelled delicious. He glanced over his shoulder as I walked in and gave me a smile. "Hungry?"

"When isn't she hungry?" Hunter asked, stepping up behind me. He took a few steps past me to try and peer over Carter's shoulder. "What's cooking?"

"Corned beef hash."

Whatever that was, I'd never had it before, but it smelled delicious. My stomach was already grumbling.

"Zee, why don't you head to the living room and make sure the curtains are closed so Javion can join us." Hunter suggested.

"And once you've done that, you can tell him and Knox that breakfast—brunch—is ready," Carter added.

As soon as I made sure no sunlight was getting into the living room, I hurried down to Knox and Javion's bedroom. It was empty. Javion's room was just a little further down. It wasn't a bedroom, but the room he had all of his computers in. And I wasn't supposed to go in there.

But Carter also told me to get the two for breakfast...

I walked further down the hallway, and as I got closer, I realized the door was open. The last time that happened, I found Knox and Javion having sex. Moving closer to the door, I peered in.

This time, the two were not having sex.

That was disappointing.

"—think you know…" Knox was standing in front of Javion, who was sitting in his chair with his back turned to the wall of TVs behind him, so he could look at Knox. "I think you both do."

"Fuck off Knox." Javion grumbled. "It's not really any of your business anyway."

"That's utter bullshit, and you fucking know it. I don't know why it's so hard for the pair of you to work out what is so fucking obvious."

Javion stared at Knox, and then his silver eyes slowly moved to fix on me. "We have an audience," he said, but I think he was talking to Knox and not me.

Knox half turned and glanced over his shoulder. "What's up, Zera?"

"Looking for a show?" Javion asked me. He shot his hand out, grabbed Knox's crotch, and started rubbing it.

"Fuck's sake." Knox hissed as he battered Javion's hand away. "This shit is exactly what I'm talking about."

"The Little Sparkler is a voyeur. Don't pretend you're not getting hard over it." He glanced back to me. "And I bet you're getting wet over there, too. You like what you see."

I wasn't sure if he was asking me a question, but I nodded.

Javion looked back at Knox and smirked. "Maybe we should do something about that?"

"So you could hide behind messing with Zera to avoid actually fucking her? Fuck off, Jay, and just admit it." Rolling his eyes, Knox walked over to me. "I assume you're here because DB sent you?"

"Yes. He said we should eat in the living room. I made it dark for Javion."

Knox nodded and then took my hand. He led me out of Javion's computer room, but when I looked behind us, Javion was following. There was a route to the living room that was mostly underground for Javion to use, and we walked down the hallway in silence.

Carter and Hunter were already in the living room. As I went to sit on the couch, Hunter handed me a bowl of food. It was probably one of the worst looking meals I'd ever seen, but it smelled good.

"Don't turn your nose up until you've tried it." Hunter scolded me.

It did taste better than it looked. I ate almost all of it before I remembered why I wanted to speak to Carter. "You distracted me with food."

"You do still need to eat. It's been a rough couple of weeks and spending fifteen minutes putting something warm and filling in your stomach is not a bad thing. I made a promise, and I intend on keeping it." Carter set down his bowl on the coffee table. "Are you still hungry? There's more in the kitchen if you want some."

I quickly finished what was left, and then put the bowl down beside Carter's. "I want to know what Dean doesn't want me to know."

Carter shared a look with Hunter, like he'd had this conversation already, and I was fully expecting Carter to say I didn't need to know.

"Honestly, I understand why that warlock said what he did, and in a way, I'm in agreement. However, I think you should know, not just so you know the truth, which I think you should, but so you understand what and why he said what he said. But Javion also needs to start with the explanation, and not me."

I looked over at Javion, who looked surprised as he stared at Carter. "Seriously?" When Carter nodded, Javion put his almost empty glass of blood down on the table beside his chair before he ran his tongue over a fang.

"This is about my astral projection?" I asked.

"Fuck it," Javion muttered. "Do you remember that time you came and saw me in my bedroom, but we didn't realize until later, that it hadn't happened yet?"

"Yes."

"That was you, somehow, travelling through time. And you've done it again."

I frowned, thinking back, and then shook my head. "No, that was it. I visited you twice, and Liberty once, and then Carter and Hunter when the Lycans had us. But the time I visited you, that was the only time it didn't happen at the same time."

Javion folded his arms, and his tongue moved back to his fang. "You've done it again," he said with a firm tone. "Only you don't remember because it hasn't happened."

My head started to hurt as I stared at Javion. "That doesn't make sense."

"You, in the future. That 'you' went to visit Javion." Hunter explained to me.

"Oh." That made more sense.

"I escaped from the power plant the Lycans were holding us in because you helped me." Javion's silver eyes were still focused on mine. "You came from the future, though I'm not sure how far in the future it was, to save my life. You said, or you from the future, said that I was dead, and so was DB."

My eyes got wide, and I turned to look at Carter. The idea of a future where Carter and Javion were dead made my chest hurt so much that I clutched at it, wondering if not breathing would help. "Why were you dead?"

It was Javion who answered. "The Lycans."

I curled my hands into fists. "I am going to kill them all."

Hunter, who was sitting beside me on the couch, muttered, "hand" before grabbing mine and gently squeezing it. "Zera."

I pulled my hand free and stood. "No. That's not fair. They are going to die. I'm not going to let that happen."

"Calm down, Little Sparkler." Javion vaguely gestured with his hand. "I don't think it's going to happen again: I think you've already changed that future."

"And therein lies the situation Dean was referring to," Carter told me.

"How do you know I've changed the future? And Dean said it was a bad thing. How is it a bad thing if I stop you from dying?"

"You stopping Carter and Jay from dying is not a

bad thing." Knox stood up and wrapped his arms around me. He leaned down, bringing his lips close to my ears. "Thank you for saving them," he whispered in my ear.

Carter cleared his throat, and Knox stepped back. "The act itself is not a bad thing. It was brave and clever."

"Then how do you know it worked, and you're not going to die?"

"You said the Lycans killed me. I didn't get out from the power plant the first time around. Only this time, I did. I'm here. Whatever happens now, it's a different future than the one you already lived."

The pain in my chest eased a little, but I still felt uneasy. I sank back down into the couch. "Good. But why was Dean so scared?"

"You have the ability to change time," Hunter told me.

That was a bad thing?

Carter moved over to me, then crouched down in front of me. "I know what you're thinking. Yes, there may be advantages to going back into the past, but changing the past, that changes the future."

"If the future is you dead, why wouldn't I want to change it?"

"The problem comes when other people know you can do this. The Lycans held you captive and used you as a power source. What do you think they would do if they knew you could change the past?"

I shook my head. "It doesn't hurt when I astral project. I can't even touch anything, I literally walk through doors and walls."

"Look at what they did to Knox in order to drain more energy from you," Javion said with one of the softest tones he'd ever used with me.

"Shut the fuck up about that," Knox snapped at Javion. "You know damn well that the Lycans chose to do that, and it wasn't Zera's fault. You fucking told us off for saying the same thing."

Javion stood up and walked over to the fireplace. "I know damn well that the Lycans are responsible for their own actions. What happened to you was not Zera's fault. But that doesn't mean they'll not try to do the same shit again. Or worse."

"Zera," Knox said. "If something ever happens to us again, I need you to promise that no matter what, you won't let yourself get hurt because of me—"

"*Any* of us." Carter finished.

I looked up at Knox, and at the scars on his face. The new ones still hadn't completely healed, and his skin was still yellow in places. Although he had a shirt on, I knew underneath, his body was worse. And he even only had one wing now.

He was asking me to let that happen again?

"No. I'm not making that promise."

"Zera." Knox's voice had a pleading tone to it.

"I'm not making that promise. I will always do whatever I can do to make sure you are still safe. All of you. You make it sound like the pain I experienced when the Lycans had me was the worst thing ever. But you're wrong. Nothing hurts me more than the idea of any of you not being here. If I felt like this when you two died—I would do anything not to feel like this. Whether that's letting the Lycans do whatever they want to me, or me astral projecting into the past to change things. I will protect you."

Carter lowered his head, muttering something under his breath that I didn't quite catch. Then, giving me no warning, Hunter wrapped his arms around me and pulled me into his lap, holding me tightly.

"You asked me once what love was. That's it. And that's how we feel about you." He pressed his lips against my temple. "I love you Zera, and that's why we don't want you doing things like that."

Knox ran a hand through his hair and sighed.

"Same. Exactly the same."

"I *have* experienced that loss before..."

"Do you want me to go back and save her?" I asked Carter.

Carter scrubbed at his face. With a weary sigh he lowered himself fully to the floor, and then leaned back against the coffee table. "I love you, Zera. And a part of me still loves Manon. I wish more than anything she hadn't died, especially the way she did, but going back and undoing that, would change everything. And I wouldn't want that."

Thirty Six

Knox

No matter how much I loved Zera, occasionally, she'd say something that made me wince.

That was one of them.

I knew with absolute certainty that she had no malice in her words, but fuck, that was a hard and awkward question to ask DB.

"Well, I think it's fair to say, that DB is a better man than all of us."

I looked helplessly at Javion and then my brother,

hoping one of them would change the conversation.

"The thing is, Little Sparkler, given the opportunity, most people would probably want to change the past."

"Why is that a bad thing?" Zera's question was innocent.

When it came to watching movies, I left the sci-fi to Hunter. Aside from the fact that I preferred action, sometimes sci-fi movies were just too hard to follow. And hell, anything involving changing the timeline, and I didn't have the patience to follow that plot.

I wasn't stupid and yet I had no idea how to make this simple for Zera to understand.

"Two reasons." Hunter thankfully came up with an answer. "Firstly, just because the future is bad for you doesn't mean it's bad for everybody else. Sometimes the bad things that happens has to happen for good things to happen."

"But Javion said he and Carter died. How could any good come from that?"

Hunter gave Zera a sad smile as he shrugged. "Honestly, in that situation, you're right. That wouldn't be good. However, that's a big thing. What if something smaller happened? What if you accidentally had a power surge and completely destroyed all of Javion's computers? If you knew it would make him feel better, would you go back in time and fix it?"

Zera looked over at Javion, frowning slightly. When Javion arched an eyebrow at her, she shrugged.

"Okay, bad example. What if you had a surge and accidentally destroyed all of Knox's cars?" Hunter asked.

Seeing where Hunter was going with this, I nodded. "I'd be very upset if that happened."

"And I had the ability to change that?" Zera asked.

"Yes, completely stop it from happening."

"Then I would go back, and I would stop myself. I don't want to upset Knox."

"Wow, I can feel the love from here," Javion muttered.

Hunter fought back his smile. "But what if you change things that, if you'd left them alone, Knox would have gone and bought new cars and ended up being even happier?"

Zera chewed on her lip, looking between me and Hunter. "Okay."

"The second problem is if somebody else finds out about your ability, they could make you do something terrible with it. Imagine if the Lycans found out, and they made you go back in time to save that piece of scum who had you locked up in the cage?"

"I would never do that," Zera said instantly. "If I had the opportunity, I would go back and kill him myself." Suddenly her eyes went wide, and her lips parted.

"What's wrong, Blue Eyes?" DB asked.

"It was me."

"What was you?" I asked.

She sat there, staring at the wall beside Javion's head, but she didn't really seem to be staring at it, so much as through it. When I reached out and touched her knee, she jumped.

"Zera?"

"The ghost."

"The ghost?" DB asked. He rubbed at his beard. "What ghost?"

"Do you mean the one Liberty thinks is following her?" Hunter asked.

"There's no such thing as ghosts." Javion leaned against the fireplace and folded his arms. "We had this conversation before. Ghosts don't exist. It was you."

"Exactly," Zera said, nodding. "It was me."

Now it was Zera who wasn't making sense...

"Wait." Something that she had said previously suddenly came to mind. "You mean, the ghost who helped you escape the Lycans the first time?"

Zera's eyes were still wide as she nodded enthusiastically. "She was so pale that I could see through her, and I couldn't see her face properly. She was clean, and her hair was nice." Her eyes narrowed. "And she wasn't wearing any clothes. It was dark, and I didn't have my glasses then. But it was me. I went to save me. I saved myself. Why don't I remember this?"

"That's exactly what Hunter was trying to explain to you," Javion told her. "You went back to change the past, so now, whatever future that was didn't happen, which is why you don't remember it. This is a different future."

"If me from the future went back to help me escape, how did I get out the first time, to be able to go back and rescue me?"

That was a reasonable question, and even I couldn't answer that. Zera and I looked expectantly at the others.

"And now, we enter the paradox that is time travel," Javion muttered.

"Unfortunately, time travel is very complicated. We can't explain it properly because we don't really know how it works," Carter told her. With a sigh, he rose to his feet and moved back to the chair he been sitting in previously. "Which is another thing that makes it more dangerous."

Javion walked back over to us and stood beside me. He folded his arms and looked over at Carter. "Let's be real here, this is Zera. Whether she means to or not, she's going to end up using her astral projection again. I agree with the warlock, that it's dangerous, and she shouldn't do it. But unless she learns how to control it, she could end up wandering into a Lycan base camp without realizing it. Or projecting into one." He shrugged. "You heard the warlock: she's got abilities she shouldn't have."

"How?" Zera asked.

"How what?" DB tilted his head.

"If I shouldn't have these abilities, how do I have them?"

"Actually, I have a theory on that," Javion said. "I'm sure they didn't intend on doing, but I think the Lycans gave them to you."

I cocked my head. "They gave them to her?" The ability to astral project and travel through time? That didn't sound like something the Lycans would do.

"Like I said, not intentionally." Javion looked back to Zera. "I think that all those years where they've been drawing electricity from you, constantly having power in and around you—your body is able to use that power differently. The warlock seemed surprised. I doubt other fae have ever been subjected to what you have been through."

"It makes sense," Hunter agreed. "That much power could be manifested in other ways."

Javion rubbed at his forehead. "Which means, the only way we're going to make this safe, well, *safer*, for Zera, is to let her learn how to control that ability correctly and make sure that nobody else ever finds out about it, and we eliminate the threat that is anybody who knows what she is and what she could be capable of."

"You're saying we go after the Lycans?" I asked.

"Don't look at me like that. We've all literally spent the last ten to fifteen years of our lives tracking them down. Our goal this whole time has been to kill them anyway. Nothing has changed."

"Something has changed," DB said carefully. "We have Zera now."

"I want to destroy the Lycans," Zera said as if we had somehow forgotten that fact. "I can help. I can kill them all."

DB shot Javion an unimpressed glare as he jutted out his jaw. "The point I'm making is that now we have you, and we want to keep you safe."

"But keeping Zera safe is going to mean getting rid

of the threat. They know where we live. We might have the wards around the castle back up, but the Lycans are not going to stop trying." Hunter awkwardly rubbed the back of his head. "I'm sorry DB, but Javion's right. They're not going to stop unless we can stop them first."

"And as Javion also pointed out, we've been hunting them for over ten years and still not found them. How do you think we're going to do that now?"

Beside me, Javion shifted his weight. The movement caught my attention, and I glanced up at him, finding him rubbing his fang with his tongue. "What?"

Javion pursed his lips. "I know where they are."

"What the fuck?"

"What do you mean, you know where they are?" DB demanded.

"Exactly what it sounds like, DB." Javion shrugged.

Hunter twisted in his seat to look up at my boyfriend. "Where are they?"

"Nebraska, Oregon, and Texas."

"How the fuck do you know that?"

In ten years, we'd barely had any clue of their whereabouts, and now he could suddenly pluck states out of the air?

"I asked Zera." Javion pointed at Zera. "Well, the one who rescued me. Turns out I was being held in a hotel, although I get the strongest impression I didn't get the four-star treatment the hotel advertises. Zera gave me a name, and I looked it up—don't worry, this time, I strengthened my VPN and bounced my search off some servers on the black web."

I was speechless.

Aside from the fact that this was the information we'd been searching for since I can remember, but before now, Javion hadn't said a word of this to me.

As if he could read my mind, Jay shrugged. "I didn't want to say anything until I had a chance to confirm. Turns out, there's a very good chance she was right. The hotel brand is small, but it's recently gotten smaller. There were two other locations. The first was in Maine: that same little seaside town where we found our little Sparkler. The second was in West Virginia where we were taken. The other three locations are all in towns with a quote-unquote nuclear power station. Zera didn't tell me which hotel I was at, but with a little planning, we can get in there and destroy them all. More importantly, if I can get on one of their computers, I bet I can find all the answers we're ever going to need."

DB, Hunter, and I all gaped at Jay. I wasn't sure if

I was supposed to be angry, amazed, or afraid.

"I like that plan." Zera declared, beaming at Javion. I think that was the first time I'd seen her truly smile at him.

Shaking his head, DB got to his feet. "Let's not get ahead of ourselves."

"Come on, DB." Irritated, Javion sighed. "You know this is our only option."

"I'm not disagreeing with you." DB shot Javion a disapproving look. "At this point, even if it was a stupid idea, you've already put the idea into Zera's head, but the thing is, it's us five against who knows how many Lycans. They are strong, but even the element of surprise won't mean shit if we're not at full strength. Gods above, it pains me to say this, but we cannot take out a hotel of Lycans if we don't have Zera and her powers at full force."

Zera stared up at DB with her eyes narrowed. "Are you saying that I get to fight with you?"

DB sucked his teeth before finally looking at Zera. "It goes against everything in me, but yes. *Only*, if I know you can protect yourself. And that means you need your powers back and at full strength."

I was a little surprised at DB's admission; however, I was more surprised at how I felt. Of course, I wanted to protect Zera, but now, after everything we'd been through, after everything she'd done, I wanted her to get back to full strength so she could absolutely annihilate the Lycans.

"Then let's start now," Zera said firmly. She rose to her feet, and I had no doubt that she expected DB to change his mind.

If I was honest, I half expected the same.

"How about you start by resting and getting better?" DB suggested.

I snorted. "Fuck that. You heard that warlock. He said fae can create their own energy. We've got to get Zera used to borrowing the energy from around her, so she can figure out have to create her own. She's not going to do that by resting."

DB's jaw was jutting out again. After making sure to give me an unimpressed look, he slowly dragged his gaze to Hunter as though he was expecting him to object.

"Javion is right. We're not going to be safe in our own home until we get rid of the threat against us. It's clear the Lycans don't want to lose Zera, and you said they know she's fae." Hunter glanced at me and Javion before looking back to DB. "They might not know about her astral projection, but that doesn't make them any less of a threat. Even if they were the bargaining kind, which we all know they're not, we don't have anything to bargain with anyway. We need to go after them, and we need to do it sooner rather than later."

DB closed his eyes, sucked in a deep breath, and when he reopened his eyes, they were resolute. "Okay, we're doing this. But, *only*, once Zera has her powers back. We are not doing this if she goes in there unarmed. That's non-negotiable." he waved towards the door. "Go do what you need to."

I had a strange suspicion that he didn't think we could pull it off.

That didn't stop Zera.

With determination etched on her face, she marched towards the door.

Letting out a sigh, I got up and followed her, catching her in the hallway before she got too far. "Where are you going?"

She frowned, glancing around. "To the gym.

The door opened and closed behind us as Hunter and Javion stepped into the darkened hallway.

"What's the plan?" Javion looked pointedly at me.

Luckily, I had one. "We're going to the gym. We're going to get Zera started on some basic fighting. You're going to go and research the hell out of whichever hotel were hitting first."

"That's not going to get my powers back," Zera said, hands on her hips.

"You need to know how to fight, just in case. But when it comes to your powers, I've been thinking about what Dean said. I think the best place to practice is going to be outside, and it's going to need all four of us—including Javion. Which means, we're doing nothing until the sun goes down."

"Why do I need to be there?" Javion eyed me suspiciously.

"Before he freaked out over Zera's ability to astral project, Dean was asking which of us she has the strongest bond with. It's you."

Javion stared at me.

"No, he's not."

I turned to Zera, reaching out to cup her cheek. "Don't worry, we're not upset. It's just that, whenever you have to use your astral projection, you've always gone back to Javion. You have a bond with him."

"She went back to herself, and she visited that ditzy witch. I don't think her coming back to me proves anything."

"She literally travelled back in time to save you." Hunter arched an eyebrow.

"Were you fuckwits not listening to anything I said? She came back to save me *and* Carter." Javion rolled his eyes.

"Why do I need to have a stronger bond with just one of you?" Zera narrowed her eyes, glaring at me. "You're all important to me. I'm going to the gym." She spun on her heel and walked off, leaving the three of us in the corridor.

"I'll be in my room," Javion muttered. He disappeared next.

I turned to Hunter and found him scratching at his head. "What?"

"She's claimed Javion."

"Yeah, and either neither of them realize it or neither of them are accepting it." I peered at my brother. "What? Do you have a problem with it?"

"It's a bit late for that isn't it?" Hunter let out a long sigh before shaking his head. "No, I don't. I guess, I just didn't see that one coming."

Thirty Seven

Zera

Hunter and Knox both joined me in the gym. This time, there was no running on the torture machine. Instead, they were teaching me how to fight.

Although my body ached, my skin was covered in sweat, and I was short of breath, I still refused to stop for long breaks. By the time the sun was setting, I could barely feel my hands.

"Let's call it a day," Hunter said. He reached for a

towel that had been left on one of the benches and tossed it to me.

I dabbed my face, awkwardly holding onto the towel thanks to the gloves I was wearing. "Let me help you with them." Lips pressed in a thin line, Knox walked over to me.

While his attention was on my gloves, I turned to his and Hunter's half-naked bodies. The two of them had shed their tops some time ago, and I was left with two glorious, glistening torsos. Although scarred, Knox was slightly bigger, with a broad chest, larger arms, and more defined muscles.

Hunter had muscles, but his body was slightly slimmer. Not that I cared. I was happy to stare at those two works of art all day. At some point, during my lessons, Carter showed me some pictures of what he called 'art.' They were strange paintings that made no sense to me, but apparently, people like looking at them.

I'd pick my mates over that 'art' every day.

"What filthy thoughts have you got running through your head?" Knox asked, before smirking at me.

"They're not filthy. I was thinking about sex. With you two."

On the other side of the room, Hunter spit out the

water from the bottle he'd been drinking.

Knox just laughed. "And that's not filthy, she says."

"There was no dirt involved," I told him.

"That's not what—why are your hands like this?" Knox had pulled one of my gloves off and was glaring at the back of my hand.

Why was he asking this? We just spent hours fighting. "I have been hitting you and Hunter."

Knox dragged his gaze from the back of my hands to my face, his lips pressing together. "Do they hurt?"

"Yes."

"For fuck's sake, Zera." He snapped.

"Hey, hey." Hunter came closer and peered over Knox's shoulder. "Why are you yelling at—Zera! You're supposed to tell us when you're hurt."

I looked at the back of my hand with a frown. My skin was red, and the knuckles, slightly swollen. They hurt, but I'd been hurt worse. "I didn't want you to stop."

With a sharp exhale of breath, Knox let go and took a few steps away from me.

Hunter stepped into his place and then picked up my hand to examine the back of it.

"You have to tell us these things. We don't feel things the same way as you do. We're made of stone.

We put gloves on and hit each other, or we hit each other without them on, but we don't hurt because our bodies are the same: we're gargoyles. You're not. Yes, you heal fast, but you can get injured just the same. We've got special bandages and thicker gloves you could wear."

"Oh."

Shaking his head, Hunter eased off the other glove. Being gentle, he ran his thumb over the back of my hands. "Honestly, how much does this hurt?"

"And don't give some bullshit evasive answer because you think if you tell us the truth that it hurts, we won't let you fight anymore." Knox glared at me as he folded his arms.

"It hurts." I admitted. "But not as much as these." I bent my elbow to raise my wrist, putting the wrist guard in front of Hunter's face.

Hunter rubbed at his forehead. "Okay. Go inside, clean up for dinner, and then we'll get some ointment on them before you eat. Next time, we will put the thicker gloves on you."

I left the twins and walked back to the house.

Outside, it was almost dark, and there was a chill in the air. Shivering, I hurried inside and went upstairs. After stripping off my clothes, I walked into the bathroom but stopped just inside the doorway.

To the side, where the shower had been, was now a large pot with a plant in it, taking up most of the small area. Carter removed the shower days after I arrived at the castle. With it gone, I was able to use the bathroom without any issue but staring at the shiny walls now reminded me of being in the cage.

Worse, I couldn't help but remember why the Lycans managed to take me, Javion, and Knox, was because when it rained, I was frozen. I couldn't let that happen again.

I just had to work out how to fix me.

After washing up and changing into clean clothes, I applied some ointment to my still healing wrists, doing my best not to look at the ugly mess and then covered them with bandages before putting my wrist guards over them. Hunter said the back of my hands needed ointment applied to them too, so I rubbed some cream into them.

I went back downstairs to the kitchen. Carter was busy cooking something, which as usual, smelled delicious. Before I could go inside to discover what it was, Hunter stepped out. Seeing me, he closed the door behind him and walked over. "We need to see to your hands first."

"I've already done it."

"Let me see." Hunter reached out and took my hands, raising them eye level, so he could examine the back of them. He carefully rubbed his thumb over the back of them. "That's already bruising. I'm sure they'll be healed by tomorrow." He turned my hands over. "How are your wrists?"

I pulled my hands away. "They still hurt."

Hunter stared at me before nodding, and then he stepped back so we could enter the kitchen.

Inside, Carter was already putting food onto plates. I walked over and looked at the meal I didn't recognize. "It's meatloaf."

"I'll take it to the table."

As I reached for the plate, Carter sighed as he reached for my hand, although he didn't hold it. "They're bruised."

"Yes."

"They should have you training with gloves on." Carter glared at Hunter.

I picked up the plate and moved it over to the cart we used to carry food into the dining room. "I was wearing gloves, but it doesn't matter."

"Of course it matters," Carter said. "And you." He pointed at Hunter with his kitchen weapon. "You should know better."

"I plan on fighting the Lycans using my powers. I won't be wearing gloves."

Hunter moved over to me and took one of the plates from my hands. "It does matter, Zee. You're training; you're learning."

"And I should be learning how to do all this without protection."

"Who's not using protection?" Javion and Knox joined us in the kitchen. They looked at the three of us.

"You should make sure Zeraora is wearing the correct protective equipment when training," Carter told him.

Javion just nodded. He walked over to the cart and placed his hands on the handle. "I'm starving. Let's eat."

"I haven't put your blood on there yet," I told him before he could walk off. What did he intend on eating?

"This is me changing the subject, Little Sparkler, so that we don't have to eat our dinner in an atmosphere again." Javion walked off, disappearing into the dining room.

Slowly, the rest of us followed him. Although the meatloaf was delicious, we ate in silence. It wasn't until Carter had nearly finished his meal, that Knox looked at him.

"We're going into the garden to see if we can help Zera get her powers back. You should come with us."

Carter turned his attention to me, meeting my eyes with his own. "Of course, I will be there."

The way he said it made it seem like I didn't think he would be there. But why wouldn't he be?

After cleaning up, Carter helped me put on my coat, and then the five of us went outside. Knox led us away from the house but kept us within the walls of the castle grounds.

I hadn't been with the Lycans for that long, but before they took me, there was snow on the ground. It was gone now, but the temperature was still cold outside.

"What's the master plan?" Javion asked Knox.

"I wanted to make sure we were far enough away from the house that Zera wasn't going to use any electricity. Out here, she will either have to draw it from us, or from whatever's around us."

I looked around. The grounds to the castle were huge, and the building itself was now far enough away that there was very little light where we were. "How do I do that?"

Knox scratched at his temple before shrugging. "I guess, you should imagine we're like the power sockets.

Find our energy?"

"And here's me thinking we were all out here to stand in a circle and hold hands." Javion arched an eyebrow.

"There's still time for that," Knox told him before turning back to me. "Give it a go."

When I had had my powers, I never knew I could sense the electricity in the castle. Once, after Javion yelled at me for shorting out the power again, Hunter tried to explain how electricity worked: the wires running through the house to every appliance to power it. There was a humming in the background that I assumed was normal.

Since having escaped from the Lycans, and my powers gone, at some point, I noticed that the thrum was gone. It was only when Dean told me to take the power from the socket that I had figured out what that was.

Out here, there was nothing.

Trees and plants—which the cold wind was blowing through. Some form of animals, insects maybe? If I listened hard enough, in the distance, I could hear the river.

But I couldn't hear that thrum.

"It's okay," Carter said, gently. "There's no rush,

and we can keep coming out here every night for as long as we need to."

Hunter was standing opposite me. I locked my gaze on him, but I wasn't really looking *at* him. Instead, I was trying to see the electricity that was supposed to be inside of him. I could barely see him in the darkness, so I didn't really expect to see any electricity.

Eventually, I blinked, bringing him back into focus. "I can't see it."

"Technically, you can't see electricity. It's like gravity..." Javion shook his head. "You can't see electricity. When you see things like lightning and plasma, it's the electricity... How do I put this simply? It's the electricity reacting with the air."

"But I could hold it. I could throw it to people." I held my hand up, but there was no electricity there.

Javion moved from around the other side of Knox and stood in front of me. Gently, he took my hand in his. They were very cold. "I think the point that fae was trying to make, is that electricity is all around you, even though you can't see it. The same applies here. Right now, you're trying to make something visible, when really, you should just be trying to feel it. Close your eyes."

Still holding onto Javion's hand, I closed my eyes.

My own hands were getting cold, but I didn't let go. Instead, I tried to feel the electricity.

And then I did.

I opened my eyes, pulled one of my hands free, and held it out, reaching for whoever was closer.

Carter took hold of it.

Just like with Javion, I could feel the electricity.

"That's a good sign," Hunter said.

Smiling, I nodded. "I can feel it."

"Good." Knox took a step closer. "Okay, now let go of their hands. Remember how that feels, and then try to find it again."

The warm hand and cold hand let go of mine, and instantly, the thrum was gone.

Javion stepped back to where he stood previously.

This time, I closed my eyes.

Nothing.

No matter how hard I tried to feel a buzz of any kind, I couldn't.

Frustrated, I opened my eyes and stomped my foot. "It's not working."

"It's okay. You don't need to get upset about it," Carter told me.

That was easy for him to say. He was a gargoyle. I hated these powers when the Lycans were using me for them. I couldn't begin to count how many hours I spent wishing they would disappear. Now they were gone.

But I needed them to destroy the Lycans.

"Why don't we head back to the house? It's late, and you spent all day fighting. Get some sleep, and tomorrow, we can try again," Hunter suggested.

"No. I want to try again now."

"Aren't you tired?" Carter asked. "Cold?"

I was both, but I still wasn't ready to give up.

"I'll stay with her." Javion's offer surprised us all. When we looked at him, he just shrugged. "I don't need to sleep."

Carter sighed, rubbing his jaw. "No. It's okay. If Zera wants to do this, let's do this."

Ignoring the cold wind that had picked up, I closed my eyes. Once again, I tried to find that faint thrum of energy.

And once again, nothing

After a while, I admitted defeat.

"Honestly, it's okay," Hunter told me as we walked back to the castle.

It wasn't though.

It was the middle of the night, and I was thirsty. I was also exhausted. Every day had been the same: fight, eat, attempt to find electricity from anywhere other than a power socket, and sleep.

Only tonight, I couldn't sleep, so I went down to the kitchen to get a drink. Wearing one of Hunter's hoodies I had taken, I brought my legs up underneath it, as I sat at the kitchen table, drinking a glass of Coke.

Every time I failed, one of them would tell me it was okay, and I would get it next time. But how many times would it take? I held my hand out and pulled electricity from the nearest power socket. The little bolts of lightning wove around my fingers before I dismissed them.

In the house, it was simple. There were always power sockets nearby, and I could summon the electricity quickly and easily. But the moment I was no longer near the castle, nothing.

Dean seemed to have some answers. Maybe I could get one of the guys to drive me back to talk to him again?

As I sipped on my drink, the rain started. It was only gentle at first as it hit the window, but my body froze anyway. It hadn't rained since we got back to the castle.

My hands started shaking, and my drink spilled onto the hoodie. As I tried to set the glass down on the table, my unsteady hand knocked it over. I stared as the dark liquid as it spread over the table and started dripping onto the floor.

This was rain. Nobody should be scared of rain.

Although my heart was pounding in my chest, and my legs didn't want to work, I forced myself to walk towards the door.

What good was getting my powers back if I was going to freeze up like this every time it rained?

"Zera, what are you doing?" Javion was by my side, grabbing my arm. "Where the fuck do you think you're going?"

My body was trembling, but his grip on my arm was strangely soothing. I looked up at him. "It's raining."

"Yeah, I can see that. The question is, why are you, the person scared of the rain, trying to go out in it?" He started pulling me away from the door.

The action snapped me out of the fear that had locked me in place, as I angrily jerked my arm back. "I can't... I need to go out there."

"No, you don't. What the hell is out there?"

"Rain."

Javion glanced at the door and then back at me;

understanding crossed his expression. "You're trying to get over your fear?" he asked. "You're not going to get over it just like that. You pretty much shut down at the sound of rain. If you go out in that, you're not going to get very far. And why the hell would you go out by yourself?"

"I have to get over it. The last time—"

"Fuck's sake, Sparkler. We've been over this. We were taken because the Lycans came here and attacked. *They* are the reason we were taken, not you."

"I know that. But I also know if I was able to attack them, they wouldn't have. They would be dead."

Wearily, Javion rubbed his face and then sighed. "Fine. But we go out together."

"You don't need to be there with me."

Javion let out a dry laugh. "Do you really think any of us would just let you go out there and do that alone?"

I stared up at him, tilting my head as I studied his face. "Not the others." Everyone else seemed to think I wasn't capable of going anywhere alone.

Folding his arms, Javion rubbed a fang with his tongue. Finally, he smacked his lips. "We didn't get off to the best start, I understand that. But I thought you knew that I don't hate you."

"Yes."

"Why would you say that the others would stop you from going outside, whereas I would let you go out and get hurt?"

"I wouldn't get hurt. And you would let me out because you don't treat me like..." I frowned, trying to think of the word.

Javion arched an eyebrow. "A helpless little female?"

"You're the only one who ever said I was dangerous."

Another dry chuckle came from Javion. "Dangerous in more ways than I first realized, Little Sparkler." He sucked in a deep breath and looked at the door. "Okay. If this is something you want to do, we're doing it together."

He held his hand out to me.

I took his hand, and then took a step towards the door, but Javion didn't move with me.

I looked up at him. "What?"

"Just because you can do things by yourself, doesn't mean you have to."

Thirty Eight

Zera

The back door had a little roof over it. We'd been standing under it, watching the rain for ages. The sound of water splashing in the puddles in front of me had my whole body trembling.

"Maybe for tonight, we should just stay here and watch the rain?" Javion suggested.

I wanted to tell him that it was okay, that I could handle it. But the words wouldn't come. I couldn't even look at him. There was this tightness in my chest still; my breathing was fast and shallow, and I didn't feel like I could fill my lungs.

Javion stepped in front of me, blocking the view of the rain.

I managed to flick my gaze up to look at his silver eyes, but I could still hear the rain.

"I think that's enough for tonight, Little Sparkler. It's spring, which means it will rain a lot more than this. We do this little and often, and it'll get easier each time."

Although I wanted to nod my head and follow him, I suddenly couldn't. My breathing was getting faster. When I didn't move, he scooped me up into his arms and carried me inside. Instead of setting me down in the kitchen, he carried me through the house. I wasn't sure what time it was, but it was dark, and the house was silent.

He kept walking, heading down to the basement to his and Knox's room instead of mine upstairs. There was a lamp on. It was the first light I'd seen for hours, and I blinked as Javion set me down in the middle of the bed

"Jay, wha—? What happened to Zera?" Knox's voice was sleepy. Almost as soon as I was on the bed, he was kneeling beside me, his hands running over my body. "What happened? Why is she shaking? What's wrong with her?"

As I curled into Knox, Javion sat down on the bed beside me. "We were outside."

Knox frowned as he looked up at the ceiling. "Is it raining? Why were you outside? "Why on earth would you go outside by yourself, in the rain, and at this time of night? Were you planning on leaving again?"

"She wants to get over her fear of the rain," Javion answered for me.

"And you fucking entertained that? Are you insane? Look at the state of her— she's shaking, and that's not just because she's fucking freezing." Knox moved his face in front of mine. Instead of asking another question, he shook his head and took one of my hands in each of his. "Look at me Zera. Look at me, and let's focus on your breathing. In." He sucked in a deep, obvious breath. "And out." And then he breathed out. "You need to do this with me. Ready?"

That was easy for him to say. Even though I was breathing quickly, I couldn't feel the air getting into my lungs.

"Come on." He inhaled another deep breath.

I opened my mouth and took a breath. It was more like a gasp than a deep breath, but it had Knox nodding with approval. Almost as quickly, I exhaled.

"That's my good girl. Try to breathe with me."

At first, most of my breaths still gasped, but eventually, my breathing slowed enough to match Knox. It was only then, as the shaking subsided, that I realized Javion had been rubbing my back.

"How are you feeling?" Knox asked

I wasn't sure how to answer that.

"What were you thinking, going outside? It was raining."

"I can't let rain stop me," I told them.

"You are practically incapacitated by the rain, and that's when you're not even outside in it." Knox looked at me in disbelief. "Why on earth did you think you could possibly take a walk in the rain?"

"Knoxlyn, she didn't go in the rain. We just stood under the back porch and watched it for a bit. She wasn't alone, either. I was with her the entire time."

With a long sigh, Knox pulled me to him, holding me against his chest. "Zera, you're not going to be able to make it disappear, just like that. The way you react to it… It's a lot. So, it's going to take time."

I pushed back against Knox's chest, so I could look him in the face. "Then I should start now."

"It's not…" Knox shook his head and then glared

at Javion.

Javion rolled his eyes. "How else do you propose we work on her phobia? We can't exactly take her to a hypnotist. A little bit at a time." He shrugged. "She wanted to do it. I didn't force her."

"There has got to be a better way to do this," Knox muttered.

"Does it hurt?" Javion asked.

I looked at him. "Does what hurt?"

"All of it. I watched the Lycans pouring water over you, and I heard your screams. Does being in the rain hurt you."

Did it? I thought about when the Lycans attacked us, and it made me shudder.

"Whether it hurts her or not, she shouldn't be doing it alone," Knox told Javion.

"The point I'm trying to make, is that when the Lycans had her, she was in pain, so why would she try to do it herself without them? I don't think the rain hurts. I think the memory of what those fuckers did to her—that's what hurts." Javion sat down beside me and stared into my eyes. "But if you've got a thing for pain, I can help out with that. Only, I can make it pleasurable."

"Now? Really? You have to be fucking kidding

me?" Knox rolled his eyes and threw a pillow at Javion's face. "Fuck's sake, Jay."

Javion brushed the pillow to the side. "I'm just trying to figure out if this fae has masochistic tendencies. If she has, it doesn't matter what you tell her."

"What's masochistic tendencies mean?"

"Someone who gets off on pain," Javion told me. "Someone who enjoys it, *a lot*."

"Why would someone enjoy pain?" I asked.

Javion just smirked.

Knox rubbed at his temple. "Zera, we will work with you and your fear of falling water. There are ways to deal with this, without throwing yourself headfirst into the deep end."

"The deep end of what?" I frowned, confused.

"A swimming pool. And I mean that metaphorically—there isn't a real pool. When you're learning to swim, you start at the shallow end of the pool, where your feet can touch the floor. It's not something we can cure overnight. It's going to take time and patience."

"Do I have the right twin in bed with me? Because you're sounding an awful lot like Hunter at the moment?" Javion narrowed his eyes and then poked

Knox's bare shoulder. "And as I pointed out, she wasn't alone, and she didn't even go in the rain. I know she's been through a lot, and that she's far from being okay, but she is stronger than you think she is."

I turned to Javion, still confused by the first part of what he said. "That's Knox, not Hunter. Can't you tell?" Knox was Javion's betrothed.

Javion shrugged. "He better be, otherwise, he's in for a bit of a shock when I fuck him."

I looked between the two of them, my body going warm, and for some reason, my mouth was getting dry. I was trying to imagine that.

"He was joking," Knox said, dryly.

"Am I?" Javion tilted his head, slowly rubbing his tongue over his fang.

With no warning, he reached for Knox, grabbed him under the knees, and then jerked him closer.

"Ja—" Knox's cry was cut off as Javion grabbed either side of his face and kissed him.

For a moment, Knox kissed him back, and then he pushed him away. "I'm not a fucking fire hydrant."

"Oh no, I'm not staking a claim. Look at her."

Knox turned his head, looking at me, and then arched an eyebrow. "Zera?"

Javion gave me a sly grin. "Turned on, aren't you?

Your pussy is getting wet, isn't it?"

"Yes."

"She's not the only one getting turned on." He turned and stared at Knox before dropping his gaze to his boyfriend's crotch. Knox had been sleeping in boxers, and we could both see him going hard.

With his gaze locked onto me, Javion reached for Knox's leg, slid his hand down his thigh and then up to the waistband before dipping his hands into Knox's boxers. Slowly, he started moving his hand up and down.

Although Javion was staring at me, my attention was fixed on his hand. Javion had been right: I was getting wet. I was also getting uncomfortably warm in this hoodie.

Finally, Javion turned back to Knox, and without stopping his stroking, used his other hand to grab the back of Knox's head. Javion shifted his weight, and then aggressively kissed Knox.

Almost instantly, Knox moaned as his hands went under Javion's shirt. At the same time, I watched as Javion's tongue entered Knox's mouth.

This wasn't the first time I'd seen them kiss each other, but my body had never felt this hot before. There was also an ache between my legs.

Javion's hand started moving faster, and Knox brought his head back and gasped.

"Fuck, Jay." This time, Knox reached for the bottom of Javion's T-shirt and then pulled it upwards and over his head. It was quickly tossed to the side, and Knox's hands were back on Javion's chest.

A growl came from Javion, and then he leaned forward to sink his teeth into Knox's neck.

"Holy fuck!" Knox's eyes seemed to roll into the back of his head.

Javion pulled back and looked at me. A drop of Knox's blood rolled down his chin. "Go into that drawer." He pointed to the bedside table. "Get me one of the tubes."

I didn't move, not wanting to take my eyes off what was happening in front of me.

"Do it, and we will both fuck you hard afterwards. We'll have you screaming for the right reasons."

Rolling onto my side, I scrambled over to the bedside table and pulled the drawer open. Inside, were various tubes, and…

"Why do you have cocks in your drawer?"

As I glanced back, Knox collapsed backwards onto the bed, covering his mouth with his hand, trying to fight back his laughter.

In the short amount of time it took me to go to the drawer, Knox was no longer wearing underwear, and Javion was in the process of pulling his sweatpants off. He stared at me, smirking.

"You can find out about those another night. For tonight, the only cocks you need to worry about are mine and Knox's. Right now, I'm hard and want to fuck Knox, so pass me the lube."

Although I was curious about the strange cocks in the drawer, I grabbed one of the tubes and threw it at Javion.

He caught it and quickly unscrewed the top, squirting a watery looking… I wasn't quite sure what it was, but he squeezed it into his hand and then started rubbing it over his own hard cock.

Without bothering to wipe what was left on his hands away, he grabbed Knox's hip and then flipped onto his front. "Show her how good this feels," he told Knox as Javion lined his cock up with Knox's ass. Then he pushed himself in.

Knox's hands fisted the bed covers. "Fuck, Jay."

My lips parted as I watched Javion moving in and out, with Knox moaning beneath him. The ache between my legs grew, and I rubbed them together to try to ease it.

A bead of sweat ran down from behind my ear, down my neck, and then under my hoodie. I'd gone from being too cold to being too hot.

And I didn't even care.

I couldn't tear my eyes away from the two men in front of me. Knox's writhing and his moans, Javion's grunts, the sound of skin against skin…

Then Javion's grip tightened, and he slowed, letting out a cry of pleasure. He pulled himself out and then slumped forward, almost entirely lying on top of Knox. Beneath him, Knox was still clutching the bed sheets, breathing heavily, with his eyes closed.

Javion kissed the back of Knox's shoulder, then with one hand, he pushed himself up, and with the other, he reached for Knox's chin, grabbed it and turned it to face him.

"Good boy." He kissed Knox, hungrily.

Thirty Nine

Zera

J avion broke the kiss, leaned forward, and then rested his full weight onto Knox. "How about we both let Zera feel this good?"

With hooded eyes, Knox redirected his gaze towards me. "Does Zera want both—"

"Yes."

Javion smirked. "You heard the woman." He lowered his mouth closer to Knox's ear. "Then let's get her ready—for the both of us." With his gaze still locked onto mine, Javion pushed back off of Knox. "Don't go anywhere."

As Javion climbed off the bed and disappeared into the bathroom, Knox rolled onto his side and then brought his arm under his head and looked over at me. "You sure? You don't have to do this because of me."

"I'm not," I said, quickly.

Knox pushed himself up to a sitting position. "What do you want, Zera?"

At that moment, still naked, Javion walked back into the room and joined us on the bed. He looked between the two of us and arched an eyebrow. "Are we having second thoughts here?"

I shook my head.

"Good." Javion gave Knox a pointed look. "I'm all cleaned up and ready to go again. How about we show this little fae how good it can be with the two of us?"

With a single look at me, Knox moved closer. As I glanced between two of them, they both grabbed the bottom of my hoodie and tugged it up over my head. Underneath, I was only wearing a short, silken nightdress.

Knox leaned forward, bringing a hand up to cup my cheek and stretched his fingers into my hair. He pulled me closer then kissed me, his tongue, plunging straight into my mouth.

He tasted so good. Knox also had a pierced tongue and the feel of the metal rubbing over me had me moaning into his hot mouth.

I placed my hands on his chest, his skin feeling warm and slightly damp to the touch as I ran my fingers over him, taking my time feeling the ridges of his scars. Knox hissed into my mouth, tightening his grip on the back of my head.

And then another hand covered the back of mine. Cold to the touch, I knew it was Javion. He guided my hand further down, until we both wrapped around Knox's cock.

As we started stroking Knox's cock, Javion reached for my other hand and brought it to his. Just like his hand, his cock was cool to the touch. He also had bars of metal running through it, which felt strange, yet oddly pleasant in my hand.

Javion leaned right into my ear. "I want you to make it hard. Let me drink from you."

Knox pulled back and glanced at Javion. "Jay," His tone sent a warning.

Breathing heavily from Knox's kiss, I looked at Javion. "It won't hurt?"

"Not only will it not hurt, but I will make you come

like you've never come before."

I tightened my hands around both him and Knox as my body went hot.

With a smirk, Javion looked at Knox, who nodded, then Javion pulled my mouth to his. He ran his hand down my neck and cupped my breast. He started squeezing it, bring his thumb over my nipple, at the same speed as his tongue.

I arched my back, moaning in his mouth.

Javion's cold hand went back to mine, moving it up and down his cock once again. As I met my other hand over Knox's cock, Javion brushed my hair from my shoulder.

He left kisses along my shoulder to the well of my collarbone. There was a brief moment of hurt as his teeth pierced my skin, but just as quickly as I felt pain, it was forgotten as the most incredible sensation spread through my body.

Javion's cock got harder in my hand, almost instantly. The pressure at my neck increased, and as though Javion and Knox were sharing the same mind, Knox's kisses became fiercer.

Like he promised, the orgasm surging through me was like nothing I'd felt before. If Knox's tongue hadn't been so deep in my mouth, I would have screamed from the sheer pleasure.

The blissful feeling didn't seem to be ending, and I felt like I barely had any control over my body, until finally, Javion pulled away. Moments later, Knox stopped kissing me.

I fell back against the bed, gasping for air.

Knox and Javion started muttering something to each other, but I didn't quite catch it. As I lay there, trying to catch my breath, a hand slid between my legs.

"You're so wet," I heard Knox say as he rubbed against me. "You think you can take us both?"

"She can." Javion answered as I lifted my head to look at both of them.

"At the same time?" I asked.

"You're not going to know anything like it." Knox promised.

My heart was still racing, but it was joined by something that had my body tingling in anticipation. Unable to say anything more, I just nodded.

The wicked smirk reappeared on Javion's face, but instead of reaching for me, he grabbed Knox, jerking him closer. With a force that made me gasp, Javion kissed Knox. Knox kissed back, just as hard.

Then, as quickly as it happened, Javion pulled away. It was the vampire who moved towards me first, bringing his body over mine. He didn't touch me; instead, his silver eyes stared down at me.

"The moment anything hurts, you tell me."

He waited for me to nod, and then he lowered his head, claiming my mouth. Although his kiss was fierce, like Knox, his mouth was soft. It was also strangely cool, like the rest of him.

Instinctively, I pushed up my arm and Knox was there, threading his warm fingers through mine.

As Javion pulled back and briefly broke the kiss so he could shift his weight, I glanced over at Knox, finding him stroking himself.

Heat seared through me, and it flared hotter as Javion's hand slipped down between my legs.

"My good Little Sparkler soaking wet for me." He rubbed his fingers over my clit, making me gasp. "I want your pussy wrapped around my dick."

"So do I," I told him as I reached down for his cock with my free hand. My fingertips ran along his shaft, and I felt the metal that pierced it. "Will that hurt?"

Javion smirked. "Quite the opposite. You're going to be begging the others to get their dicks pierced too."

"You'll love it." Knox promised me.

Batting my hand away, Javion then grabbed his cock, and lined it up with my entrance before pushing it in slightly. Then, with his gaze locked onto mine, Javion pushed in.

My eyes rolled back in my head. I had never felt anything like it. Just like every other part of his body, Javion's cock was still cool, making me feel even hotter. And I felt every one of his piercings as he slid into me. Deeper and deeper, he pushed, filling me.

"How's that feel?"

When I opened my eyes, Javion's face was above mine, his silver eyes looked like liquid. He didn't move.

"I want more."

Javion smirked. Slowly, he pulled himself out, and once again, I felt each of those pieces of metal. My head was spinning, and my body was tingling. And then, with no warning, Javion thrust harder into me. My body actually moved back over the bed, but as the pleasure mixed with the pain, I let out a loud cry.

Javion grabbed me by the hips.

Over and over, he thrust into me, and each time, it felt like he was somehow going deeper. I could barely breathe, distracted with the whimpers I made with each thrust. I wasn't sure if it was me or Knox, who was holding more tightly to the other.

"Javion, I... I..." My free hand grabbed the bedsheet.

His hands went lower, grabbing my ass and raising me slightly. He thrust in again, this time, from a slightly different angle. Finally, Javion started to slow, coming to a complete stop, but he didn't remove himself from inside me.

"Oh, we're not done yet, my Little Sparkler."

Although my entire body was tingling, I opened my eyes just in time for him to flip us both over. He immediately sank deeper inside me, and my arms were too jellylike to even keep myself upright.

Somewhere in that movement, I let go of Knox's hand, but he was able to grab my waist to keep me from falling. His bare chest pressed up against my back, then he pressed kisses along my shoulder blade.

"I'm going to need you to bend forward."

With help from both Knox and Javion, I leaned forward, unable to stop the moan of pleasure as Javion shifted inside me. "What are you doing?"

"We're both going to fuck you," Javion told me. His hands went to the bottom of my nightdress, and he quickly pulled it off over my head. The only thing I was left wearing were my wrist guards. "Now, come here. Knox is lubing his cock up for you and I want to make sure you've got all the endorphins you need inside you."

Considering I was very firmly impaled in place, I

wasn't sure how they were going to accomplish that. Then Javion's hands went straight to my breasts, rubbing my nipples, and twisting them as he pulled me towards him.

There was pain, but it also had me moaning in pleasure.

Javion released one of my nipples, but only so he could grab my breast and pull it towards his mouth. He latched over my nipple and ran his tongue around the tip, before sinking his teeth in, at the same time, twisting the other nipple.

In an instant, he had my body feeling like it did just before an orgasm. I arched my back, pressing my breast into his mouth, wanting more.

And then I felt Knox. His hands spread my ass cheeks, and he slowly started pushing his cock into me.

This time, there was pain as my body resisted, despite the slipperiness of his cock. But as I started to cry out, Javion sucked harder. Like ointment being rubbed into a wound, the pain eased.

"Fuck, that's a good girl." Knox's voice sounded strained. "Relax. Take it all, good, good girl."

He continued to push himself in, slowly. With Javion continuing to drink my blood, and his cock seeming to pulse inside of me, the pain was starting to mix with pleasure again.

Finally, it felt like Knox was as deep inside of me as Javion. The two of them stilled, and Javion stopped feeding and leaned back. His hand returned to the breast that he had been biting, and he continued to pinch and pull.

"How does my Little Sparkler feel?"

My blood was dribbling down the side of Javion's chin.

"Full. I can feel you both."

"Fuck me, so can I," Knox said, his voice, still strained. "I don't give a fuck about the others getting piercings, I think you should get the underside of your dick pierced too, because fuck me, I think I could feel it too."

"Give me your wrist, Knoxlyn."

Reaching around me, Knox held out an arm.

Javion grabbed it and jerked it to his mouth, the action, sandwiching us together. My moan was joined with Knox's as Javion bit down on Knox's wrist.

"Fuck, Javion! You're going to make me come already."

Smirking, Javion released Knox. "You two taste like a whiskey sour."

Knox snatched his hand back. "You fucker, you're

going to make me come before Zera does."

Javion bucked his hips, and my fingers curled, scratching his chest. "Let's see about that."

Muttering curses in my ear, Knox started moving, pulling himself in and out of me as he did, which set my body working up against Javion. A moment of pain quickly followed with a moment of pleasure. Digging my fingers into Javion's chest, I closed my eyes.

One of Knox's hand's left my hip, sliding around my body, down to my clit. He applied pressure, rubbing at the same speed he was thrusting into me.

My breath was coming out in sharp gasps. Gasps combined with groans. Both men were deep inside me and I had never felt this sensation before. There was still a hint of pain but it was quickly being dulled. I could feel my orgasm building, like it was calling for my body's release.

"I want to come. Let me come," I begged.

"You like this?" Knox asked, grunting in my ear. "You want to come?"

"Yes. Please, yes."

The hands on my breasts hadn't stopped teasing my nipples, and then suddenly, there was a sharp tweak, and Javion jerked beneath me. "Fuck."

I slammed down onto him, crying out as my body

was forced to take him—and Knox—deeper. I clenched, and then Knox seemed to mimic Javion's action.

This time, there was a sharp pain. But as much as it hurt, it felt good. "Oh, yes!"

As I cried out again, Javion grabbed my wrist. Before he could bite down, I was already throwing my head back and enjoying the orgasm as it spread through my body.

My thoughts left me, and although I was ready to collapse, Javion kept me upright. As I struggled to catch my breath, I closed my eyes.

That's when I felt it.

The thrum.

But it wasn't coming from me.

I opened my eyes, but what I saw in front of me wasn't Javion. Well, it was, but it wasn't. It was the outline of Javion, only he was made of tiny lightning bolts—more than I could ever count.

When I gasped, he tilted his head.

"Yes, I have always been this handsome."

"You're electricity."

Knox pulled out of me. Only once he rolled to the side, Javion slowly eased himself out too, laying me down on the bed between the two of them.

I couldn't stop looking between them. It was like their bodies were nothing but swirling balls of electricity, and yet I could work out their muscles and the features on their faces.

"What do you see, Zera?" Knox asked.

"Electricity." I held out my hand and watched as an arc of electricity jumped from them and into my palm.

"Well, fuck," Knox muttered.

"Can you see it too?"

"Only what's in your hand," Javion replied.

The longer I looked at him, the more his strange electrical outline faded and returned back to normal. I turned my attention to my palm, and I could still see the current until I closed my fingers. The electricity disappeared. Opening my palm again, I focused on trying to bring the electricity back, trying to pull it from Knox and Javion instead of the electrical things in their bedroom.

A ball of electricity reappeared in my hand.

"Where did that come from?" Knox asked.

Letting the electricity vanish, I turned to him. "You two."

With a grin, Knox grabbed my cheeks and kissed me. "That's my clever girl."

We lay there, trying to catch our breath, or at least, Knox and I did. While we did, I kept opening and closing my hand, summoning the electricity.

It came every time.

Eventually, Javion rolled onto his side and leaned over to kiss me, and then stretched over to kiss Knox.

"How are you feeling?" Javion asked.

Leaning back into Knox, I wiggled my toes. "Sore, but good. We should do that again, but not right now."

Behind me, Knox chuckled, his vibrating chest, rubbing against my back. "Agreed."

"You and Knox should go get a bath together, and cleanup. You'll feel better after that, and you both need to get rid of all the lube that Knox's cock is coated in."

I shook my head. "I don't want to move."

"Tough luck." Knox shifted and then scooped me up into his arms. He slid off the bed and carried me into his bathroom. Keeping me in his arms, he leaned over and turned on the faucet, running water into the bathtub. When the tub was only half full, Knox eased us both into it.

Relaxing into Knox, I let out a sigh. I didn't think the water would feel so good.

We stayed like that for a while before Knox finally spoke. "Did you mean what you said?"

"What did I say?"

"About wanting to do it again?"

Frowning, I looked over my shoulder at him. "Why wouldn't I mean it?"

"No, I suppose that's not what I mean. What I mean is, how do you feel about Javion?"

"He is very…"

"Cold?"

I nodded. "He is. Is that because he's dead? At first, his cock felt very strange, but I enjoyed that cold."

From behind me, Knox laughed, making me bounce against him. "Yes, I guess he is. But I meant his personality."

"Personality can be cold?"

"That he can sometimes seem hard to get to know. That it's hard to read how he's feeling. He can be unemotional." Knox ran his hand up and down my arm.

Thinking about it, I shook my head. "No, not really."

"Not so long ago, you didn't like him."

"Yes. But I don't not like him now. He wanted to protect you. I know Carter thinks he's the reason that the vampires came here, and the Lycans, but I don't think that's his fault. He was trying to help me. And he is the only person who really thinks that I'm dangerous.

He was right about that."

"I think you're right," Knox murmured, hugging me to him.

Starting to feel sleepy, I eased myself lower into the warm water. "Javion belongs with us. I claim him too."

Forty

Hunter

I woke to the sound of rain falling against the window, and I couldn't stop my sigh. Even though time had passed, Zera was still no better with rain. She would want to train but be unable to and get frustrated.

If she was anybody else, I'd take her to some kind of therapist. What she'd been through was a lot, and it's no surprise she had all kinds of trauma as a result. It wasn't her fault.

More than anything, I wanted to take that away from her, wave a magic wand, and have it gone. But even the witches didn't have a spell for that.

Zera needed to work through it, and even then, there's a chance she'll never get past it. But of course, being Zera, she won't accept that.

Phone in hand, I did a quick internet search, trying to find suggestions on how to tackle this. It wasn't the first time I searched this, and none of the results had changed. Almost all of them said professional help is required.

Did I have enough time to get a psychology degree?

After another unhelpful search, I grabbed a quick shower and dressed before heading downstairs. DB was already up, as usual, cooking breakfast. He glanced over as I walked in.

"It's raining," I said, stating the obvious.

DB nodded. "Forecast says it's here for the rest of the week."

Rubbing the back of my neck, I leaned against the kitchen island, watching DB cook. Today he was making something Zera hadn't tried before—breakfast burritos—probably in attempt to distract her from the rain with food.

"We are going to have to do something about it."

"We are," DB said, knowing exactly what I was talking about. "Any suggestions?"

"The best I can find, is trying to desensitize her. We take it slow, and it takes as long as it takes." I sighed. "And we try to get her to accept that this is a fear she might never be able to completely eliminate."

Nodding, DB pointed his spatula towards the dining room door. "Go draw the curtains and get some music on. This is almost ready, and I'm sure Zera will be down soon."

"Up. I checked in on her. She wasn't in her room, which means she's down with Knox."

After tending to the dining room, I turned the music on just as Zera walked into the dining room, holding Knox's hand. Although she looked uncomfortable, there was also something different about her. If I didn't know any better, she seemed excited. Which of course made no sense since it was raining.

"DB has a new breakfast treat for you today," I told her over the music.

Zera took the seat furthest from the window and sat down, then let out a subtle wince.

"Do you need me to turn the music up more?" I asked.

She shook her head.

DB walked into the room pushing a cart with all the breakfast food on it. "Good morning, Blue Eyes," he said, cheerfully. "I have breakfast burritos for you this morning."

"I can get electricity from you." She held up a hand, and a glowing plasma ball hovered above it. "And I had sex with Knox and Javion. It was good, and I want to do it again. I'm claiming Javion as my mate."

All I could do was stand there, blinking at her. When I glanced over at DB, I found the same applied to him.

Knox's eyes went wide, looking between the three of us. Surprised that he wasn't, I could tell he was trying not to laugh.

"Okay," was all I could manage to say. I didn't have any objection, and if I was honest, I saw that one coming. Maybe not the threesome... No, maybe I saw that, too... I was just more shocked at Zera's declaration, even though I probably shouldn't be.

Zera looked at DB. Her bright, blue eyes remained unwavering. "You don't want this?"

"I'd be lying if I said I hadn't expected this. Zera, I love you, and I want you to be happy—gods above, you deserve it—and if Javion is part of what makes you happy, then he's part of this relationship too."

"Then why do you look…?" Zera tilted her head.

DB scrubbed his face with his hand.

"Speechless." He lowered his hand. "That was at you announcing that you, Knox, and Javion just had sex. It's not something I expected while eating breakfast."

"But we're not eating." With a frown, Zera pointed at the still full cart. "You haven't served it yet."

That was enough for Knox to start snickering.

"How about we all sit down. I'll serve breakfast, and we can move on to discussing how you have your powers back?" DB suggested. "And you must be hungry?"

Zera nodded, hastily taking a seat. "I'm very hungry. Last night—"

"We don't need to know the details," DB said quickly. He picked up one of the plates, walked over and then set it in front of Zera.

Helping DB, I handed out some plates of food, and then took my seat beside Zera. That was the moment Javion walked into the room. When we all looked at him, apart from Zera, who was busy eating her breakfast burritos, he arched eyebrow.

"What did I miss?"

Knox didn't bother hiding his smile. "Everyone

knows what we did last night."

With a strut, Javion went over to the cart and picked up the glass of blood. "Ah." And then he took a long sip of his drink. "What did she ask you?"

"Ah i-unt asgs bow og earring."

DB, who was about to place a forkful of food into his mouth, lowered his fork. "Finish what's in your mouth first," he told Zera.

Zera hastily swallowed her food. "I haven't asked about the cock piercings."

Knox finally burst out laughing.

That was enough for DB to set his knife and fork onto the table. Templing his hands, he looked at Zera sternly.

"While I am absolutely fine with you calling Javion your mate, let me be clear: under no circumstance am I getting *any* part of my anatomy pierced."

"So," I said, happy to change the subject. "You got your powers back?"

Instantly, Zera's attention was diverted. She set down her cutlery and raised her hands. Electricity danced over the top of her palms, but she was frowning. "It's not the same as before. I have to think about it, and I have to pull it from something. This came from you."

When the fae warlock said Zera would be able to take energy from us, I expected to feel it, or at least be sensing it somehow. Either she wasn't pulling that much from me, or the act was unnoticeable.

"Are you saying the secret is sex?" DB asked.

"I considered that, but I don't think so," Javion said. "I mean, kind of, but not."

I stared at him and arched an eyebrow. "And that's a helpful analysis. No, but yes?"

Javion shrugged. He'd yet to sit down, but instead, went to go lean against a wall. "I don't think it's the act that did it, so much as Zera being able to relax and not think about it. That warlock said she was the block." He shrugged again. "Can't get more relaxed than with multiple orgasms."

DB slammed his hand against the table, making us all jump. "Was that necessary?"

A smirk grew on Javion's face. "The point is that the Little Sparkler has her powers back. It won't be long before she's back to just creating it and becoming that little nuke of mass destruction." For the first time, the look he gave Zera wasn't one of mistrust. If I wasn't mistaken, that was pride.

Zera's eyes were wide. "Now we can go destroy the Lycans."

"That won't be happening this week," DB told her, firmly.

The excitement disappeared from Zera's face in an instant. "But I'm ready."

"We currently have…" DB frowned. "Whatever this noise is—"

"Noise?" I asked, outraged. "This isn't noise. This is Lil Nas X." I was asked to put music on, and my choice was this. I already knew Zera liked it, otherwise I wouldn't have played it. And DB didn't like anything released after the 80s anyway.

DB pinched the bridge of his nose. "This *noise* is on to drown out the sound of the rain. Rain, which is going to be here for the rest of the week. I know you're eager, but you're not ready for that yet."

Zera glanced at the curtains, and then shuddered. Almost at once the familiar sight of tiny little electric bolts on her bare skin appeared.

Her powers really were back.

"I can't let it stop me."

"Hand," I muttered, before reaching over and taking one of Zera's hands. "We spoke about this before." I reminded her. "I know it's a very extreme reaction to rain, and when we consider what you've been through, it's completely understandable. But it's not something you can just get over."

"We want to help you, and we will work with you to see if we can change how it makes you feel," DB told her. "And before you ask, you can start today. I need you to understand that there's a strong possibility we're not going to be able to just 'fix it.' If we do, it's very, very likely, that it's going to take a long time."

"We don't have a long time. We need to destroy the Lycans and—"

"We can wait until it's not raining."

Somehow, hearing DB say that was more surprising than Zera telling us she'd had a threesome last night. Even though DB said we could all go after the Lycans together, I guess I was somehow expecting that when it came down to it, that wouldn't happen.

I clearly didn't give him enough credit.

"Really?" Zera asked.

DB nodded, then he turned his attention to Javion. "You said there were three locations for the Lycan's hotels. The closest, being in Texas." He waited until Javion nodded a confirmation. "While I wouldn't normally suggest we plan an attack based on the weather, I think, in this instance, we can be afforded the luxury. And being in Texas, we might have an advantage on that front."

"Really?" This time, it was Knox asking the question.

Rubbing his face, DB turned back to Zera. "You have to give us a month. We need to work on this fear and your fighting skills, and I want all of us to be as healed as we possibly can be. And we also need to research the hell out of this hotel, so we know exactly what we were up against. I don't want any of us getting hurt or worse. And I don't want you in a situation where you're trying to travel back in time to change things again. Understand?"

"Yes."

A rare smile appeared on Zera's face.

"And then we're going to destroy them."

Forty-One

Zera

It rained a lot.

Every day that it rained, one of my mates would sit with me underneath the porch by the back door, holding my hand as I tried to get used to the sound, the smell, and the falling water itself.

They all kept telling me it was okay when I stood there, frozen in place, struggling to breathe, struggling to keep my powers under control.

But it wasn't.

I was spending so much time in the rain, that things should have been improving better than they were. But I couldn't even manage to have the same reaction each time.

"I think that's enough for today," Hunter told me.

My teeth were chattering and my hands were shaking despite them being balled into fists. Little bolts of lightning were shooting off me, hitting a stone wall beside me. I shook my head. "Longer."

"You've been out here for a couple of hours now. That's enough. It's going to rain tomorrow, so we can try again then. Let's go inside, get something warm to eat, and then you can have your lesson with DB. I'm going to take your hand now." Hunter reached for my hand, also putting another on my shoulder, and then gently pulling me back inside.

I had to eat almost all of the sandwich Carter made before the shaking eased.

"You are glaring at that sandwich like it personally wronged you," Knox told me.

At the other side of the table, Carter set down a mug of coffee he'd been drinking. "I know you're frustrated, but we did say there was a strong possibility this wasn't going to be something we can fix easily. What we need is for you to not get upset about it. You might not see it, but you have made progress."

"No, I haven't," I muttered, darkly. Nothing had improved. On days it rained, I couldn't go to the gym to practice fighting. Instead, I had to spend time in the library learning how to read.

"You haven't noticed that there's no music on today," Carter said before smiling. "Not only that, but the curtains are open."

Looking out the window, the rain was hitting it heavily, making my mouth drop open as I shuddered. And it was just a shudder.

"That's amazing progress, Zee." Hunter gave me a proud smile.

"End of the month is coming up."

I looked at Carter. "We're going to destroy the Lycans?"

Carter nodded. "This afternoon, the five of us are going to sit down and start working out a plan. Javion said he has all the information we need."

Ready to start that, I shoved the sandwich into my mouth as quickly as I could. That earned me a look of disapproval from Carter, but I didn't care. It was really going to happen.

Impatient, I had to wait for Carter and Hunter to finish their meals, and then we had to clean up before I was finally allowed to go to the library.

"I don't think I've ever seen you look so excited to come in here," Knox said as I walked in.

I'd gotten used to being taught in the library with the curtains closed and the lights on. Today, they were still closed, but that was because Javion was in there. He was sitting at the head of the table behind his movable computer.

Javion looked up and pursed his lips. "You got those powers under control? As in, do I need to be worried about the laptop being nuked?"

"Javion." Carter used his warning voice.

It wasn't like I ever intended on destroying his computers, but there had been a couple power surges over the last few weeks while I was out in the rain.

"So, what's the plan?" Hunter asked.

"If the weatherman can be trusted, the sun is coming out next Tuesday, and it should be staying out. Even better, it should stretch all the way down to Texas, where there are a couple days when we might get afternoon showers," Javion said. "Which means, that's going to be our first opportunity."

"And what about nighttime?" I asked Javion. "You're a vampire. We can't do this during day."

Javion gave me a smile which showed off his fangs.

467

"Don't worry, my Little Sparkler, there won't be any rain at night either. We'll drive down there and attack at night. We have a better chance of a surprise attack with less people—humans or Lycans—being up and about."

"Humans?" I was confused.

Knox reach over and patted my thigh. "It's a hotel. It's Lycan owned and controlled, and it sounds like there's a high chance its clientele are also Lycans, but we can't ignore the possibility that there may also be humans staying there."

"Does it matter?" I asked.

"Zeraora, our issue is with the Lycans, nobody else. Humans don't know about supes. They wouldn't know who owned and ran that hotel, so we need to do everything we can to ensure there are no human casualties."

I was going to tell Carter that the humans still shouldn't have made a decision to stay there, but the look he was giving me made me keep my mouth closed.

"Maison des Loups is a hotel with fifty-two rooms. I tried to book a room, and they still have vacancies; however, we can assume that we're probably expecting at least fifty Lycans being there, if we try to account for staff and humans," Javion said before smirking.

"Let's create some fake accounts and book some

rooms. As many as we can. That way we can stop the hotel getting filled—"

"No," I said cutting Hunter off. "We want to get as many Lycans as possible."

"I know that," Hunter said. "But there are only five of us. That's ten Lycans each."

"Actually, this is something we should discuss." Javion sat back in his chair and rubbed his chin. "We have been after the Lycans for a very long time. We all have our own reasons, but ultimately, what we want is for them to be gone. We need to take out this hotel and stop them from getting any word to the other hotels. We still don't know how many there are, or where across the country they're hiding. No one does. And if we're not one hundred percent successful, this could be our only shot."

"There is nothing to discuss here," Carter said before I could agree. "Zeraora, I understand how you feel, I do, but we're not going in with the intent of destroying every single Lycan."

Slamming my hands on the table so hard that Javion's computer jumped, I stood up. "You said—"

"I know exactly what I said. And yes, we will stop the Lycans. But what you and Javion are essentially doing is condemning an entire race of supes. And that has never been our goal. We want to stop the Lycans who are kidnapping and torturing other supes, but this is a hotel. There could be families staying there. There could be Lycans who have no part of what's going on. Our goal shouldn't be to destroy all Lycans, but to stop those who are working to hunt and hurt others."

"Lycans are Lycans. They're all evil."

How could Carter possibly think otherwise? How could he change things now?

"The ones doing this, yes. There's no doubt about that." Carter got up and moved around to my side of the table before standing beside me. "But children? They're not evil. And what we've seen, the women aren't taking part either."

"It was a woman who hurt me." Pretty, with blonde corkscrew curls. "She made it so that if I didn't keep the blinds open, Javion would burn."

Carter slowly nodded. "Our goal should be to get information. We need to know where the Lycans are, what they're doing, and who is doing it. We go in, and we get access to their computers. If anyone tries to stop us, then we kill them. But if we come across anyone trying to escape, not trying to hurt us in the process, we let them go."

"I'm with DB on this. Sorry, Zee."

Hunter sounded apologetic, but he and Carter were still making me angry. "No. No, you can't change things. They took me, and they used me. They had me in chains in a glass prison, where they poured icy cold water over my head every single day, ignoring how much pain it caused me, just so they could steal my power. Until I got out of there, the *only* thing I wanted to do was die. And when I managed to escape, I saw that it wasn't just me in there. They were doing it to others too." I pointed at Javion and then at Knox. "And then they hurt my mates just to make sure they could keep stealing my power from me."

"Yeah, I've got to say, I agree with the Little Sparkler. Those fuckers aren't going to stop unless we end them first." Javion sat back in his chair and folded his arms.

"Of all the things for you two to be agreeing on, it's this?" Hunter arched an eyebrow.

"Even children?" Carter glared back at Javion. "During our entire time together, as we've been hunting the Lycans together, you have *never* been okay with us hurting children."

Javion remained silent.

"Jay, do you really want that? Really?" Knox's voice was quiet, but Javion's gaze flicked over to him. Knox

471

turned in his chair to face me. "All of us have been hurt by the Lycans, some more than others, but what you're suggesting is fucking genocide. We don't want to kill an entire race of supernaturals."

"They did it to me," I said.

Knox stood up and took my hand, shaking his head. "They killed your family, but Dean said the fae retreated to a different realm. That's not the same." As I glowered at him, he sighed. "Don't look at me like that," he said, gently. "They killed my family too."

"Would you have stopped me from destroying the place they held us?" I demanded.

"Fuck no," Knox said, quickly. "That was a facility where they were doing god-awful fucking shit. It was a place like that where they kept you most of your life. The Lycans in there are evil fuckers doing evil shit. They knew what they were doing. They know what they signed up for. As far as I'm fucking concerned, they got what was coming to them. But we're talking about going into a hotel, where families stay, and children might be sleeping, and annihilating everyone in it."

Javion let out a loud sigh before looking away. "Fuck." He sighed again before looking at me. "We can't do it. They're right."

Knox gently squeezed my hand. "You know this

too, right, Zera?"

"What happens when they grow up? We need to stop them, and we need to stop them all." I pulled my hands free. "If you don't want to do this, I can do this without you. I will stop them all and make sure they never hurt anyone again."

Why couldn't any of them see how dangerous the Lycans were? Why did they all look at me like that? All I wanted was make sure that these four, the ones who I needed in my life, were safe.

"Our plan…" Carter said firmly, but gently. "Has been and always will be to find the Lycans who are taking other supes and stop them."

"You know how vampires need to drink blood to survive?" Hunter asked me suddenly. I glanced at Javion and nodded. "Well, some of them are utter dicks about it. They make it hurt, and they can often kill their victims."

My hand went to my neck and rubbed at the spot a vampire had once bitten me. Those marks were no longer there, but I can still remember how much it hurt.

"But we know not all vampires are evil." He pointed at Javion. "What if someone who had been hurt by a vampire decided they were going to kill all the vampires? That would include Javion."

"I would destroy them before they came close," I said with conviction. "I would destroy anyone who tried to hurt any of you."

"To them? All vampires are evil."

"No, they're not. Javion is not evil."

Hunter held his hands up. "I know that. But if Javion isn't evil, do think it's possible there are some Lycans that aren't evil?"

I thought it over. Maybe Hunter was right, but... "What happens if they grow up and become evil?"

"Then once they do, we get to go and kill them too," Javion said, a small smile on his face.

"We just want to give them the chance to not do evil first," Carter told me.

Although I was sure the best choice was to stop them all *before* they could do any evil, if we were allowed to go after them in the future, then maybe this plan wasn't too bad.

I sat back down. "Okay."

Knox let out a sigh as he sat beside me, and then glanced over at Javion. "And you don't need to ever doubt how Zera feels about you."

As Hunter and Carter both sat down too, I frowned. "But how am I supposed to know who are children? When do they stop being children?"

"I guess we could change our target?" Javion suggested.

"To what?" Knox asked.

"The Lycan facility in the same town masquerading as a nuclear power plant."

"Just because there's a power plant, it doesn't mean it's Lycan controlled. If it's not, we're going in and attacking innocent humans, in an actual nuclear power plant," Hunter said. "It's not worth the risk. We need to get into the hotel so you can get access to their computers in order to confirm this first."

"Only, I already have access to their servers."

Carter, Hunter, and Knox all glanced towards the door.

"Do we need to be worried about the Lycans coming here again?" Knox asked.

"No more than we already did. Now that I know how they work, I set up the necessary precautions. They have no clue I'm in their servers."

"How?" Hunter asked.

"How'd I get access?" When Hunter nodded, Javion smirked. "I went spear phishing."

"When did you go fishing?" I hadn't seen Javion leave the house, nor had I seen any fish. "Do Lycans eat fish?"

Javion's smile grew, but he shook his head. "They probably do eat fish, but this is a different kind. This is a digital kind."

"Spear phishing as in P-H phishing?" Hunter asked.

Javion nodded. "Phishing emails get sent to everyone. Spear phishing is targeted."

Carter rubbed his temples. "I'm old. Zeraora isn't the only one you need to explain this to."

"Everything is digital these days. Almost everybody has an email, including companies. I did some digging around on the hotel website and found some email addresses, searched on social media for people who work at the hotel, figured out their work email addresses and then sent them an email pretending to be someone in the company. Poor old Louise who works on the reception desk has not been taught to be wary of cyber-attacks and responded to the email, giving me all the information I needed." Javion sat back in his chair, putting both of his hands behind his head. He looked very proud of himself.

"Was there a fish in the email?" I asked, still confused. I wasn't entirely sure what an email thing was, but I knew that involved a computer, and the one in front of Javion didn't look like you could put a fish in it.

"No fishes at all," Javion said. "It's called phishing because it's like going to a river and casting a line to catch a fish, but what we are doing is sending an email, and instead of catching fish, we're trying to catch information. In this case, I got the login credentials, and through privilege escalation, I got administrative access, and boom. Full access to the Lycans servers."

"So there are no fish involved?" Well that sounded boring.

Javion gave me a soft smile. "Next time, I'll put a hide a fish in it."

"And they really have no clue?" Knox sounded doubtful.

"None at all, I promise."

"You should have led with this." Carter pressed his lips into a thin line.

Javion just shrugged. "Anyway, the point is, that fake powerplant is a confirmed Lycan facility, which means everyone in it is Lycan. Those fuckers know exactly what they're doing." Javion grinned. "So Zera can take out anyone and everyone, and we don't have to worry."

Finally. I was going to get my revenge.

Forty-Two

Knox

It took two days to get to Texas. Although we drove in the van, during the night, DB wanted us to stop at a hotel so that he and Hunter, who had also been driving, could rest.

Now that Zera had her powers back—most of them—she was a different person. Fidgeting in the back of the van, it was like she had an unlimited reserve of restless energy.

Last night in the hotel, she was awake most of the

night. Like a kid on Christmas Eve night, she tossed and turned, afraid if she fell asleep, she would miss Santa arriving.

By the time we stopped on the second day, she couldn't keep the electricity from dancing over her. I asked at one point if she was creating the electricity, but she just shook her head and said she'd been pulling it from me and Javion for the past few hours. It felt like we were strapped to a bomb but we couldn't see the timer counting down.

The back door flung open, and Zera scrambled past me, almost crashing right into DB.

He set his hands on her shoulders to steady her. "Easy there, Blue Eyes."

"Where is it? Where are they?" She looked around, confused as to why we were surrounded by parked cars outside of another hotel. "I thought you said we weren't going for the hotel?"

"This isn't Maison de Lupes," Carter told her. "This is the hotel were staying at today."

Zera frowned. "No. We're going to the Lycans."

"It'll be sunrise in a couple of hours. I'll be useless, and daylight means there'll probably be more Lycans around." Javion got out of the van and stood beside her.

"And you didn't sleep at all last night. Tossing and

turning, all fucking night." I grumbled as I got out and shut the door behind us. I yawned and stretched my arms.

Hunter scoffed. "You weren't the one sharing a bed with her."

"No, because if I was, I would have held her tightly all night, so she couldn't wriggle around. She was on the other side of the room and still kept me awake. Just because you sleep like an actual fucking rock…"

Big brother never had a problem falling asleep.

"While you guys figure out tonight's sleeping arrangements, I'm going to get us a room." Javion rolled his eyes, and then headed towards the hotel. I watched him go, wondering why he was keeping up the pretense of being vaguely irritated by Zera. He was just as addicted to her as the rest of us.

I sighed and leaned back against the side of the van, folding my arms. "You know, if you ignore the fact that we're about to take on a pack of murderous, monstrous Lycans, this kind of feels like a road trip."

Hunter tapped the side of my head. "Did you whack this at some point?" he asked, as he dodged out of the way of my fist. "A road trip?"

"Fuck off." I grunted. "Usually, when we're tracking down the Lycans, Javion's at home and talking to us through earpieces, and we have gone straight to our target. Obviously, we're not on a fucking vacation."

"Enough," DB said in the tone that had us both going quiet. He looked over at Zera and tilted his head. "What are you thinking about?"

"I'm hungry. If we're not going to destroy the Lycans yet, can we eat instead?"

Neither me, DB, nor Hunter could stop the bursting out laughing. I clutched at my side as Zera looked at the three of us in confusion. Fuck me, I love this woman.

"Sure," DB said, still chuckling. "As soon as Javion's back, we'll head to that diner over there. Looks like it's open."

It didn't take long for Javion to return, although with Zera dancing from foot to foot you'd think we'd been waiting for years.

"What's wrong with her?" Javion asked me.

"She remembered she was hungry."

It was some ridiculous hour in the morning: too late for kicking out time, not that there were any bars around here, and too early for most people to be up for breakfast. So I was surprised when we walked in and there were four men in a booth at the back, even if it was a twenty-four hour place.

"Take a seat wherever you want to," the server hollered at us. "I'll be over in a minute." She headed over to the other table, carrying a pot of coffee.

Although Zera managed to get her powers under control, DB led us to a table on the opposite side of the diner, the counter in the middle of the room separating us, just in case.

The server came over a few moments later and handed us some menus. "What brings you to this neck of the woods?"

"Passing through on the way to visit family," DB lied, smoothly.

"Well, in that case, can I get you guys some coffee to start?"

We ordered drinks and food, and then the server disappeared behind the counter to give the order to the cook. I leaned back against the booth, stretching, but also craning my neck to check out the other table. The four men were still here.

There was something about them that had the hairs on the back of my neck rising. I caught Javion's eye, and he nodded. While Zera was busy in conversation with Hunter and DB watching them with a soft smile, I leaned forward towards Javion.

"Supes," he mumbled.

It was stating the obvious, really. And I knew both DB and Hunter had picked up on it too: Hunter was keeping Zera distracted, and DB was listening to our conversation.

"You recognize them?" I asked.

Javion shook his head. "Given that we're in the next town over from one of their facilities, we should probably assume they're Lycan." They were too far away to get a good sense of what type of supe they were.

We had a plan for this. One from way before Zera joined us, and back when we were hunting the Lycans.

We do nothing.

Or at least, we didn't run, nor did we confront. Instead, we carry on doing whatever it was we're doing. If we're around humans, we don't want to risk them getting hurt. Instead, either DB or Hunter would follow them when they left, taking to the air, to see where they went.

Although that was the plan, this was the first time we'd ever encountered supes when there was a legitimate chance they were actually Lycan. Aside from Maine, we'd never come across a Lycan pack, and they'd all been together inside the facility at that point.

Glancing at DB, I caught his eye, and he just nodded.

The original plan stood.

The server returned with our drinks, looking around the table as she handed them out. "You poor folks must be exhausted."

"I'm not," Zera told him.

"Well, I guess one of these gentlemen isn't doing their job properly." The woman winked at her.

I didn't care if the woman was harmless or not. I was ready to rip her throat out.

Lips pursed, Zera stared at her, blinking slowly. "Is this one of these times where you say something, but mean something else? Are you talking about sex?"

Of all the times for Zera to pick up on sarcasm... Strangely, my urge to cause bodily harm ebbed.

"Because if you are, you're very wrong. I have lots of sex with my mates. And it's very good: I have lots of orgasms."

The woman barely had the chance to hurry away before I laughed. "I fucking love you."

"I don't like her. She insulted you. I want to kill her." Zera tried to push past DB to get out of the booth.

DB didn't move. "There's no need to be killing anybody."

Shaking my head, I leaned back. That's when I glanced over to that previously occupied table, only to find it was empty. "Fuck."

Hearing me, DB looked over.

"They're gone," I muttered.

Although no words were uttered, we came to a silent agreement. I slid out of the booth to let DB out, and then quickly slid back in to keep Zera where she was.

"Are you going to go kill him?" Zera asked.

"I need to get something from the van. I'll be back." DB hurried out of the diner.

A good forty minutes passed before DB returned.

By then, Zera had devoured her meal, along with the meal Javion ordered. She looked up, pouting as DB sat down on the other side of me. "Your food is cold."

I passed DB the plate of now cold meal that he had ordered. Probably for Zera's benefit, he picked up his knife and fork. "It's fine."

The pout turned into a frown. "How long have you been gone? What were you doing in the van?"

Instead of answering, DB took a bite of his chicken fried steak. "Mmmm," he mumbled as he chewed. "I've never cooked chicken fried steak for you, have I?" he asked Zera. DB cut a slice and offered it to her.

The distraction worked perfectly.

I couldn't help but frown. I thought, that at this

point, we weren't going to keep secrets from Zera.

Judging from the expressions on Hunter and Javion's faces, they agreed. With Zera's attention still on helping DB clear his plate, he gave the three of us a knowing look, and gently shook his head.

Un-fucking-believable.

It didn't take long for the final plate to be cleared and the bill to be paid, then we headed back to the hotel. The room had one queen bed, and one foldout sofa bed, which, when out with five large adults in the room, didn't leave much space.

We were used to working with less.

At that point though, I didn't care. I was still irritated with DB. While Javion collapsed on the bed closest to the door, I went to the windows to make sure the curtains were tightly closed for the sun which would soon be coming up.

When I turned around, Hunter and Zera had already claimed the pull-out bed. DB was stood between the two beds, arms folded, as he leaned against the wall. Intentionally ignoring him, I went to join Javion.

"The sun will be up in about half an hour," DB announced.

The only reason he was saying that, was for Zera's benefit.

"Did you notice the other occupants of the diner?" DB asked, although his attention was on her.

Zera wriggled into a sitting position beside Hunter and nodded. "I saw them."

"The reason I left you wasn't to go to the van. They were supes, and we needed to find out which kind. I followed them. They were Lycans."

The mild confusion on Zera's face darkened into anger. "How could you kill them without me? Why didn't you tell me? You said—"

"I did not kill them, I only followed them. There were four of them and one of me." Not that it'd ever been his intention to do anything more than follow.

Before Hunter could stop her, Zera was already scooting her way off the bed with electricity crackling over her hands. "Then let's go. Let's go get them."

"Calm down," DB told her. "The sun is about to come up."

And then I realized why DB had waited until now.

Zera looked between the window and Javion. "Why didn't we all follow them? Why didn't you say anything?"

"Because it is too close to dawn. I didn't know where or how far we would go, but if we had all gone, we would have risked Javion getting burned." DB gestured to the bed where Zera had been curled up with Hunter. "We agreed that we would all do this together. Together includes you, but it also includes Javion."

There had been tension in my body for a while now. I initially assumed it was from the injuries the Lycans gave me, but as DB said those words, I realized it was from something else entirely.

Things between DB and Javion hadn't been great for some time now. In fact, I worried that their friendship—a relationship that existed, even before mine and Javion's—had been damaged irrevocably.

Sure, DB still had his reservations about going after the Lycans with Zera because he, like me, wanted to protect his mate. But once he agreed to do this, I knew he was going to keep his word.

However, we'd had an opportunity to take out a pack of Lycans—or part of one—and allow Zera to be present. But the fact that he'd hesitated, and part of that reason was Javion?

Maybe things *were* going to be okay between them.

Forty-Three

Zera

Waiting for the sun to set was very frustrating. I'd gotten some sleep, and then Hunter took me to a local store to buy some food. We'd come back and eaten, and still, the sun hadn't set.

I didn't ever want to be a vampire. Waiting for the sun to go down was boring, and I felt trapped.

By the time it was dark enough for Javion to walk around outside, I felt so charged that no Lycans would stand a chance against me. Tonight, I was going to destroy them all before they even came close to hurting my mates.

Javion had picked this hotel because it was about twenty minutes from the Lycan's base, which was close enough to not waste time, but also a safe distance away that we wouldn't be at risk of being caught unprepared. Twenty minutes still felt too long, so I jumped out of the van the moment Carter open the door.

We were on top of a hill, staring down at a strange-looking building. I never saw the first one I escaped from, and the second, I had pretty much destroyed by the time Carter and Hunter pulled me and Knox out.

This building was ugly. I wasn't going to be sorry when I destroyed it.

We had come up with a plan before we even drove down to Texas. My plan was simple: just blow it up, but none of my mates agreed.

"Most of what should happen here doesn't need many people. It's all controlled in that building," Javion said, pointing at one particularly ugly building. "But here, there's a lot going on beneath the ground. It's hidden away. If we want to destroy it and everything in it, we need to go inside."

"We also need to see if there are any other supes

being held prisoner in there," Hunter said. "They had you guys." He shrugged.

They had others too. In the first place, when I escaped, I ran past corridors of rooms. A lot were empty, but some had people in them that I'd never seen before. People who Lycans were hurting too.

"There's also the other thing to consider," Javion said. "The Lycans had five facilities they were passing off as nuclear power plants. They might not be nuclear, but they're still power plants. We can't ignore the fact that there might be other fae like Zera in this one too."

Even now as I stared at the strange building, I didn't think there was another fae like me inside. The Lycans told me I was the last, that there *had* been one other, but she was dead.

"Okay, before we do this, do you remember the plan?" Carter asked me.

Although I was aware that Carter asked a question, my attention was on the power plant. Something didn't feel right.

"Zeraora? You need to pay attention."

I pointed to the strange buildings. "What is it supposed to do?"

Hunter glanced at the power plant and then back to me. "The Lycans say it's a nuclear power plant but is not nuclear."

"Or at least not anymore," Javion corrected him. "They once were, but I discovered that the Lycans took over decommissioned plants back in the sixties. I don't know if it was lack of the internet or they paid a witch or two, but they still have the local populations convinced they're still active."

"What is a nuclear power plant?" I asked.

Hunter had once tried to explain what something nuclear was, but it was confusing. And what I understood from his long explanation was that it was very dangerous and could kill a lot of people and supes.

"How does it work?"

"I have no idea how to make a nuclear reaction simple." Hunter looked helplessly to Javion.

Javion shrugged. "You take one source of energy, if it's a nuclear power plant, a nuclear source, if it's a normal power plant, probably coal or sometimes gas, and it's used to create heat to boil water. The water gives off steam which powers a turbine that converts the energy. The water is then cooled in those big cooling towers so the process can…" He stared at me and then sighed. "They make electricity."

I still wasn't sure what half of what he said meant, but I think it was starting to. make sense. "So, there should be a lot of electricity there?"

"If it was being used as an active power plant, yes. If they have a source... if they have another fae in there, yes." Carter arched an eyebrow. "Isn't there?"

I closed my eyes and tried to see the electricity. It was there, and there was a lot of it, but the place was big. "It's like the castle. I can sense it, but it's being used."

"A decommissioned power plant using electricity and not creating it? At least we don't need to worry about nuking the state." Hunter rubbed the back of his neck. "But the lights are on, and someone's home, which means the place is being used for something. Fuck. They could actually have imprisoned supes in there."

"Which is something we considered. We already knew we had to go in, and if anything has changed now, it's that we make sure to get everybody out first." Carter looked at the four of us. "Unless any of you want to back out?"

"No," I said, firmly. I curled my fingers into fists, allowing the electricity to surround them.

"Then the plan remains the same. We all go in through the old water disposal tunnels, where me, Javion, and Zeraora head to the control room. Javion does his thing on the computers..." Carter wiggled his fingers, which had Javion arching an eyebrow. "He'll work out how to release any potential prisoners, who Hunter and Knox will help escape, and then, once they're clear, we let Zeraora loose on the reactor."

"And if we meet any Lycans on the way—?"

Carter nodded. "You can kill them if they try to stop us, provided..."

"Provided I don't destroy the whole place in the process," I said, sullenly. It wasn't that I disagreed or didn't understand, I just wanted to use all the power I had on each and every Lycan because it was nothing less than they deserved.

"Don't worry, you'll get your chance to show us your full firework display," Javion told me, grinning. He pointed down at the power plant. "We've got a few CCTV cameras, but as it's not a real nuclear plant, it doesn't have the same level of security. Let me know when we're ready to go, and I'll hit the button."

According to Javion, he had the ability to turn off the cameras, but only for a short period of time. But the most difficult part was going to be getting to the tunnels.

Raising his hand to his ear, Carter touched the earpiece he was wearing. "Comms check."

Although we had practiced with them before, Carter's voice in my ear still made me jump. "Yes."

"Received," Javion, Hunter, and Knox said, almost simultaneously.

Carter crouched down and looked back at me, waiting. Carefully, I climbed up onto his back, between his wings. My legs didn't make it around his waist fully, but I clung on.

Beside us, Hunter grabbed his brother's hand. "Ready when you are."

Javion had already pulled out his phone, and he pressed something on it. "We have ten minutes." As he put his phone back in his pocket, he reached for Carter's hand, then the five of us took to the sky.

This power plant was on the edge of a cliff. Like the one I had escaped from, it was by the sea. We flew down, landing on a ledge just above the water. Almost at once, a terrible smell blew out from the cave.

"What the ever-loving fuck is that god-awful stench?" Knox covered his nose.

The smell not only turned my stomach but also made me feel lightheaded as the memory of me plummeting into a pile of dead bodies hit me. "Death."

I slid down off Carter's back.

Carter reached for my hand, taking it in his. "You

don't have to do this."

"Yes, I do."

Giving my hand a gentle squeeze, Carter nodded. "We don't have long until the security cameras will be up and running again. We should move."

We had come prepared. My mates were wearing black pants that Hunter called cargo pants, and black tops. Hunter had offered to get me something similar, but I refused. I liked the way the leather felt against my skin because it made me feel more powerful. Dangerous. But I did agree to wear black.

Although my mates were gargoyles and a vampire who could see well in the dark, I couldn't. From one of his pockets, for my benefit, Carter pulled out a flashlight. It didn't shine that brightly, but it was enough to light the ground under my feet.

The deeper we got into the tunnel, the darker it became. And the stronger the smell got too. There was a strong breeze blowing into our faces.

Finally, we'd come to the end.

"Gods above," Hunter muttered. He'd been taking the lead.

"What is it?" Knox asked from behind me.

"Death. A huge, decaying pile of death. Literally." Hunter's expression wasn't visible, but he sounded like he was ready to punch his fist through someone's face.

Even though I knew what I was going to see, I raised the flashlight. It was Javion who step forward and stop me from bringing it up fully. "You don't need to see this."

"Are the cameras still down?" Carter asked before I could tell Javion I had fallen into something similar before.

"Yeah," Javion confirmed after checking his phone.

I was ready to climb back onto Carter's back, expecting to fly up to the entrance the bodies were dropped from above us, but from the side of the room, Hunter pulled at a door. "Keypad access."

"And for once, I get to do this in person." Javion moved over to the door, his body, blocking what he was doing. Not that I would be able to see anything well anyway. A few moments later, something clicked as the door unlocked.

"We split up at the top of the stairs. Keep radio silence unless it is urgent. We will wait for the signal," Carter said in a low voice.

We all nodded. Knox followed Hunter up the stairs as Javion turned to me. "You ready to destroy some Lycans?"

"I've been ready for a long time."

"Let's do this." Carter took my hand, and then we followed the twins up the stairs with Javion right behind us. When we reached a door at the top, Carter let go of my hand. He carefully opened the door and peered out. Then he stepped back to allow Javion to take the lead.

All the corridors we walked along seemed the same to me, but Javion knew where we were going. We didn't come across any Lycans as we made our way to the control room. With it being nighttime, Carter said it would be unlikely, though not impossible.

I was disappointed.

That is, until we got to the control room.

Forty-Four

Zera

"Who the hell are you?" There were two Lycans inside, and one of them looked up as we burst into the room.

The other was asleep, laid back in a chair with his feet on the desk in front of him. At the shouts from the first Lycan, this one practically fell off his chair.

Although I was ready and willing to kill them both, I hung back in the doorway: I promised not to use my powers in the control room unless absolutely necessary, just in case I destroyed everything before Javion could pull out the information he needed.

Instead, I had to watch Javion break the first Lycan's neck while Carter fought with the second. This one was strong despite being startled, and he recovered quickly, ferociously fighting Carter.

Still in his human form, though with hands like paws with sharp claws out, the Lycan swung time after time. Most of his attempts, although tearing clothing, bounced off Carter's toughened skin.

Until the Lycan got lucky.

Carter yelped as three streaks started seeping blood from his arm.

With a step forward, I raised my hand, ready to completely destroy the Lycan hurting my mate.

But Javion grabbed my hand before I could get close. "You'll destroy everything in this room. It's too soon for that."

Although I still wasn't convinced that wasn't a bad thing, I reluctantly held myself back. I'd been told, repeatedly, that releasing any potential prisoners, as well as allowing Javion to extract important information, was essential.

For some reason, Carter did not kill the Lycan. With a roar, he lunged, his hand circling the Lycans neck. But it was the force at which the Lycan flew backwards, his head smacking against the wall, that had him collapsing to the ground, unconscious.

"You should kill him." I folded my arms and glared at Carter.

"Until we know we don't need him, he stays alive. And then, you can kill him when we destroy this power plant."

That didn't sound completely unreasonable.

Javion pulled the chair towards him and then sat in front of the computer. He pulled a small black stick from his pocket and stuck it into the computer. "I was right. They have information on a local network that's not accessible remotely." His fingers flew over the keyboard as images flashed across the screen too quickly for me to be able to work out what they were.

"What are you looking at?" Carter asked him.

"Aside from a fucking inventory of supes that have been rounded up and brought here to experiment on? I'm not sure. I'll have to study it more carefully, back at the castle. There's too much information here. No wonder it's not on the network, though. If someone—supe or human—were to hack into this... They have so much information on so many supes, that I don't even need to look deeper to know this wasn't obtained through simple observation."

"Are there any more like me?" I asked.

Glancing over his shoulder, Javion shook his head. "Not that I can see. Not here, at least. I don't think that warlock was lying when he said the fae are either well-hidden or just not here anymore."

I nodded. Strangely, at that point, I didn't really care anymore. Maybe I should have, but now, the only people I wanted in my life were my mates.

"How many supes are they holding here?" Carter asked.

Javion's fingers flew over the computer. "Twelve. Fuck me, they even have a mermaid."

A mermaid was half fish. "How will Knox and Hunter get a mermaid out?"

"Like most shifters, they have a limited ability to appear and be human. But if they, or any supe for that matter, is injured and unable to shift into a human form, the twins will get them out." Carter placed a hand on my shoulder. "They will get them all out."

As he said that, a loud wailing sound started ringing through the air. Red lights began flashing around us. I covered my ears, cringing at the noise.

"And they know we're here." Without looking back, Javion continued to do things on the computer.

"Including these two, there are currently eighteen Lycans in this facility."

"Can I kill them now?" I looked up at Carter.

"What do you still need to do?" Carter asked Javion.

"From here, I can control all of the cells, but I need a little bit more time. The system looks like it was created in the nineties. Nothing fucking intuitive about this shit."

"How long do you need?"

"Five minutes. It's Hunter and Knox that need help. The Lycans are heading to them."

Carter pressed the thing in his ear. "You're going to have company."

Suddenly, Hunter's voice burst loudly into my ear. "We already do." His voice was breathy, like he was running.

"Go help them," Javion said without looking up from the computer.

I started to move towards the door, but Carter stopped me. "You need to speed up," he said, directing the comment to Javion. "And we'll go help them together. We are not splitting up and that means we are not leaving you."

I wasn't sure if Javion took five minutes or longer,

but eventually, he pulled his black stick out of the computer and stood. "I've just opened all the remaining locked cell doors. The Lycans are going to know we're in here now."

"Now can I kill them?" I asked.

"Yes, my sexy Little Sparkler, you can kill them all, but try to refrain from blowing the building up before we can all get out, please." Javion grinned. "Let's go kill these Lycan fuckers."

We left the room, and almost immediately, a group of Lycans jumped on us. At the last minute, Carter shoved me out of the way, taking the full force of two Lycan bodies slamming against him.

Seeking out the energy from around me, I raised my hand, ready to destroy the monsters that were hurting my mates, but I stopped as Javion got between me and Carter. He was busy fighting two Lycans himself. My energy would bounce off Carter, but if it hit Javion, it would destroy him, too.

I needed a better angle.

Dodging around them, I tried to get to the other side, making sure the Lycans and Carter were in between me and Javion. As I raised my hands again, a Lycan leapt at me.

Unable to move out of the way fast enough, the

Lycan fell on top of me. The impact from the fall knocked the breath from my chest. Pinned under his heavy weight, I struggled to fill my lungs.

My focus wasn't on breathing but keeping my head away from his snarling fangs. He was still in his human form, but his mouth had taken on a more wolf-like appearance with long, sharp teeth trying to tear at my throat.

I wasn't going to be able to push him off, and with how I'd fallen, my arms were trapped between us, so I wasn't able to hit him either. Just as fangs grazed my neck, I pulled an electrical current to me, drawing it from the Lycan itself.

His body went stiff, jerking above me, until the scent of charred flesh filled my nose.

There was something surprisingly satisfying about frying him with his own energy.

Just as I stopped, and his body went limp above me, Carter shoved it off me.

"Zeraora? Are you okay?"

I sucked in a deep breath. As Carter pulled me to my feet, I was only able to nod back. The two Lycans he'd been fighting were also dead, so I turned to Javion and watched as one of the Lycans who'd attacked him fell to the floor, next to the other. blood spraying everywhere.

"What does it taste like?" I asked, looking at the blood dripping from Javion's chin.

With the back of his hand, he wiped the blood away, a sneer replacing the blood. "Like the fuckers smell: wet dog."

I was still curious, but now wasn't the time. "We need to help Hunter and Knox."

"That, we do." Carter wrapped his hand around mine, and we hurried down the corridor. "Be prepared. They know we're coming."

We ran along more corridors and down more stairs. Everything looked the same to me, especially with the lights flashing and the alarms blaring. I had no idea how Javion or Carter knew where to go, but somehow, we arrived at the same floor as the twins.

It was chaos.

Doors were open, and I could see fighting everywhere I looked. There were a lot of Lycans in a mixture of wolfen and human form, but they were fighting people and creatures I'd never seen before.

In one room, there was a wolf fighting something which I was certain was a dragon. In another, two blonde women, wearing scraps of cloth leaving them almost naked and all their injuries visible, were attacking a human Lycan, only it looked like they were just screaming at them.

"Sirens," Carter said, pulling me past them. "Don't get in the middle of that. Their screams hurt."

The area was full of people, and I couldn't see my Hunter or Knox anywhere. "Where are they?"

"This is more than twenty Lycans, Javion," Carter snapped as he ducked from a fist that was flying towards him.

"It's what their computers said," Javion yelled back. "You got an issue, take it up with one of these fuckers." He jumped into the air, kicking a Lycan who was fighting with a guy who'd lost an eye.

These people, the supes that were fighting back against the Lycans, had been here for who knows how long. There wasn't one of them not injured in some way. And yet, they were doing their best to kill the Lycans.

My mind was on my twins. With Carter and Javion busy helping to fight the Lycans, I slipped away, pressing forward to find my missing mates. The easiest thing would be to just send a charge down the corridor, but as I looked at the freshly released prisoners, I knew my power would kill them too.

Until that moment, I hadn't cared. I was prepared to kill everything if it meant destroying the Lycans.

Now, I cared.

Now, I wanted all these supes to survive and have their lives back.

I passed another room with another dragon in it, bigger than the last one. One on one with a Lycan, it would probably have destroyed it alone. This one was pinned down by four, all trying to pierce the scales.

Without giving it a second thought, I ran into the room and pressed my hand against the back of one of the Lycan's neck. That wolf was big, and my hand barely wrapped around its throat, but it didn't need to.

Just as the Lycan turned, snarling, I found its electrical current and sucked it out, forcing it back into another wolf. Transfixed at watching each hair singe away, I didn't see the third Lycan lunging at me.

Claws raked down my thigh, shredding the leather like it was nothing.

The scream that left me wasn't of pain, but rage.

Letting go of the dead Lycan, I swung my arm around and shot electricity at the one that attacked me. Its body lit up like I turned it into a lightbulb. Still enraged, I turned my arm back to the final Lycan, my electricity passing straight through it, and thankfully, bouncing off the scales of the dragon.

As that Lycan fell to the floor, dead, I stopped,

clutching at my thigh. Now I could feel the pain.

"Are you okay?" The dragon had turned back into a human. He had golden skin, covered in as many wounds as the other prisoners, with dark eyes and a strange accent.

"I am going to kill them all." The blood was running down my leg, but after all the pain I'd suffered from the Lycans, this was nothing.

"I… I don't doubt that."

I straightened my back, testing the weight on my injured leg. When I was sure it was going to hold, I turned back to the dragon. "You should leave. I'm going to destroy this place."

After wrapping his hands around his rib, the dragon shifter nodded. "Good luck."

He followed me out of the door but went in the opposite direction as I continued down the corridor. I saw Carter and Javion fighting with the Lycans, but I still hadn't spotted the twins.

My counting skills had improved, but it was difficult to count while avoiding the vicious fighting and flying bodies. There were dead bodies, mainly Lycans, but some other supes too, all over the floor. With those still fighting, all I could say with certainty was that the number Javion gave us was much lower than the reality.

Shocked

As I continued down the corridor, stopping occasionally to satisfy my urge to destroy a Lycan and help a struggling supe, the pain in my thigh went numb.

My heart pounded the further I moved, still not seeing Hunter or Knox.

Until I did.

Forty-Five

Hunter

Our destination was one of the lower floors. Knox and I only had to climb a couple of flights before we exited into a corridor. Being nighttime, everything was dark, lighting only coming from the occasional emergency light.

Light wasn't necessary for us. Well, for me. My eyes were certainly better than Knox's, but he was keeping up. Besides, lights out meant we were undetected.

Javion had found some floorplans when he hacked

the facility. They were dated several years ago, but so far, things were playing out. The most important thing was that although there was a master override in the main control room where he was headed with DB and Zera, each cell could be opened at each door.

And each door shared one master code.

Or, at least, that's what the old files said.

Whether or not they would still hold up was another matter entirely, but Javion also provided us with a backup plan: a device unscrupulous humans used to break into luxury cars. It worked on these keypads the same way. They just took a bit longer.

Behind me, Knox let out a long sigh, and I turned back to him. "You okay?" I asked in a low whisper.

"I will be once we've freed everyone in here. Can't even fucking imagine what they've been through."

Knox's description of what the Lycans did to him was brief and vague, but after treating his injuries, I could see they were barbaric. Whether they'd done it to torture him or to find out more about gargoyles, as was their usual motive, clearly, the end result was the same.

Devastating pain.

Glancing down the corridor, it was much longer than the plans made it out to be, with more doors than I'd counted back at Castle Viegls.

Which meant at least some of the information was wrong.

Sucking in a deep breath, I turned to the first door and peered in. A man was curled up in a corner. I couldn't see much to tell even how old he was. The light in the room was dim, and he was hunched over. But even with the limited vision, I could see his wounds. Chunks of skin were missing, and the wounds were open and wet. Either they were fresh, or they did something to him to stop them from healing.

I jammed my finger against the keypad, only just refraining from punching it.

The code didn't work, either.

Turning to Knox as I pulled out the universal key, I couldn't stop my scowl. "The information is old. Don't let down your guard."

Knox nodded, and then glanced past me down the corridor. "This will be quicker if we each take a side." Not waiting for a response, he pulled out the backup universal key and moved to the door across from us.

I returned my attention to the door in front of me. The device probably took less than a minute to read the door code before it pinged open, but every second was going to count in this rescue mission. Particularly because I knew Zera was itching to destroy everything.

As I pulled the door open, the man in the corner looked up, cowering back. I held a hand up as I shook my head. "Friend, not Lycan. It's time to get out of here."

The man's eyes went wide. "You're not a hallucination?"

I hurried over. "I'm sure your brain can hallucinate something better than me. You okay, or do you need help walking?"

Leaning to the side, the man glanced past me to the door, his eyes still wide, though this time, in fear. "The Lycans?"

"They don't know we're here yet. We need to move quickly and get you all out of here before they realize their base has been breached." I held out a hand, and he took it so I could pull him to his feet. "Can you walk?" I looked down at the injuries on his legs. Whatever they'd done to him, I didn't need the details.

Although he wasn't putting his full weight on one of his legs, he nodded. "You know what's going to happen if they catch us, right?"

I shrugged. "Then let's not get caught."

Without another word, he followed me out of the room.

Knox was also exiting the room he'd gone into,

with a female in tow. She looked over at me and then looked up and down the corridor. "This is it? This is the rescue party?"

"There's a few more of us, but yeah. Feel free to stay if you want." Knox didn't look back as he moved on to unlock the next room.

"That door leads down to an overflow tunnel. Follow it out, and you're going to be on a cliff If you can fly, do so. Otherwise, it's about a forty-foot drop into a lake. The water's cold, but deep enough. Just don't stop—I don't know how long we have until they realize we're here." I had no idea what supe they were, but if they couldn't fly, they *should* be able to survive the fall. Forty feet wasn't too far for a supe with advanced healing, even if they had been kept prisoner by the Lycans.

The man I'd freed didn't give us a second look as he limped towards the door. The woman just stared at me.

"You're staying?" I didn't have time to give her a pep talk.

"It will be safer if we all leave together. If the Lycans come, we'll all need to fight, and it will be easier if there's a lot of us than them picking us off, one by one. Send them down to me."

I nodded, then hurried on to the next door.

Knox and I got about halfway down the corridor when the alarms went off. As the device in my hand was unlocking a door, I froze, glancing up at the ceiling, as though I could see through the floors above to the room Zera was in. *Was it her? Had they found her? Or was it us? Had the security cameras just kicked back in?*

Either way, the Lycans were aware of our presence.

The door clicked unlocked, but I glanced over at the door Knox was at. He was just leaving with a guy draped over his neck. As he handed him over to someone else that we'd released, he glanced at me. He didn't need to say anything for me to know he was thinking about the others.

I managed to get the door open when, from the far end of the corridor, Lycans started pouring in.

Abandoning the cell I was at, I charged down the corridor, toughening my skin. Only a few of the Lycans were armed—weapons were of no use when in their wolf form, and teeth and claws were more deadly—but the few in human form had guns. From long range, they would be deadly to most of the supes we'd freed so far.

Dodging wolves, I set my sights on the human Lycans. A gun fired, and the bullet ricocheted off my arm. I ignored it, punching a Lycan out of the way so I could reach the one firing at us.

Part of the reason they favored their wolfen form was because they were stronger. The human Lycan's neck broke easily in my hands.

As I dodged another wolf to reach the next human, I caught a glance of Knox from the corner of my eye. He was following me, clearly thinking the same. I didn't have time to think about the other supes, save for vaguely acknowledging those that could shift had already changed forms and joined the fight.

Taking out another armed Lycan, I finally glanced back as a ball of fire soared down the corridor. A dragon. One of those we'd freed was a freaking dragon!

As the realization that we had a dragon on our side lifted my spirits, more Lycans poured into the corridor.

"Where the fuck are they coming from?" I heard Knox yell, although I was unsure if he really wanted an answer.

The facility was teeming with wolves: more than any of us wanted to fight. But equally, I wasn't completely surprised. Or at least, it wasn't unexpected. We'd all agreed that the plans we'd found may have been out of date, and that also included the number for Lycans on site—even during the night.

But I don't think any of us had been prepared for

this number.

Gritting my teeth, I prayed to any of the gods that were listening that with the few we'd freed, we would be able to defeat them.

Something—a fist or elbow—slammed into the back of my head. The blow wasn't hard enough to knock me out, or to give me double vision, but it did make me stumble. The next thing I knew, a wolf was pinning me to the ground, and teeth clamped into my neck.

The bite didn't break the skin, but I could feel how close it was.

Instead of trying to pull the wolf off me, I pushed, flipping myself up, and then slamming myself down with all my weight, onto my back—and the Lycan. Almost instantly, the pressure at my neck disappeared.

Scrambling to my feet, I reached up, feeling at my neck. When I pulled my hand away, there was blood. The Lycan had broken my skin...

I didn't have time to think about it. I was surrounded by six snarling Lycans.

Raising my hands, I readied myself for an attack. One on one, I would stand a chance, but if they pounced together... I backed up so that there was no space between me and the door behind me. It didn't leave me room to maneuver, but it also meant that a Lycan wasn't going to get me from behind again.

As my gaze swept over the Lycans in front of me, the corridor was continuing to fill.

Where the fuck were they coming from?

The other supes were fighting, but we were outnumbered and going to be taken out before long, at this rate.

A Lycan leapt at me, and I batted it to the side as a second one jumped moments later. This one hit my chest, but I went flying backwards.

Someone had unlocked and opened the cell doors.

Javion.

I wasn't sure how aware of what was happening in the corridor the cell's occupier was, but all of a sudden, the Lycan was yanked off me.

Rolling to the side to avoid another Lycan, I caught a glimpse of the cell's occupant.

A berserker.

Fuck yes!

The rage demon's skin was glowing from the heat it was producing, and he had no issue fighting the Lycans. No doubt, he'd been waiting for this moment.

The Lycans fucked up capturing one of these.

A berserker, dragons and Zera… for the first time,

this mission didn't seem completely hopeless.

That was all the thought I gave to the berserker as I focused on fighting the Lycans coming at me. They seemed to keep pouring through the door into the cell like ants finding a picnic.

Slowly, I was tiring. For every Lycan I killed—bodies were literally piling up around us—another appeared.

"Back away from my mate." Zera's voice, low and rough from years of screams destroying her throat, filled the room.

Let's go baby!

Forty-Six

Zera

The further down the corridor I got, the more Lycans there were. Even with every one of the supes that were freed, we were still outnumbered, and we were falling quickly.

All I wanted was to raise my arms and electrocute everything in front of me, but there were other supernatural creatures—some I didn't even recognize—and I couldn't bring myself to kill the ones that were also trying to fight.

Instead, I walked with my hands out, making sure the only thing I fried was something I touched.

That was still satisfying, even if it didn't eliminate them as quickly as I wanted to.

Finally, as I neared the end, I saw a glimpse of Hunter just before he disappeared behind a snarling Lycan.

No.

No Lycan was allowed to hurt my mate.

"Back away from my mate," I shouted. Not that I was going to spare any of them.

I moved to the door, raised my hands, and blasted every wolf in the room. I enjoyed the acrid smell of burning fur almost as much as I enjoyed watching their bodies twitch and dance under my command.

From the corner of the room, another monster appeared, moving towards me. I'd seen a volcano on a television show once. This looked like it was made from one of them.

And it was walking towards Hunter.

"No, Zee," Hunter shouted before I could raise my hands towards this new monster. "He's a friend."

The 'friend' had eyes like they were made from fire. "You're quite impressive."

"What are you?" I asked.

The fire monster chuckled, but it was Hunter who answered. "A berserker—a rage demon. Probably the only thing in here as powerful as you."

Seeing the dead, charred Lycans around the room, I glanced back to the berserker. "I doubt it."

The berserker chuckled again. "Let's get out of here, and then we can test that theory." He walked out of the door without waiting for a response.

Jumping over a dead wolf, I flung myself at Hunter. "He wouldn't stand a chance against me."

Hunter stroked the back of my hair. "No, he wouldn't. But he has the right idea. Let's get out of here. There are way more Lycans here than we anticipated."

"Where's Knox?" I pulled away.

"He was out there." Hunter stated, grabbing my hand and leading me out into the corridor.

The chaos was finally more controlled. Any fighting was mainly at the far end—by the escape. Dead bodies covered the corridor, but there were far more Lycans than anything else.

From here, I could see Carter and Javion. Two completely different supes and body types, and yet their fighting was fluid. Lethal. Each move somehow seemed both effortless and planned.

The dragons, the sirens, and the berserker were

helping, and one by one, the Lycans fell.

But I still couldn't see Knox.

Turning to Hunter, I found him looking towards the end of the corridor we were in. As he turned back to me, frowning, he raised his hand to his ear. "Knox? Location?"

The thing in my ear remained silent, but at the other end of the corridor, both Carter and Javion turned their heads sharply in our direction.

"Knoxlyn, answer the damn call," Javion said, his eyes fixed on me.

"Missing someone?"

The voice that came through wasn't Knox. It wasn't even male. But I would have recognized that voice anywhere.

The female Lycan with corkscrew curls: Scarlett.

I thought she was dead.

A shiver ran down my spine, but it was from rage, not fear.

"Where is he?" Javion demanded. He and Carter were already moving towards us.

"I don't want him. I only want the fae."

"You can go fuck yourself," Hunter responded with a snort.

"I'll be doing that after. But if you want your poor

excuse for a gargoyle back, all of you need to leave—
take the other subjects with you for all the fucks I give—
but the fae stays."

With my hands clenched into fists, I started to
move towards the door that was open at the end of the
corridor: I could see stairs, and I was ready to search
every inch of this place to find Knox.

Hunter grabbed my shoulder before I could get
close. "Where do you think you're going?"

"I am not letting that Lycan bitch hurt Knox
again," I said through gritted teeth as I tried to shake
Hunter's hand off me.

"Easy Little Sparkler." Javion and Carter joined us.

I turned back to them and glared. "You're not
going to stop me."

"Like fuck we are," Javion snorted. "We're not
going to let you go alone." His voice had a deadly edge
to it, but I could see worry in his eyes.

I looked at the three of them and then nodded.

Hunter let go of me and then stepped back.

Knowing my mates would follow me to the ends
of the earth, I walked towards the door before stopping
in the doorway.

This time, Carter grabbed my shoulder. I turned
and glared back. "I was going to suggest we go back to

the control room and find him on the CCTV. This is a large facility," he said.

"We don't need to do that. We have Zera." Javion's silver eyes were locked on mine. "She can find him."

"How?" Hunter asked before I could.

"His current. You could see that this place wasn't being used as a power plant, and the other night, you saw me and Knox." He stepped towards me, blocking the other two from my view so I had to focus on him. "You can find him quicker than we would if we went back."

"I've never done that before." My heart was racing. What if I couldn't find him?

"You can do it. You've got to." Javion's tone was firm. And then it wavered slightly. "It's Knox."

"He's right. It's the quickest way, and I know you can find him, Zee." Hunter stepped to my side and placed his arm around my shoulder. "We've got you."

Taking in a deep breath, I closed my eyes. At first, all I could hear was the fighting at the other end of the hallway. I wasn't worried about the Lycans. If the supes down there couldn't stop them and they came down this way, I'd just destroy them.

Still, the noise was distracting.

"Just think about Knox," Javion whispered in my

ear. "Nothing else."

With my eyes still closed, I focused on the electricity around me, specifically from Carter, Javion, and Hunter. I could feel it, just like I could feel them next to me.

Slowly, their energy took shape until I was seeing them with my eyes closed. Their bodies were made of thousands and thousands of bolts of electricity bouncing around in a contained form.

If I thought my mates were handsome, it was nothing compared to their beauty when they looked like this. Better still, it didn't even matter that my eyes were damaged. I could see them perfectly.

Moving slightly, I focused on the other energy around me—the Lycans and the other supes at the other end of the corridor—until the wires were no longer hidden in the walls or to the lights above.

Slowly, the hallway took on a different form. Only, it wasn't solid. I could see the energy continue on, like all the walls were see-through. I knew where they were because of the currents passing through the wires, but they weren't really there. As I looked further, through the walls, I could see more energy sources of other Lycans—above us, below us—in other parts of the building. This floor was underground, and as I looked past the walls, I could sense the energy in the dirt, even the insects under there.

"Do you see him?" Javion's voice stopped my mind drifting, and I focused on searching for Knox.

Finally, I found him. I'd recognize his energy anywhere. He was a fair distance from us, and above ground. "This way."

Without opening my eyes, I ran.

There wasn't a word of doubt or hesitation from Carter, Javion, or Hunter. The three just followed after me as I led them through a maze of corridors, pausing only when one of the guys held me back to knock down a door I hadn't seen.

Finally, I felt the wind on my face. We were outside. Knowing where I needed to go and that I could easily find Knox like this again, I opened my eyes, wincing at the bright floodlights lighting up the area.

"Where is he?" Carter's eyes were searching the area.

I pointed at a strange pale building in front of us.

"The cooling tower?" Hunter sounded doubtful.

"He's in there. He's not alone, though."

"How many are with him?" Javion asked. He curled his fists like he was prepared to take on a hundred Lycans to get Knox back.

Luckily for him, so was I.

"Two. One of them is the woman who hurt us before. Scarlett, her name is." I didn't know who the other one was. I think they were female, but that was irrelevant. Very shortly, they'd both be dead.

"There's no one else in there with them?" Carter asked.

"Just them and Knox."

"I am going to pull her spine out through her ass." Snarling, Javion stepped towards the tower, but Carter moved in front of him.

"You realize we're probably walking into a trap?" Carter asked the question, but somehow made it sound like he wasn't asking anything.

Knox's scream rang out, amplified in the quiet night.

Javion was moving before I was, but only just. Neither of us cared about traps. Carter didn't stop us, or Hunter. He didn't stop any of us after that as we all ran towards the cooling tower.

There were stairs to one side, and Javion beat me to them. We darted up, through a door, and into the tower. Inside was strange. There was no roof above us, and I could see the night sky, but there were dozens of pipes, crisscrossing to obscure the view.

"Javion, Zera, slow down," Carter called.

I could sense him slowing behind us. I did the same, glancing around.

Something didn't feel right.

There were pipes above us, but below, we were walking on a giant metal grate that clinked with every step we took. Below that, maybe two heights of Carter, was a black abyss. From the way it reflected the moon and the shadows of the floor under our feet, I guessed it was water.

Alone, chained to a grate in the center of the tower, Knox was laying on his side.

Forgetting Carter's warning, I ran over, just behind Javion. "Is he okay?" I asked as Javion dropped down beside him.

Knox's eyes flew open as Javion's cool hands touched his face. "You need to get out of here. It's a trap!" His gaze locked with Javion's. "Get Zera out of here."

Glancing back at me, Javion's mouth parted as something above us caught his attention.

"It's too late for that."

Looking up in the direction Javion was staring, I found Scarlett and a woman I didn't recognize standing there. They were on a platform above the woven pipes, sheltered behind a glass wall.

Squinting, I peered up at the woman. "Wait, I know her."

She was the mongoose shifter. What was she doing here?

"I don't like this. Get him out of those chains now," Carter told Hunter who was already working to free them.

Somewhere, deep underground, something started rumbling, making the pipes above us hiss and creak.

"I don't like this either," Hunter muttered.

"Now, I'm a reasonable woman," Scarlett said, making me scoff. "So, before we make any irrational decisions, let me offer you a way for you to walk out of here right now." She pointed at me. "The fae stays, and the rest of you can leave."

"Fuck off," Knox snapped at her, the pain evident in his voice.

"I thought you might say that, but here's the thing. If you all stay, she's going to have to watch as she kills you."

"The only things I'm killing are you two." I summoned electricity to my hands and launched it at the Lycan.

It hit the glass and bounced off.

"After all this time, you've still not realized that glass doesn't conduct electricity." The mongoose shifter tutted and then laughed. "Idiot."

Glass might not conduct electricity, but if I hit it hard enough, it could still shatter.

"You know what does?" Scarlett asked. She titled her head and then reached for something beside her. "Metal."

Whatever was on the wall, as she lowered her hand, the creaking and screeching in the pipes got so loud, I had to cover my ears.

Javion looked up and then at me, his eyes wide. "Zera, get the fuck out of here, right—"

Before he could finish, water started raining down on us. At each point where the pipes crossed, there was a small nozzle spraying water, harder and faster than anything I'd ever been under.

I froze, unable to breath. Pain ripped through my body, forcing electricity to explode from me.

I couldn't control it.

All I could do was watch as my energy hit the grate below us before shooting out in all directions...

Straight towards my mates.

Forty-Seven

Zera

J avion's cries of pain were deafening.

The thought of hurting my mates with my power had terrified me, but Carter, Hunter, and Knox all promised they could barely feel it.

Javion wasn't a gargoyle. He might have been undead, but his skin wasn't tough like my other mates.

After Knox had told him to get me out of there, he'd taken a few steps towards me, and now he was locked in place between us both. Javion's body was rigid as he screamed.

Tears fell from my eyes, not from my own pain, but from his. And the pain the others were feeling.

None of the gargoyles were screaming, but their bodies were stuck in place, frozen like my electricity was holding them there, muscles, tight and taut. Carter was the only one of them who had been looking at me when the water started pouring down, and his eyes were wide, teeth gritted.

They weren't the only ones locked in place.

I felt like invisible chains were clawing at my wrists, trapping me in place. Electricity poured from me. With no glass cage to keep it in place, it traveled everywhere there was metal. With a metal grate for flooring and pipes running all around us, almost every inch looked alive, lightning bolts electrifying everything.

I can't make it stop.

I tried to say that to Carter, to Javion—to let them know I wasn't hurting them willingly—but no words came out.

Above us, all I could hear was laughter. I wasn't sure if it was coming from the Lycan or the Mongoose.

Then the water stopped.

All five of us slumped to the floor. Javion's screams stopped, and his eyes closed. Unable to see a rising chest, I wasn't sure if he was still alive.

Hunter, in my line of sight, turned his head to look at me. He was breathing heavily, and even though there was still pain in his eyes, he somehow managed a crooked smile. "You pack quite a punch there, Zee."

My body was still silently screaming in pain. The falling water might have stopped the electricity from spewing everywhere, but my clothes and my body were soaked. Lightning bolts that normally danced harmlessly over my skin were still attacking me.

"You all need to get out of here," I mumbled.

If I could have moved, I would have. The urge to fling myself out of the tower was overwhelming. The fall could kill me, but at least it would take my power away from my mates and save them.

Only, all the energy was on top of my skin and not in my body. I could barely move my head. Which meant they needed to. "You're not leaving."

"It's the metal," I heard Carter say to Hunter. "If we can get Zeraora in the air—"

"No!" I shrieked, panic swirling around inside of me again. "I will hurt you. Get Javion and Knox and go!"

The Lycans wanted me. They could take me *willingly* if I could get my mates out of there safely. If they stayed, I was only going to… they were going to be in more pain.

"None of us are going to leave you, Sparkler." Javion's voice was weak—but he was alive.

"Then the four of you are idiots," the mongoose declared.

"Fuck off Catherine," Knox called weakly.

"It's Caitlyn. Though I'm certainly not surprised at how hard it must be to get information through that thick skull of yours. Living up to your reputation as the dumbest of all the supernaturals."

"Your name is irrelevant. You'll be dead soon and forgotten quickly enough." Javion struggled to his feet. Although he was looking up at the two women, he was moving towards me.

"No, get Knox and go," I begged him. "I can't stop it. I'm going to hurt you more. Get away from me!"

"What are you gargoyles hoping to accomplish right now?" Scarlett sounded irritated.

Although I needed Javion to focus on Knox, I couldn't help but look past him at the others. Hunter was still with Knox, but Carter was trying to haul himself up between the pipes that ran everywhere.

"Are you trying to distract us with boring conversation while one of you somehow manages to get up here? Please. That battery you've sided with is going to be the death of you. I've given you an out, but you're not taking it."

Her words sparked a reaction in me, fury rippling down in my gut.

"Don't call me battery," I spat. Water splashed off me as I put my hands on the grate to push myself up. Gritting my teeth against the pain, I glowered up at the Lycan. "I am not a battery."

"Oh, but you are," Scarlett informed me as Caitlyn burst out laughing again.

The laugh was high pitched and squeaky, and it made me twitch.

"Again, what are you trying to accomplish right now?" Scarlett moved slightly on her platform, following me as I struggled to walk towards her instead of my mates.

"Where are you going, Sparkler?" Although clutching at his side and breathing heavily, Javion staggered to my side.

"I am going to kill both of them."

Laughter once again echoed around the tower. "How?" Scarlett asked. "If I turn the water back on, I'll just leave it on until your friends are dead and you've passed out. There is no 'winning' here. Not for you, at least."

"Why have you always got to be like this, Scar?" Caitlyn asked. Her arms were folded and she was glaring at her companion. "Just turn the damn water on and be done with it. Let her kill her pathetic friends already."

Summoning the electricity to me, ignoring how it ripped down my arm, I raised my hand and sent a large bolt of lightning at the two women. It smacked into the glass and bounced off.

Just like it did before.

If I could just get the glass to break… I'd done it before—my powers were strong enough to have gotten us out of a Lycan facility. And if I could do it again, those two women wouldn't stand a chance.

I'd send so much electricity through their bodies they would light the world up.

I just had to get through that glass.

This time, with a scream at the effort, I threw another lightning bolt.

The glass didn't shatter.

But Scarlett's eyes went wide. "What the fuck?"

"Just finish them," Caitlyn said, panicked.

"That's it," Javion said, making my heart leap with hope. "It cracked."

Before I could throw another bolt of lightning,

Scarlett slammed her hand against the switch on the wall.

At the last second, I managed to turn back to see the others, just before the water started pouring down again.

This time, I screamed too.

Tears poured down my face, lost into the water. My vision became blurry, but I didn't need to see anyone to know my mates were in pain. What's worse, I could sense their energy getting weaker, especially Javion's, without the same natural protection as the others.

All I had wanted to do was protect my mates.

Protect them from the Lycans.

All this time, I should have been protecting them from me.

I was going to be the one to kill them.

That realization had me dropping to my knees. The pain the electricity was causing me was *nothing* compared to the agony that flooded me.

Me. They were going to die because of *me*.

"Zera." Javion said my name in an anguished gasp. "Little Sparkler. Look at me. Whatever you're thinking you've got to stop."

I wasn't sure how he was managing to speak.

There was a loud crash behind him as Carter fell

from the pipes and landed heavily on the grate beside Knox and Hunter. Heavy enough for me to feel the vibration where I was. If he couldn't take the electricity, how could Javion?

Movement from Javion had my attention back on him. He was twitching, his face contorted, but he was still trying to move to me. "You can fight this. You control the electricity, remember?"

There had been a noise in the background, echoing around the tower, that had started up as the water had begun pouring down again. As it fell silent, I realized it had been coming from Knox.

I couldn't save them.

Not this time.

"I'll go back for you," I whispered.

"You can't."

I didn't realize Javion was close enough to hear me. Not that it mattered.

The four of them could tell me not to, but I would.

I would come back as many times as necessary to protect them.

I wasn't going to live in a world without them.

"I mean it, Zera. You can't mess with things like that. The consequences could be a million times worse."

There's nothing worse than a future without any of you in it.

540

I wanted to say the words, but the pain was so bad, I couldn't get the words out anymore.

The water didn't stop until Javion collapsed in front of me.

Was he…?

Were the others…?

I fell to the floor, coughing and gasping for air. I didn't move, but instead, just lay there.

The pain inside me was becoming unbearable. Before it consumed me, I bit down on my lip so hard that I tasted blood. I focused on the energy that was still whipping the area around me, willing myself to go back to some point in the past.

To do this again…

To save them.

But as I closed my eyes, I realized something was different.

Forty-Eight

Zera

I could see Carter, Javion, Hunter, and Knox, as well as the two women above us, and the dozens of Lycans who were still in the facility…

I could see the various power lines that ran around giving the facility shape…

I could see the energy all around me.

Raising my hand off the ground, with my eyes still shut, I waved my hand through the energy.

It was fluid, just like the water... Only this didn't hurt.

I felt a slight tingling sensation, like fizzing on my tongue when I drank Coke.

"Scar, they're not dead yet—look, that one is moving."

"The vampire fell to the floor. I thought they *were* dead."

"Just leave it on until they're all crispy like what she did to your pack. You won't get more revenge than that."

Moments later, the water turned on again. Somehow, I knew it wouldn't be turned off until my mates were dead. And I watched as the energy shot from me, travelling across the floor. It had been visible when my eyes were open, but closed, the sight was mesmerizing and... beautiful.

Reaching out, I ran my hand through it.

More tingling—*tingling*, not pain.

Water gushed down over me, so heavy, it pinned my body to the metal grate. But for some reason, it didn't hurt me anymore.

So, I focused on the electricity moving towards Javion, willing it to obey me. *Protect him.*

The energy listened.

Rising up into an arch around him, the energy surrounded Javion, but didn't touch him. Almost instantly, I sensed his energy change. He was still alive.

Without moving, I focused on the other three. With the same plea, I urged the electricity to do the same.

It listened.

Just like with Javion, it rose above my mates, surrounding them without touching their skin. Almost at once, I could see their bodies' energy level rise.

"Something's happening down there."

I didn't move an inch, even though I was aware of the other three getting to their feet. Except for Knox. He was still chained to the ground.

Not for much longer...

The energy listened to my command and snapped through the lock with a pop.

"It's her. Turn the water up!" Caitlyn shrieked.

Fear.

I could hear it in their voices, and even in my weakened state, I smiled.

"It's up as high as it will go," Scarlett told her.

"Then send your Lycans in."

I laughed.

The sound was strange and gurgled. Somehow, that

made me laugh harder.

Summoning the energy around me, I created my own protective barrier. As I did, Carter, Javion, Hunter, and Knox reached my side, helping me to my feet. They were injured, pain making their movements jarred and clumsy.

But they were alive.

"Zera, what are you doing?" Knox asked.

"Don't hurt yourself." Hunter added.

"We need to leave," Carter told us. "Now."

Eyes still closed, I shook my head at Carter's energy source. He had a slight blue tint to him, just like his eyes. "No. I'm ending this."

"You've got this, my amazing Little Sparkler. You destroy those bitches."

To everyone else, it looked like I was just standing there, laughing to myself. What they couldn't see was the energy I was controlling all around me. I sent it seeking out every living thing, silently wrapping them in a shell they couldn't see or feel.

Not until I wanted them to…

Finally, smiling wide now, I opened my eyes and stared at the two women above us. The mongoose looked worried—as she should. The Lycan was staring, rage burning in her eyes.

"You want my energy?" I grinned. "It's all yours."

Summoning everything—every charge from every cable, from every living creature and plant—I turned their invisible shells on.

Just like with myself and my mates, the supes that were held captive, along with the stray animals that wandered too close to the facility, the energy protected them.

It protected the Lycans, too.

"Zeraora, what are you doing?"

Ignoring Carter, I focused on the energy. Not just calling it to me but creating it. I wasn't sure how I knew what I was doing, but sensing it appear out of nothing just felt completely natural to me.

Like breathing.

Like loving my mates.

My hair was flying around me even though there was no breeze. Even the air felt thicker.

"What's she doing, Jay?"

"She's about to show us all just why you shouldn't fuck with her," Javion said, proudly.

Carter stepped in front of me. "Zeraora, you need stop." he said, the same tone he'd use when he wanted the others listen to him. "You're going to kill us all."

Glancing at him, I met his gaze and smiled. "No.

I'm going to destroy the Lycans."

Before he could say anything else, I let the energy free. Explosions rang out everywhere. Suddenly, we were surrounded by fire, dust, flying metal, debris...

With the exception of Javion, my mates tried to duck for cover.

I didn't move.

I wasn't scared.

The energy shells I'd created weren't letting anything pass through them unless I wanted them to.

Staring up through the fire and confusion, I saw the terror in the eyes of the Lycan and the mongoose shifter.

And then I let their shields drop.

In less than a second, the energy tore through them, completely destroying everything about them. There wasn't even a drop of blood left.

I smiled.

It took a long time for the fires to stop burning and the dust and debris to settle. Keeping the shields up, I walked us through the flames until we reached the edge of the destruction that I'd caused.

Here, there was an uphill climb which, in the end, Carter and Hunter flew us all out of. But the other supes hadn't all made it out, so Carter and Hunter went back in, finding those who were still there and pulling them out.

"Holy motherfucking fuckballs," Knox said. Again. He'd been saying that a lot as we stood on the top of the cliff, staring at the destruction in front of us.

"You've said that forty times already," Javion told him.

"And I'll say it again: holy motherfucking fuckballs." He pointed in front of him. "It's a crater. A fucking crater. It's not just a dent in the earth, she fucking annihilated an area the size of…" He ran a hand through his hair. "Ten football fields."

"More like a hundred," Carter said, finally landing beside us. "That crater is the size of… Gods above, it's huge."

Hunter landed beside him. "And the emergency services are heading towards it. Now is a good time to get out of here." He pointed into the sky. "That, and the sun will be rising soon but our van was somewhere in that."

"Ooops." I giggled, not feeling the slightest bit sorry.

With a quick scan of the area, I didn't sense any more energy points in the crater that shouldn't be there, so I dropped everyone's shields.

"I just want to take this moment to remind everyone that I said Zera was unbelievably powerful and none of you believed me." Javion folded his arms and smirked. He leaned over and ruffled my hair. "I'm so proud."

"I did." I frowned. "I said it a lot. I also said I was going to destroy the Lycans."

Knox draped his arm over my shoulder. "To be fair, I think *destroy* is very, *very* much an understatement. You obliterated them. We don't need to worry about a human finding any evidence of the Lycans, because you haven't left anything to be found. And I doubt any managed to escape—"

"No Lycan escaped." I corrected him. "I felt all the energies around us… Nothing escaped unless I let them." With a sigh, I sank to the ground. Instantly, all four men were crowding me.

"Zeraora? Is everything alright?"

Frowning, I tried to wave him to the side. "No."

"What's wrong?" Hunter demanded, running his hand over me, looking for something.

"It was over too quickly."

Hunter's hands froze. "What?"

"Are you…?" Carter peered at me, the concern replaced with confusion. "Are you… pouting?"

"We all almost died. What do you mean it was over too quickly?" Hunter asked, glancing at the others with the same look of bewilderment as Carter.

"They didn't suffer. They hurt you. They hurt me." I could feel the anger growing inside of me as the electricity began crackling around my curled fingers. "They nearly made me kill you. And I just…" I waved my arm at the crater, stray bolts of lightning flaring from my fingertips. "I didn't let them suffer."

There was a moment of silence then Knox snorted before he stepped away, laughing.

Carter and Hunter shared a look, but it was Javion who spoke. "You are the most incredible woman I have ever met. You have wiped out—completely annihilated one of the most savage and dangerous species on the planet—and you are sulking because you didn't cause them enough pain?"

"I wanted them to feel what you felt." I folded my arms and glowered at the crater.

Javion crouched down, gently grabbing my chin to turn me to face him. "You saved us. *You*. The only thing more dangerous than a Lycan." He turned and pointed at the crater. "How isn't that the most beautiful thing you've ever seen?"

Barely giving the crater a glance, I instead stared at Javion in confusion. "How can you ask me that when you four are stood beside it?"

"We're keeping her," Knox said, instantly. "We're keeping her forever."

"You say that like you have a choice," I muttered. Keeping *me*? They were my mates.

"Good Little Sparkler." Javion smirked.

Hunter reached down, placing his hand on my head. "Zee, you are the most remarkable woman I have ever met."

"While I don't disagree on any point, you're going to be down a mate soon if we don't move. We need to get a little further away than the next town to lay low for the next couple of days," Carter said. "And as Hunter said, we don't have long before the sun will rise."

"Can we get something to eat too?"

All of that had worked up my appetite.

As Knox started laughing at me again, Carter helped me back up.

"We're in Texas," Carter said. "You can have all the food you want."

I took one last look at the beautiful devastation in front of me and then climbed up onto Carter's back, ready to leave.

"What about the other supes?" Javion asked. He glanced at Carter. "Do we need to be worried about them?"

"I didn't let them die," I said.

"I mean more about them telling anyone what happened."

Carter shook his head. "Not a single supe I pulled out had any idea what happened. They were all underground. I told them it must have been witches."

"Same." Hunter looked at me, now with a proud smile. "I think we're safe."

Safe.

That was a new feeling.

I liked it.

And I was going to make sure the five of us would always feel that way.

Epilogue

Zera

It hadn't stopped raining for four days and nights. Despite what I'd done at the Lycan facility, once I was out, I hadn't been able to avoid my reaction to rain again. The progress I'd made before going there, being able to stay inside without destroying all the electrical equipment in the castle was the best I could do.

And even that was a stretch.

If anything, I felt like I'd taken two steps back. If

the rainfall was heavy enough, when it hit the roof in certain parts of the castle, it sounded like the water was hitting metal.

Carter said the castle was old, and that in places, the tiles in the roof were held in place with lead sheets, so that's why it made that noise. Come spring, he and Hunter were going to retile those parts of the roof so it wouldn't sound like that anymore.

In a few months, it wouldn't matter too much as the mountain would be covered in snow again. But for now, I was trying not to get frustrated every time Hunter reminded me that I had been through a lot, and it was completely normal to still be suffering.

What it did mean was that on days it rained, my mates were always with me. Or at least, until sex was involved, we were all together.

Carter and Hunter were adamant that sex was to be with just one of them at a time. Although Javion and Knox were more than happy to both have sex with me at the same time.

"Zee?" Hunter waved his hand in front of my face, and I blinked. "You spaced out there. DB is asking if you want duck pancakes or tacos for dinner."

"Yes," I said.

From the other side of me, Knox laughed. He'd

been doing that a lot more recently.

I liked the sound of it.

"It was pancakes *or* tacos," Hunter muttered.

"Oh, let her have both. You know she can eat more than the three of you combined." Javion smirked.

Raising my hand, I stuck my middle finger up at him.

"Of all things, you thought teaching Zeraora to flip the bird was essential?" Carter's lips thinned as he stared at Javion.

I looked over at Carter. "I would zap him, but Javion likes that."

Holding his hands up, Carter shook his head. "I don't need to know that kind of information."

"What were you thinking of, anyway?" Hunter asked me. "Not liking the show?"

The show we were watching was paused, yet I hadn't even noticed.

"Sex."

Knox laughed.

"Sex?" Hunter repeated. He shifted his weight. "You aren't tired from earlier?"

"I won't be after pancakes and tacos."

Javion, who had been lying down with his legs hanging over the edge of the couch and his head lying in Knox's lap, propped himself up by his elbows so he could look at Carter. "And to think, at one point, you were worried we wouldn't be able to keep Zera occupied if we killed the Lycans."

Carter folded his arms, his lips, still pressed firmly together.

We had defeated the Lycans... but we hadn't. There was still at least one other power plant and their hotels, but after we returned from Texas, Carter started working with the Council. I didn't really know what or who they were, other than they kept the supes in check...

Considering they'd let the Lycans do what they wanted for the last twenty years, I wasn't really sure 'keeping supes in check' was something they did well...

However, Carter said that since I'd wiped the Texan facility off the map, there were no more reports of supes going missing. At least, not any they suspected because of the Lycans.

Once we'd gotten back to Castle Viegls, while we were all trying to rest or recover, Hunter asked me what I wanted to do next.

Before we went to Texas, my answer was always to make sure every last Lycan was dead.

But at some point, that changed.

I didn't care anymore.

No, it wasn't that I didn't care.

I wanted to destroy all of the Lycans that had hurt me and my mates. Maybe there were a few that had gotten away.

But I left a crater in the earth.

According to Javion who had been keeping an eye on the internet, no one was able to explain the size and depth of the crater because there was no trace of radioactivity. Something that should have been there if it was a nuclear power plant, which it wasn't. And no radar—whatever one of those was—had picked up on a meteor hitting the earth. In fact, people ruled out the meteor because one that left a hole that big should have done to us what it did to the dinosaurs.

If there were Lycans out there who were plotting to come after me and my mates, they'd best hope that's the smallest crater I'd leave when I killed them.

And if the Lycans started hunting supes down again, well. I'd stop them.

For now, I just wanted to be with my mates.

And have a lot of sex.

And food.

But mainly sex.

I liked that more.

"I'm going to make dinner," Carter said, earning him a smirk from Javion.

As Carter left the room, I snuggled into Hunter's side. "I think Carter wants sex."

"I think he's not the only one," Knox muttered.

Dinner wasn't tacos or pancakes. Instead, Carter came back with hot turkey sandwiches, made from leftovers, with gravy for dunking. Or for Javion, his usual glass of blood. I was busy dipping my sandwich into the yummy liquid when Carter set his sandwich down on the plate in his lap.

"Have you thought about what you want to do next?"

"Sex."

Javion snorted into his blood, sending it splashing over the side and onto Knox's face.

"Fuck's sake," Knox grumbled.

Before he could wipe it away, Javion leaned over and licked his face clean.

Intentionally not looking in their direction, his lips back in a thin line, Carter sighed. "I mean long-term. We've not wanted to bring this up, because in the past, you only ever wanted to destroy the Lycans, but we've done that. What do you want to do now?"

"Am I supposed to do something?"

"Have you thought about looking for your family?" Hunter suggested.

"Hunter." Carter used that tone again.

Gravy was dripping from my sandwich, but I was too focused on Carter to care. "Why can't Hunter say that?"

"It's not that we can't look for your family. It's just that the warlock said almost all the fae were in another realm, and unless you were of royal blood, which you aren't, we would never be able to unlock the gate." Carter picked his plate up and placed it on the floor beside him before wiping his hands on his trousers. "On top of that, looking for your family, when we don't even know what your name is, would be impossible. I don't want you to get your hopes up, spending years searching for something we might never find."

Javion cleared his throat. "Actually, I know Zera's name. Her real name."

All four of us turned to stare at him. Even Knox was glaring like Javion had hidden that fact from him too. "You do?"

Javion nodded. "It was in the data I pulled from the facility."

"You've known all this time and not told us?" Carter's eyes narrowed.

"Look, if I was going to tell anyone, it was going to be Zera." Javion rolled his eyes. "But it's not something that's easy to bring up and I don't exactly want to lose Zera."

"You're not going to lose me." I shrugged. "I don't care."

"You don't... care?" Hunter turned to face me fully. "Zera, it's your family."

"No, you are. You're the ones I want to be with."

Javion tilted his head. "You don't care about your parents? Or if there are more like you?"

"No." The way they were all looking at me made me feel like that wasn't the answer I was supposed to give. "I want to be with you four. You make me happy. I am happy here. I've chosen you."

Knox reached over and took my hand in his. "Hey," he said softly "It's okay. You don't need to get upset. We're not going to force you to look for them. Are we?" He looked at Javion.

"Of course not," Javion said. "I mean, look at me. I don't want anything to do with any of the other vampires."

"That's not quite the same," Carter told him.

"You think I should find the fae?"

Carter's gaze met mine. Eventually, he shook his

head. "I don't want you to do anything you don't want to. I just don't think it's fair to compare Javion's vampire family to your real family. If you don't want to know more about them, you don't have to at all."

"I don't want to."

Carter nodded. "Then we won't. But I want you to know that you're allowed to change your mind at any point, and if you do, we'll be right here to help you find out what you can about them."

I picked my sandwich back up and took a bite. It was getting cold because I wasn't eating it quick enough.

"Why would I want to find people who don't even eat." When I'd been held captive by the Lycans, they never fed me. Fae didn't need to eat. Which meant, if I was to go to their realm—wherever that was—there probably wasn't even going to be food there.

Knox burst out laughing again. "Fuck, I love you. Here, finish mine, baby." He leaned over and placed what was left of his sub on my plate.

"Zee, I know you don't want to know anything about your family, but can we at least find out what your name is? It's not fair that Javion knows, but we don't." Hunter pouted.

I shrugged, grabbing the sandwich Knox gave me.

"Spill," Knox demanded, poking Javion in the side.

Shocked

"Euforia."

Wrinkling my nose up, I looked at the vampire. "Ew."

"You don't like it?" Carter asked.

"My name is Zeraora." I bit into the sandwich.

Knox leaned forward, rubbing his hands against his temples. "You mean, instead of the name your parents gave you, you prefer the one Hunter picked?"

"Zeraora is a beautiful name." Carter was glaring at Knox.

Raising his head, Knox stared at the older gargoyle. "He named her after a fucking Pokémon," he said, his tone flat.

Slowly—eerily slowly—Carter turned his head so he was looking at Hunter. "Is that true?"

"It suits her!" Hunter's voice was strangely high pitched.

"What's wrong with my name?" I liked Zeraora. I liked how, when Carter said Zeraora, he somehow made it sound like a hug. Hunter called me Zee, which sounded like the electricity humming in the air. Knox called me Zera, and the *a* came out like a sigh.

Javion mainly called me Little Sparkler. I hadn't liked it when Knox called me Tric, but it was different with Javion.

But Zeraora, Zera, Zee, or even Little Sparkler… that was who I am.

"Nothing is wrong with your name." Carter promised me. "It's just not the most conventional way of choosing one."

"Is anything conventional with Zera?" Hunter asked.

Javion rubbed his tongue over his fang. "I see what you're trying to do there, Hunter, but you should probably just shut up now."

"I am Zeraora, not Euforia. And I don't want to know anything else about the fae because they're not my family. You are. What I want is to be with you and protect you and keep you safe." I tilted my head. "And have sex with all of you. Preferably at the same time."

Carter let out a long and weary sigh as Knox and Javion burst out laughing. "I'm going to go do the dishes." He got up and walked past the back of the sofa behind us.

"At least she didn't ask you to get your dick pierced," Knox told him.

He was rewarded with a smack to the back of the head before Carter walked into the kitchen.

"Keep working on it," Javion told me as he rubbed the back of Knox's head. "For you, he'll cave."

Returning my attention to what was left of my sandwich, I settled back into the couch, smiling to myself.

I had all the time in the world to work on it.

The End

ACKNOWLEDGEMENTS

When I started this series, I never thought I'd end up here. The main reason was that this was supposed to be a (maximum) forty-thousand-word standalone story. Over three books and three hundred thousand words, here we are. The end of the Elemental Magic Unleased trilogy.

Another reason was because of the horrific burnout I've been suffering from. My plan for Shocked was to have released the book six months ago. And then I spent several months sitting in front of the laptop, crying, just because I couldn't get the words out.

Thankfully, I finished and this ending is how I saw it (back when I knew Grounded was never going to be that short standalone...). So my first acknowledgment and eternal thanks go to you who is reading this right now. Thank you for giving Grounded a shot. Thank you for sticking around to read the last book, and thank you for being patient with me while I got here. I cannot express how much that means to me—you really did keep me writing!

Sarah, my bestest friend in the whole wild (not a typo) world, who puts up with me and my crazy author antics far more than a sane person really should. Thank you for letting me call you at random hours of the day and night to talk at you as I try to figure out a plot point I'm stuck on. For proof-reading and finding all those typos. For giving me the best, honest feedback. And for making sure I leave my laptop alone and have some downtime. You are the best thing in my life and I love you.

The other person who helped me get this story written is Caia. Aside from your amazing (and fast) editing skills, I swear, writing sprints are the only way this book got written at times. I can't wait to work with you on our project. We're going to kill it!

This book cover was created by Moorbooks Designs and it's gorgeous. And it was done with minimal input from me. I trusted them to deliver, and they did. Thank you, guys!

A huge thanks must go to my beta team: Sarah, Tanisha, Elizabeth, Karissa, and Angela. You are wonderful! I was so nervous about sending out this book but you all read and responded so quickly and your comments were incredibly helpful. You really have helped shape this series and make it as good as it is. I appreciate you all so much!! Thank you!

I actually don't like writing this part because I'm always paranoid that I've forgotten someone. If I have, please forgive me. I promise it was not intentional. I am just a dumbass.

So, what now? Well, there are a few series that I'm working on—it depends on how the muses play as to which one gets the word count. One is with a character who has been in this series. Another was mentioned so briefly in Grounded, and the third… you've met her harem. You just might not have realized it yet. There's also another series I'm working on, but I'm not giving anything away on that one yet, other than it not being related to anything I've written yet because it's contemporary…

So, Zera's story may be over, but there's more to come in this little world. I hope you'll stick around and join me on their crazy adventures!

Serenity xx

NEWSLETTER

The best way, hands down, to stay in touch with me, is through my newsletter.

Facebook has a terrible habit of suppressing posts, and as for notifications, I don't get them half of the time either!

While I will post occasionally on FB, and I will try to be active in my group, you can guarantee an email from me once a month.

What's more, each month, there will be a giveaway to win—it could be a signed paperback, gift card, or some other fun goodies.

So please sign up using the link below:

Find out more at:

http://eepurl.com/gJhECL

ABOUT THE AUTHOR

USA Today Bestselling author Serenity Ackles writes both contemporary and paranormal romance stories. With a long-standing inability to choose a book boyfriend, and always rooting for the 'second lead', she mainly writes reverse harems.

As such, Serenity's stories contain a lot of men, just as much cock, and a liberal sprinkling of profanities.

More importantly, the contain (eventual) happy endings, where, if the girl doesn't want to choose between the men who like her, she damn well doesn't.

WAYS TO CONNECT

Facebook:

Page: www.facebook.com/SerenityAcklesAuthor/
Group: www.facebook.com/groups/SerenityAcklesRebels

TikTok:

@author_serenity_ackles

Bookbub:

www.bookbub.com/profile/serenity-ackles

Amazon:

www.amazon.com/Serenity-Ackles/e/B081F8D5FK

Newsletter:

www.subscribepage.io/SerenityAcklesNewsletter

Printed in Great Britain
by Amazon

84110610R00332